This book should be returned/renewed by the latest date shown above. Overdue items incur charges which prevent self-service renewals. Please contact the library.

Wandsworth Libraries
24 hour Renewal Hotline
01159 293388
www.wandsworth.gov.uk

Wandsworth

the rivers, lakes and seas of his home country (the UK) but has ventured further afield to countries across Europe and the USA.

DISCLOSURE

THE FUTURE IS NOW

DR GRAHAM CLINGBINE

Matador
9 Priory Business Park,
Wistow Road, Kibworth Beauchamp,
Leicestershire. LE8 0RX
Tel: 0116 279 2299
Email: books@troubador.co.uk
Web: www.troubador.co.uk/matador
Twitter: @matadorbooks

ISBN 978 1784624 262
ISBN 978 1784624 507

British Library Cataloguing in Publication Data.
A catalogue record for this book is available from the British Library.

Printed and bound by CPI Group (UK) Ltd, Croydon, CR0 4YY
Typeset in 11pt Aldine401 BT Roman by Troubador Publishing Ltd, Leicester, UK

To my daughters Lorraine and Gemma and grandchildren Jade, Rebecca and Hayley.
Thanks too to Bibi Rabeya, my parents Rose and Joe (no longer with us), David and Pam, family, friends and ex-colleagues.

CONTENTS

FOREWORD

Scientific discoveries have provided the means for wondrous technological development. Novel inventions have produced instruments and equipment which could only have been dreamed about a few generations ago. Motorised vehicles were unknown just a short step back in historical time when horses and carts were the common mode of transport. Flying craft like present day aeroplanes and helicopters could only have been dreamed about. Satellites orbiting the Earth and vehicles which can travel to other planets and land on their surfaces would have been objects of fantasy. So many current common technological items would have amazed our ancestors of just a relatively short time ago. Consider a few diverse items that have only been in use by mankind for a relatively short period but are taken for granted in modern life: television, radio, wrist watches, mobile phones, refrigerators, computers, lasers, navigation devices and so on. The list is huge and diverse.

In the more mirky recesses of human history many modern daily commonplace activities might have been ascribed to divine actions. If a spacecraft descended to Earth the culture of an ancient civilization may have described what they saw as a 'fiery chariot' or some other expression within the range of their understanding. Any beings with advanced technology coming into contact with ancient peoples would be considered to be 'Gods'.

The knowledge of sophisticated technology may have been known, lost and rediscovered. Human observations of strange sightings in the past may have been recorded and then forgotten. How did ancient Egyptians and Mayans produce megastructures like pyramids with intricate placement of massive carved rocks without sophisticated technology? Why do some mediaeval paintings depict objects flying in the sky? Why do ancient texts and scripts often refer to visitors descending from the stars? These questions and many more like them remain unanswered.

The diversity of documented paranormal events is enough to give interested researchers a lifetime of work. To name a few there are mysteries relating to ghosts and hauntings, life after death, cryptid creatures, observations of strange animals, time slips and time travel, alien abductions, UFO sightings and many more. Evidence for the reality of such phenomena is often presented but falls tantalisingly just short of scientific proof.

Tangible proof of various strange phenomena may never be obtained. Would an advanced race of aliens with technology thousands of years ahead of human understanding wish to share their knowledge with mankind? Do humans try to teach our primate cousins to use mobile phones, drive cars and build submarines? The answer is not just in the negative. Consider the case if an ant colony was being addressed. There would be no technological interaction at all. Is this the relationship between present day occupants of UFOs and humans? If UFO phenomena are unreal then some other kind of psychological phenomenon is afflicting mankind as reports are so widespread. If such inexplicable craft are nothing to do with human military technology, they could be time-travelling, interstellar, intergalactic, interdimensional or something else. Modern theories relating to 'string theory', warping spacetime and jumping through wormholes makes the impossible achievable in the future.

Consider a story involving your son or daughter. A small

child having strange experiences would not know they were abnormal. They might not even be worth sharing with family or friends. Perhaps everybody's life was the same.

Slipping into the future could be a normal part of life. Advanced technology might seem stranger than 'magic spells' but no doubt would be more effective in outcome. The question arises as to the consequences of living in the future. Can the past be altered? Can the future be altered? Imagine being pitched head first into a mixture of the maelstrom of future technologies and exotic experiences: time portals, UFOs, abductions and a changed Earth. If you cannot imagine yourself in this predicament then follow the life of Kevin in this book. He was given no choice in the matter.

CHAPTER 1

An Innocent Genesis

The handle on the door turned. The movement was so slow, it was almost imperceptible. Kevin lay in his bed, sleep washing over his tired eyes. He just caught a glimpse of the rotation of the handle out of the corner of his eye. Who would be coming into his room at this time? It was just 5 am. A sliver of sunlight crept through the darkened room, filtering through the small gap between the heavy bedroom curtains. For sure, something had woken Kevin from his slumbers. Did he really see the handle rotating and then turn back on itself to the closed position? He was not sure. Something had disturbed his sleep. Perhaps he had been dreaming but he could not clearly remember his dreams, they were quickly forgotten.

No doubt he had imagined what he thought he had seen. He decided to forget about it and go back to sleep. It was warm and safe under the duvet. It was still too early in the morning to get up. It was the school holidays and his mum was going to take him to the local fairground that had arrived a few days previously at the far end of town. There was a day of fun ahead to look forward to. The attraction of the warm air generated by his body heat under the duvet bedcovers was too much to resist. He decided that the best course of action in the circumstances was to roll over and snooze until being called downstairs for breakfast by his mum. This call would set in motion the daily routine of the bathroom chores, the toileting, the washing and the cleaning of teeth. Kevin's mum loved to spoil him. She would help him to dress, brush his hair and make a hearty breakfast. He was only eight years old and an only child. He needed a bit of spoiling.

Kevin sat bolt upright. It was a sudden reflex movement. He was still in bed but his eyes were now not only wide open but firmly transfixed on the bedroom door. All his senses yelled 'be alert'. The door had made a faint rattling sound but it was loud enough and real enough for Kevin's ears to detect. Kevin pulled the warm duvet fully over his head. Perhaps this would protect him from whatever was scaring him. He cautiously allowed his right eye to peek out from under the duvet and view the culprit of this unexpected disturbing event but the door handle remained motionless.

Who would want to enter his room at this time of the morning? His mum was a heavy sleeper and Kevin could hear faint female snoring sounds coming from his mum's room at the end of the landing. No-one else was in the house. Kevin's mum was a single parent. She slept alone. There were no cats or dogs in the house and the fish in the downstairs goldfish bowl were very unlikely candidates to want to visit him at 5 am on this late summer morning. The rattling had stopped. It had only lasted for a second or two. Kevin quickly sought a logical cause to this odd event.

Perhaps it was caused by vibrations from a passing car or lorry. This seemed unlikely. The farmhouse was located along a narrow country lane away from the main road which was positioned several hundred yards away. No traffic passed along the rural lane except on rare occasions when farmer Jones's tractor trundled along the lane and across the ditches into his fields when the potato harvest was in full swing. This was not a likely time to hear that faded, red and muddy old machine's diesel engine struggling along noisily and puffing oily smoke.

Besides, farmer Jones had told Kevin's mum he would be away for a while, taking a short trip to visit an elderly aunt who had taken a bad fall. The old lady was already diabetic, had leg ulcers and high blood pressure. Now she was bedridden and needed some home help with her chores while support was sorted out by the local social services. Much of the potato crop had already gone to market although the small remainder still lay unscathed in the rich soil of the surrounding fields.

Another explanation flashed through his mind. Maybe a breeze had penetrated an open window on the upstairs landing. That was it. This explained the rattling. He was less sure why the door handle would have turned. Kevin told himself he obviously had imagined everything. Very old wooden doors always misbehave and creak and do things. That's how it is. His desire to seek a logical cause was very short lasting.

Maybe he should arise early from his bed, tidy the bedclothes and set about his daily ablutions and routines. He would mention the business with the door to his mum later on in the day… if he remembered. After all, there was nothing to be concerned about. Many strange things can pass through the mind of an eight year old. Not everything required the rational explanation needed by an adult. Odd things might happen from time to time but these were just accepted as part of daily life. Besides, Kevin had other things on his mind. The funfair only visited the town once a year. It had arrived on schedule two days ago. He could not wait to get on the rides. He particularly liked the Ferris Wheel and the Helter Skelter. Anything that rose high above the ground had a great fascination for Kevin. Why was that? Why was he never scared of heights? The higher the better, there was no fear in Kevin. A vertical sheer drop was… well… awesome.

Kevin got out of bed and slowly, cautiously, turned the bedroom door handle and peeked out onto the landing. If

7

'something' or 'someone' had been trying to enter his room, there was nothing there now. Everything was in place though he did think the mirror on the landing wall outside his door was slightly askew. There was no point wasting his thoughts on something so unimportant as rotating door handles and rattling doors when there were more important things to apply one's mind to... like the smells, sounds and sights of the fairground. Kevin had been saving up his pocket money for some time in anticipation of his visit to the funfair in the late afternoon that day. He would be accompanied by his mum as she wanted to ensure his safety. She liked to keep a discreet eye on him but she would allow him limited free reign to have fun and 'act like a boy' with his mates. Several of them would be gathering at the funfair keen to give the rides a turn and be boisterous and noisy as a way of letting off steam before the summer came to an end and the restrictions of school behaviour became a reality once again.

Kevin made his way to the bathroom and carried out industriously all the hygiene activities his caring mum had shown him to do since very early childhood. These were now repeating automatic habits he would perform every morning that would benefit him for the rest of his life. She wanted her son to grow up with all the best social habits which would lead to him becoming a good citizen in later life and set the mould for him as a future father when he would one day have kids of his own. Kevin's dad was absent. He knew absolutely nothing about him. Perhaps one day in the future he might develop a 'need-to-know-more' desire but for the time being he was content with the support and attention of his mum. His mum would frequently talk to him about developing his social skills so that one day when he was a big man he would know how to best help his future sons or daughters. In truth, Kevin was still on the young side to consider such events. They seemed so far distant in time that such things seemed unreal. He wondered why his mum brought the topic up so frequently. Kevin knew that his mum loved him and was aware of her need to look out for his well-being and welfare. It was nice of his mum to worry about his life as a grown-up… but this was all a long way ahead in the future and he did not dwell on such matters. The funfair later in the day was a much more important event for taking his eight year old imagination into the realms of fantasy. Soon he would be at the very top of the Ferris Wheel, looking down at 'planet Earth' and all the ant-like beings so small below while he hovered high overhead in his swinging chair dangling precariously over the funfair. Maybe his mum would allow him to go up by himself if he promised the man who sold the tickets that he would behave responsibly and would ensure he remained tightly strapped in.

Kevin was still in his pyjamas. He had a little time to kill. He knew his mum liked to assist with his dressing. Even after she had had helped him successfully don his shirt and trousers, his mum would always do a little tweak of his clothes here and a little pull there until she was entirely satisfied with his appearance. Then came the routine hair combing and all was not done until on her instruction he had to take a final look in the mirror to confirm that she had done a good job and every hair was in place. That signalled a little freedom opportunity to do what he liked for ten minutes while his mum started to prepare breakfast for them both. Typically it was tea and toast. Invariably it was real butter that was spread on the toast, not margarine. The choice of what was spread on top of the buttered toast varied from day to day. Typically it was strawberry jam or marmalade, sometimes the dreaded Marmite appeared. This was an acquired taste for Kevin but one that he had not yet come to appreciate. Maybe once a week he could request a boiled or scrambled egg and on more rare occasions he was allowed a small fry up of bacon, sausage, mushrooms, grilled tomatoes and fried bread. On these days if he was not in the mood for a full cooked breakfast he might alternatively eat some porridge oats or one Weetabix in warm milk.

Kevin had a full life. He had nice clothes, plenty of good food, lived in a quiet rural town and had a fussy if not devoted mum. He was doing well at school and had some early childhood interest in subject areas of basic science and nature. To some extent he was a bit of a loner but he could count a couple of lads in his school class as friends. The future was looking bright for Kevin. The only thing missing was a father figure. There was no masculine presence at home. It did strike Kevin that it was slightly strange that his mum would never mention his father. There were no stories of him being an absent father, a drunk, a criminal or a two-timer. There was just not a single word ever spoken about him. Not a word! There was no point worrying about such things. Maybe there was something about talking of his father that might be upsetting his mum. It was best to just leave that subject alone. Inevitably, the matter did sometimes cross Kevin's mind but it was rapidly dismissed. Kevin found that if he tried to think about his unknown father he would get a strange feeling as if a switch had been activated which turned his thoughts elsewhere. One or two school classmates occasionally brought up the matter of his absent parent either innocently or with more malicious intent. Each time, the mysterious switch would turn on and direct him to change or ignore the subject. In fact the subject never cropped up as a serious issue until Kevin reached the age of twenty four and had an unpleasant verbal exchange with the goalkeeper of an opposing football club.

Kevin took a little time out waiting for his mum to come down the stairs, give him his morning kiss, say "Hi" and go into the kitchen to sort out breakfast. He had gone downstairs rather early due to the 'door incident' which had slightly unsettled him. He spent some time playing with his toy soldiers which had been randomly tidied away into a big cardboard box which sat in the corner of the room. They were a mottly collection of German and British soldiers from World War II. They had seen better days. Some were twisted, some had arms, legs or even heads missing and all of them were in a big jumble. He soon tired of these and began playing with a few of his collection of toy racing cars. He lifted the cardboard toy box onto the lounge table to make room on the floor carpet for his imaginary grand prix racing track. Several cars were lined up on the starting grid. There were various model soldiers still scattered around the room hiding in their foxholes and trenches.

Where was his mum? It was around 8-30 am and she would normally be up and around by now. He wondered if he should call up the stairs to her. Perhaps she was tired and having a 'lie in'. It would be selfish to disturb her. The best thing was to remain patient. His mum would be up sooner or later and he would have to control his morning appetite until she was ready to make her appearance. Kevin had heard his mum in bed earlier-on breathing heavily in her sleep. In truth it was only a mild snoring sound but it was a reassuring one. Kevin knew his mum was fast asleep and getting her rest, snoozing safely away in her own upstairs bedroom.

Kevin noticed something out of the corner of his eye while busying himself with his toy racing cars and making a loud 'brmmm brmmm' noise as his cars revved up. He saw his mum... but she was going up the stairs towards her bedroom. Where had she come from? Had she emerged from the kitchen and gone straight upstairs without so much as a word to her boy? She was moving rather strangely, Kevin thought. Her head looked fixated and stared straight ahead. She did not turn to look at him or anything else in the house at all. He noted that his mum was wearing her pink dressing gown with rabbit patterns along the sleeves as she climbed the stairs. It was her favourite dressing gown. Kevin could not see his mum's legs or feet as they were hidden behind the wooden bannisters of the stairs. Her movement looked rather different to usual. It almost looked as if she was floating up the stairs like how those seeds with a hairy parachute-like 'pappus' float up and down in the air currents when they are being dispersed. "Mum, are you all right?" His mum neither blinked nor turned her head. She continued her slow progress up the stairs and onwards across the landing and into her room. Kevin heard the door close gently behind her. His mum had not acknowledged him at all. Maybe he had done something naughty and his mum was cross with him. Still, it was not like her to ignore him. On those odd occasions when Kevin's more boisterous behaviour came to the fore, his mum would admonish him in no uncertain terms. It took a long time for her to quiet down once she got angry. So what was going on? Kevin was becoming rather concerned. Why was his mum still in her room? How come she was going up the stairs rather than coming down? Not long ago he had heard her sleeping soundly upstairs in her room. Why was she not talking to him? It was also past breakfast time but he now had a hollow feeling in the pit of his stomach. His appetite had waned.

"Kevin"! Kevin heard his mum call him. All was well. There was always something reassuring about his mum's voice. It empowered him with confidence. It was the voice that had nurtured him through his infancy. It was the voice of constancy and security in a young child's life.

"Hello Mum! I heard you sleeping. I got up a bit early this morning. I'd love a scrambled egg on toast for breakfast this morning. I'm really hungry."

"What are you talking about?" Kevin's mum replied. "You only just had your lunch. It won't be long before I take you down to the funfair. Don't forget to sort out the pocket money you have been saving. Maybe you should give it to me to look after for you. I have been a bit lazy today and I am still in my dressing gown but I'm going to get dressed in a minute. If you're still hungry you can have a bar of chocolate or a bag of crisps. There's a cheese and onion flavour bag on the living room table you can take."

Now this was very peculiar. Kevin's young mind could not comprehend the situation. He had finished eating his lunch? His mum's voice was coming from the kitchen. He had not noticed her come downstairs. Perhaps he had eaten breakfast and snoozed off. His mum had been lenient with him about staying up late and watching TV. Normally he would be tucked up in bed by 8 pm but this was the school holidays. Last night he had gone up to bed about 11 pm. He never tired of the endless reruns of *Tom & Jerry* animations that ran on the twenty-four-hour cartoons channel (which probably attracted as many adults to it as kids). There was no need for the frantic 'rush-to-get-ready' that was not uncommon in the mornings during term time. Kevin did not like being late for school. In the summer holidays, mornings were somewhat more leisurely.

Kevin decided to distract his thoughts from this anomaly. He must have gone back to sleep while playing with his soldiers and toy racing cars. He knew his mum would get cross if he did not pack away his toys after he had finished playing with them. She was a tidy person but he had not inherited that trait. Everything had its own place, according to Kevin's mum. He decided he would tidy up and put away his things, giving his mind a chance to clear and come up with the explanation of his absentee breakfast and lunch. 'Displacement activities' came in handy when things did not make sense. Kevin's box of toy soldiers and his racing cars were sitting neatly in the corner of the lounge. This was his private area, his play area. How come his things were already neatly stashed away? He had not tidied up yet.

Kevin's mum emerged from the kitchen. She was wearing her pale green, plain dressing gown. "I am going upstairs to get dressed properly for going out. I think we can leave in about an hour. The sun is still out but you can take your light beige jacket with you to the funfair. It might get chilly later. Change your trainers and put your old ones on. They will do for today. I don't want you scuffing up your new pair. Don't forget to pass me your pocket money for the rides and I'll look after it ."

Kevin was now puzzled. He was more than puzzled. His pulse rate began creeping up. It was racing now. His dilated pupils gave away his inner turmoil as did the sweaty beads beginning to drip down his forehead. An adrenalin rush was bombarding his blood. Systolic blood pressure was on the rise. His mum must have changed dressing gowns from the pink one to the green one before going up to get dressed for going outdoors. Why would she do that?

It was at this point that a hammer blow fell. The shock was like a thunderbolt descending from a clear blue sky. It was as if ball lightning was circling round and round his head. It was like getting a personalised 'wow' signal received at SETI from the depths of the galaxy. Kevin was fully dressed. He could not remember getting dressed. A moment ago he was in his pyjamas playing with his toys contemplating breakfast. Now he was wearing his white koala tee shirt and blue denims. It was the afternoon. His mum had told him he had already eaten lunch and it would soon be time to go out. What? If Kevin had known the appropriate swear words, he would have made good use of them at this point. There must be an explanation for this memory deficit. Where had the time gone between playing with his toys and now? Should he cry? It was an option he seriously considered. Should he talk to his mum about it? She would surely not believe him… this was a bizarre occurrence. His mum would start up in arms about him having too many late nights. She would tell him he has a vivid imagination, he is a day dreamer. Maybe it would 'all go away' if he ignored it.

The fairground beckoned. It was late afternoon. The sun was still out in the clear blue sky. It was a warm dry day. This was a rare event for the British climate. It was a piece of good fortune. Kevin was keen to take full advantage of this piece of good luck. Maybe he could take his time looking round the fairground and stretch things out until it was dark. The flickering lights and colours made the whole thing so much more exciting once the sun had set. There were so many rides to go on. He would also visit the little stalls with their games of skill. Try to knock off the coconut from its stand. You have five plastic balls to throw, five chances. Win the teddy! There would also be the food stalls selling hot dogs, burgers (with or without fried onions) and chips. He could already smell the cooking food and hear the noise of the fairground visitors. The shrill musical tones of the rides and shows were in the air. "Let's go, Mum." The unusual happenings of earlier in the day were long gone. The fairground was a safe place to be. All was well.

Kevin's mum was ready. She was wearing a pale blue summery dress. Her purse was firmly gripped in her left hand. It contained the monetary efforts from Kevin's good endeavours. Helping with chores and housework had contributed to this fund. He had earned some money here and some extra there. Now it was time for Kevin to blow his fortune… at the fair. One or two of his classmates were probably there already, having the time of their lives. His mum's right hand firmly gripped his left hand and with a little yank they were off. He did not need much encouragement to make the fifteen minute walk. Down the country lane they walked, passing the remnants of farmer Jones's potato plants still showing in certain areas of the field. They reached the T-junction at the bottom of the lane and turned left towards the village centre. They walked along the main road. In reality, it wasn't much of a main road. It was only a bit bigger than the country lane alongside Kevin's house. Every two or three minutes a car or lorry would rumble through the village centre on the old tarmac surface trying to avoid the increasing number of new potholes that had been alarmingly opening up over the previous couple of months.

They strolled along chatting in the mode of mother and young son. Of course he would be careful on the rides. Yes, he would steer clear of any strangers who might decide he needed company and talk to him without any invitation. From time to time Kevin had enough childish enthusiasm to abandon walking mode and replace this with a couple of skips, ensuring he did not break free from his mother's grip. They passed all the familiar landmarks. Peter Barnes, the village butcher's shop passed on the left. A little way along and the local grocery shop was open, its door ajar, as if inviting customers to come in. There was a little baker's shop where they offered mean hot pies... then the corner post office and sweet shop, Meads. The pair walked along taking in the local sights and landmarks. Kevin's school lay a little way down another lane on the left. He didn't want to dwell on Marwick Junior and Prep School. Time to think about that on another occasion, this was the school holiday period. The foot journey continued down the village centre.

Places of significance were also passing on the other side of the road. There was the little community centre in which two small brick buildings housed both the local doctor's surgery and the dentist. There was even the fish and chip shop, Fred's Finest. No doubt Fred used the best potatoes available from farmer Jones. He would have to get his fish delivered by van as the sea was twenty miles away... but the cod, haddock, plaice and so on always arrived fresh and on time. There were always the sausages, sausages in batter, fish cakes and fish roe to fall back on, for a change. Today, Fred's customer numbers would be down, the village folk were heading for the fairground and its fayre. Eventually they reached St Benedict Parish Church of the Holy Trinity, at the far end of the village. They took the footpath that ran alongside the church grounds and past the small number of gravestones in the cemetery plot... these were mouldy and unkempt. At one time they had been loved and looked after. The people buried below their markers would once have hoped their memories would be cherished and held in perpetuity for the world to see and think of them and their deeds in life. Now the stones were faded... new times were underway. At last, in front of them, a wonder-world of noise, smells and movement opened up ahead of Kevin and his mum. They had arrived at the funfair.

The hours passed as planned. Everything lived up to Kevin's expectations. No, his expectations had been surpassed. He noted that the bulge in his mum's purse which he was now holding had gone right down. His money was mainly spent but he did not regret it at all. He had met a friend or two from his class and shared some rides and some food with them. He was not gregarious by nature and also spent a lot of time wandering around on his own. He investigated everything and tried his hand at lots of games and tasks. His mum had met some of her own friends, mainly mums of the kids, or from her part time job in the day nursery where she watched over young children while the parents were away working and earning money to survive the daily cost of living. She had busied herself chatting and even tried one or two of the rides herself. The Dodgem Cars had been a bit scary. How come everyone smiled and seemed to enjoy crashing into each other

17

as often as possible? She had given Kevin the freedom to move around independently but he was under strict orders of behavioural correctness.

It was dark now and the stars blinked… off and on. There were so many of them in the night sky. There was something strangely familiar about some of the shapes and patterns he could make out. It almost felt like he was being called. Maybe when he grew up he would learn more about them. He had heard his science teacher at school Mrs Brown talk a little about them. They were suns? He could not understand, there was only one sun that he knew about and it had been shining down on him all day. Now what was that word Mrs Brown had used about studying the stars? Kevin thought it was 'astrology'… or maybe it was 'astronomy'? Perhaps they were the same thing. His attention span was that of an eight year old. His thoughts soon wandered away to having a final ride. Time was running out. He had been up and down the Helter Skelter several times. That was just about done and dusted. He had loved going up high above the ground in the Ferris Wheel even though his mum had insisted that she accompany him on that particular ride.

Perhaps there was just enough time left (and money) to go on the Rocket Ship ride. These were model rockets that went round and round but you could pull a lever and a compressed-air system would make the rocket rise as it rotated in a great sweeping circle. Depressing the control made the rocket sink. He stepped into the rocket and buckled up. There was enough money to pay the man to take one trip. He was in a nice sparkly yellow rocket. There were many others in front and behind him in lots of nice shiny colours… red, green and blue. The ride started. He pulled on the lever and his rocket rose… higher and higher. He could see the people far below. Was that speck below his mum? It felt like his rocket was still ascending. He was well strapped into the canopy with a safety harness. How come his rocket had gone so much higher than all the others? Higher and higher he went. He felt like the stars were coming to meet him. One star in particular above his head flashed and twinkled as if it were sending him a personalised Morse code message. This star was so bright. It remained stationary overhead for some time. Kevin felt compelled to give the star a wave. It unexpectedly moved off at high speed and seemed to drop down to earth in the vicinity of the woods at the far end of the village.

Kevin had a tremendous time on the rides. He had no hesitation using up his saved pocket money. His mum was happy to see her son enjoying himself. Kevin raced from ride to ride. His pocket money dwindled rapidly. Eventually the time came to go home. Kevin went over to the snack stall selling hot dogs (onions optional), burgers, ice cream and canned drinks. It was here that he bought a large purple and sugary candy floss on a stick. This would occupy him on the journey home. He had a distinctive smell of the funfair ingrained into his clothes, skin and hair. There was a strange mixture of odours deriving from fast foods, sweaty bodies and oily engine smoke from the motors that ran the rides. Kevin took his mum's hand and they made their way home. "Thanks for taking me" said Kevin. His mum smiled.

The next morning the daily routine of everyday life resumed. Kevin's mum busied herself tidying away the breakfast plates, cups and saucers ensuring that the blue-and-white checked tablecloth was crumbless. All the dishes were scrubbed by hand... no fancy dishwashers for her. Each item was scrupulously examined and not returned to its resting place until it was back in pristine condition. Kevin's mum placed a high value on cleanliness and orderliness. Everything had its place. She was a lady who ran her home according to her rules. As far as Kevin was concerned, she was a good mum. After all, he was the apple of her eye. Her strict household regime did tend to waver somewhat when it came to Kevin's requests to eat certain less-than-healthy foods such as chocolate buttons and cough candies or take out various messy or noisy toys to play with which he would spread around the lounge floor. She would also on occasion bend to his bedtime requests. Kevin was never keen to 'go up to bed' and he would relish negotiating another ten or fifteen minutes of 'staying up time' to play a little longer with his toys or watch some TV programme that had taken his fancy. However, he had to make allowance for 'tidying up' time. That was still his chore and was rarely left to his mum.

Kevin was eight years old at this point in his life. His mum was thirty eight. Although Kevin's mum was still young there was a slight generational gap in attitudes already present between him and his mum at a subliminal level. The kids at school and the programmes he watched on TV painted their own pictures of the outside world and reality. Although his young mind absorbed the views and attitudes of the real world, his main focus of attention was directed on his mum. She was his rock, the centre of his Universe. Kevin knew his mum's name. It was 'Sylvie'! To Kevin, the name was a meaningless title… 'mum' was the correct way to address his female parent. Sylvie herself was devoted to Kevin. She was basically a housewife but did help out from time to time at the Mount Joy Day Centre in the village centre. This was dependent on getting Kevin sorted out for school. She would see him off on his journey every day and sometimes walk along with him. She liked to be at home when Kevin returned from school to greet him. Alternatively, if pre-arranged, he would go into the Mount Joy building and meet up with her there. He would invariably sneak a chocolate biscuit or two before leaving for home with his mum.

Kevin's mum was friendly but rather conservative. There was nothing flamboyant about her. She preferred to wear long dresses that were past knee-length. Her shoes had flat heels and were chosen for their ability to last rather than their fashion appeal. She did wear some white trainers with a blue flash occasionally which she would combine with over-long shorts and a baggy tennis shirt. These were likely to appear on a hot summer day. Most of the time she preferred to wear long skirts and dresses. She did not keep stiletto heel shoes, real furcoats, fashion 'shades' or lacy underwear. Practicality was the name of the game. Her hair was brunette and shoulder-length but it was usually neatly tucked back into a bun and held in place by a clip or small ribbon. She did make use of make-up but this was used very frugally. No use was found for thick mascara or eye liners. She considered her lashes and eyebrows to be fine as they were. In truth, she was an attractive slim woman and make-up would have distracted from her natural looks.

Sylvie was careful with her money. She was great at budgeting. She and Kevin never went short of anything. Sylvie did not receive any financial assistance from the State or the Local Authority. She was financially independent. Kevin never used to think about money matters or where the money came from that supported both him and his mother. It just seemed 'normal' that his mum should have the finances to cover their bills, food and other expenses. The origin of any household money was of no interest. However, he did like to receive his weekly pocket money which he stashed away in a little ex-jam jar.

Sylvie preferred to be known as Mrs Powell. Bills would be posted to her in the format of 'Mrs S. Powell'. Acquaintances would acknowledge her formally. She did not have many friends but of these only one or two would address her as Sylvie or 'Syl'. In general, Sylvie preferred to 'keep her head down' and mind her own business. She liked her privacy. She liked her independence. She liked her peace of mind.

21

Sylvie never discussed her marriage. People assumed she had been married, after all, she used the title 'Mrs'. She lived alone with Kevin in their farmhouse. She owned it. It was a freehold property in her own name, not leasehold. There was no rent and no landlord. The house was fully paid for. On rare occasions someone would ask Sylvie about her life before she was married. This would initiate a stony silence. Her eyes would become transfixed. There was a hint of a tear but her expressionless face gave nothing away. It was a 'no-go area'. Kevin had not developed any great curiosity about the former life of his mother, before he was born. He knew that his grandparents were 'no longer with us' and that other relatives were 'far away'. So he was content to get on with his own life. He was busy enough to put such curiosities as might arise to one side. He had a moment from time to time when he had asked about his dad but these were infrequent. Sylvie would immediately switch to blank mode. If he persisted she would quickly change the subject to distract him. He decided there was no urgency to know about his father, at least not for the time being. He was having a happy childhood... there was no point looking for entropy... he preferred his life to remain stable. Maybe some time as he became older it might become more important for him to know more. He felt his mum would impart knowledge about his ancestry to him when she deemed it to be the right time. He trusted her in all things. Kevin Powell was content to wait until his mum decided it was a good time to talk to him about her background and his relatives. What Kevin did not know was that Sylvie had no intention of telling Kevin anything... ever. The only way she might speak about such things would be if somehow she was forced to but she could not at this time envisage any situation which might arise that could force her hand or encourage her to talk. It seemed likely that Kevin would never be enlightened about his roots and that the identity of his father would remain unknown.

Kevin Powell's life continued in a rather uneventful way. In fact, nothing out of the ordinary disrupted his childhood development and the one or two occasions of strange occurrences in his younger days were forgotten. He had continued to achieve good grades at school and had an excellent attendance since he remained in good health. There were very few 'unauthorised absences'. He did not stand out in any particular way from the other boys in his cohort. As he got older he developed interests in some sports like football and had an academic liking for the sciences which he enjoyed studying. He scored straight 'A grades' in physics, chemistry and biology but was also strong in maths, English and foreign languages. By the time he reached teenage and beyond he had become a mature and well-balanced intelligent young man. His domestic situation had not really changed very much. Kevin was still supported by his long-serving mum who took on the brunt of domestic responsibilities like cooking and laundry. The only main visible environmental change was that the fields near Kevin's house were now overgrown with weeds and shrubs. The potato crops had long been abandoned since the passing away of farmer Jones some years before. No-one had come forward to claim the land so it just remained *in situ* unattended and left to its own devices.

Kevin Powell had reached the age of sixteen. He now had to focus his mind on further studies. He knew he would like to take a degree course at University but was not quite sure as to what ultimate career he would like to do. Various science-based professions crossed his mind... these included medicine, pharmacy and optometry. At other times his mind went off at a tangent and he looked at options such as law and accountancy. His visits to careers advisors were helpful but he could not make any final decision. It was important to plan ahead in his life as his school would only allow a maximum of three subjects to be studied over the next two years. The choice of these advanced level options was important because in some of his potential degree study areas he could only gain entry to the University course with appropriate exam subject choices. Kevin was an excellent student and was highly self motivated to study.

Kevin had begun to experience a minor distraction, however. Each day on leaving school while walking home, he would invariably notice a blonde blue-eyed girl going in the opposite direction. She was about the same age as himself and was, like him, apparently making her way home after school. This young lady walked along briskly on the opposite side of the road to Kevin. The realisation dawned on Kevin that this girl was extremely pretty. He was beginning to feel a great attraction towards her. However, she did not notice him looking at her. She always moved onwards, eyes focussed on what lay ahead. Kevin was far too shy to cross the road and say "hello." What would he talk to her about? Maybe she might think he was molesting her? Even in the unlikely event that she did speak with him, he would be too nervous to ask her out. Most likely she would not like him. It was much safer to concentrate his mind on his studies. This continued for some time until one day two events occurred which would have a big impact on his life.

Kevin was taking his usual walk home after school. On the other side of the road going home was the blonde girl. For a moment he thought he had imagined it. Did she just look across the road and give him a quick smile? No, surely not. "Hello, how are you?" The girl shouted across the road to him in a sweet high voice. It must have been aimed at him, there was no-one else in the same proximity. Kevin gulped and took a breath.

"I'm fine thanks. I'm Kevin."

"I'm Jane" the girl replied, "see you again soon" and she then continued on her way. Kevin's heart skipped a beat. He barely remembered the rest of the walk home. He arrived home and sorted out his school things but his imagination was about to run away with itself as various scenarios with himself and Jane filled his head. The second event then took place.

"Kevin! Please come here." Kevin's mum's voice did not have its usual calm and melodic tone. There was a hint of fear in the voice and a touch of distress. Kevin entered the kitchen to see his mum sitting on a bar stool, head orientated downwards, as if she were examining a spider making its way slowly across the kitchen floor.

"Mum! Are you ok?" His mum slowly raised her head and looked at Kevin. He thought it was more like she was looking through him as if searching for something behind him in the lounge. At first there was no reply. "Mum?" Kevin thought his mum looked pale and withdrawn.

Then she spoke. "I started feeling unwell a few minutes ago. I tried to take some cold orange squash from the fridge to drink. I could barely swallow it. My breathing is not right. I am finding it difficult... heavy." Kevin could see beads of sweat on his mum's face. Kevin was a very sensible young man. He remained calm and did not panic. Kevin came to a rational conclusion.

"Oh mum! Try to relax. Maybe you should lie down. I think you need to see a doctor. I better phone our surgery."

"No! I am sure I will feel better soon," his mum replied, in a whisper. Kevin made his own assessment. His mum's breathing had declined further. It appeared laboured and shallow.

Kevin decided that the local doctor was not the right choice. Not only did Kevin not listen to his mum's protestations regarding not getting medical assistance but he felt emergency services were appropriate. "Stay just there, mum. Do not try and move. I will be back in a moment."

Kevin quickly entered the lounge and used the family phone to call medical emergencies. After a few quick questions about the identities of the caller and patient, symptoms and location, an ambulance was dispatched. His mum was saying very little. Kevin was used to his mum being fit and well. He had noticed variable changes in her behaviour and activities recently but as is often the case, he did not put any importance on it. Kevin had noticed that his mum's neck was looking somewhat swollen recently but it was often kept hidden below some high neck blouses and cardigans.

It seemed an eternity while Kevin stood by his mum to support her while he waited for the ambulance. However, the ambulance crew were soon knocking on the door. It had only taken seven minutes to arrive but to Kevin it had felt longer. Two crew members entered the house and were directed into the kitchen where Kevin's mum remained in the same position on the bar stool, once again surveying the kitchen floor with her head drooped. The crew were very well-trained paramedics. One man remained in the ambulance in the driver's seat. The two paramedic crew that entered the house looked very smart wearing green shirts and black trousers. One was a big man: in truth he was rather overweight. His partner was a very slender blonde woman who was very pleasant but seemed subservient to the big guy. He took the lead and spoke to Kevin and his mum and did a physical examination. The two crew members reminded Kevin of old comedy duos he had seen on TV from years before his birth. Were they reincarnations of Abbott and Costello? Maybe it was a return of Laurel and Hardy in a new guise? Kevin's mind snapped back to the present. This was no comedic situation.

The medical assessment was over and Kevin's mum was whisked off in the ambulance to the Marmaduke Centre in the Royal Hospital located in a nearby town. Kevin accompanied his mum in the ambulance and onwards into the hospital. An assessment was done by the hospital emergency staff. Kevin's mum was admitted to the Observation Ward. After a while Kevin said goodbye to his mum and wished her better. By this time she had got very sleepy. The doctor in charge said they would have to keep his mum in the hospital for a time and would have a further word with Kevin in the waiting area.

After ten minutes one of the ward staff came to see Kevin to update him. He said any initial diagnosis needed to be confirmed by some tests which would then be reviewed by Mr Sharpe, the resident consultant. After the tests were done the appropriate course of treatment could be undertaken. In the meantime Kevin did not need to worry, his mum was not in any danger but would be admitted. The doctor asked Kevin what he wanted to know. Obviously Kevin needed to know what was wrong with his mum and what it would mean for the future.

The doctor then gave Kevin a simplified explanation of the situation. "We think your mum has a thyroid gland problem. It is a gland found in the lower neck region. It has a shape rather like a bow tie. It releases chemicals into the bloodstream we call hormones, including one called thyroxine which controls our metabolic rate, the chemical reactions going on in our bodies. Things like our heart rate and amount of sweating our body does are included in its functions. The gland is below the voice box and folded over part of the windpipe. It is made up of two interconnected lobes."

Kevin interrupted the doctor. "Please tell me what is actually wrong with my mum. I want to know exactly what is going on." The doctor asked Kevin if there were any other relatives that needed to be informed, preferably adults. What about his dad? Were there any other family members to contact? Kevin explained there were no other significant adults in his life… it had always been just him and his mum. The doctor continued his medical assessment.

"Usually we cannot feel the thyroid gland. Your mum has an enlarged thyroid gland. Swellings can occur due to both underactivity of the gland, which we call hypothyroidism and overactivity of the gland or hyperthyroidism. Our initial assessment leads us to think that your mum has an overactive gland. There can be various causes of this. It could be an illness called Graves Disease or what are known as toxic nodular goiters. We have to check for malignancy too… cancer. Your mum will stay here for a while so we can carry out further tests. You can phone the ward directly or visit. What about you coping? I may have to inform social services to keep an eye on you." Kevin assured the doctor he would be fine and could stay with his friend and his mum in the village. He had fibbed and told a few more white lies as he did not want to be supervised. Finally, he got away from the hospital. He had money on him and took a ride on the local bus which was waiting outside the hospital. This was a piece of good fortune as the service was very infrequent. It took him to the village centre and after a short walk gained entry to his home. Kevin was alone. He was feeling upset but he decided he would cope… and he did.

Time moved on and Kevin managed very well. He made a number of visits to see his mum and she seemed much better. As he was a mature lad and spoke well he gradually gathered together further information. Various lumps and nodules had been detected on the thyroid gland but one of these was sizeable compared to anything else detected. Some imaging was done using CAT scan technology. Other tests were done: blood tests and chest X-rays. This was followed by a tissue biopsy. A fine hypodermic needle was inserted into a nodule using an ultrasound technique to guide the insertion. The cells in the extracted tissue fluid were passed through to the Pathology Laboratory and the cells examined for malignancy.

On Friday evening Kevin visited his mum in the ward.

She seemed quite cheerful and had only been an inpatient for a matter of days. The tests done on her had been carried out very quickly as well as very effectively. Her main concern was for Kevin's well-being rather than for her own problems. The consultant Mr Sharpe came to see them both on the ward. The curtains were drawn round them for privacy and some ancient wooden chairs put in place so they could be seated for a chat. Mr Sharpe had a broad Welsh accent. He was very slim and tall, probably over six feet. His hair was greying. He wore a well-fitting grey suit and yellow tie which seemed very flamboyant and did not match the rest of his clothing at all. On his face sat a pair of thick black rimmed spectacles balancing precariously on the bridge of a long pointed nose. He spoke very calmly which put both Kevin and his mum at ease. Mr Sharpe updated the medical findings, options and treatment.

"You have a hyperthyroid condition. The gland is overactive. Sometimes we give patients medication. The point of this is to reduce the amount of thyroid hormone being made by the gland. Your symptoms relate to your thyroid function and gland size. In some patients we make use of radioactive iodine which we introduce into the bloodstream. The thyroid hormone contains iodine but when the radio-isotope is given it is absorbed into the tissue and destroys all or part of the thyroid gland. In your case we looked at the cells in case there were any signs of cancerous cell division. You told us that there was no family history of thyroid cancer, which is good to know. We looked at your Pathology Report and the results were indeterminate. In other words we do not think you have cancer, which is good news. Sometimes we see some abnormalities in thyroid cells. These could become malignant in the future. We do not want to get to that stage. There is some kind of sizeable nodule present in your thyroid in the left lobe. We have decided on a treatment plan. It may be the wisest course to surgically remove all or part of your thyroid gland. There is a definite lump in the gland that is rather worrying and that probably needs to be removed. We will not remove any tissue unless it is required. This procedure does require a general anaesthetic. You may or may not need thyroid hormone medication in the future. We will make a final decision to remove nothing, one lobe or the whole gland at the time of surgery. We will take another cell biopsy during or shortly before the surgery. There is certainly some kind of lump sitting in your thyroid gland that should not be there."

After the initial shock had worn off it was agreed that Mr Sharpe knew best and his advice would be followed. Consent forms were agreed and signed. Kevin's mum was allowed out of the hospital… her condition had stabilized. She would have to wait for an admissions notice in the mail. She made good use of her time back at home sorting out chores and bills. She would not be a long-stay patient: hospital bed space was in demand. She was likely to be out within twenty four hours of the surgery. Kevin was not worried about looking after himself, he just wanted his mum to get better. It was not long before the date of admission came by, there had been a cancellation and Kevin's mum was going to be fitted into the surgical schedule early. The operation was going to be carried out by Mr Sharpe himself. She did extra cooking for Kevin and checked that he would manage on his own for the short time during which she had the surgery and was an inpatient.

Kevin's mum had some pre-operative tests and she had to answer some health questions. Kevin sat-in with his mum while a staff nurse went over some issues. After discharge she must watch for possible complications. These could be things like a hoarse voice, swallowing problems, bleeding and loss of feeling in the neck area. Her calcium levels might have to be checked for a time after the surgery. If she experienced anything out of the ordinary she should contact the hospital. Things such as fever, breath shortage and pain were mentioned as examples.

The awaited surgery was performed without any hitches. Kevin's mum woke up in the recovery room and after an hour the anaesthetic had blown off sufficiently for Kevin to join his mum in the room and reassure her. She was feeling surprisingly well and pleased it was all over and done with. At the end of the afternoon Mr Sharpe entered and after some informal chat and reassurance that all was well he sat down between Kevin and his mum. Kevin's mum asked about what had been done. Mr Sharpe took a sideways look at Kevin's mum. The thick black frames of his spectacles seemed to be balancing more precariously than usual on the bridge of his nose. He paused before speaking. For a moment Kevin felt a cold chill run up his spine, like when you are about to hear something very bad.

"When we took a look at your thyroid gland we only removed a tiny sliver of tissue. That is because we found 'this' embedded in the left lobe of your thyroid gland. I have never seen anything like this in my whole surgical career." Mr Sharpe opened his hand and inside was a piece of lens tissue on which sat a dark object. It was very small. Nevertheless, it was clearly a tiny pyramid shaped object.

"What is that?" asked Kevin.

"You must have some idea" added Kevin's mum.

Mr Sharpe replied: "I have no idea at all. In fact, I cannot understand how this object came to be embedded in your thyroid gland. Whatever it is, it is possible if not likely that it caused the symptoms you experienced by having an adverse effect on your thyroid structure and function." Mr Sharpe went on to explain that the object had had some kind of organic layer over the top of it, seemingly protecting it. This layer was very tough and resembled keratin, a protein that is found in nails and hair. The object had been carefully removed from a nerve bundle that supplied the thyroid gland and the outer layer dissected away.

31

"How on earth did such a thing get into my thyroid gland?" Kevin's mum wanted an answer.

Kevin's mum was bemused. What was this thing that had been hidden away inside her body? Mr Sharpe offered Kevin the object to keep as a 'souvenir'. "It is very odd" said Mr Sharpe. "I had a good look at that object under the microscope. It seems to be metallic in nature. I was guessing something like titanium but one of my colleagues thinks there is more than one element present and there might be some iron. He may be right because we did a little investigation and found that it is magnetic."

Kevin was intrigued and he spoke up, cutting Mr Sharpe's sentences short. "Doctor, this is a tiny object but has a perfect shape. The sides are regular triangles. It must have found its way into my mum's neck somehow."

Mr Sharpe's eyes peered over the top of his glasses. "It is most peculiar. It does not look like a natural object to me, rather it looks like something that has been manufactured. Life is full of mysteries. We will probably never know how it ended up in the thyroid gland. If I did not know better I would say it was implanted surgically... but this is impossible. Well, you keep the object Kevin and if anyone asks you or your mum about it you can refer to it as an implant."

It was not long before Kevin's mum was out of hospital and home. She had no complications from the surgery and no follow-up procedures were required. After all, only a tiny piece of tissue had been removed. It seemed like the absence of the implant had made a big difference. The thyroid size soon returned to normal as did its function. Life returned to normal and the implant was put in a little empty match box and stored away in a non-used drawer in a bedside locker.

CHAPTER 2

Life before Life

Kevin lay prone on top of his bed. He was fully clothed except for his trainers which he had placed out of the way to one side of the bed. This was mainly done in respect of his mum's sense of neatness. She had trained him to be a tidy person from an early age. This was the same bedroom as he had slept in since his childhood. The wallpaper was a rather mundane pattern of stripes while the ceiling was covered by matt white Dulux paint. This contrasted with how things had once looked, years ago. In his young days Kevin had demanded and been given a mosaic wallpaper to line his bedroom walls. The pattern included all kinds of craft whizzing around the sky with a yellow sun and blue sky as a backdrop. He could remember that most of these craft were printed in such a way as to almost make them appear animated. They were present in bright if not gaudy colours which were aimed at attracting the attention of a small child. There were red, green and blue biplanes, jet aircraft, rockets and even flying saucers. The latter seemed oddly familiar even though they did not 'connect well' with the other more terrestrial and worldly flying machines on the wallpaper pattern.

It was 11-30 pm and the house was quiet. His mum was already asleep in her own room as had always been the case. Sometimes Kevin would listen to music in bed through headphones. He liked several genres of music but he was especially attracted to rock. By its nature, this music was best appreciated at high volume, hence the wearing of headphones. Kevin did not want to wake his mum from her slumbers. This evening was not one for listening to music. Kevin was feeling tired and sleepy which was something quite unusual for him as he was something of a night owl. He did not feel like getting up off the bed to do the normal washing, teeth cleaning and day-clothes removal before sleep. He was already beginning to drift in and out of light sleep. In his moments of waking he dreamily reflected on his life.

Kevin was now eighteen years old. Various past times and events flowed through his mind, flicking from one thing to another, rather like quickly turning the pages of a book. When a large river flows downstream it develops eddies and back-flows, makes sharp bends, flows over shallows and deeps until splitting into tributaries. This is how Kevin imagined his life story… ups and downs, twists and turns. He had been lucky, his life river had been mainly flowing at medium speed and with just a few ripples to disturb it. More unlucky folk had to suffer maelstroms and rapids. He pondered his future through glazed sleepy eyes. Which route would the water choose next?

He began to recall dreamily and rather vaguely the day his mum had taken him to the funfair. He had enjoyed that experience very much but his memory of it was hazy. He could remember going up high above the ground on the rocket ride and the feeling of ascending towards the stars. He could also remember being high above the ground in the Ferris Wheel and looking both down at the tiny people below and upwards into the night sky. It had seemed so 'normal' somehow, so 'right', hanging up high in the heavens and observing the ether of the Universe. Of course, one thing stood out vividly in his memory. The sudden illness of his mum when he was sixteen was firmly embedded into his mind. It had come as a great shock, maybe even a life wake-up call.

Kevin's mind then jumped to the 'in-between' years. Kevin had a very stable childhood during the years between his funfair experience and his mum's illness. This was a formative time in which Kevin had built his personality and interests. He had learned how to interact with others and was respectful of those 'in charge' such as his teachers. However, he would not be cowed by anybody and would always stand up for himself. His mum had continued to give him all her love and support as Kevin progressed through ages nine, ten, eleven and onwards. He had an interest in learning and reading and could be a bookworm on occasions. Life had mainly consisted of school lessons, homework and having fun-times indoors. He had a reasonably free run to do what he wanted at home provided he was not too noisy and tidied up any mess he made. He was able to preoccupy himself without becoming bored. His mum fed him well. There were occasional trips to the coast for holidays in the spring or summer. Days out made use of the coach route which had a pick-up point close to Meads, the village sweet shop and sub-post office. It was a convenient walk from and to home to pick up or get off the coach. Most holidays were at Warner's or Butlins Holiday Camp sites. Sometimes Kevin shared a room with his mum at the coast near the sea in cheap hotels or guest houses that catered for bed and breakfast. There were lots of activities to keep him busy on seaside trips and the sandy beaches represented challenges to him to make sandcastles which would resist the wave action of the incoming tide for as long as possible until the inevitable happened and they were swept away. Kevin had not been the type of child to worry about anything. His childhood had been there 'for his pleasure'. His mum was his rock. The first time he had experienced insecurity was two years ago when his mum was unable to fulfil her usual domestic roles due to her illness. Kevin had been maintained in a safety bubble away from any bad influences or dangers. It was the first time that he had thought about mortality.

Kevin was now fully asleep. He went into a deep 'comatose' state. His clothes were still on but he had turned all the room lights off. His began to make rapid eye movements... this REM sleep reflected the fact that he was now dreaming. He would rarely be able to remember his dreams after he woke up. They very quickly faded away. His dreams ranged across all kinds of events both real and imaginary. His body made occasional twitching movements. The night wore on and the house was cosy and warm. The house had a central heating system and the radiators had been left on.

Kevin was rudely awakened at 3 am. There was a small window in the wall adjacent to the main bay. The headlights from a car shone through this window. The beam was focussed on Kevin but it was so bright that his whole room was illuminated. It was a very intense white light. It was so bright that Kevin could not see anything clearly. Everything was a blur. He raised his right arm and used his hand to cover his eyes. He tried to get up to see the source of this nuisance light. He could not move... not even a finger. He wanted the light to go away but it stayed on. Kevin was becoming petrified. What the heck was happening? He was afraid he was experiencing a 'night terror'... a kind of nightmare where people act out terrible deeds. He did not think people were able to remember their night terrors after they woke up. He was sure he was awake. Maybe he was experiencing 'sleep paralysis'. He knew that people in this state think they are awake but are actually still asleep and dreaming and usually have paralysis of movement. So what was this humming noise now filling his head? Kevin stared as best he could into the glare coming from outside. It looked to him like the light was coming down from somewhere up in the sky. As he strained his eyes upward he could just make out a tiny shimmering object just beyond the light beam. It appeared to be the source of the illumination but this object had a redness about it... whatever it was. Then the light beam abruptly turned off and the humming noise stopped. The room returned to its normal illumination and Kevin felt so weary that he immediately went to sleep despite the distressing experience.

Kevin stirred out of his sleep at 7-30 am. He was still dressed from the night before. His bedclothes were somewhat 'rucked up'. He had set his alarm clock to go off at 6-45 am. As an eighteen year old he had embarked on a course of study with the aim of getting himself into University. He had mock exams coming up shortly and he was taking his revision extremely seriously. It was Saturday morning and he intended to wake up early, shower and eat breakfast before doing a few hours revision. He had always found it easier to revise and learn information during the morning between around 9 am until around 11 am. After that he would take a break. The weather was kind and he considered taking his pedal bike for a ride into the village. He felt an urge to take the footpath alongside St Benedict Parish Church of the Holy Trinity and round the park behind the church where the funfair had once been located.

He emerged from underneath the duvet though he did not remember covering himself with it. He rubbed his eyes which were slightly sore and inflamed and then yawned. He noticed that his alarm clock had apparently not gone off as it did not wake him up at 6-45 am as anticipated. Perhaps the clock had malfunctioned or he had not heard it and slept through the buzzers of the clock. Kevin noticed that he was wearing his trainers. Had he gone to sleep with them on? There seemed to be a few mud-like marks on his jeans and a couple of blades of grass stuck to the soles of his trainers which had some dried muddy deposits attached to them. He brushed these off into the bedroom waste bin. He remembered nothing of any events that had occurred during the previous night. He had slept well. Today was another new day. The sun was rising. It was going to be a scorcher.

Once his revision session was over Kevin decided it was time to go outdoors and have a change of scenery. He donned his light blue tennis shirt that he invariably wore for cycling and a pair of navy blue shorts. They were not really colour co-ordinated but Kevin was not aware of this. He was not the sort of person who felt the need to dress in a certain style and he was not self-conscious at all. He was not bothered about how other people viewed him. This was consistent with other aspects of his personality since he was not too bothered about what other people thought of him in general either. His own view of himself and life was paramount. This did not mean that Kevin was self-centred or arrogant. Far from it, he was merely self-assured and confident. However, he had maintained his shy streak and reluctance to speak to strangers, traits carried forwards from childhood. He enjoyed his own company but once his barriers were down he was actually very easy going and friendly, if not charming. He decided he would change his trainers… there were some scuff marks and discoloured patches on his main pair. He had only given these a cursory cleaning since noticing their state earlier on. He could clean them up properly later. On went the spare pair of trainers over his pale blue cotton socks. They were looking immaculately clean with their broad red stripe which looked most pronounced. Finally, the shades were put in place over his eyes and the baseball cap put in place. Of course, the rim was facing to the rear of Kevin's head. There was a plastic water bottle in place in the small bag behind the saddle. It was ice cold having just been taken out of the kitchen fridge. The Evian liquid refreshment might be needed if he began to sweat and get thirsty. It was gone noon and the sun was beginning to beat down. Kevin was ready and raring to go. He yelled a quick "bye mum" and a "see you later" and he was off.

Kevin raced along the lane running by his house and turned left into the main street. He quickly reached the village centre. He wanted to take a ride round the park behind St Benedict's. The area where the funfair had once been located now mainly consisted of flat low-cut grassland which was maintained by the local council. In one corner there was an area of black rubber matting on which stood four swings, a slide, two see-saws and a roundabout. This area was used by the local children to have some fun, usually under the watchful gaze of an anxious parent. The rubber matting provided an extra safeguard against unexpected accidents occurring such as falling off equipment. Health and Safety regulations ensured that such issues were taken seriously. The council had no intention of getting sued for damages relating to any kind of mishap that might happen to the children which could be laid at their door for negligence. There was also a football goal located a little further on past the play area. It only consisted of two vertical poles and one horizontal crossbar. There was no netting. This was where the older kids and adults spent time kicking a football and chasing each other, whacking their opponents ankles to get the ball at any cost. Somebody would go in the gap between the horizontal posts to act as the goalkeeper. The other participants would split up into teams and have 'matches' that were quite competitive. Many make-believe matches were fought out here… one day it was Man Utd v Liverpool, another time it would be Arsenal v Chelsea. Many alternative and fantasy parkland 'cup finals' and 'league matches' were played out here. Sometimes the results were unexpected. Kevin himself had in the past spent some time here kicking a ball around with some mates.

Beyond the football goal and at the far end of the flat

grassy area stood dense woodland. Between the trees lay various well-worn bumpy cycle tracks. Kevin's stamina was good and his calf and thigh muscles strong so it was possible for him to cycle well off the beaten track. Some areas within the wood did get rather swampy and it was necessary when cycling along not to get embedded in such muddy, sticky water-filled depressions. There were also pot holes and fallen branches to look out for. Kevin headed for the trees. He liked cycling in this area. Sometimes, he had in the past dismounted from his bike and stood still. The woodland wildlife would soon expose itself. There were the usual wood pigeons and even cuckoos. One time on a previous visit he thought he had seen an adder slithering along but he did not approach it knowing that it was poisonous. He had also spied Muntjac deer and the odd fox. The woodland floor was surrounded by ferns and in the spring bluebells proliferated, coating the land with their blue sheen. There were insects galore to be seen. He did not have time for the gnats and mosquitoes but there were some other more interesting creatures to see like the huge dragonflies. These would lay their eggs in the pond at the boundary of the woodland and private housing which was fenced off except for a small gate beyond the trees, separating them from the properties on the estate. The eggs hatched into ferocious aquatic predatory larval nymphs. Woe-betide any tiny fish or invertebrate that crossed their path. Sometimes Kevin would lift up any stones or piles of leaf-litter he spotted on the woodland floor. Numerous beetles and spiders would be revealed. Lifting up rotting pieces of damp fallen wood would expose numerous woodlice scuttling around, trying to figure out what this big upheaval to their world was all about.

Kevin enjoyed his time cycling round the woodland and looking at the living showcase it offered to those who had the patience or interest to look. A couple of hours had nearly passed and he had not eaten. He was quite hot but he was untroubled by thirst because he took frequent swigs of water whenever he felt the need. It was time to make his way back home, he was starting to get a little hungry and he thought he would make one last stop before going home. He decided to take a look at the pond close to the houses. The gate in the fence allowed limited access to the pond and woodland for the residents of the housing estate. The gate was kept padlocked but the local residents had been given the combination code. Some of the pet owners liked to walk their canine friends in the woods. The local children were generally discouraged from entry. Most parents feared that their kids might fall into the pond and drown. Most of the time the gate was kept locked and it was rather a quiet relatively undisturbed area.

The pond maintained a good water quality since it was stream fed and regularly topped up with incoming clean water. It was bounded by water rushes and reeds. Floating on the water surface were beds of water lillies… pinks, whites and yellows. These hydrophytic *Nymphaea* imparted vibrant coloured areas to various regions of the pond. The Canadian pondweed below the surface bubbled out life-giving oxygen into the water as a by-product of its photosynthesis. Kevin had always been fascinated by the natural world and this included diverse ecosystems and ecological niches. Kevin's shades were polaroid and took the glare away from the water surface where the water boatmen scudded their way along using their trapped air bubbles for buoyancy. His polaroid glasses would allow him to peer deep into the depths of the pond. He knew sticklebacks and minnows abounded, feasting on the millions of water fleas. There were also some small red-finned rudd and stunted striped perch. There had been occasional large swirls seen in the water and matts of weed had been seen moving around as if disturbed by some unseen force. There had been rumours that a large pike was living in the pond. Perhaps a big old *Esox* had been put in there by a mischievous angler. The pond was less than half an acre in size and would not support a large population of top predators. Kevin had heard that one day a mother mallard duck was swimming across the pond followed by a row of fluffy ducklings. Suddenly there was a big swirl and a duckling vanished. Kevin thought he might be able to spot any pike if there was one in the water with the aid of his polaroid 'specs'.

Kevin burst out of the woodland cycle track and arrived at the pond. There was somebody there already, standing on the opposite side adjacent to the entry gate in the fence, which was open. The resident female mallard and her duckling brood were being fed small pieces of bread which were thrown out across the surface after which they chased greedily in their competition to get to the food first. Kevin's own hunger pangs were immediately forgotten.

Kevin had seen Jane off and on for a long time during his trips to and from school and very occasionally in the distance during trips into the local village centre. Other than the one occasion they had exchanged names she had remained a ship passing in the night. He did not know how he had managed to contrive not starting a proper conversation with her. Now she stood face to face on the opposite side of the pond staring directly into his eyes. She was a sight to behold. Jane was wearing a white, light summery blouse neatly tucked into faded blue jeans. Kevin wondered if her gaze had penetrated through his eyeballs and delved somewhere into his very soul. She was such a beautiful and mysterious creature. Kevin did not have much experience dating girls or even chatting with them. He was a late starter. This new situation put him in a position where some form of interaction was called for. He took a deep breath and addressed Jane with a twinkle in his eye which unknowingly to Kevin she had noticed. "Hi! Do you remember me? I'm Kevin. I believe you are Jane." These brief words were to spark a whole new chapter in Kevin's life but at this point he had no idea of the significance of this encounter.

"Yes! You surprised me when you crashed out of the trees. Would you like to help me feed the ducks?"

Kevin joined Jane and they spent an hour feeding the feathery residents of the pond and chatting. Large amounts of information were exchanged. They talked to each other as if they were old friends. Jane explained to Kevin that she lived on the housing estate behind the pond. She liked to wander through the woodland or walk round the pond from time to time to get some thinking-time to herself and relax her mind. Like Kevin, she also lived alone with her mum but her dad had run off many years before with someone he had met during his rounds as a van delivery driver. Her mum and dad had divorced when she was small but he abandoned them both and she had no idea where he was. He did not even step up to his duties to pay alimony payments but just disappeared without trace. Jane was well-adjusted to life and like Kevin's mum, her mum had also been supportive and loving. It turned out that Jane was the same age as Kevin and was also studying. She was considering the possibility of making a career in nursing. Although Kevin had remained in the village to take his advanced studies in the Sixth Form of the senior school adjacent to Marwick Junior and Prep School, Jane had chosen to go to a Sixth Form College to undertake her studies. This was located in a nearby town. She felt too mature to remain in school and was too independent of thought to put up with school discipline and rules. Kevin walked alongside Jane pushing his bicycle along with one hand gripping the handle bars. They walked through the gate in the fence. Jane closed the gate, snapped the padlock shut and scrambled the combination. They took a slow walk to Jane's house on the estate, chatting continuously. Kevin asked Jane if they could meet up again. She replied that they could meet the same night. Kevin had not expected her to say yes. He certainly did not think they might meet up again the same evening. Kevin's eyes twinkled.

The community centre now had an annexe dedicated to the small number of youths in the village and surrounding area. There were a couple of table tennis tables, three pool tables and a snooker table, the green baize of which was in surprisingly good condition. There was even an old-fashioned juke box available which would churn out current and recent hits for a nominal fee at high volume. Soft drinks could be consumed on the premises. The annexe had really been put in place to prevent bored local youth becoming antisocial and to distract them from aberrant behaviours. The local area was relatively vandal free and had never suffered from youthful misdemeanours but whether the facilities in the annexe of the community centre had contributed to this tranquility was a matter for debate. The community centre was well-situated for Fred's Finest so once the delights of the annexe were finished with it was easy to access some great-tasting fish and chips though sometimes the fish was coated by excessive crispy batter and the chips were somewhat greasy. This somehow contributed positively to the unique taste of Fred's take-outs. Nowadays Fred's had a good alternative to the usual fayre with the choice of the new chicken or doner kebabs which rotated endlessly around the spit of the vertical grill above the gas-fired flame, dripping fat onto the metal plate below. The kebab was eaten inside a piece of hot pitta bread. There was a choice of adding nothing extra or filling the cut bread with salad, choosing from green and red cabbage, onions, cucumbers, tomatoes and hot green chilli peppers. These 'extras' came with the kebab and there was no additional charge. It was also possible to smother the final end product with a sauce… chilli sauce was the most popular but there was also English mustard, ketchup and 'burger sauce' to choose from. The kebab was often consumed with an ice cold coke or lemonade to complete the feast. With this in mind, Kevin and Jane decided to meet at the community centre at 7 pm.

Kevin and Jane soon 'became an item'. They would maximise their time together and shared their ideas and dreams. One afternoon they decided to take a walk together through the woods. They would do some exploring. The plan was to proceed off the beaten track of the usual cycle tracks and walkways and investigate the dense foliage and undergrowth for any long-abandoned and discarded items or interesting wildlife hiding in the interior. Old clothes and heavy boots were the order of the day. Kevin met-up with Jane outside her house and they took the short walk to the fence that held back the woodland process of ecological succession by which new species radiate outwards to occupy other environments in waves, each species in turn changing the conditions and replacing the previous one until the climax vegetation is reached, such as the oaks, hornbeams and beech trees which dominated the woodland. The overhead canopy was quite thick in some areas, blocking out most of the light so that only the shade plants like the ferns could flourish. These areas could also become quite swampy, even in the summer, since the soil never seemed to dry out properly in such places. Jane fiddled with the combination on the padlocked gate, opened it and they stepped through. She turned and fiddled with the combination code again. The gate was firmly closed and shut behind them. They strolled hand in hand around the pond and then they forced their way through the brambles and shrubs into the morass of tangled branches. They knew they would need to be careful to avoid scratches from brambles and stings from nettles. They had taken the precaution of wearing their sunglasses as a protective barrier to their eyes rather than an aid to reducing the glare of the sun, plus gloves. Very little skin was exposed. Nevertheless, they proceeded with great caution and slowly moved deeper and deeper into the wood. Kevin took the lead and Jane followed close behind. As they moved forward they came to a small clearing where the overhead canopy was not quite so dense. This gap had allowed extra rainfall to reach the ground and the woodland floor looked slightly muddier than before and it also had a darker tinge. However, Kevin was undeterred and unconcerned. He was leading the way. He confidently strode forwards into the clearing. His right leg sank down into a boggy quicksand-like hole. He tried to pull his leg out of the bog but was unable to do so. Suddenly he became aware that this boggy area stank. It was an awful smell of decay and rotting leaves. His leg sank deeper and deeper into the mire. Kevin's left leg still had some measure of grip. It was located on a drier patch of soil. He tried and tried to lift out his right leg. It was an impossible task. Cold damp water was trickling over the top of his boot. His face was getting red with the efforts of trying to extract his foot and leg. Some of the colour was due to the embarrassment of his predicament.

"Ha ha ha ha." Jane's laughter rang out. This was so amusing. The more Kevin tried to lift up his foot the more it sank into the dark brooding muddy bog. Kevin turned to Jane and meekly said "help." Jane was now in hysterics. "Ha ha ha ha." After a measure of her mirth had died down she asked Kevin to take her hand. She pulled with all her feminine strength. Kevin's foot seemed to move slightly. She grabbed hold of his jacket and yanked and yanked. Suddenly she felt Kevin moving. She pulled even harder and in a flash Kevin came flying towards her. She fell backwards onto a mat of weeds, leaves and twigs which covered the ground with Kevin lying on top of her. His right boot was still stuck in the bog, the top of which was only just showing above the surface. His right leg was wet and black and smelly. Jane now had hooked burdock burrs in her hair and her back lay in the dirt. They both laughed for another minute or so and then their eyes met. There were a few moments of silence.

Jane's lips tasted of nectar. Kevin became bolder as instinct told him how to kiss. He felt Jane's tongue inside his mouth. It was sweeping left and right, investigating his oral space. The two tongues intertwined. Kevin could feel his heart rate speeding up. His heart was beating so fiercely he thought it might burst through his chest wall. His breathing was deep and shallow. Their caresses turned his mind to jelly. They lay there in a crumpled mass for some long time. In fact, the world seemed 'timeless'. The afternoon drifted past. In later years they would talk about this event recalling that Kevin's boot was abandoned in the bog and perhaps still lay there for posterity unless some other hapless individual stumbled into the same boggy area and discovered it. Kevin somehow eventually got himself home with just the damp muddy sock on his right leg. He took it off before entering his mum's house.

Time moved on and in due course both Kevin and Jane obtained University entrance having both done well in their respective advanced studies. Kevin had finally opted to take a degree in pharmacy. He was interested in the therapeutic and preventive role of drugs and medicines. Perhaps one day he might use his knowledge in the field of medicinal research. Jane had maintained her interest in nursing and took a degree route to get her knowledge, training and qualification. Both of them successfully graduated with good honours. All the way through their undergraduate lives at different colleges they had stayed in regular contact and met up whenever they could. Both of them had brief flirtations and liaisons while at college but these did not break the bond that had developed between them and it was inevitable that they would get back together.

Life after University brought both Kevin and Jane into the realm of adult reality. Both Kevin's and Jane's mothers needed help to pay the bills and cope with the rising cost of living. Neither of them wished for maternal subsidy of their living and social activities. The need to secure their own income became increasingly relevant. Jobs were not easy to come by and this applied both to humble occupations and professional careers. Both Kevin and Jane were not oriented towards entrepreneurship nor were they business-minded so they needed to embark on a course of paid employment.

Both of them were independent and responsible young adults. In fact, Kevin and Jane had many characteristics in common and they held somewhat similar moral, political and general life views. Their personalities were not just compatible but they complemented each other. A long-term or permanent relationship was enveloping them without any conscious effort on their part to cement any ongoing future commitment or partnership.

Jane undertook some nursing hospital placements, work experience and post-graduate training. Job-seeking became increasingly serious. Kevin and Jane helped each other prepare a meticulous resumé. They utilised advice from the careers service regarding the format of the document and the need for a covering letter. The curriculum vitae (CV) needed to impress any potential employer. There was a need to get noticed when applying for a job to have any chance of success. The CV had to stand out from possibly hundreds of others that were sent in to potential employers by applicants. It was necessary to 'sell yourself' without coming across as arrogant. The document had to include not only personal contact details but information on places of education, academic qualifications and full-time or part-time employment. Most important was to include a section outlining personal skills and why they suited the applicant to the post applied for. Their CVs included comments on areas such as their communication skills (written, verbal and listening), self motivation, time-keeping and ability to meet deadlines. The skills section also referred to both working within a team and also being able to act independently and show initiative. These skills supplemented the more usual brief comments of many applicants which referred only to hard work and punctuality. A short section followed their skills on the document which outlined some personal aspects about them such as hobbies, sporting, musical and reading interests. The document concluded with a list of three referees. One referee was an academic one, another was from a previous employer and the third was a personal referee that could vouch for good character, sociability and honesty.

The CVs were posted off 'on spec' to various potential employers. Kevin and Jane also responded to any relevant vacancies they could spot being advertised in journals and publications. Both of them experienced one of the realities of job-seeking. Being invited for an interview did not guarantee that a job offer would be forthcoming. They dressed 'suitably' and usually formally when interview occasions came along. The failures were disappointing but the experiences did hone both of their interview techniques. They learned to listen carefully to any questions and take their time before replying. Answers became measured and less likely to stray away from the subject area. They had both mastered the art of hiding their nervousness so that their body language and eye contact were positive. The eye twitching, shaking hands and mumbled speaking often evident during interviews were gone.

Their persistence in job searching paid off. In due course Kevin obtained paid employment with a pharmaceutical company involving the testing of potential new medications and also pesticides pre-licence and not yet approved for use in the public domain. This involved various toxicological studies mainly on microbes, non-living systems and computerised models though there was a little testing of laboratory animals. The latter aspect was the only negative part of Kevin's work and he decided that at some point he would move on to new employment that did not involve those components of his job that he was uncomfortable with, including any animal testing. Much of Kevin's work involved looking for malformations and abnormalities in cells due to exposure to the chemicals in the proposed medications and pesticides. Kevin was shown novel investigation techniques including aspects of gene manipulation with a view to possible gene therapy in future times where treatment could be given to the unborn foetus before the process of parturition. On some occasions his colleagues demonstrated how to undertake new cutting-edge and state of the art procedures of studying reproductive development. These procedures seemed surprisingly familiar to Kevin. He did not only get the strange feeling that these techniques were known to him, it seemed that they were actually very primitive modes of study and there were far more efficient and sophisticated systems of investigation. Just what these better procedures were was unclear in his mind. It was as if he had a blanket thrown over his head which was hiding his eyesight. Whenever he got these odd thoughts he quickly shrugged them off but sometimes these ideas lingered in his mind longer than he wanted. Anyway, he was happy to receive a pay cheque at the end of each month. In the meantime, Jane had secured a paid post within the nursing profession and she developed a growing interest in midwifery and also paediatric care.

It was rather ironic that both Kevin and Jane were involved on a daily basis in areas that covered embryology, birth and childcare. Fate can have cruel tendrils that wrap around its victim and keep the person on-track for what awaits them in the future.

CHAPTER 3

A Loud Quiet Time

They reached St Benedict Parish Church of the Holy Trinity at the far end of the village and took the old footpath that ran alongside the church grounds and past the gravestones in the cemetery plot which remained in their mouldy and unkempt state. They walked slowly, hand in hand, fingers intertwined. Their conversation was light hearted and optimistic for the future. Kevin and Jane at a still youthful twenty four years old had many happy years ahead of them and time to plan their future lives. They had already had a couple of informal chats with the vicar in the small house adjoining the church. The vicarage was subsidised to ease the living expenses of Father Williams and the close proximity of the house to the church allowed him to keep an eye on the building and its holy contents. Today the formalities of their proposed marriage were arranged and their joining would be officially sanctified within the stony walls of St Benedict. Dates had been set for the ceremony. The task remained of deciding which guests to invite to join them on their special day and for their post-marital celebrations. They also needed to finalise where these should be held. Kevin had also been pondering on suitable destinations for the honeymoon but he had not made up his mind at this point. Jane was proudly wearing the engagement ring that Kevin had carefully selected for her. He had travelled out of the local village to seek something fit for his beautiful fiancée in a large jewellery store in a nearby town. She now sported a gold ring with a beautiful central sparkling diamond complete with a cluster of small stones surrounding it. These made the main stone stand out visually. The ring had dented Kevin's finances but Jane was deserving of the best. He really loved her.

The two mothers of the happy couple had been introduced. Kevin had long since met Jane's mum at her house and they got on very well. Once it had become clear to Kevin and Jane that their relationship had become serious they decided early on that the two mums ought to meet up. One evening Kevin had gone over to Jane's house taking his mum with him. Kevin's mum was known in the village as Mrs Powell and that was the way she preferred it. Kevin diplomatically mentioned to his mum that perhaps on this occasion it would not be a term of endearment to introduce her as Mrs Powell. His mum gave him a cursory sideways glance and said nothing. Jane's mum opened the door. Before Kevin could speak, his mum spoke out in a friendly tone. "Hello, it's nice to meet you. I'm Sylvie." Sylvie and Emma quickly hit it off and it was not long before the two mothers became good acquaintances if not friends in their own right. Sylvie was now fifty four and Emma two years her junior.

Emma was an attractive slim woman with blonde hair and blue eyes and the resemblance to her daughter was clear for all to see. There were a few wisps of greying hair and a wrinkle or two in the brow which hinted that the ageing process was at work. The two mums met on a number of occasions sometimes in the absence of their progeny. They chatted about many things though Sylvie still had nothing to say about Kevin's dad. This was a topic which she avoided or, if this was not possible, she would manage to turn the conversation along a different route. Both women were in good health but Sylvie did recount to Emma the time she had been taken ill and had to have a thyroid investigation and surgery. She told how she had experienced some soreness in the neck after coming home but no mention was made to Emma of the removal of a 'mysterious' implant by the surgeon.

Unlike with many families, there were no issues about who to invite to the wedding. The guest list would be very small. Neither Kevin nor Jane had attachments to any relatives of their absent fathers. Sylvie had no extended family to speak of at all and though Emma had a brother, he had taken the decision to emigrate with his wife to Australia many years before in search of a better life and he was rarely in contact these days. Emma did remain in touch a few times each year with a cousin. Cousin Meg lived far away and was a spinster. She was much older than Emma but they made an occasional phone call to each other and exchanged Christmas cards each year. Emma had become slightly concerned over Meg as her health had been declining due to a combination of hypertension and angina. A guest list was gradually put together but it consisted of just a few friends of Kevin and Jane and some local people suggested by Sylvie and Emma. Cousin Meg was included in the guest list and Emma hoped she would be well enough to attend the marriage service and celebrations. The two mothers decided to split costs as money was not in abundance and a small celebratory wedding party was booked in the community centre's main hall.

Philip Barnes now managed the local village butcher's shop. He had inherited and taken over the business when his dad Peter passed on. Emma was a regular customer at the butcher's and Philip had suggested a caterer friend of his should supply the food for the happy occasion. He was sure his friend would offer his services at a value for money rate and of course he would supply any meat products required personally. It did not matter if it was cold meat or poultry needed for sandwiches or if the food needed cooking for serving hot or cold. Anything they required would be organised by him personally or his mate. The meat or fowl would be guaranteed to be locally slaughtered, fresh and tasty.

As for liquid refreshment, Kevin himself organised the delivery on the appropriate date of various drinks. Most of the drinks were soft drinks... he did not envisage nor desire anyone getting drunk and out of control. Plenty of fruit juices, cokes, squash and also bottled water was ordered with a special purchase option including an ice delivery. Some alcohol was ordered and this mainly consisted of lagers, beers, ciders, Guinness, some wines, a few Babychams and a large bottle of Champagne. Suitable glasses, plates and cutlery were soon also ordered. The lady in Meads sweet shop assured Kevin that she would be happy to help out at the party reception assisting guests with the drinks, food and clearing up. One or two of her mates would also help out for a nominal fee. The event was going to include buffet-style dishes set out on a couple of long wide trestles in the community centre hall. The trestles would be covered by two new sparkling white giant tablecloths overlapping with each other.

Everything was coming together. Jane discussed the design of her wedding cake and this was soon undergoing the process of manufacture at the local bakery. It would be handmade to Jane's specifications. A rather upmarket mobile music system company was booked and they would supply suitable music and light effects. Their 'PA' system could also be utilised for any speeches though Kevin hoped these would be few and far between. His best man was a friend from childhood school days and he was briefed by Kevin on his preference for keeping speeches minimal. Kevin himself did not intend to talk for long, he did not like public speaking, even though this was a very special occasion. He would say how much he loved Jane and how beautiful she was and then go on to say some words of thanks to his mum for her efforts in bringing him up so well. He would also say something nice about Emma, Jane's mum and how he looked forward to having a great mother-in-law despite all the nonsensical jibes of comedians on television and entertainment shows about them.

Time moved on. Kevin selected and purchased a lovely wedding band from the same store as he had obtained the engagement ring. Both Kevin and Jane continued their daily routines going back and forth to work. Their minds were not so focussed as usual on their jobs, their thoughts kept drifting towards the soon-to-be nuptials. Both of them were a little nervous about the life changes that lay ahead but such worries were brushed away as soon as they set eyes on each other or spoke. In fact, they spent a lot of time after work in each other's company or talking on the phone and other electronic devices.

Time moved slowly towards the great day. Both excitement and trepidation built up in Kevin and Jane. The two mums busied themselves assisting with the preparations. Invitations had been sent out following the joint consultations with the happy couple. All of the reception requirements had been sorted out and St Benedict Parish Church of the Holy Trinity was 'booked'.

In due course the great day arrived. All the carefully planned preparations worked to a tee. The limousine booked to transport the bride and her mum the short ride to St Benedict's turned up on time. The food was great, the music was lively and all the guests attended except for poorly cousin Meg. The formal speeches were short, just as Kevin had hoped. Even the sun shone. Kevin and Jane were now Mr and Mrs Powell. They had arranged time away from work to enjoy a honeymoon. They were not going on an exotic far away trip. Perhaps that was something they would reserve for the future. They did have a beautiful bridal suite booked at The Plaza

Beach, a luxurious five star hotel on the coast a couple of hours drive away. The hotel had a spa with all manner of facilities. There was a gymnasium with health and exercise machines, indoor heated swimming pool, jacuzzi, solarium and sauna. There was also bookable whole body, facial or Indian head massages. Beauty treatments available included manicure and pedicure and there was even a mini hairdressing salon. Two restaurants provided sumptuous meals. There was the choice of the posh 'La Maison' restaurant or 'Joes' which provided large portions of bar-style meals in less formal surroundings. The TV lounge and 'Rose's Bar' completed the main facilities.

Before the occassion of marital celebrations, Emma's cousin Meg had been taken seriously ill. Unfortunately, a few days later Meg passed away. Her angina had been getting worse and worse and even placing her small medication tablets under her tongue when she felt breathless was barely supressing various unpleasant symptoms. Eventually she had a massive heart attack and died in the lounge with the television still playing. She was found by a district nurse who used to visit Meg at home to assist her with putting on her compression stockings which had prevented the occurrence of leg ulcers caused by poor blood circulation in the legs. The nurse had failed to gain entry on two occasions despite the background sound of the television programmes. Meg was found following forced entry by social workers and the local police constable who found her sitting upright in an armchair as if still watching the television. Some twisting of the corners of her mouth gave a clue to the bad pain she had experienced very briefly during her last moments.

Meg had lived in a substantial house. It was somewhat old and rickety like its owner. The contents were also very dated and old fashioned. She had never been engaged nor married. Meg was fiercely independent but more than that she was intolerant of other people's faults and what she perceived as annoying habits. This did not mean that she had not had her share of boyfriends in her younger days but she soon tired of them and moved on to the next. Meg did not have any children and her maternal instinct was unusually limited. She could tolerate other people's kids for a while but she would rather lavish her attention on a succession of cats and dogs. Meg was an eccentric old lady and was rather reclusive being happy with her own company. She did like to keep tabs on her cousin Emma from time to time just to see if anything of note had occurred. This was more an idle curiosity rather than a desire for familial well-being. In the event, Meg had died intestate. Following due proceedings after some time a large inheritance passed down to Emma. Jane's mum had no ambitions regarding big changes to her life. She was not well-off but was stable financially. Her house was enough for her as it was and she liked its location. After receiving the inheritance money, Emma did treat herself to a few extra domestic items, paid off some long standing credit card bills and took a short break with a friend to a guest house on the sea front of the popular coastal resort not far from Kevin and Jane's honeymoon hotel. Emma decided the young couple were more in need of financial support than she was and she generously donated the bulk of the financial windfall to them. The money was used as a deposit for a house and Kevin and Jane soon were the proud owners of a modern small two-bedroom semi-detached house at the far end of the village not too far from Jane's mum.

The house was in good condition and needed no internal or external work or improvements doing to it. In fact, the paintwork and decorating were immaculate. The previous owner was a builder and handyman and had maintained the property in excellent order. There was both a front and back garden. The front garden was small and included an area of lawn surrounded by flower beds. A low lattice-style fence stood adjacent to a neat privet hedge, shrubs and hydrangeas. These formed the main boundary between the property and outside pavement. A little yellow-painted wooden swing gate filled a gap in the fence and this led to the front door via a pathway consisting of a mosaic of paving stones. The back garden was about forty feet long and had a high wooden fence along one side and wire mesh fencing along the other, separating their property from the adjoining neighbours. There was a small pond which retained a few old and wise goldfish left there by the previous owner. A small green mesh net covered the pond to keep any invading herons at bay in case they fancied a quick fishy snack away from their usual haunts on local lakes. The back garden also had a small outhouse reached by a concrete pathway running down the centre of the rear lawn. There was a miniature apple tree in the far left corner of the rear garden and a large olive-coloured water butt. One thing missing was a garage but the absence of this was not a problem and parking was available outside the front door. The spare bedroom was handy in case anyone wished to stay over but more importantly it was there for any baby that might make its appearance with the passage of time.

Kevin and Jane checked-in at the Plaza Beach Hotel as the new Mr and Mrs Powell. The honeymoon suite was very luxurious with a large double four-poster bed draped in pink, lacy attire. The available space in the suite was substantial. There was a machine to press trousers, tea and coffee-making facilities, satellite television and a large bathroom and shower area. On the coffee table at the foot of the bed was an ice bucket. The freezing ice cubes enveloped a large bottle of Champagne. The cold bubbly brew was quickly consumed. Kevin and Jane had a wonderful time. Day time was filled with excursions to local places of interest, while the afternoons were filled up by making full use of the hotel spa facilities. In the evenings sumptuous meals were eaten with relish. This occasion was not one in which healthy-eating featured highly on their priorities. Night times were filled with romancing and marital conjugations. The idyllic life continued for ten glorious days before they returned home to take a few days reorientating themselves and preparing for a return to work.

After returning from their honeymoon, Kevin and Jane quickly settled down to everyday life. The general pattern of events involved taking an early breakfast in good time to leave for the daily commuting to work. Once a week, usually on a Friday, they would indulge themselves and have a hearty cooked breakfast. Making Friday breakfasts somehow evolved into a weekly task for Kevin. He enjoyed cooking in general and he also took his turn making evening meals. This was particularly important on certain weeks when Jane had to work on a late shift. There was a rota and weekend work was a part of her nursing job that had to be accommodated. Jane was also on call and at times of staff shortage she would be asked to go into work as emergency cover for a colleague who was off sick or who could otherwise not attend for personal reasons. After all, babies would insist on being born when they were ready which was not always at a convenient time for hospital doctors, midwives and nurses.

Kevin and Jane at this point in their lives were still both twenty four years old. Kevin continued with his reproductive toxicology work which included drug testing. Various studies were contracted by the pharmaceutical company from external sources to check the efficacy and safety of proposed new medicines and environmental chemicals like pesticides and fertilisers. Without proper scientific testing such agents would be unlicenced and illegal to use in the public domain. Some contracts came in directly via the Government in association with various national and international companies requests for safety testing. Kevin's company undertook behavioural, biochemical, anatomical and genetic studies. Some of the testing required Home Office licences since some vivisection procedures were occasionally undertaken. Kevin detested this part of the work but fortunately for him he mainly was concerned with tissue testing and certain molecular biology studies and gene manipulations. Genetic research was undertaken in a state-of-the-art biotechnology laboratory. He did not have to play a direct role in any animal killing or vivisections. There were possible advantages to society if animals could be bred to resist any toxic effects to certain environmental agents that might destroy pests so agricultural stock and yield could be increased. However, most of Kevin's work was related to studying the human genome and looking to find ways of resisting various biochemical anomalies which could cause defects even before birth.

Kevin's expertise lay in the field of genetic engineering. This speciality allowed genetic modification to take place. He carried out various techniques allowing novel sequencies of DNA to be inserted into the DNA of an animal under test. Sometimes genes were removed using chemical enzymes like nuclease which acted like scissors at the molecular level. These kinds of studies had previously produced many benefits to mankind such as the production of non-bovine insulin. However, sometimes Kevin involved himself with more controversial studies mixing animal genetic material with human DNA. Of course, no transgenic offspring were generated but it was an area of great interest to Kevin. He had a feeling in the depths of his mind that he knew a lot more about this subject than his conscious thoughts would reveal. He frequently had thoughts of how useful these techniques could be for the survival of a species, even human-kind, should their environment change. New human characteristics might help them adapt to changed conditions. These thoughts had been flashing through his mind with increasing frequency during the last few months. He had even dreamed about this several times including one night on his honeymoon. Jane had to apply a gentle elbow in the ribs to waken him from his mutterings about visions of strange places and weird beings. They had somehow seemed not only real and familiar to Kevin.

Kevin's research projects had been numerous and varied but his managers had recently put him in charge of a team to concentrate on a particular study area. The work was focussed on human gene therapy. This aspect of genetic engineering allowed defective genes to be substituted by correctly-functioning versions. Tissue removed from the body had new genes inserted into their genetic component and this 'germline' tissue could be passed along future generations. It seemed apparent to Kevin that he could use similar techniques to go further than the guidelines provided by his managers for his work studies and research. There was no necessity to limit this work to defective genes. He speculated in his mind about replacing normal healthy genes with new variants. Perhaps if such tissue were inserted into the egg of a surrogate mother, humans could be born with very new traits and characteristics which might have survival advantages for them. It could lead to a modified form of humanity. He realised that his fantasised dreams and reality were beginning to overlap. These thoughts were leading Kevin into a world of eugenics and designer children. Of course such work could be deemed by some to be unethical if not illegal but it lingered in his mind and refused to take a back seat.

Jane had become a very dedicated and conscientious nurse who was very empathetic with the patients under her care. She was interested in paediatric development but had followed a midwifery training route which she had successfully completed and she now was registered and legally qualified to practice. She was active via her hospital links with pregnant women giving them support and advice. She had become proficient in assisting birthing and she was always vigilant to look out for medical complications in the mothers or offspring which might call for emergency action by one of the doctors. Jane gradually expanded her professional role and spent regular sessions during the week in the ante-natal clinic at the hospital. Her work there had many facets including counselling, education and preparing potential mothers (and fathers) for parenthood and child rearing. Jane loved her work and as time went by she became extremely interested in looking for any preventable defects. She liaised with colleagues involved with screening the unborn babies using ultrasound studies, providing that the mother-to-be had given appropriate permission. It was a coincidence that Jane's interest in developing and screening for health issues in the unborn and newborn rather mirrored the ideas passing through Kevin's mind regarding the genetic studies he was immersed in. In later years Kevin and Jane might reflect that these interests perhaps were not quite so much of a coincidence as they seemed at the current time.

Kevin and Jane had purchased a second hand Ford which was parked outside their front door. The car was in good condition and turned out to be reliable. Jane had not liked its sky-blue colour too much but decided that this car was a 'good buy' and excellent value for money so she had agreed to go ahead and buy it. Kevin did not mind the colour and his only reservation was that he would have liked the engine to be more powerful. He liked speed and was not too impressed when the car slowed down and huffed and puffed its way up steep hills. In the event, Jane became the main user of the car. She had to work shifts and was not happy commuting to and from the hospital during early or late shifts and in the dark. Jane was much more relaxed inside the safety and security of her own car and this allowed her to worry less when being out and about during anti-social hours. It also helped with shopping. She could pop into the grocery and butcher's shops when she was not working and pick up what she wanted without having to drag Kevin with her. Sometimes he would get impatient in the shops and at other times would spot things he thought were worth buying or bargains but to Jane's shrewd eye were simply a whim and waste of money. As far as Kevin was concerned, he was content to let Jane make full use of the car while he travelled to and from work on his bicycle. This had the extra bonus of giving him regular exercise and keeping him fit. There were some downsides to cycling especially when it was raining or cold but he would adjust his clothing to suit the prevailing conditions.

Cycling helped to keep Kevin in good physical shape. He sometimes turned out for the local village football team when a team member was off sick or injured. Kevin liked to play as a striker. He enjoyed playing up-field and loved it when he managed to score a goal. It is fair to say that his rate of goal-scoring compared to the number of matches he had played was quite poor. However, Kevin did not worry about the statistics. He just enjoyed the competition and exercise. Jane was rather ambivalent about him turning out for football matches. She was pleased that he enjoyed playing but worried in case of him getting injured. Football is a contact sport and Jane's nursing knowledge had brought her into direct contact with patients displaying sports injuries. She had seen a good crop of broken legs, broken noses, strained cruciate ligament and other tendon and muscle pulls and sprains.

One cold and dull Sunday morning in November, Kevin was invited to play a home league game against a rival visiting club. The opposition team were riding high near the top of the local league table whereas Kevin's side were right at the bottom. This was somehow reflected by the team's kit colours. The rival team were dressed in bright yellow tops and shorts with scarlet socks. Kevin's team wore dark green tops and brown shorts. Their socks were dark green with horizontal brown hoops. The 'yellows' had a reputation of being a loud-mouthed arrogant bunch whereas the 'greens' were short of confidence and the team spirit was poor. There were one or two good players in Kevin's side but they tended to play as individuals rather than as a coordinated team group. The match that day included an unsavoury incident which left its psychological mark on Kevin.

Kevin's side gave a good account of themselves during the first half of the match. They had mainly been pinned back in their half of the pitch by the opposition side. When the half-time whistle blew, Kevin's side were down by two goals. However, they could not be criticised for their efforts. They worked very hard chasing the ball around against a side which was a class above them. The second half duly arrived and the match continued. In the sixty-third minute, one of Kevin's team-mates centred the ball from the wing. The ball flew across the goal area at pace. Without thinking, Kevin launched himself instinctively into the air. Both legs were off the ground when he got a good connection on the ball. Perhaps more by luck than judgement, the ball went flying into the opponent's goal. Kevin was ecstatic. He raised his right arm into the air in triumph.

The opposition goalkeeper was less than impressed. He was a well muscled man over six feet tall with substantial beard and face stubble growth. The goalkeeper secretly was not pleased with his own inability to stop Kevin scoring but he decided Kevin was the cause of his shame. The goalkeeper grabbed the ball and ran straight at Kevin. He stopped right in front of him and eye-balled him. "Your father's a gorilla" said the goalkeeper, adding a few swear words to his comment.

"What did you say?" asked Kevin.

"You heard me" said the goalkeeper, "your father belongs in a zoo and you need to be there with him."

"You don't even know anything about me or my father" said Kevin angrily.

"I do" retorted the goalkeeper, "his son was a chimpanzee wearing football boots who couldn't decide whether to swing about on the goalposts or eat bananas on the side lines." The two men squared-up to each other but fortunately the referee gave a few shrill blasts with his whistle and intervened to separate them. Both players received a yellow card warning. The game continued to the full ninety minutes closure without further incident and the final score remained the same at 2–1, a narrow winning margin for the visitors.

After the match, Kevin could not get the goalkeeper's comments out of his mind. He knew the comments were stupid and mindless. However, the part that kept ticking over in his head was his own comments about the opposition goalkeeper not knowing anything about his father. It was a fact that Kevin himself did not know anything about his dad. Anytime he tried to think about it, right from his childhood days, some kind of switch clicked in his head and told him not to pursue the matter. His mum would not talk about the issue so he had managed to ignore the topic until now. Kevin felt quite emotional about this gap in his life history. The mental switch which inhibited his thoughts about the matter seemed to have temporarily at least, turned off. Kevin decided to pop into his mum before going home to bring the matter up.

Kevin duly arrived at his mum's house. After the customary warm greeting, tea and biscuits and chit chat, Kevin decided it was time to bring up the subject of his father. He pre-warned his mum that there was something bothering him which he needed to talk to her about. Kevin finally asked Sylvie to tell him about his father. Sylvie's body language immediately showed tension and anxiety. She could not look Kevin in the face. His mum complained that she needed to go to the bathroom but Kevin insisted that she stay where she was and answer his questions. A minute of stalemate followed with mutual complete silence. Finally, Kevin's mum asked him if he was someone who would believe the unbelievable. He replied that of course he wouldn't. The response from Sylvie was "in that case, you have no need to know."

Kevin was less than happy with his mum's answer. He did not wish to argue with her but he suddenly needed to know the truth. Rather than race headlong into a full blown argument, Kevin decided to rest the matter for the moment and bring it up again when the tense atmosphere had gone. He walked over to the bay windows and noticed that it was almost dark outside. For some reason, he could not clearly make out anything along the outside lane. The yellow neon street lamps did not appear to be working in the village across the fields. He noticed that the sky was unusually dark and cloudless. Strangely, he could not see any stars in the clear sky but even more baffling was the absence of the moon. Kevin turned round to face his mum in the living room and she asked him to turn on the room light. He clicked the wall switch and the overhead ceiling light came on with an unusual dark red glow instead of the usual colour.

The next thing Kevin became aware of was Jane's voice asking him how the football match had gone. Kevin felt slightly disorientated. He had a slight tingling in his head but he put this down to heading the ball in the football match. He knew that he had scored a great goal but did not recall paying his mum a visit. Kevin went into great detail with Jane about how he athletically headed a high-quality consolation goal. He continued "you'll never guess what. After I scored the goal, the opposition goalkeeper came charging out towards me. He told me I had scored the best goal he had seen all season and patted me on the back. That was so great." Kevin noticed that his watch was two hours ahead in time compared to what he thought the time should be. It seemed he had lost a couple of hours somehow but his mind was totally blank regarding this missing time.

CHAPTER 4

A Celebration: Feeling the Fear

It was early December and the days had been drawing in. The final autumnal resistance to lowered temperatures and shortened day length was all but over and leaf fall from deciduous trees was nearly complete. The leaves had changed colour from their various shades of green to reds and yellows. They now lay in the hedgerows, gardens and streets as crumpled brown masses. In some places the rainfall had made them slushy and slippery.

Kevin was up early. He shaved, washed and dressed before Jane was ready to join him. It was Friday and he set about his task of cooking a full breakfast for them both. It was about 7 am and still dark. The street lights would soon be turned off as the dawn light filtered weakly down from the rising sun. Kevin noticed through the gloom that the windscreen of their car was iced over and some five extra minutes of scraping with the little plastic implement would be required to clear it off. He would do this after he had made breakfast so Jane would be able to go straight off on her way to work.

The inside of the house was chilly. However, the central heating timer had clicked round to the 'on' position and it would not be long before the house warmed up. Jane would soon be forcing her way out from underneath the warm duvet and Kevin was in the mood to prepare a filling breakfast to see them through to lunch when pre-packed sandwiches were the order of the day. Kevin really 'went to town' on his breakfast. The frying pan sizzled with spluttering hot oil. It was joined by several rashers of bacon and a couple of chipolata sausages. This was just the start. Button mushrooms and scrambled egg and tomatoes joined the culinary delight. Kevin had not finished yet. Baked beans were added to the mix. Sometimes hash browns were also included and black pudding. Jane was not partial to black pudding, a strange mainly British delicacy made from dried pigs' blood and oatmeal. Kevin quite liked it but there was none in the fridge so it did not feature in this early morning fry up. Next came the time for the production of toast. Four cut slices of wholemeal bread sank into the fiery red grill of the toaster and it was not long before it noisily popped its way out to freedom in preparation for consumption. Butter already lay on the kitchen table in close proximity to the two bar stools they used to seat themselves. Both marmalade and strawberry jam were available but these might not be needed due to the extent of Kevin's chef-like efforts. Usually it was tea that brewed in the old-looking brown tea-pot with the bent spout but on this day Kevin decided upon having coffee for a change. He was no coffee expert and was content with a heaped half teaspoonful of instant Nescafe for speed. The hot brew would be consumed with a touch of milk and a spoonful of sugar. Jane soon joined Kevin in the kitchen. She looked very smart in her hospital uniform. Kevin got a sweet peck on the cheek as a thank you for making breakfast. They both had their own personalised drinking mugs. Kevin had them made on a whim but they were now used every day. Kevin's one was light blue and engraved with the words 'Kevin... World Class Boffin'. Jane's mug was pink and customised to read 'Jane... Trust Me... I'm a Midwife'.

Breakfast small-talk ended and most of the food was eaten. It was beginning to get brighter. Kevin thought how attractive his wife looked in the morning light. Kevin offered to do the washing up and Jane gladly agreed to this proposition. It was now 8-35 am and time for Jane to make her way to work. She was expecting a busy day ahead of her. She noticed that the ice had been scraped off the windscreen glass and she appreciated Kevin's thoughtfulness. Jane had made a good choice of Kevin for her husband. Not only was Kevin her soul- mate but he was also kind, loving and caring. He was a gentle person but could always be relied upon for support in a crisis. His inbuilt self-confidence seemed to 'rub off' on Jane as she went through the daily stresses and strains at her workplace and no-one there, neither staff nor patient, was ever unpleasant or uncooperative. She was well-liked and respected by staff colleagues and her patients loved her. The car engine burst into life and Jane was away. She reckoned to arrive at about 9-15 am. This would give her a little time to settle down and maybe grab another coffee before starting her duties at 9-30 am. If it was a busy day as expected, the time would pass more quickly and the day would feel like it had rapidly gone by. She hoped to get home around 6-30 pm. She wanted to relax and get plenty of sleep that Friday evening so she could make the most of the coming weekend. Fortunately, she was not on a duty roster and would have the whole weekend with Kevin to do as they wished.

Kevin soon finished washing the breakfast dishes. He even tidied a few things up. He liked everything to be put and kept in its correct place. This was a habit he had picked up from his mum during childhood. Jane had left fifteen minutes beforehand. Kevin now placed a strong white cycle helmet on his head and buckled the strap under his chin. He wore warm clothing with a waterproof outer plastic cover over the top in case of rain. He was able to dress more informally for work compared to Jane. His home clothes would be enveloped by a long white lab coat. This was the appropriate attire for his research work. This needed to be donned before entry into the research lab where Kevin would spend most of his day. He was wearing casual blue denim jeans, a Kashmir woolly jumper over a tee shirt and vest. This was topped off by a leather jacket. He wore special cycling boots. Kevin took with him some trainers in the saddlebag behind the cycle seat. In perhaps too close proximity to the trainers, he had placed some home-made egg mayonnaise sandwiches wrapped in silver foil, for lunch.

Kevin had always enjoyed cycling and he was happy to use this mode of transport to and from work. Besides, it was cheaper than petrol or using public transport. He was content for Jane to use the car and travel in relative safety and in the warmth provided by the car heater. Kevin hoped to get home a little earlier that day. He had worked some overtime hours helping out a colleague whose project was approaching a deadline and preliminary results were due to be published in a report. If the report deadline was missed, Kevin's company would be fined a penalty payment reduction in fees as per a clause in the contract between the company and client. Thanks to Kevin's assistance the report was produced in time. Kevin had been given a little time off 'in lieu' by his grateful company. He expected to be home around 3-30 pm giving him a little time to himself. Kevin, like Jane, was also thinking of having a relaxing evening in anticipation of an enjoyable weekend.

Kevin set off on his usual journey to work along the familiar country lanes and rural tracks he used as shortcuts. He travelled the same route back and forth each day. He was feeling content with life and was close to whistling a little tune while his feet did the hard work of pedalling. As he passed down the lane beyond Jane's mother's house his mind drifted to thoughts about Emma and then on to his own mum. Sylvie was now fifty five and coping well with her own independent life without Kevin and she was in good health. Kevin's thoughts drifted back to his childhood days at home with his mum. He recalled the occasion of going to the funfair and how he had strangely seen his mum in her pink dressing gown ascend the stairs when he had believed her to be still in her upstairs bedroom. Oh yes, he recalled how he had later seen his mum in a different dressing gown, a green one. "That's right" he mumbled to himself. "I could not remember having my breakfast and I was feeling hungry, yet mum said I had not long had my lunch."

Kevin's thoughts became more and more random and all kinds of memories began to flood through his brain. As his mind brought forth further long-forgotten experiences, he suddenly glimpsed something strange in his mind's eye about the day he went to the funfair. A buried memory suddenly revealed itself. He continued mumbling to himself. "Bloody hell! Now I remember that I was waiting for mum to come down and do breakfast and it suddenly got quite dark. I looked outside through the window and everything looked... wrong." He remembered how it had felt so still and quiet. Even the sun had changed colour to a shade of red. Soon after that, time itself had jumped ahead and he could remember nothing until he was about to go off to the funfair. "Strange I have just recalled this. Why now"? Kevin tried to rationalise this newly-emerged memory. "Maybe it is some kind of false memory" he told himself out loud. Kevin realised he was talking to himself.

Suddenly he began to feel somewhat disorientated and confused. He could not see very far along the lane. A mist had appeared from nowhere obstructing any long-distance views. He became aware that everything seemed very still. There was no wind. No sounds could be heard, not even from birds or distant traffic. Kevin's eyes were drawn skywards. Now this was odd. In fact it was very odd indeed. Peering upwards through the mist the sky looked strangely dark. The pale yellow wintery sun had risen some time ago but this looked more like a weird night sky. He could not see any sign of the moon and there were just a few stars. In fact there was no sign of the sun in the sky, it had 'gone'. The only thing he could make out was a small overhead globe. It resembled an orb of some kind and it glimmered with a most peculiar colour that Kevin could only describe to himself as blood red. It reminded Kevin of his newly-discovered recent memory of his childhood funfair day when he had looked out of the window and gazed skywards.

The next moments were unclear but Kevin had crashed into a shallow drainage ditch. He opened dazed eyes and everything had returned to 'normal'. There was a pale yellow wintery sun and whispy white clouds. He could hear birds singing and calling to each other from their territories and the sound of occasional cars and trucks on the main road in the distance near the village centre.

Kevin stood up. His first thoughts were worries that he might have damaged his bicycle. He thought the drop down into the ditch might have buckled his front wheel. Fortunately the bicycle was undamaged. Kevin then turned his thoughts to himself in case he had been injured. He felt fine. He was unaware of any cuts, bruises or pains. The only odd thing was that he had a slight unpleasant tingling in his neck. This was in front of his windpipe in a similar area to where his mum had suffered discomfort years ago before being diagnosed with thyroid problems. There was no mud or debris on Kevin's clothing. He was extremely baffled by the incident. Since he was feeling generally ok he decided to continue on his journey to work despite feeling a little bit shaken by the experience. The rest of his journey was uneventful. Kevin arrived at work and decided not to recount what had happened to anybody. His colleagues would probably only laugh at him if he told them he had ridden his bicycle into a ditch on the way to work. He would keep the incident to himself.

Kevin was soon at work in his lab and did not get much

time to reflect on what had happened on his way to work. He had a lot to do that day and he wanted to get his tasks finished so he could leave early in the afternoon. In his lunch break Kevin did spend a little time thinking about his experiences earlier that day. He was slightly concerned in case some illness had caused him to crash his bike and hallucinate. Something more sinister crossed his mind. He felt that the experience was familiar to him, not so much the crash but more the visions he had seen in the sky. It was a kind of *déjà vu*. He would confide what happened to Jane when he got home. Maybe she could provide some kind of rational explanation. Kevin instinctively rubbed his neck. He must have bruised it when falling into the ditch with his bicycle.

Jane's day was uneventful but busy. She was relieved when the time came to go home. Although Jane enjoyed her job, enough was enough. It could be emotionally draining being supportive to so many pregnant ladies and to be in a reassuring mode for much of the day. There were sometimes pre-natal problems or health issues *post partum* but these were few and far between. Usually she had to just encourage the more mature matrons who had been through the childbirth experience all before. The newly-pregnant mainly younger women needed her instruction and guidance. Some of them were surprisingly ignorant when it came to biology and bodily functions. If there were issues beyond her personal expertise she would refer the problems to others such as the doctors or counsellors.

At last the weekend was near and she would be able to relax and do what she wanted to do. Shopping crossed her mind. This was not something that Kevin would enjoy but maybe she would leave him at home for a few hours and wander round the shops to her heart's content. Even better, she would write out a shopping list for groceries and meat and ask Kevin to get them. This would leave her free to do some window shopping and perhaps a little purchasing. She began considering shoes, dresses and blouses. She could not afford to buy too much but maybe she would spoil herself for a change. There was always the credit card in her purse. She was always frugal with spending and there was very little debt owing on the card. She could pay for some things on this. Then she began to feel a little guilty buying things just for herself without getting something for Kevin. On the other hand, maybe she would get some new sexy underwear, perfume and lipstick and other cosmetics. Kevin would surely appreciate these in the marital bedroom. Jane arrived home a little later than she had anticipated but after a change of clothes, coffee and general 'winding down' she found the energy to cook and make a nice evening meal.

Kevin had managed to get home early as he had hoped. Jane had told him she would cook the evening meal so on arriving home he just busied himself with small jobs like doing some household tidying and putting away various pieces of crockery and cutlery that had been left on the drainer by the sink to dry themselves. He changed his clothes and took a shave... he had not bothered that morning and beard growth was already slightly evident. Normally Kevin shaved every morning but it had been a funny kind of a day. Something in Kevin's mind had suggested leaving the shaving for later and that was what he had done. He reflected that other than this, the morning had started very normally. He had not had any premonition of feeling unwell which might explain his accident on the way to work. Nothing could explain his strange thoughts and visions. He relaxed and played music eagerly anticipating Jane arriving home from work. He would tell her about what had happened to him.

Jane duly arrived and parked the car outside the front of the house. Kevin opened the door. He was very pleased to see her. When they met they undertook the customary hugs and kisses. Perhaps the initial excitement of their first meeting had waned a little but they were still madly in love with each other. Jane's kisses and hugs almost overwhelmed Kevin. He changed his mind about telling Jane of the earlier events in his day while cycling to work. He could tell her all about it later or even the next day. There was no rush. Jane's meal was delicious and after some joint dish washing they sat down to watch some evening television. Jane mentioned her proposed shopping trip and Kevin happily agreed she could go on her own. However, he did suggest that the following evening would be a good time for them both to go out and forget about work for a while. A movie and restaurant outing was suggested. Jane agreed and it would distract her from any residual guilty feelings following her shopping spree. She would treat Kevin to the night out and pay for everything.

They watched television and as the evening wore on they both became more and more tired. They felt both fatigued and sleepy. This was very unusual. They would usually stay up quite late watching a TV movie or soap opera. They also liked to listen to the late News as they were interested in current affairs locally and internationally. Kevin snoozed off during what had been an interesting historical documentary prior to the 10-30 pm news summary. Jane woke him up but she had tired eyes herself and her eyelids drooped. Maybe their workloads had caught up with them both. Work plus daily travelling was an energy drain which by Friday would often start to demonstrate its effect on the human body.

Kevin had been harbouring some secret thoughts about lovemaking but this drowsy feeling rapidly dampened his libido and testosterone influences. Jane was also now more or less devoid of the desire for romance. A bottle of chilled red wine lay unopened on the glass coffee table between the two armchairs which faced the TV and contained the sleepy couple. "I think we should turn in" said Kevin.

Jane replied "Me too! I am so tired. I just want to sleep."

Kevin thought it would be a good idea to take the wine up to the bedroom. His sleepy mind told him that perhaps they would reawaken and could sup the red brew in bed. The TV and lights were turned off except for a small onyx lampstand with a red shade in the corner of the lounge controlled by a dimmer switch. This would act as a 'nightlight' to warn off any would-be intruders that somebody was home. Jane made her way up to the bedroom closely followed by Kevin. His right hand held two wine glasses and his left hand held 'le vin'. The wine had a screw top and would be easy to open. There was no cork so a bottle-opener was not necessary.

Kevin and Jane were soon in their cosy bed. They snuggled up closely together and shared their body heat. Their lips pecked at each other and soon they were both fast asleep. They had not planned on an early night but drowsiness had overwhelmed them. Both of them were in a deep sleep. At about 3 am Kevin woke briefly. Something had disturbed his slumbers. The bedroom was very dark as the couple preferred not to use a bedside lamp. He opened his sleepy eyes and perceived a small round red glow on the bedroom ceiling. It must have been something coming from the street, probably a car headlamp. He was too tired to consider the fact that headlamp lights were not normally red. He rolled over, put his arms round Jane and went back to sleep.

At 5 am Kevin awoke again. He thought he could hear the bedroom door making a faint rattling sound. He peered towards the door and glimpsed a small rotation of the door handle which quickly returned to the starting position. Perhaps he was dreaming. Who could possibly be trying to come into the room? Jane was fast asleep next to him. A sliver of sunlight crept through the darkened room, filtering through the small gap between the heavy bedroom curtains. Had he imagined what he had seen? A horrible reality swept through Kevin's body. He had been in this situation before. He recalled the same event when he was an eight year old child. His memory of this situation suddenly became very sharp and his childhood experience became clear in his mind. As a child he had peered out from behind the duvet. On that occasion he made a conscious decision to ignore it and go back to sleep. Nothing nasty had happened to him except that there were some confusing observations of his mother being 'in the wrong place' in the house and some kind of time loss and memory deficit which he had put down to inadvertently falling asleep.

Kevin sat bolt upright. There appeared to be lights flashing which were coming from the landing under the door and into the bedroom. The illumination continued in sequential flashes of red, green and blue lights. The display continued... red, green, blue... red, green, blue... red, green, blue. What did it mean? Kevin had not wanted to disturb Jane. She was still fast asleep. As a child he had hid under the duvet during his bedroom experience. This time he did not think that was an option. What the heck was going on? He decided that he better wake Jane up from her sleep. He would call her name. He tried to mouth her name. No sounds came forth from Kevin's throat. His larynx was not cooperating. Again he tried to call out to Jane but this time more forcefully. No sound whatsoever came out of his mouth. He decided to shake Jane. He rubbed gently on her shoulder not wishing to startle her. There was no response. He tapped on her back... nothing. Jane's eyes were still tightly closed. She was breathing quite deeply and appeared to be still deeply asleep. Kevin wondered if she was in some kind of trance. Maybe he was hallucinating or still asleep and dreaming. He recalled the strange things he had experienced shortly before he crashed on his bicycle. Maybe he was suffering from delusions of some kind. Perhaps he was having a nervous breakdown. Maybe he had some psychological or mental problem all the while since childhood.

Kevin decided he better get out of bed and investigate. He

was getting quite nervous and anxious. What was the source of the lights? Who had turned the door handle? He could not move. His body was 'frozen'. He was not sure why he could not move. His brain was giving out instructions from his motor cortex to his limbs to move. He was not knowingly suffering from motorneurone disease or any other nervous affliction. How come his body refused to move? His pupils became mydriatic… they dilated wider and wider. Red, green, blue… red, green, blue… the frequency of the flashing was increasing. There was also a faint but distinct background humming sound. The door handle rotated and then closed. The door began to rattle. Kevin could not figure out what was going on. He had a minimal interest in paranormal events but he was generally sceptical. Was there any possibility that the house had a poltergeist? Perhaps some ghostly entity long-since passed away was returning in spirit form.

Kevin sat 'paralysed' in bed. He had to do something about this predicament. Indeed, time seemed to be passing but nothing was changing. Red, green, blue… red, green, blue… the flashing lights and humming sound continued.

The situation was becoming surreal. Even the environment was changing. He raised his eyes to view the ceiling. This was the only movement his body could make. Where there should be a ceiling was a night sky. It was not a night sky he could recognise. For a start, he could not see the moon. The normal night sky was full of a multitude of shiny glittering stars. This night sky, if that is what it was, contained just a few pin pricks of shimmering light. Some were very faint though a few were somewhat brighter. However, he could count them. There were less than a hundred, there should have been a countless array.

Kevin peered upwards. One object stood out from the rest. It was not very large but it was round and red. The redness was quite deep. It reminded Kevin of blood red, the

79

kind of shade he had seen from time to time on unfortunate experimental animals undergoing vivisection. The object glowed but its illumination was very weak. It occurred to Kevin that it somehow resembled the sun but it was not the sun he was familiar with. His astronomical knowledge began fluttering through his mind. Thoughts about phenomena such as pulsars and red dwarfs coursed through his head.

Kevin's neck muscles began to relax and he was able to make some small rotations of his head. It was rather like he had consumed or been injected with some drug or chemical agent which had affected him but was now beginning to wear off. He could still perceive the bedroom door. The flashing red, green and blue beams continued to pulsate. They seemed to be increasing in intensity. He felt that his whole body was enveloped by a haze of pulsating light. Perhaps it was some kind of plasma, a field of earthbound ionising radiation, like an anomalous *aurora borealis* of Northern Lights. For a few moments he felt the surrounding coloured mist dissipate. The red, green and blue flashing lights were still present but they were shining straight ahead like long distance car headlamps. Were they were emanating from Kevin's eyes? Was he the source of the energy beams?

This was inexplicable. Kevin was now becoming agitated. His emotions had been on a rollercoaster. He had been fearful at first. Then he had experienced the feeling of amazement and wonder. Any curiosity about his predicament was starting to wear off. He was beginning to get angry. Surely he was dreaming. It was about time he woke up. He again tried to shout out to Jane who was still fast asleep in bed next to him under the nearly starless night and red orb above. No sounds emerged from his mouth. He just could not speak. As this scene continued Kevin started to feel mental confusion. It was hard to cope with what was happening. Was it really happening at all? He wondered if he was going crazy. In fact, he was becoming convinced that this was the case. Kevin Powell, the crazy scientist. He needed rescuing but there was no saviour, he had to deal with this alone.

Kevin's confusion mounted. His conscious mind was having a major problem dealing with this reality. Did he exist? Had he ever existed? Who am I? What am I? What is this place? "Keeeeevin!" He heard a voice in his head. "Keeeevin... Keeevin... Keevin... Kevin." The voice in his head continued.

"Yes Dad, it's me." Who was he talking to? Was he having an imaginary thought conversation with a father he had never known?

"Time to do it" the telepathic voice said.

"Ok! I am ready." Kevin had spoken out loud but who had he spoken to?

Kevin felt his body muscles relaxing. He was able to make bending and straightening movements of his right arm. The antagonistic flexor and extensor biceps and triceps muscles were definitely getting their strength back. His scientific mind wrestled with itself looking for explanations. Perhaps something had disrupted the physiological contractile process. Maybe that was why he had been unable to move his muscles. Perhaps some inhibitory chemical had somehow got into his system at work and was having a delayed effect. This did not explain his 'hallucinations', however. Both his arms were improving in their mobility but his legs were quite leaden and heavy. He still could not walk.

The humming noise had vanished but the glowing and flashing coloured lights were still visible but were less intense than earlier. At least they no longer felt like they were derived from his eyes. He could now make partial rotations of his head. The room was still very dark and the overhead view still did not look right. He could make out the bedroom walls, they were in place as they should be. The bedroom door looked fine but there was still the faint glowing of sequential coloured light beams which filtered below the door between the frame and carpet on the floor.

Kevin tried in vain to turn his head. He thought he could just make out a shadow on the wall to his left nearly behind him. It had the shape of a man. There was a visible head and torso. He wanted to call out but still his vocal cords would not do as they were bid. The shadowy figure made a few gestures with slowly waving arm movements. The figure then seemed to float upwards to where the ceiling should have been and disappeared.

Kevin immediately became aware of something to his right side barely in his line of vision. Something was standing there motionless. Horror was beginning to fill his soul. Once again he tried to move and this time he had some success. His legs had moved on his brain's command. His brain's motor cortex was back in business. He managed to launch himself off the bed with the aid of a push or two with his arms and hands. He felt rather disorientated at first. His movements were uncoordinated. His balance was precarious. All of a sudden he felt fine. The cerebellum of his brain was released from its inhibitions and fired into action. His balance, movements and posture were back under reflex control. He turned round fully to face the stationary object standing motionless next to the bed.

Jane was wearing her newly purchased partially see-through white nightdress. She stood there without blinking. Her breathing movements were minimal. "Jane" he stammered. Jane did not move or reply. Her eyes were fully open, her arms at her side. Kevin stood right in front of her. He made strong eye-to-eye contact but Jane was expressionless. Her eyes were blank. There was no recognition of Kevin nor of anything else. Her gaze passed right through him. Kevin gently lifted her up and lay her on top of the duvet where she remained prone and motionless. Her long blonde hair cascaded over her shoulders but this version of Jane was eerie and reminded Kevin of the 'living dead' he had seen in many horror movies.

Kevin was in turmoil. He was pleased to get his senses back but he did not know what had been happening. Yet something in his head told him that he did know. He looked down at Jane. She was so beautiful. He loved her so much. He immediately realised he had to strangle her. What? It seemed his thoughts were still not under control. How could he think such a weird and wicked thing? He decided it would all be fine after he dissected her and took some of her DNA from her cells to study at work the following Monday. Kevin's thought processes were getting out of control. Was an *alter ego* trying to take over? Maybe he had a multi-personality disorder. Kevin tried to discard any wayward thoughts and get his mind together. He would figure this situation out in due course. His immediate concern was for Jane's welfare and safety so the sooner he killed her the better. No, he could not do that, death was not the task he had to accomplish. Whatever was he thinking? He sat astride Jane. Various implements were in his hands. He did not know what they were. He had to find the right place. He examined Jane's neck area and decided that a few sites would be suitable for inserting... something. The thyroid area was one choice, just like it had been in his mum. Another choice was to work on the cartilage discs between the vertebrae in the neck region. He decided to use this cervical region and set to work.

"Kevin! Kevin!" Jane was screaming.

"Quiet" said Kevin, "the neighbours will hear you."

"What are you doing? Why are you doing this to me? Stop it!" screamed Jane.

"You should be grateful" said Kevin, "especially with your interest in child development."

"Have you lost your mind?" asked Jane.

"Our future baby will love us for this" said Kevin.

"You are hurting me. Leave me alone" complained Jane. She tried desperately to push Kevin off. "My neck is so sore. Please Kevin, stop. You know I love you with all my heart." This phrase shook Kevin to the core. He realised he was still not thinking normally. He thought perhaps he was having sex with his beautiful wife. He realised that this was not the case at all. He had been doing something to Jane's neck. He might have been strangling her. As he thought more about it, he considered that he had been carrying out some surgical procedure in Jane's neck region. How could that be possible? He certainly had no anaesthetics or aseptic instruments. Why would he attempt anything like that, especially at home? Besides, Jane was well and there was nothing that required treatment.

Kevin lay in bed. He turned his body round to face Jane. She was fast asleep with her back to him. He passed his right arm across Jane's sleeping body as if to protect her. He listened to his wife breathing. He could feel her heart beating. He was so lucky to have such a wonderful soul mate. One day she would bear him children. She would be an excellent mother to his kids. He was glad it was the beginning of the weekend. He could have some quality time with Jane and forget about the working week. He would get the household shopping done while Jane contented herself window shopping and making a 'wish list'. He knew she would buy some things for herself but she deserved it. Later on in the day or evening they would go out together and do something interesting.

Kevin had been woken up by the wind and some draughts which sometimes permeated through the house via small openings in window frames and such like which needed filling and repairing. The draughts on the landing had caused the door to rattle. This had startled him and woken him up. He decided to get up although it was just 7 am. He would let Jane have an extended laze in bed and some extra snooze. Although he regularly made breakfast on Friday mornings this Saturday he would make breakfast again. He would deliver it to Jane on a tray while she was still in bed. He liked to spoil her and give her little treats and surprises. She would not expect breakfast in bed on Saturday morning.

Kevin finished in the bathroom. He had shaved, washed and dressed. He decided on making tea and buttered toast with a couple of semi hard boiled eggs. The egg cups had been customised like some other items in the house such as their drinking mugs. One egg cup was inscribed 'Kevin' in light blue while the other was inscribed with 'Jane' in pink. Now this was hardly original or unusual but the practicality of it appealed to Kevin's orderly mind and he found the personalisation appealing. The kettle was soon steaming away and the tea bags were in place in the pot for brewing. The egg-timer did its work for two and a half minutes before Kevin removed the eggs from the boiling water. They both preferred them on the soft and runny side. Kevin still enjoyed dipping toasty 'soldiers' into his egg just like he had done as a child.

Kevin ascended the stairs and walked the short distance along the landing to the bedroom. He carefully balanced the silver tray in his left hand while he juggled with the door handle with his right hand. On the tray were the tea, toast and egg in Jane's personal egg cup. The bedroom door handle rotated quite easily provided it was gripped firmly. The bedroom door opened smoothly and noiselessly. There was no rattling. There was Jane. She was laying on her back peering at the ceiling. It was now 8-30 am. Her eyes were only half open as Kevin entered the room, now holding the tray with his two hands. "Good morning" said Kevin. Jane's eyes opened fully. "Did you sleep well?" asked Kevin.

"Hello darling" said Jane. "Yes, I was so tired last night. I think I must have dropped off very quickly once we came up to bed" she continued.

"Did you enjoy your lie in?" asked Kevin.

"Yes, thank you so much for letting me sleep on longer than usual. I must have needed it" said Jane.

"I've brought you up your breakfast so you can eat it in bed" Kevin proudly announced.

"So I see" said Jane. "Oh Kev, you do spoil me."

In due course Jane was up and dressed. Breakfast was over with and they began to plan their weekend. Jane would use the car to travel into the nearby town and have a look round the shops. She wanted to do some window shopping and see the latest fashions and styles. She was especially interested in dresses and shoes but she also wanted to look at perfumes and cosmetics including lipsticks, blushers, eye shadow and eye-liners, mascara and foundation creams and powders. Jane did not normally use a lot of make-up but just now and again she liked to indulge herself. Most likely she would make a purchase or two. While she was immersed in her shopping spree Kevin would go into the village store and pick up some groceries. Jane decided it would be best to give him a shopping list on paper so he could not forget what to buy. She also wanted to prevent him from purchasing things which were not needed… or so she hoped. She knew Kevin well and even a shopping list was no guarantee that he would not make his own amendments to requirements. Jane diligently wrote out her list on a scrap of paper and it gradually expanded from general groceries to specific vegetables and meat.

There was no discussion of any unusual events during the previous night. Not only this, Kevin had no inclination to discuss the accident with his bike. He had previously been keen to discuss the matter with Jane. Now he could barely recall the incident at all. He did have a vestigial memory of something wayward happening. He remembered very vaguely that he had fallen from his bike but got up, remounted and rode on again. It was hardly worth telling Jane about it. He did have a feeling that there was more to what happened but it had vanished from his mind. This did not bother Kevin except that he felt as if something was 'blocking' his memory but he could not put his finger on what it was. Anyway, it seemed insignificant in the context of the greater scheme of things and it was dismissed from his conscious mind.

Kevin and Jane decided to go out individually and use up the coming afternoon. They would get back together later and go out for an expensive meal on that Saturday evening. Sunday's daytime would be a leisure period but they would go out again in the evening and watch a movie. The weekend outings would make a nice break from the weekly work routine.

Saturday morning passed by. Kevin yawned a few times. He felt a little sleepy. He could not understand why this should be. To his best knowledge he had slept quite well during the night. He had a slight memory of tossing round a bit in his sleep due to being disturbed by headlights from a passing car. He knew that he had also been dreaming about something but the memory of that had long since dissipated.

Jane did some washing up and vacuum cleaning during the morning. In the fridge was their unopened bottle of wine that Kevin had taken up to the bedroom to drink. The wine glasses were in the bowl in the kitchen sink for washing but they appeared completely clean and unused. Jane thought this was slightly strange but assumed Kevin had put them here for some reason. This was unlike him as he did not usually leave things lying around or chores unfinished.

Kevin liked everything to be in its 'right' place and he did a little tidying up. He gave his main attention to their bedroom. A few things were slightly out of position. The bedside locker had moved out of place by a good foot so he slid it back to its correct location. He noticed that the bedside lamp bulb had stopped working and needed to be replaced. The alarm clock lay face-down on the table. It had stopped at 3 am. He would have to put new batteries into the clock and would have to remember to add these to his shopping list as there were no spares in the house. He always stored his shoes neatly on a shoe rack but somehow one pair of his cycling trainers had fallen off onto the bedroom carpet. He opened his bedroom wardrobe. All his clothes were kept dangling neatly on hangers hooked over a shiny metal support rail. He had suits, jackets, ties, shirts, tee shirts and trousers. All these were maintained in a logical and unchanging order so he could choose his items quickly and easily when dressing. Several items were not in the right position. Perhaps he had unwittingly moved some things around or maybe Jane had done some tidying up or rearranging in his wardrobe. In particular there was a pair of denim blue jeans and a round-neck yellow tee shirt at the end of the rail sitting proudly on their own just beyond his small collection of suits. This was anathema to Kevin rather than just a trivial matter. He really did like everything to be in the right place as this contented his orderly mind. Soon everything was put back in their rightful place.

The afternoon was soon upon them. Jane duly went off in the car on her shopping quest. She really enjoyed her time in the shops. The afternoon passed quickly and her credit card now held the expenses from a number of purchases. Jane had come across some items on 'sale price' and she could not resist the temptation of getting some bargains.

Kevin used his bicycle to go down to the local stores in the village. He dutifully obtained all the items that Jane had requested. On this occasion he resisted the temptation to deviate from the shopping list. They both got home a few hours later. Jane showed Kevin her purchases and gave him a rueful look. He quickly smiled and Jane knew she had his approval. Jane was also pleased with Kevin for getting all the correct items on her list for a change with no extra purchases.

They sorted out all the shopping things and Jane's purchases and everything else was put away in the 'correct' place. After a time 'chilling out' with tea and biscuits they changed into some fresh clothes and were soon readying to go out for an evening meal. Jane had decided to let Kevin choose where they would go. He had seen a new Indian Restaurant which had opened in the village. Its patronage was still rather low as it had not yet built up a repeat customer base. It had only been open for a matter of weeks. The restaurant did take-out food which could be ordered by phone or online and they had a delivery service to local addresses. They also had tables for guests to eat 'in-house' but it was not busy enough yet to require pre-booking.

Inside the restaurant the walls were covered by carpet-like thick red paper. Images of men in turbans sitting astride elephants, dusky maidens and golden temples were everywhere. Kevin had previously popped in to see what it was like inside the restaurant and had a chat with the manager. He left with the menu on a printed brochure so they were able to consider their choice of food at home before they entered the premises.

The menu was extensive and included most of the 'usual' things. Kevin had noted some typical 'starter' choices such as samosas, onion bhajis, Tandoori chicken and various kebabs. Less well known to non-Asian diners were pakora, idli and dosa. In addition, there were a few soup alternatives like daal and mulligatawny. The main dishes came in all kinds of degrees of 'hotness' and this could be amended according to individual customer taste and tolerance to chillies and other spices like garam masala, saffron, cumin and jeera etc. There were many dishes to choose from. Not only were there numerous types of curries but there were also baltis and biriyanis plus a few English dishes like omelettes. All kind of breads were available such as naan, chapati, roti and puri.

There was an array of rices and side vegetables like saag, aloo, chana and okra.

Kevin wanted to try a 'chaat' like des bhalla. He had seen someone eating this in the restaurant as a cold dish when he had popped in previously. He asked the manager what it consisted of. He found out it contained pieces of cooked potato mixed with crisply fried pieces of bread and chickpeas. These were covered by a slightly sour and tangy tamarind and ginger sauce, coriander leaves and yoghurt. It appealed to him.

About 8 pm Kevin and Jane entered the restaurant. They were greeted by the manager who was very friendly. He was keen to grow the reputation of the restaurant. Besides advertising in local newspapers, dropping brochures through letterboxes and mailing leaflets, the manager Mohinder Singh knew that word of mouth and personal recommendation were probably the most effective ways of getting more clients. They were also just putting the finishing touches to a new website for promoting the restaurant.

Mohinder had a very relaxed manner and he showed Kevin and Jane to a candle-lit table for two in the corner. There was a romantic ambience about the place. Mohinder took their jacket and coat and hung them away safely on the wall at the far end of the restaurant adjacent to the bar. Mohinder delivered the food menu and wine list and told the couple to take their time before choosing what they wanted... he would come back to them in due course to see what drinks they wanted and to take their order for 'starters'.

Kevin was feeling very relaxed and happy to be out with Jane. They both had an idea as to what they might eat but they still scrutinised the menu in case they wanted to change their mind. A bottle of cold house wine was not long in being delivered in an ice bucket. Two crispy popadoms were placed on the table with a metal tray of 'chutneys'. There were dips of spicy yoghurt, lime pickle and mango plus diced onions.

These would keep them busy while they decided on what to choose for their main order. They dipped the fried crispy popadoms into the shiny bowls. They also noticed they had been given a spicy red dip which neither of them were familiar with.

Kevin and Jane sat opposite each other. Kevin extended his arm across the table and Jane took his hand. They were still in love. Their eyes met and the corners of Kevin's lips twisted into a smile and Jane responded with a pout and mock kiss. Other customers in the restaurant included one other young couple seated further along the wall at a table near the entrance door. Near the bar at the opposite and far end was a family group. There was a man and woman in their late thirties and two older people, a male and a female. Kevin assumed that this group were a couple probably out with one of their parents. There were also a couple of children, one boy aged about ten and a girl who looked just a little bit younger. It seemed that it was the occasion of either a birthday or an anniversary as a cake duly arrived and was placed on the table but Kevin was unsure about whose honour it was in. The children were well behaved and it occurred to Kevin that perhaps this was the first time they were being introduced to 'curry'. Kevin did not allow his curiosity to take over and he did not want to stare at them or any other people. He needed to mind his own business.

Overhead was a rotating chandelier which had long drop-down shards which sparkled rather like long earrings. The shards were crystal-like and teardrop shaped. They glimmered and somehow spread the light coming from three coloured bulbs mounted on the ceiling in a holder. The chandelier turned very slowly. As it did so, beams of light shone down onto Kevin... red, green and blue. The colours alternated and shone in sequence. Kevin fixed his gaze upwards at the ceiling.

"Jane, I am not feeling too well" said Kevin.

91

"What's the matter?" she asked in a concerned voice.

"I'm not sure" said Kevin. "I feel a little light headed and nauseous" he continued.

"Maybe you should come outside with me and get some fresh air" said Jane.

"I'm sure I will feel better in a minute or two" said Kevin.

Kevin beckoned to Mohinder to come over to their table. He arrived pen in hand and with a notebook ready to take their order. "Sir, are you and madam ready to order?" Kevin asked the manager if they could change tables. He said the flashing lights were bothering him. "No trouble, sir" said Mohinder and he immediately took them to another table away from any overhead lighting. In fact Mohinder had no idea what the problem was and he just assumed that the couple were fickle. On the basis that the 'customer is always right' he decided that politeness and remaining agreeable was the best response and this would benefit the restaurant in the long term in its search for referrals and new customers.

Immediately Kevin sat down at the new table he started to feel better. There were no immediate light sources to bother him. "Are you ok?" asked Jane.

"I feel perfectly normal again. I don't think there is anything to worry about. Maybe I should have eaten a little snack earlier on before we came out."

"If you are not feeling right we can go home" said Jane.

"No, I am fine now. I am actually very hungry. Let's order and eat."

The meal went ahead without any other problem. The food was delicious. Kevin and Jane agreed they could recommend the restaurant to friends and colleagues. They were also impressed with Mohinder. He had been very polite, patient and helpful.

Kevin and Jane arrived home feeling very full. They had enjoyed a great Saturday evening meal. It was nice to get out of the house and do something together. They would spoil themselves this weekend. They decided that they would go out on Sunday too and go to watch a movie. Jane wanted to wear one of the new dresses she had purchased. They had slightly different tastes in movie choice. Kevin preferred thrillers, science fiction and action films. Jane preferred something more romantic or comedies. They took a look at the movie guide. Jane decided she wanted to see a comedy movie that was showing in the nearby town. Kevin agreed to watch this movie and so the decision was made. They decided to go to the 7 pm showing. The movie would last for a couple of hours. By the time they came home it would not be especially late. They could turn in to bed and get some good sleep before starting another hard week at work.

After some time chatting they began to feel the onset of sleep requirements starting to nag at them. Jane changed into her night dress and went up to bed. Kevin checked all the doors were closed and locked up. Everything seemed fine. It had been a good Saturday. He soon followed Jane up to bed. He had put a new low wattage night bulb into the bedside lamp and he turned it on. The bedroom was dimly illuminated. Kevin was dressed only in his underpants which is how he preferred to sleep.

Kevin and Jane faced each other and chatted in whispers. They snuggled up together and gently kissed. Although they were both sleepy Kevin suddenly realised that he was becoming aroused. Jane responded and their kisses became more passionate. What had been hugs gradually changed into caresses. The tempo of activity was increasing and Kevin decided to kiss Jane's neck. She immediately let out an 'Ouch' yell.

"Whatever is wrong?" asked a startled and worried Kevin.

"My neck feels very sore" said Jane.

"Are you ok? Do you want me to stop?" asked Kevin.

"No, carry on from where you stopped" laughed Jane, "but be careful of my neck."

"I sure will" said Kevin. There followed a night of passion and energetic sex. At some point sleep took both of them over and they slept through the rest of the night undisturbed.

On Sunday morning they were in no hurry to get up but in due course they dressed and had breakfast. They were in the kitchen having tea. "How's your neck this morning?" asked Kevin. "Maybe you strained a muscle or slept on it in a funny position."

"Oh Kevin" said Jane. "How could you have forgotten?"

"What? What have I forgotten?" asked Kevin.

Jane did not look too pleased. "You know" said Jane.

"What do I know?" asked Kevin.

"On Friday night you woke me up and gave me a love-bite" said Jane, rather indignantly. "You started to make love to me. Then you bit my neck."

Kevin had no recall of this event. It was not part of his usual lovemaking repertoire or skills. "Let me take a look at your neck" said Kevin.

Jane duly pulled her hair to one side to clearly expose her neck. Kevin observed her neck closely and it was easy to see a large black and blue bruise. How embarrassing for Jane and for him. He would advise Jane to wear a high-necked jumper or blouse to hide it at work the next day. He could not see anything that resembled teeth marks. The contusion looked slightly unusual to Kevin. He thought there were indications of some kind of piercing or puncture wound more like a minor surgery mark than a toothy bite. He said sorry to Jane and that he did not know what had made him do such a thing. He wasn't into neck biting. Jane managed a slightly wicked-looking smile and decided to forgive him. She did not want her weekend to be spoiled by getting into an uncomfortable conversation with Kevin.

Sunday's weather was on a decline. The cloud cover gradually built up as the morning continued. The wind direction swung round and blew in from the east. It was distinctly chilly. "It's going to rain" said Kevin.

"Are we still going out later?" asked Jane.

"Of course we are" replied Kevin.

"I will make a small cooked lunch" said Jane.

"We still have plenty of time. The film does not start until 7 pm. They usually show trailers for the movies they will be showing during the following week as well as adverts. The movie itself will probably not start until 7-30 pm" said Kevin.

"Ok" said Jane. "Why don't you go and feed the fish in the pond while I sort out lunch? Do it now before the rain starts" demanded Jane.

"Will do" replied Kevin.

Kevin slipped on his old 'garden shoes' and proceeded along the central concrete pathway. He opened the locked padlock with a tiny key. The padlock gave protection from kids or burglars entering the outhouse though there had never been any trouble. There was nothing of huge value in the outhouse though Kevin would usually store his bicycle in here. Also in here they kept a small step ladder and an electric lawn mower. There were a number of shelves along the wall. His eyes moved along the objects stored on the shelves. There were several cans of partly used paints with their lids firmly replaced. He could see some grass seeds destined for the lawn to improve it... he would sprinkle these on the bare patches in the warmer weather. There were some flower bulbs like daffodils and tulips. Next he spied a plastic container of weed killer and then a packet of mixed seeds for the wild birds. Finally his eyes settled on the fish food.

Kevin liked to feed the fish floating flakes when the weather was kind. The fish would come up to the surface and dart about greedily chasing the food. The surface would ripple with activity and sometimes there would be the occasional unexpected big splash from one or two of the larger occupants. When it was windy it was not practical to feed flakes as they would blow all over the place as soon as they were released from his fingers. Kevin settled on a sinking variety of pondfish pellets as these could be gently lobbed into the water without much problem from the wind. He pulled up a small section of the covering green mesh net which had protected the fish from fish eating herons. He noticed the fish gathering under his feet even before he had thrown any food into the water. These fish had learned a thing or two over time. One thing they had learned for sure was that the appearance of Kevin at the side of the pond meant that dinner was on its way.

When they had first moved into the house there was a small resident stock of goldfish already in the pond. Kevin and Jane had 'adopted' these fish and took over their care. Not all these fish were the usual orange colour since there are several varieties of *Carassius auratus*. Some of Kevin's fish were combinations of red, yellow, white and even black. Kevin had not been content to only keep goldfish in the pond. Unknown to Jane he had also stocked some expensive colourful koi carp into the pond. He had not stopped there. The residents also included blue and golden orfe and a few mixed ornamental orange tench along with their naturally coloured green kin. These were mainly bottom feeders. His pride and joy were some mirror and common carp. He had stocked these fish by hand and they were growing large. They made loud slurping noises when he threw pieces of bread crust into the water. These floated on the surface until the carp came along and sucked them in. A pair of leathery lips would rise up from below the bread and it would vanish into the 'depths'.

The rippling and swirling of the water indicated that the fish were gratefully feeding on the food pellets. Kevin re-entered the outhouse and replaced the box of fish pellets onto the shelving. The door was closed and padlocked. At that moment the rain began to bucket down. The fish would be pleased but Kevin did a sprint down the concrete path and through the kitchen door back into the house. "You just made it without getting soaked. Lunch will be ready in ten minutes" said Jane. Kevin removed his slightly wet garden shoes and sat down near Jane on the kitchen bar stool while she finished making some pasta with home made cheese sauce.

By the time 6 pm came round the rain had turned to drizzle but it was still not very inviting outdoors. The wind was howling and blowing objects around. Some waste bins had blown over and were rolling around in the road. Pieces of paper and rubbish were blowing along the road like tumbleweed. Other debris flew up into the air and swirled about in spiral patterns. They decided that they would pick-up some fast food on the way to the cinema. Kevin decided on a cheese burger with fries and a soft drink. Jane chose a fish fillet plus an apple pie.

They arrived at the cinema and joined a small queue to purchase their tickets. The cinema was a 'multiplex' showing several different movies. There was a choice of seats at the front, middle and back row. Not many other people had chosen to see this movie. A bigger queue indicated a preference by a large number of teenagers for the horror movie which was showing in the adjacent auditorium. On their way into the auditorium Jane had paused at the stall selling popcorn. There was a choice of salty or sweet. The size of the popcorn containers was huge.

"Go on" said Kevin, "treat yourself."

Jane hesitated and thought about it. "I am tempted" she said, "but I think I am still too full after my fish burger." She decided against it. They watched the movie and both of them enjoyed it. They had some good laughs during the show so Kevin and Jane were in a happy mood as they drove home.

Both the wind and rain had died down and the stars were beginning to show through the scattered clouds along with a crescent shaped moon.

It was not long before they were home. They sorted out what clothes they were going to wear the next day. A working week was approaching yet again. The weekend had passed quickly. It did not take long before their clothes, documents and other bits and pieces were ready to pick up the next morning ready for work. They managed to get things sorted out before they became tired and sleepy.

About 11-30 pm they both had a milky warm chocolate drink and sat in the lounge exchanging small talk before retiring to bed. "I hope we sleep well tonight, especially having work tomorrow" said Jane.

"I'm sure we will get a restful night" said Kevin.

"I hope you are feeling ok. I was worried when we went for our curry and you felt unwell for a short time" said Jane.

"I feel fine now. It could have been anything that affected me. The rotating overhead lights on the restaurant ceiling gave me vertigo for some reason plus I got light headed but it did not last long. I feel good now. Don't worry darling. It was just one of those things" said Kevin. Kevin continued "there is no reason for our sleep to be interrupted."

Jane looked lovingly at her husband. "I think there is something you missed last Friday night. You were fast asleep in the middle of the night and I heard a humming noise. It woke me up. I didn't want to disturb you so I let you carry on sleeping. I got out of bed and there was something in the sky. I could not make it out clearly but I guess it was some kind of helicopter. It was sending out beams of flashing red, green and blue lights. I went back to bed and at one point the lights were reflecting from across our landing and were entering our bedroom. They were quite pretty actually. Anyway, after a while the humming noise stopped and the lights disappeared.

Just before the lights vanished and the sound stopped you spoke to me. I must have gone straight back to sleep after that."

Kevin laughed at Jane. "Ha ha, you were probably dreaming. I'm sure flashing lights and humming sounds would have woken me up. I don't remember a thing."

"Maybe you are right" said Jane. "Anyway, goodnight darling" said Jane. She then continued "and don't forget to ride your bike more carefully tomorrow while you cycle to work. You don't want to have another accident."

Kevin thought about what Jane had just said. He was sure he had not mentioned his accident to Jane. "My accident?" queried Kevin.

"Of course! Just as I was getting sleepy again you spoke to me. I do not clearly remember hearing your voice funnily enough. Your thoughts just appeared in my mind. You must have spoken out loud though. You told me how you had ridden into a ditch on the way to work. You didn't make up the story did you?"

Kevin felt confused. Had he forgotten telling Jane about his bike accident? Surely not! How could she possibly know about it? Kevin asked Jane if he had told her anything else. "I have no idea" said Jane. "As soon as the humming sound went off and the flashing lights disappeared I went straight back to sleep."

Kevin snuggled up to his wife and wished her goodnight. They were both twenty five years old at this point in their lives.

CHAPTER 5

Excellent but Improving

The doorbell rang. At first there was no answer. Emma pushed the doorbell button again but this time it was a more vigorous push and longer lasting. Faint footsteps approached the front door and a moment later the door opened widely. "Hello! So nice to see you" said Sylvie.

"You're looking well" said Emma. Sylvie beckoned Emma to enter. They shared a quick hug and Emma pecked Sylvie on the cheek. Emma took off her coat and gave it to Sylvie who hung it away on a hook on the coat rail in the hallway. They went into the lounge and sat down to chat. The two mums liked each other and stayed in regular contact. They found each other easy to talk to. As well as talking about their married offspring, they liked updating each other with any other personal 'news' and chatting about local and world issues.

Just more than a week previously, Sylvie had gone to visit Emma at her home at the other end of the village where Jane had previously lived on the housing estate. Kevin's mum still resided in the same house down the country lane where her son had grown up. It was not long before the kettle was steaming. Tea and digestive biscuits were soon placed on the glass top 'coffee table' ready for consumption. Both ladies sipped their tea and drank it white with milk. Sylvie had got used to drinking tea without any type of sweetener but Emma added a teaspoonful of granulated white sugar and stirred it rapidly in a counter clockwise direction.

The conversation was brisk and cheerful. All kinds of things were discussed and when one subject area became exhausted another one soon took its place. The topic of grandchildren was raised and the two mums speculated about when pregnancy might happen, how many children the couple would have and whether they preferred boys or girls. Neither Sylvie nor Emma had been given any clue regarding any possible increase in the Powell family. Both Kevin and Jane kept their cards close to their chest and gave no hint about any 'little ones' being on the way or even planned. After all, this was a private matter between the two of them. Certain intimate details could not be shared, not even with mothers.

The two mums had decided to have their get-together on a Tuesday morning at 10-30 am. Emma arrived and rang the doorbell very punctually at the exact time they had arranged. Emma planned to stay and chat for two or three hours and then make her way home walking through the village centre. Perhaps she would pop into one or two of the shops on her way home and buy a few bits and pieces that she needed, especially potatoes and onions which were running low.

This current meeting of the mums occurred only two weeks or so after Kevin and Jane had their weekend sojourns to the Indian restaurant and cinema. Kevin and Jane were still twenty five years old and Sylvie was fifty five. Emma had moved on to fifty three. The general health and mobility of the two ladies was still pretty good.

It was very rare these days for Sylvie to wear trainers, shorts or tennis shirts as she had done sometimes in the past, not even on hot summer days. She had become progressively more conservative in her dress style than she used to be. She continued to wear long dresses beyond knee length and 'maxi' skirts. Her shoes were still low or flat heeled and not chosen with any reference to current fashion trends. Practicality and durability were more important to Sylvie. Blouses and jumpers were very plain and not 'patterned' and it would be fair to say that her dress code was rather 'dowdy'. Sunglasses were only produced and worn on rare cloudless sunny days to keep down any glare rather than as any 'fashion statement'.

Emma on the other hand was much more 'young minded' and she was fashion conscious to an extent but limited her clothing collection to items she considered to be suitable for her age. She did not want the old saying 'mutton dressed as lamb' to apply to her. She did possess a couple of pairs of high heeled shoes which made an occasional appearance in public. When she wore a skirt it was quite short and barely knee length. She considered correctly that she still had nice legs and could see no reason for not displaying them. Her tops and blouses were colourful and quite tight fitting as she liked to display the womanly curves which had been developing each year as she matured and aged. In her mind she still felt she was ageing gracefully. Unlike Sylvie, she continued to wear denim jeans and trainers when she wanted to. The difference in dress code had no effect on the closeness of the friendship which had developed between Sylvie and Jane. Their personalities seemed to complement each other.

Sylvie had retained the attractive facial features that she possessed in her younger years. She was still slim but she had put on a few pounds compared to her size some years earlier. She still had brown hair which had so far resisted the usual greying process but she secretly checked in the mirror once a week for any signs of discolouration. Sylvie was not bothered about fashion crazes or styles nor about covering her lips, face or skin with all kinds of cosmetic products. However, although she preferred a natural look and had her own taste in clothing style and dress sense, she still liked to appear well presented in public. Greying hair was not necessarily part of this ethos. She had secretly considered using some hair dye products if grey hairs started to appear even though this went against her natural instincts. Sylvie's hair was no longer shoulder length or styled into a bun. She had her hair cropped rather short a year or so previously and she kept it like this as it was easier to manage.

Sylvie was a familiar figure walking around the local village and she had gone outdoors more and more frequently after Kevin had got married and left the house. She still did not stand and chat with local people in the shops or street and had become increasingly aloof. However, local people often greeted her with "Good afternoon Mrs Powell, how are you?" She would often reply "Fine thank you" and walk on. The getting-together of Kevin with Jane had 'thrown' her and Emma into contact with each other 'like it or not'. However, she had quickly come to like Emma and was pleased to have her as a friend.

Emma put on several pounds in weight after her daughter got married. She was pleased to see Jane happy and she liked and approved of Kevin. Her feminine shape had become more pronounced but in some ways she liked this and her tight-fitting clothes made her feel sexy. She was pleased to see that she could still turn men's eyes towards her in the street but they stopped short of wolf whistling. Emma was energetic and unlike Sylvie was very outwardly extrovert and garrulous. She was happy to stop and chat with anybody about anything and in general exuded warmth and friendliness. Although there had been some increase in her girth, Emma was still attractive to the opposite sex. She also had a great sense of humour which increased her social popularity. She applied anti-wrinkle cream to her forehead before going to bed and had numerous creams, powders and lotions in a large cosmetic box that Jane had got her a while ago as a Christmas gift. She also had a separate cosmetic bag containing lipsticks and several perfumes which lay on a little shelf in her bedroom. These were applied liberally as and when required. She did not like the greying streaks in her blonde hair but was happy that peroxide colouring preparations could come to her aid.

Emma had enjoyed chatting with Sylvie but she did not want to overstay her welcome. She decided she better start making her way back home and she could also quickly pop into a few shops to get a few items on her way back. Sylvie told Emma she was welcome to stay longer but Emma had decided it was time to make a move.

The two ladies stood by the front door of the house and Sylvie opened it. As they were saying their goodbyes Emma turned back to face Sylvie and spoke. "Oh my goodness! I nearly forgot to tell you" said Emma.

"What is it?" asked Sylvie.

"I don't know how this slipped my mind" said Emma. "I have a brother who lives in Australia. We somehow lost track of each other many years ago. He emigrated donkey years ago to start a new life. I knew he was in Perth for a time but all communications suddenly stopped. I would have loved to have invited him over to our kids' wedding but all my contact details were out of date so I could not add him to our guest list." Sylvie asked Emma to continue. "Well" Emma said, "yesterday I got a letter. It had an air-mail sticker on the envelope. It had lots of franking ink all over it and the stamp was Australian. I quickly opened it and to my surprise it was a long letter from John… my brother."

"How wonderful" said Sylvie. "I hope it was good news."

Emma offered to show the letter to Sylvie next time they met up so she could read it in full herself. She outlined his story. John had got sick and then lost his job. Not only was he unemployed but he had become close to ending up homeless. He had been too ashamed of his circumstances and fall from grace to let Emma know. He had recovered from his illness but spent his time on the streets roaming around looking for odd jobs or more permanent work.

It was during this low point that an aboriginal friend he had made on the streets introduced him to a retailer who owned a food mart. Now this retailer was well off financially and often gave away free food handouts to people down on their luck. As well as fresh food items there were always shelf-life foods about to go out of date that could be given to needy individuals. He gained personal satisfaction by acting as a benefactor and he was helped out in these generous activities by his daughter.

John had been reluctant to take free handouts... he was not a beggar. He decided discretion was the better part of valour and one day had gone with his aboriginal mate to the food mart premises. After all, although he was not starving, a few bonus food items would be more than handy. It was better he had them rather than knowing that perfectly edible food was going to be dumped or confined to the waste bin. It was inside the premises that he first set eyes on Maria, a beautiful curly haired redhead with slightly freckly skin. She had a number of wide gold bands on both wrists. Her smile was warm and welcoming. Maria was the daughter of the food mart owner. They got chatting and it was not too long before John became a regular visitor. After a while John began to help Maria and her dad handing out the food gifts to others. After some weeks had passed, a relationship developed between John and Maria. Her dad subsequently offered John a permanent managerial job in the mart. Time moved on and the couple decided to get engaged. John's life was not just on the mend but he was reclimbing the ladder of success, thanks largely to Maria and her dad. John now had the funds to invite his sister Emma over to Australia and pay for her flights and accommodation.

Emma could not wait to go. She was keen to see her brother and meet Maria. She also wanted to update John about Jane and Kevin and tell him about her own life. She would write a letter back as she did not have any electronic contact details and she would accept his kind offer. Hopefully he would reply and sort out flight tickets and other arrangements. She would have to organise her passport, insurance and any required visas. When she replied to John, Emma would include Sylvie's name and home address in case there were any issues she could help with while she was in Australia. Sylvie agreed that it was fine to do this. Emma decided to wait a short while before passing on Jane and Kevin's home contact details. She had not even told Jane yet about the letter but she would inform her of events shortly. The more Emma relived the contents of her brother's letter in her mind the keener she became to write a reply and send it off in the post the same day, provided there was time before the mail was picked up from the village post box near the post office.

Sylvie congratulated Emma on her good news. She asked Emma whether Jane knew anything about it. Emma was sure that Jane would be surprised and pleased to hear the news. Sylvie asked Emma how long she thought she would be gone. Emma was not sure and said she would have to arrange the details with her brother. Apparently he was now based in Alice Springs where he lived with Maria. Emma would take the opportunity to do some sightseeing while she was over in Australia and there was no rush to come back. She could stay in touch with her daughter from time to time while she was away but knew she could rely on Sylvie to keep an eye on the couple without any obvious intrusion into their privacy.

Emma duly exchanged messages with her brother and detailed arrangements were made regarding meeting up, accommodation and so on. John and Maria had purchased a large downtown apartment and it had plenty of space for guests to stay over. Two spare bedrooms were available. Flight tickets arrived and all the relevant documents were acquired. The dates of flight transfers back and forth were finalised but there was some flexibility in the return date. When Emma told Jane and Kevin about the mail she had received from her brother, Jane was thrilled. Kevin was happy that his wife was pleased. Kevin even considered the possibility that at some future time he and Jane might be able to make a trip to Australia and visit his wife's uncle.

It did not take long for the time of Emma's trip to come round. Since the get-together with Sylvie in which she had mentioned the receipt of her brother's letter, Emma had spent further occasions socialising with Sylvie and the young married couple. Emma had told John the news of Jane's marriage to Kevin. John also had been given Jane and Kevin's home contact details and also those of her good friend Sylvie. The 'big day' finally arrived. A cab arrived at Emma's house to take her to the airport. The driver helped Emma to load some large and heavy suitcases into the cab's boot (trunk).

Sylvie had seen Emma the previous day to wish her good luck and a safe journey. It was now early evening and Kevin and Jane had gone over to Emma's house after work to see her off. Emma hugged Kevin and then had a more extended hug with her daughter Jane. Jane's eyes were watery with emotion at saying goodbye to her mum but she was happy for her and asked her mother to pass her own and Kevin's love on to her uncle John. Emma was taking with her some photos of their wedding day to show her brother. Tears began to flow down Emma's cheeks but she knew it was time to leave. A long flight lay ahead of her and she did not want to be late checking-in at the airport flight desk. It was time for her to go. Emma asked Jane to keep an eye on her house while she was gone. She also asked Jane and Kevin to take care and look after themselves.

The driver politely guided Emma into the front passenger

seat of his cab and she strapped herself in firmly with the seat belt. Just before they left the cab driver said a few comforting words to Emma. He could see it was an emotional departure. Maybe his pleasant demeanour would earn him a bigger tip. Emma waved goodbye and the cab accelerated away. It was quickly out of sight. Kevin and Jane returned to their own house. Little did Jane suspect that this was the last occasion she would see her mum.

The following weekend Sylvie visited her son and daughter-in-law at their house. Jane always made Sylvie welcome and liked to make her feel at home. Kevin was always pleased to see his mum. He had felt slightly guilty when he moved out of the childhood home into his new house with his wife. There was no logical reasoning to these thoughts. They were caused by some emotional factors. His mum was getting a bit older and he had always been at home with her. Now he was gone from the house and he worried in case his mum might start to feel lonely even though he did not live very far away. What would happen if she was unexpectedly taken ill again? Of course, there was no question in his mind that residing in his own property was the correct and only thing to do. He was not going to share his mum's house with both his mum and his new wife. It was a prospect he might have considered had he had financial problems but due to Meg's legacy they could afford their own place. There was no question in his mind that he and Jane were better off in the privacy of their own home. Nevertheless, a nagging doubt haunted his thinking for brief moments of time.

Sylvie and Jane chatted away to their hearts' content. In fact, after a prolonged period of chit-chat about 'female stuff' Kevin was beginning to feel like an outsider in his own house. As the morning turned into the lunch period, the two women disappeared into the kitchen to do some baking. This was not in Kevin's realm of interest though he was perfectly happy to eat any freshly baked cakes they might generate. Some pleasant cooking smells were soon emanating from the kitchen. Sylvie was an 'old hand' at baking and also decorating homemade cupcakes and on this occasion she was keen to demonstrate her skills in the production of cup cakes to Jane.

Sylvie liked Jane and the feeling was mutual. Since the departure of Emma to Australia, Sylvie found her maternal instincts had focussed on Jane. She somehow felt more responsible for Jane's welfare and guidance now that Emma had gone. They knew that Emma had arrived safely and was staying with her brother John and Maria. However, she was not physically available to Jane and Sylvie wondered whether Jane was harbouring some hidden worries and anxieties about her mum. Australia was far away and there was no set date for Emma's return. Jane was becoming more like the daughter that Sylvie had never had rather than a daughter-in-law.

Jane asked Sylvie if she would like to go to the next town with her and do some window shopping. She had always enjoyed looking at items close up in the shops and checking whether the advertising slogans bore any resemblance to reality. If something was a bargain or good value for money she sometimes would expose her credit card and the sale was secured. Jane was aware that Kevin's mum was an attractive mature lady but thought her dress style was very conservative, old fashioned and 'frumpy'. She never overtly said anything about this to Sylvie as she did not want to hurt her feelings or cause embarrassment, if not an argument. Everybody had a right to dress as they wished. Still, perhaps she could treat Sylvie to a 'make over' as a surprise. Jane was not sure what Sylvie would say in response to this shopping trip offer. Jane was aware that Sylvie was known in the village as the rather aloof and somewhat cold Mrs Powell. However, she was very personable once you got to know her. Once the protective emotional defences really came down she was a sweet person and loyal to anyone she considered to be worthy of her trust.

Sylvie told Jane she would love to spend some time out shopping with her. Jane was delighted. The two women were united in agreeing that Kevin was not to accompany them. He was far too impatient and would be agitating them to keep moving on. This was to be a 'girl thing' and Kevin was excluded from the trip. Jane had a free day off work on the coming Friday due to not being required to work at that time on her rota system. That is when they agreed to meet and go on their venture. Jane would drive over to Sylvie and they would go by car into town, have lunch out and then head for the shops. Kevin feigned disappointment at not being able to join them but really he was pleased to have avoided hours of window shopping. In any event, he would be at work next Friday and could not have joined them anyway.

The week progressed but it felt like time was dragging to Sylvie. She was looking forward to spending time out with Jane. She had not had the pleasure of taking her time looking round the shops with Kevin when he was younger. On the few occasions she tried to take him on long shopping trips it was not long before he was being 'dragged round' and nagging to go home. Sylvie soon realised it was a pointless exercise trying to get Kevin to accompany her on her shopping trips. She did wonder whether had she been gifted with a daughter her experience as a mother might have been rather different. Surely a girl would have relished the chance studying all the exciting items on display in the shopping malls. This did not diminish her love for Kevin as a child. She loved her son deeply but did not always understand the male *psyche*. Now Jane was in her life she had the chance to catch up with a few experiences she had previously missed out on.

Jane's week was a busy one. This was good in some respects as time seemed to pass more quickly. She had been busy with meetings, training and birthing and the week flew by. Jane did not have too much time to think about the forthcoming shopping trip though it was definitely engraved on the back of her mind. Friday came along and Kevin made a nice breakfast and went off to work. Jane did the washing up and a little tidying and then changed into some outdoor clothes. She picked up the car keys and checked her handbag to ensure everything required was present. It would not be great to attempt to buy something without any cash or credit card being to hand. She also wanted to treat Sylvie to a surprise make over.

It did not take very long and Jane was at Sylvie's door. After some friendly greetings and hugs they went straight off. Jane and Sylvie chatted and gossiped small talk during the short drive and they soon arrived in town. Parking space was limited to a few meter pay-machines, a multi storey car park and a local council-run municipal car park. Traffic wardens patrolled all of these parking points on a regular basis, notebooks and pens poised and ready to write down car registration numbers of those who had not paid or who had outstayed their welcome. After a short time yellow parking tickets were attached to the windscreens and a hand held camera took evidence of the misdemeanour in case of dispute.

Jane found a parking space in the municipal car park. She purchased a ticket which would last for a full five hours. She did not want to become a member of the 'pay cow' club funding the local authority with her hard earned money. A parking fine was not on her plans for the day. She already paid more than enough in local taxes. Five hours was enough time for her and Sylvie to get through everything they wanted to do.

Jane and Sylvie had a plan. They set about the programme with enthusiasm. Events started off very slowly with a quiet lunch in a small café. Sylvie footed the bill. The afternoon went as well as expected if not better. Despite Sylvie's protestations, Jane persuaded her to have a make over and

111

paid all the expenses. She was fond of her mother-in-law and her own mum was not around. Sylvie emerged a 'new' woman. A 'pageboy' hairstyle, low cut blouse and skirt only up to the knee. She also wore various cosmetics and lipsticks upon her face. Sylvie was concerned that she might be looking ridiculous but the finished product was greeted by enthusiasm by Jane who kissed and hugged her. This gave Sylvie some extra confidence. She looked in the full length mirror and could hardly recognise this other person staring back at her. After a few minutes thinking about it she smiled. She began to wonder why she herself had not done something like this a long time ago. She liked what she could see. She did start to wonder what Kevin would make of it. Probably he would be shocked.

The afternoon passed pleasantly. Jane dropped Sylvie home. They thanked each other for a nice day. Sylvie was especially enthused. Jane's insistence on her make over was a revelation to her. Sylvie did not really want to have it done but she did not want to upset Jane so she had gone ahead. Now she was pleased. Jane returned home and after Kevin had come in from work and eaten, Jane told him all about the afternoon she had with his mum. Kevin found it hard to take on board the apparent change to his mother's style and appearance. This was something he could not wait to see. He did wonder whether Jane was fibbing and 'pulling his leg'.

At 8 am on the following Saturday morning Sylvie's phone rang. Sylvie picked up. There was a brief silence. Then Jane spoke. "I just had a phone call from uncle John in Australia."

"Is anything wrong?" enquired Sylvie.

"My mum… is dead." This statement was followed by terrible sobbing the like of which Sylvie had never heard before. Kevin took the phone away from his wife.

"I'm afraid it's true" said Kevin. "There was an accident."

"I am coming straight over to you. You can tell me the details later. The important thing is to help poor Jane." Sylvie immediately dressed quickly and headed over to Kevin and Jane's house. Sylvie entered the front door. Her heart was racing. Kevin barely noticed that his mum had a new look about her. He had more important things on his mind. He had been trying to calm his wife but had not been too successful. Jane was sitting on the sofa with both hands cupped around her face. Her nose was buried in the palms of her two hands. She was weeping. Sylvie sat down with Jane and surrounded her in a giant hug with both her arms around her. Sylvie did not say anything to Jane, she just held her tightly. The two women sobbed together.

Jane was twenty five when the news of her mother's death was learned. She was devastated. Growing up with Emma as an only child she had developed a close bond with her lone parent. Jane had been used to the idea that her mum was always around to support her if need be. Kevin was very supportive of his wife after the death of her mother but he came to realise that only time would be a 'cure'. The death of a loved-one was never to be forgotten but the pain did diminish with time to the extent that a normal life and daily routine could begin again. The trauma Jane was suffering in her grief was held in check by Sylvie who used much of her time and energy to support her daughter-in-law. Sylvie decided the best approach was to let Jane cry and express her emotions. She would 'be there' for Jane as needed. She was needed rather a lot. Jane became reliant on Sylvie for her support. Whilst Jane greatly appreciated Kevin's efforts to comfort her there was something about the feminine support offered by Sylvie that helped her paper over some of the emotional gaps in her heart produced by the unexpected loss of her mum.

Jane needed some time to herself after hearing of her mother's death. She went through a depressive period and discussed the matter with her doctor. Medication was suggested such as a tranquiliser. Diazepam was available in different doses as white, yellow and blue pills but after some hard thinking she decided against taking the medication. Jane did not want the crutch of medication despite the value it might provide. She decided to face the demons of her grief and depression face on. The doctor decided that the decision not to medicate was up to Jane to decide though he thought it might benefit her. The outcome of the visit to the GP was that they agreed Jane should return for a consultation at the surgery once a week for four weeks and the doctor would spend ten minutes counselling time with her. This was not really adequate but it would allow the doctor to monitor her depression. Jane did not wish to be referred to any specialist services including bereavement counselling. If Jane's depression deepened then the doctor would insist that she start a course of antidepressants such as Prozac but this would be a last resort.

Jane was given a period of compassionate leave from work because of her bereavement. She needed some time to come to terms with the shock of what had happened. She could not behave in a professional manner with her patients while under stress. The time off work was helpful to Jane allowing her to regain some composure. Several sympathy cards arrived by mail from colleagues and some patients who had got to hear about what had happened. Jane did visit the doctor regularly as agreed but valued more the time she spent with Sylvie who was very patient and kind. Sylvie turned out to be a good listener to Jane who poured out her heart and sorrow.

Being able to confide with Sylvie was of great benefit to Jane. It helped her grieving process. Jane knew that time would reduce the sharpness of her loss though the pain remained below the surface. Jane tried to cope with her grief as best she could and she was in fact somewhat in control of her tears on some occasions but at other times not all. She decided she would get Kevin to discuss funeral details with uncle John and that would take the pressure off her to some extent. Even though Jane remained grief stricken, she was strong minded and determined to cope. Therefore a most odd and frightening event which Jane was about to experience would be inexplicable to her. As to why it occurred was somewhat of a mystery as the grief of Emma's death was now more manageable and did noteasily explain away what Jane was about to experience as a stress related hallucination.

One afternoon, Jane had a few hours to herself. She decided this would be a good time to get some chores done. Doing the laundry would occupy her mind and distract her from mourning. Anyway, the laundry bag was full and the washing needed to be done. It could not wait any longer. Jane entered the utility room and took a peek inside her large laundry basket which had a pretty blue flower pattern around its sides. It was full to the top with bed linen, towels, blouses, shirts, trousers, socks and so on. Doing laundry washing was not Jane's idea of fun but was a chore that needed to be done. She opened the door of the washing machine and pushed item by item into the machine through the open door. When it was full she clicked the door closed. She adjusted the settings on the machine to the best temperature and appropriate fabric types. Finally, she took a scoop of washing up powder and dropped it into the machine via a sliding tray. Jane was not particular about which brand of powder to use but on this occasion she decided to use up the remains of a packet of Fairy. Like most other mainstay brands, the soap powder could be relied on to produce clean, fresh smelling garments and other items. Jane turned on the machine and watched the water flood into it while the machine made the usual whirring sounds as the drum began its spin programme.

Jane had intended to retire to the living room and find something on television to keep her occupied while the washing was being done. She stared at the washing machine and listened to its varied noises. She checked out the time on her watch and it was precisely 2-05 pm. The spinning drum fascinated Jane and strangely she could not take her eyes away from it. The noise of the machine became more shrill and then altered into a low, rhythmic, humming sound. Jane forgot her intention of watching television but concentrated instead on the rotating drum. Jane became less aware of her surroundings and her mind felt like it was entering a hypnotic trance. The drum spun quickly round and round. Jane stood in front of the machine though her mind felt strangely detached.

The passage of time did not influence Jane. She felt content to stand directly in front of the washing machine and observe its actions. She began to focus her attention more powerfully on the wash and closely scrutinised the clothes as they whirled before her. Jane's gaze was focussed straight ahead but her peripheral vision suggested that the room was getting dimmer. However, she could not turn her head away from the washing machine situated just a few feet in front of her. The utility room appeared to be quite dark but she was able to raise her eyes to the ceiling. The overhead electric lamp was on but for some reason it had a red bulb. Perhaps Kevin had changed it and put a coloured bulb in the light socket.

The washing twisted and turned as it revolved and Jane could see it clearly through the glass of the front door. Jane's body suddenly tensed. The laundry did not look quite right. Where there had been clothes and bedsheets and so on was something else. It resembled a face. The face rotated, round and round, keeping pace with the movements of the drum. The eyes were closed. There was something about the features that Jane recognised. She could see that the face belonged to a female. As Jane concentrated further, she realised whose face it was. It was Sylvie, Kevin's mum. What was going on? Jane knew that something was wrong with her perception of reality.

She tried to free her mind from the scene. At that moment, Sylvie opened her eyes and stared directly at Jane. Sylvie's head was now visible inside the washing machine whose drum had ceased turning. The head was orientated the correct way up and the face was pushed up tight to the glass of the washing machine's door. No torso was visible. Jane was horrified. She tried her best to scream but no sound would come forth from her throat. All Jane could do was watch and see what happened next. She felt frozen to the spot.

Jane felt as if she might pass out with fear. Kevin would not be home for some time. There was nobody to wake her up out of this nightmarish daydream. As she watched, she once again could not believe her eyes. The washing machine was slowly but surely stretching and changing shape. It formed initially into a cuboidal box shape and then rose to form a rectangular cabinet-like object. Jane estimated the height to be a little over six feet tall. It resembled an upright freezer chest with the facing surface transparent and sealing off the contents with its glass like or synthetic clear material. It was the contents of the chamber that raised Jane's heart rate to 150 beats per minute.

The washing liquid was visibly changing within the cabinet. It started off with a colour change. The liquid medium had been quite clear and watery with some soapy foam. Now, the liquid was taking on a pinkish hue. As Jane watched, the shade passed through salmon pink and on to a final bright pink. The aqueous medium also then began to change its constitution. The normal flowing movement of water was replaced by a runny viscous material rather similar to jelly when it is heated and becomes runny.

Jane stood fully face on to the chamber. No longer was Sylvie's face the prime object of Jane's gaze. The pink viscous material now enclosed the whole of Sylvie's body. She was completely naked. Her arms and legs thrashed around like when a non-swimmer falls into a pool of water and struggles

117

to try and avoid drowning. The limb movements were slowed down by the thickness of the liquid medium. There was sufficient room in the cabinet for Sylvie to remain upright. Occasionally she rotated revealing her bare buttocks to Jane. She mainly seemed to prefer facing directly towards Jane, squashing her breasts against the facing transparent casing. Sylvie was expressionless. Her mouth opened and closed like a fish breathing in water. Her eyeballs moved up and down exposing the white sclerotic coats of the outer eyeball. Jane failed to comprehend how Sylvie could remain alive but small respiratory thoracic rib movements were visible as she somehow extracted oxygen from the fluid medium. Jane noted a very fine stream of bubbles passing upwards from the base of the cabinet through the pink liquid towards the surface. Perhaps the liquid was being oxygenated.

Once again, Jane tried really very hard to scream. She wanted to scream and scream again. She felt complete despair and terror. She prayed for Kevin to save her. This was the scariest situation she had ever experienced. It was total terror. Jane felt a stream of wet, warm urine soak through her panties and trickle down her leg to form a small pool on the kitchen floor.

Jane decided to use every ounce of her willpower to get away. Her legs were like lead pillars and had no interest in locomotion. Jane managed to tilt her head upwards. She noticed that the lamp bulb had been replaced by a rather larger overhead object. It quite resembled the sun in the sky but she could look directly at this orb without hurting her eyes. It had no glare and rather than the usual bright yellow colour she was familiar with, this object had a distinct red glow.

Jane lowered her eyes away from the overhead orb and once again looked ahead. The freezer-like cabinet was still there and full of the pink liquid. Sylvie was gone. Jane was both relieved and puzzled. A voice then entered her mind. "This one is for you" said the voice.

Jane was beginning to think she was going crazy. She decided to try and respond by thinking of a reply in her mind's eye. Jane's thoughts formed in her head. She responded with "leave me alone. I do not want one of those things."

Another thought appeared even more strongly in Jane's brain. "Oh, but you must want it. You have to enter it, right now. You must remove your clothes first." Jane decided that in no way was she going to strip naked in her kitchen, whatever was happening to her. A few moments later, all her clothes were strewn around her. Her naked body was fully exposed.

Suddenly, Jane's body felt very light. It was as if the force of gravity had been removed, or at least reduced. She realised her feet were floating off the ground. Her whole body slowly levitated and positioned itself over the top of the cabinet with the pink liquid. The top of the cabinet seemed open and Jane feared she was going to be lowered down into the chamber. She hovered over the top. At any moment she might fall into the syrupy matrix below her. Finally, she let out the loudest scream of her whole life. "Kevin!"

Jane heard the doorbell ring. Kevin decided to use his door key and was now in the hallway heading for the utility room. Kevin saw Jane and his eyes opened in amazement. Jane was stark naked. The washing machine door was open. "Hi sexy" said Kevin. "This is a great greeting. I did not expect to come home and find you nude."

"I'm glad you like it. I might do it more often if you are a good boy. By the way, I think the washing machine is leaking. Maybe the door seal has corroded."

"Don't worry about that, I'll get it sorted out. Just come and give me a hug" said Kevin. Jane duly obliged.

"I'm so glad you're home" she said. "I was missing you."

"It's good to know you care" said Kevin. "Are you ok?"

"I'm fine" said Jane. "I think I snoozed off and had a bad dream. I really can't remember what it was about. The funny thing is my watch shows 4 pm. I seem to have missed some time during the afternoon. I thought it was earlier than that."

"Don't let it bother you" said Kevin. Jane's naked body was having an effect on Kevin and he began to become aroused. "Now I'm home, maybe we can go and have a lie down together" said Kevin, with a cheeky smile and twinkle in his eye.

"I wanted to have a chat with you about mum's funeral" said Jane. "Sorry to be a misery but it is hard to keep what happened off my mind. I need to be in contact with uncle John in Australia and sort out what to do."

"Don't worry about anything, darling" said Kevin. "You go and lie down. Leave the washing. I will deal with your uncle so there is no need to stress yourself about that. I love you."

"By the way" said Jane. "How's your mum? I thought of her today."

"I spoke to her earlier" said Kevin. "Apparently she's trying out some new pink bath salts and quite likes the feel of the liquid on the skin."

Jane did her best to continue with her normal married life though floods of tears still occurred from time to time when her psychological defences faltered and she thought dark stressful things related to her mum's passing.

Kevin liaised with Jane's uncle John. Kevin looked into the circumstances of Emma's unexpected and sad demise. Alice Springs was located near the middle of the Australian continent in the Northern Territory. Uncle John and partner Maria had relocated and flown there from Perth and set up their own retail store. It was a popular tourist venue and the population numbers varied from time to time. The Flying Doctor service had been operating from there and it had built up its infrastructure over the years. It was in an arid area of a usually dry river bed. John and Maria had welcomed Emma on her arrival and they took her to see several places of interest. Emma had then begun to look round the town on her own while her brother and Maria were tied up with their business activities.

This area of Central Australia varied in temperature at different times. It could drop to just a few degrees above freezing point at night. Emma decided to visit the Botanic Gardens but this was a hot day with a temperature around thirty five degrees Celsius. Emma was feeling rather dehydrated despite taking occasional sips of bottled water. Emma did not notice the 'insignificant' pebble she had stepped on as she tipped her head back to drink from the plastic bottle. Her ankle twisted and she fell. Her plight was not helped by hitting her head heavily on the ground. She quickly felt very unwell and became dizzy and light headed. She was soon unconscious. She was never to regain consciousness. Bystanders called an ambulance but she was pronounced dead on arrival at the hospital. Emma had suffered a major and fatal brain haemorrhage.

Following the death, it was decided by Jane and uncle John that Emma would 'rest' permanently in Australia. Jane and Kevin flew out to Australia for a short cremation service and scattering of ashes. Jane was distraught and she was not in the emotional state she would have liked to have been in for her first meeting with uncle John. This ought to have been a happy occasion. Sylvie did not accompany the couple to Australia but stayed at home to keep an eye on the houses and collect mail. Kevin did a good job supporting his wife through this difficult time. Jane and her uncle John determined to remain in contact with each other after she returned to England. Kevin and Jane were soon back in England. It was not long after their return that Jane paid the first of several more visits to her doctor for depression and sought solace with Sylvie, her mother-in-law. Jane began to regain her energy and zest for life and was grateful for the compassion and support of the people near and dear to her. Her thoughts began to extend towards the future and what life still had to offer.

"How about getting a little Powell on the way?" asked Jane.

"Errr! I am still not sure I am ready" replied Kevin.

"I see so many babies being born at work. I am beginning to feel like having one of my own" said Jane.

"Do you have any preference for a boy or a girl?" asked Kevin.

"I really don't mind. I am surprised you haven't thought about it Kevin."

"Well I have… a little bit" replied Kevin.

"We can afford it" said Jane. This was certainly true. Following the death of Jane's mum, the probate had been sorted out. Emma had left her property and assets in favour of Jane as her sole beneficiary. "I have even been thinking about names" said Jane. "I would quite like the name to be derived from my mum's name, maybe something like Gemma if it is a girl. What about Emmanuel if it is a boy?"

"I quite like the name Lorraine for a girl" suggested Kevin.

"Why is that?" asked Jane. "Do you have an ex-girlfriend named Lorraine?" Kevin laughed at Jane's question.

"Ha ha! You are jealous. Anyway, no, I never had a girlfriend called Lorraine. I just like the name" said Kevin.

"I don't know if I believe you. Perhaps we could use both names and call the baby Gemma Lorraine" responded Jane. "What about if the baby is a boy?" continued Jane.

"Kevin Junior sounds good to me. I am not sure I am ready to be called 'dad' yet. I don't mind practicing making one though" giggled Kevin.

"Typical you" said Jane. She smiled at Kevin with a naughty grin.

The conversation about babies took place some years after

Jane had lost her mum. It took her quite a long time to come to terms with what had happened. Jane had taken some time off work and when her official leave elapsed she took an extra week off. She had been depressed but in the end she decided it was time to go back to work. She found she could cope a lot better than she thought she would. In fact, going back to work had been enough of a distraction to take her mind off her personal loss. Kevin had been very strong and supportive and as for Sylvie… she had been an emotional rock. Jane's doctor had also played a role in getting her back on track to deal with everyday life.

Jane had lost her mum at age twenty five. Following the loss, although Jane recovered gradually from the shock and coped with her grief, she had become more emotionally vulnerable. Any thoughts she may have had at that time about getting pregnant were put to one side. She did not have a sufficient level of emotional investment to put into a child. Her inner strength was at a minimal level. It was better to concentrate and consolidate her relationship with her husband. Children, if there were to be any, would come along later.

Jane was now in her early thirties. She began to think that perhaps she should not wait too much longer to start a family. The older a pregnant mother was, the greater were the risks of health problems for both the child and the mother. There were various methods in place to test for abnormalities even before birth like ultrasound scans and the more old fashioned amniocentesis testing procedure. A long syringe removed foetal cells from the amniotic fluid in the water sac and these cells could be observed under the microscope. A normal nucleus within the cell should have the diploid number of chromosomes which in humans is forty six. If the count revealed a different number there would be a genetic problem. Having forty seven chromosomes in the nucleus was one of the more common genetic errors and this often indicated that the foetus had Down's Syndrome. Expectant mothers over forty had increased chances of having this condition and screening techniques were a useful early tool of detection. If this condition was detected then counselling protocols were in place and decisions on any intervention would have to be made.

Jane did not want to wait until she was in her early forties to have a child. Kevin would make a great dad. Their finances were secure and their house had room to accommodate a child in a separate bedroom. Jane knew that Sylvie would be pleased to have a grandchild and would spoil him or her rotten. She herself would be a doting mother. Jane's mind tossed round all kinds of imagery about babies, nappies, cots and sleepless nights. It would be a cause for regret that Emma would never get to see her grandchild. Nevertheless, maybe she would wait a few more years to go ahead and try for pregnancy. After all, once the baby was born, it would most probably be around for the rest of her life, there would be no going back.

Both Kevin and Jane were secure in their careers and had made several jumps up the promotion ladder. It was getting on for almost a decade. Both Kevin and Jane were thirty four. They still lived in the same house but they had some building work done on the property and it had been extended. It had also been repainted and decorated and was looking very nice. The years following Emma's death were ones of 'consolidation'. The relationship between Kevin and Jane was still excellent. They had a very strong bond between them. Neither of them was 'interested' in other members of the opposite sex. Kevin and Jane were still soulmates. Admittedly, their sex life had declined a little under the daily pressures of work. Kevin did his best to give romantic surprises to his wife especially when they were least expected. Bottles of Champagne, boxes of chocolates and bouquets of flowers all featured. Jane liked to entice Kevin by wearing sexy underwear in bed and putting out delicious candle-lit dinners for them both. If their eyes did stray towards another individual of the opposite sex they were both confident in each other that it would be a case of 'look but not touch'.

Kevin and Jane were still fit and well at thirty four. Kevin had continued to use a bike for work and his circulatory system was healthy and working well. He was well toned and muscled. Jane remained slim and active and possessed considerable stamina which helped her at work, especially during times which required hours of standing up. Sylvie was also well though her speed of mobility had slowed somewhat. Her mental capacities were still as sharp as ever. She was sixty-four and she did not expect to remain a 'spring chicken' for much longer. In fact, her 'prime' had already passed-by some years earlier. Since the day of her make over with Jane, she had made some effort to continue to dress in a more flexible and younger style but she was still relatively conservative in her appearance. Sylvie had remained in frequent contact with both her son and Jane and she felt that the latter was not just a friend but more like an 'adopted daughter'.

Kevin and Jane were twenty five when Kevin had come off his bicycle and crashed. The strange events that followed on an evening over that weekend may have been real or imagined but little or no memory traces of what may or may not have happened remained in either of their minds. However, an event was about to unfold which would bring back some distant memories into Kevin's mind. They were ones from a significant experience in his earlier life at the age of sixteen.

The memories of his mum becoming ill and having a neck operation began to trickle back. He also recalled a strange object being removed from his mum's neck region which the doctor could not explain. He suddenly recalled that it had been put into a bedside drawer as a souvenir in his childhood house where his mum still lived. It was unlikely but perhaps the object was still there after all those years hidden in the drawer. Sylvie had retained a lot of her old if not antique furniture. It was her nature to maintain the *status quo*. There was no point updating or changing household items provided they worked correctly or still looked in good shape.

Kevin was relaxing in an armchair. It was late on a Sunday morning. He was scrutinising the football results from the previous day and looking at the Football League tables to check which club now had enough points to top all the others. He also was scanning the also-rans and looking at which clubs were in a mid-table position and which ones were propping up the others in the 'relegation zone'. Jane had just gone into the kitchen. She was about to prepare lunch for both of them.

"Kevin! Please come here." Jane's voice sounded strained and anxious.

"What's up?" asked Kevin.

"Just come here" answered Jane. Kevin entered the kitchen to see his wife standing at the cooker with her head orientated downwards. Her right hand was placed on her neck, the fingers partly wrapped around it and gripping hard. A few teardrops slowly trickled down Jane's cheeks.

"Are you ok?" asked Kevin.

"What does it look like?" Jane's response was very snappy. Clearly, something was wrong and Kevin felt rather silly for asking such a dumb question. "I have an awful pain in my neck. I can't turn my head, it hurts too much. My left arm has gone numb" continued Jane.

Kevin suggested that Jane should lie down. He could massage her neck and apply some soothing heat rub. Jane had great difficulty moving. Her head felt locked in position and the pain was worsening. She sat upright in a lounge chair for ten minutes. Kevin tried his best to massage the pain away but without success. Jane was now crying more profusely. She was obviously in a bad state and could not be left to suffer. Medical intervention was necessary. Being a Sunday, the NHS services might take somewhat longer to arrive than normal. Staffing was more skeletal over the weekend. Kevin did not want to wait for an ambulance to come. If he could manage to get Jane into the car he would drive her to the hospital himself. There might be a prolonged wait in the Accident and Emergency Department but perhaps as Jane was in bad pain the wait might not be as long as he feared. Surely she would be seen quickly, even though her condition did not appear to be life-threatening. Kevin considered asking Jane to take some painkilling medication. He had paracetamol tablets and also steroid anti-inflammatory capsules. Kevin knew that should surgery be required it was not always a good idea to pre-medicate a patient as the drug might delay any action required until the medication dissipated from the system.

It took a long time to get Jane into the passenger seat of the car. Kevin supported her as she very slowly made her way to the vehicle. She sat in the front seat still holding her hand to her neck. Kevin quickly rushed back into the house and retrieved Jane's handbag in case she needed it. He also checked to see that he had money on him and his cell phone. He would have to phone Sylvie later on to let her know what had happened. Jane was very quiet and non-talkative on the journey to the hospital. Jane could still barely move her head and the pain was excruciating. Each time the car bumped over some obstacle in the road the intensity of Jane's pain increased and she had to suppress a scream. Kevin was very supportive and talked to his wife all the way on the journey in an effort to distract her mind from the pain she was suffering.

Kevin headed straight for the Royal Hospital in the next town. He went through the pay-on-exit barrier at the car park and picked up the parking ticket. On leaving he would have to insert the ticket into a machine and insert a monetary payment.

The machine would then electronically authorise the ticket to be used to allow the car to exit the car park provided that the correct fee had been paid. Inserting the ticket into a slot would cause the exit barrier to rise and allow the motorist escape from the car park.

Kevin was fortunate as he found a vacant car-parking space near the entry barrier. Jane was still in a lot of discomfort though there was a slight reduction in pain level and a small amount of rotation and flexion movements had returned to her head. Her left arm was still numb and tingled. They walked twenty yards and entered the Marmaduke Centre. Perhaps Kevin should have dropped Jane off first at the entrance to the centre and then gone off to park the car. She would not have had to walk hardly any distance to the entrance at all. However, Kevin was distressed at seeing Jane's condition and he was not thinking very clearly. He did his best to remain calm and reassuring in front of Jane.

After some initial administrative information was taken at Reception, Jane was asked to see a triage nurse who assessed her. She then returned to the waiting area where she and Kevin remained seated. After a twenty minute wait, Jane was called forward into a private cubicle. Kevin accompanied her. A young boyish-looking doctor examined Jane and asked various questions. She was asked to go for an X-ray. She was still in considerable pain but it had eased up compared to how she had been suffering in the kitchen at home. It took thirty minutes for the X-ray pictures to come through. The young doctor held them up to a bright light and had a close look. He then gave Jane something to take away the pain and suggested that it might also make her drowsy.

The doctor told Kevin that he wanted to admit Jane to the Observation Ward overnight. Kevin could return home and come back later with Jane's night clothes. They would do further investigations including a scan of Jane's neck area. The young doctor had conferred with the resident Consultant and had confirmed what he had already diagnosed. It seemed that Jane had cervical disc disease.

Jane quickly started to feel drowsy due to the effects of the medication. She was taken to the ward more or less asleep. At least she was out of pain for the time being. It did not look likely that she would be working for a while. Kevin would have to let her clinic manager know the next day. Kevin let Jane sleep. On returning home, he phoned his mum. Sylvie was alarmed and upset by what had happened to Jane. After Kevin had managed to calm his mum down they came to an arrangement regarding visiting. Sylvie would make her way over to the hospital about 7 pm. She wanted to take Jane some fruit and sandwiches in case she did not like the hospital's cooking. These and some squash drinks could be left on her bedside locker. Sylvie did not mind making her own way home. She was sixty four but still mobile and happy to take a taxi home. Sylvie suggested that Kevin go up to the hospital at around 8 pm and spend some time with his wife alone. He agreed to this and determined to pick up a bunch of flowers from somewhere on his return. These could be deposited in a vase of water next to Jane's bed. Kevin would really have preferred to drop his mum home by car but she insisted he should take some time to be with Jane by himself. She would take the bus which still stopped outside the hospital entrance.

In the evening Kevin met his mum and they exchanged a hug and had a quick chat. Sylvie departed and Kevin made his way to the ward. Jane was feeling better and sitting up in bed. She hoped to go home the next day. She beamed a smile at Kevin as he walked into the ward with a large mixed bunch of flowers he had picked up at a corner shop. The big supermarkets had closed early on Sunday as trading was not allowed by law after 4 pm. They had a warm kiss and the flowers were put in the vase. Jane loved the flowers but she had been cheered up by Sylvie and now that Kevin was there she felt even more positive minded and cheerful.

Jane apologised to Kevin for spoiling the weekend. Kevin told her not to be silly as she could not help what had afflicted her. The main thing now was to get her neck sorted out. Jane looked at Kevin and speaking in a non-punitive gentle voice told Kevin that it may have been due to him that she had ended up with this problem. Kevin looked bemused and had no idea what Jane was alluding to. Jane pointed to her neck and told Kevin that the pain was coming from exactly the place he had given her a love bite on her neck. Kevin looked rather guilty and thought it highly unlikely. He could not even remember doing this deed. He did recall that when he had observed Jane's sore neck the marks he saw resembled puncture wounds as if a surgical procedure had been carried out rather than something he had done. He let her comments pass by but did look a little sheepish.

The following day Jane was given the all clear to be discharged. She would have to wait until Kevin had completed his day at work and then come to pick her up. She did get a little impatient but she would 'grin and bear it' until Kevin showed up and could lift her home by car. She was feeling much better. She had some scans done during the day and was told she might have to attend outpatients for further assessments.

Kevin made his way towards the hospital in the car to pick Jane up and take her home. Jane's comments about his role in causing her neck pain were bothering him. He kept on getting the feeling that there was something more to what she had said but he could just not remember what it was. He also had an uneasy feeling. The events relating to Jane's neck and admission into hospital seemed to mimic what had happened to his mum so many years ago. Not only had the events of that time returned to his conscious memory but also he recalled the emotions and stress of what had happened. The situation felt very much like history repeating itself. Of course the hospital admission of Jane was not exactly the same as had occurred with his mum. For a start, his mum was admitted with thyroid problems and Jane was admitted with disc problems. Nevertheless, both of them had issues with their necks and the 'general scenario' was rather similar.

After parking the car Kevin entered the swing doors and before going into the main ward where the beds were located he came across the same young doctor he had seen previously. He must have been doing an extended shift or overtime hours. He called Kevin into his private office to discuss Jane's condition more fully. He had already spoken to Jane and she was happy to share the medical situation with her partner and next of kin.

The doctor explained the situation to Kevin. Kevin already knew some of the information but decided it was polite not to interrupt the doctor. He explained that there were discs made of cartilage between the vertebrae. These were like little 'cushions' between the neck bones or cervical vertebrae. They enabled a limited amount of movement to occur in the spine and reduced friction between the neck bones. Sometimes a disc could be damaged. Arthritis was one possible cause of disc damage but this seemed unlikely in Jane's case. She was rather too young and the damage was most likely due to something else. Quite often the cause of the injury was unknown. The pain and stiffness Jane had experienced in her neck was due to a combination of muscle spasms and inflammation. Most likely the disc injury had exerted pressure on the nerve roots as they emerged through a small hole in the backbone from the spinal cord. This would account for the pain and numbness in Jane's arm.

The young doctor went on to reassure Kevin. Apparently, the vast majority of patients recovered on their own without any major medical intervention. He put this figure as over

90%. A conservative approach was always the best. There were surgical procedures available should the problem persist or return.

Kevin thanked the doctor and felt reassured. He entered the ward. Jane was already dressed and ready to go home. They said their goodbyes to the staff and Jane gingerly walked to their car with Kevin in support. She took her time and was careful not to lift anything heavy or strain her neck. She had a support collar round her neck and had been given a few exercises suggested by the physiotherapist. Jane was helped at home by Sylvie while Kevin was at work.

Jane had to take a lot more time off work than she had expected. The initial optimism which she shared with Kevin for a quick recovery was misplaced. Unfortunately as the week continued, Jane's neck pain returned. She was not in agony to the extent she had been in previously but she was in no state to go back to work. She could neither comfortably cook nor do housework. The painkillers and other medication seemed to make little difference. Jane was given ongoing help from Sylvie at home and she was more than pleased to help out. After three weeks with little or no progress or improvement in her condition, Jane phoned the hospital and an appointment was made in the outpatients department. Kevin took some leave from work and accompanied Jane to the appointment.

The appointment lasted some hours. A scan was done of Jane's neck. Eventually they were called into an office by a specialist in back and neck problems. The doctor was a female who looked strangely familiar to Kevin. He could not figure out what it was and he stared intently at her. She introduced herself. She was Dr Sharpe. She had a distinctive Welsh accent. Kevin realised that she closely resembled the Mr Sharpe who had operated on his mum's neck some eighteen years earlier. Kevin excused himself for asking but he enquired if she had a male relative who had also worked at the hospital. She replied that it was her dad who had now retired. This seemed to be a very strange coincidence to Kevin.

After reading the case notes, she listened to Jane and noted that she was still in pain and relatively immobile. After examining the scan results, Dr Sharpe went through her recommendations. She came to the conclusion that cervical disc surgery would be necessary. There was a slight risk of permanent injury such as paralysis from the surgery but this was extremely rare. Jane and Kevin were rather shocked but they were both realistic in their views. If surgery was required, so be it. Jane could not continue the way she was feeling. Her quality of life had been diminished by the neck problem. The process of getting osteoporosis in later life was not desirable. Infection and inflammation did not seem to now be Jane's main issues. Antibiotics had been taken to clear away any infection and steroid anti-inflammatory tablets had also been prescribed.

Two options of surgical procedure were offered. These were disc replacement or fusion. Some patients were not appropriate for having an artificial disc inserted. This procedure often allowed a quick return to work. The surgery took longer than the alternative method and blood loss had to be carefully monitored. Since the disc was pinching a nerve or pressuring the spinal cord, it would be removed under general anaesthetic. This 'discectomy' involved removing the disc via an incision. Sometimes it was done from the anterior or front region of the neck, at other times from the posterior or back of the neck, whatever was the easiest. After removal of the problematic disc an artificial one was put in place.

A cervical fusion technique was also available. This also involved removal of the disc causing the symptoms. A piece of bone would then be grafted in the gap between the vertebrae. The graft would be held in place by a supporting metal plate and screw while it healed and fused with the backbones. It was sometimes the case that the outcome resulted in reduced neck movement compared to normal.

Jane and Kevin took some time deciding if they had a preference. Dr Sharpe in her clinical judgement had recommended that in Jane's case, a disc replacement would be suitable. They decided it would be best to follow medical opinion.

Jane and Kevin had been made aware of various risk factors should things go wrong. There was always the risk of an adverse bodily response to the general anaesthetic. Other risks included ongoing neck pain, infection and bleeding. Some serious risks included damage to the vocal cords and gullet. If any surgical slip damaged the spinal cord or spinal nerves then paralysis could result. This was a frightening prospect. However, Dr Sharpe was very confident that everything would be fine and after some recovery time had passed Jane would be as good as new plus she could get back to work fairly quickly after the operation.

Jane had to attend the hospital outpatients department for pre-operative tests and to answer some background health questions. Jane was reminded of the risks of having the surgery and the possible side-effects that might follow on afterwards. Consent forms were produced and signed. In due course a date was set for the surgery.

Kevin again took time off from his job and waited anxiously while the surgical procedure was done. A nurse came to see Kevin and said that the surgery had gone well. It had been successful. Jane was resting and after the anaesthetic wore off she would be able to take some sips of water. Her head would take a little time to clear but if she felt ok she might be able to go home the next day. She would be kept in hospital overnight as a precaution. Kevin stayed a while and held Jane's hand. She was light-headed for quite a long time but her head slowly cleared.

She was happy it was all over and glad that Kevin was with her. The following morning Kevin sat at Jane's bedside. Her discharge had been approved and authorised. Midday was approaching but they could not leave yet even though Jane had changed into her normal outdoor clothing. There were two things delaying their departure. Firstly, they were waiting for some prescription medications to be processed through the hospital pharmacy. The medications had been prescribed the previous evening by the ward doctor for her to take home. After what seemed like an age a nurse arrived with a small paper bag containing a couple of small bottles of tablets. That was one delay over and done with. They also had to wait for the surgeon to do a ward round. Jane's Consultant wanted to speak to her before she left the hospital. Eventually, just before the hospital served lunch to the inpatients, Dr Sharpe appeared and visited each patient in turn surrounded by a group of junior doctors, house doctors, nurses and physiotherapists.

Finally, Dr Sharpe arrived at Jane's bed. She spoke in a broad Welsh accent. To Kevin's ears it almost sounded like her speech had a singing rhythm to it. Perhaps Dr Sharpe had once been in a Welsh choir or had lived in the Rhondda Valley where nearly everybody enjoyed singing, largely as a legacy of the coal mining communities which were now decimated. Dr Sharpe assured Jane that the surgery had gone very well. Jane mentioned that her neck was rather sore but this was to be expected. She was to refrain from bathing or showering for a short time but as healing proceeded she could bathe in some 'salt baths'. The stitches were self-dissolving and should not need any further attention. If any problems or side effect symptoms occurred, Jane was told she must phone the hospital immediately or pop into the clinic.

Jane and Kevin gave their thanks to Dr Sharpe. Kevin gave her a large box of chocolates as a 'thank you gift' for her support and surgical skill. The doctor was pleased but gave the box to the ward 'sister' to share out with the other members of the care team. Just as Dr Sharpe was leaving she turned round and told them there was something she had nearly forgotten to tell them though it was not of any importance. She rummaged in her pocket in her white medical gown and withdrew a small object.

Dr Sharpe told Jane and Kevin that when she removed the troublesome disc in Jane's neck, she had noticed something unusual about it. It was something she had never seen before. In fact, it was something she could not explain. Dr Sharpe opened her hand and on her palm was a very small dark pyramid shaped object. The doctor went on to explain that this object had been buried deep inside the cartilaginous disc and perhaps had distorted it. It seemed likely that this object had caused Jane's neck problems by causing the disc to bulge and put pressure on a nerve. Jane was dumbfounded and wondered what the heck the object was and how it could have got into her neck vertebral cartilage. Kevin was surprisingly silent. This revelation reminded him of the anomalous object removed from his mum's thyroid gland in her neck region many years ago.

Kevin then spoke up and asked Dr Sharpe if he could keep the object. Dr Sharpe agreed but she suggested he wait a few days and then pop into the clinic to pick it up. She would leave it in Reception for him to pick up. She wanted to ask a forensic colleague she worked with from time to time to take a look at the object and try to identify what it was and where it had come from. Kevin agreed to this and he then proceeded to take Jane home.

Jane's neck remained rather sore but she took her medications and after a few days was on the mend. She was totally baffled by what the doctor had excised from her neck cartilage. Kevin was also keen to know more about the object and it was not long before he managed to take a quick visit to the clinic Reception and waiting for him in a sealed envelope was the object and also with it was a very brief handwritten report.

The report was on headed paper with a 'lab address'. It started off with 'To Whom It May Concern'. There followed a single short paragraph. The object had been observed under the high power lens of an optical microscope. Various special techniques were also used such as oil immersion and phase contrast. The sides were regular triangles. The object seemed to exhibit an overall pyramid shape. Its texture and density suggested it was made of some kind of alloy or metal compounds. There had not been time to do any substantial study but the object had magnetic properties. Some kind of weak electromagnetic field existed around the core. The object was so regular along its edges that it looked as if it had been manufactured artificially. There was no clue as to who may have made it, nor the purpose of this object. It was perplexing in that it would have needed high technology equipment to make something so small and precise but nobody came to mind as the manufacturer. The most mysterious thing about this object was how it had made its way into Jane's cervical vertebral cartilage disc. The only logical answer was that it had been placed there by some surgical procedure. There was no indication of the purpose of such an implant. Speculation about this would need investigation by somebody in a different specialised field of study. The only people with such expertise were those who had knowledge of dealing with alien implants but these were few and far between and unlikely to be of any help or relevance. The report was signed off and dated by the investigating scientist.

Kevin was amazed at the report. He thought twice about telling Jane. He did not know what she would make of it. On the other hand, the object had been inside her body. She had the right to see the report. On his way back from the hospital clinic, Kevin popped into his mum's house for a cup of tea and chat about Jane's recovery. Kevin decided to mention the object removed from Jane's neck to his mum. Sylvie looked at Kevin with a wide-eyed stare while her face was expressionless. Kevin found this slightly disturbing but his mum did have some quirks and eccentric streaks. He asked his mum about the object that had been removed from her neck many years previously. He wanted to know if it was still in the upstairs bedside locker. His mum told him to go and take a look. She had moved the locker around a few times over the years but had not thrown it out. It had become superfluous to her needs and it had hardly been used. She had dusted it on the outside but the drawers were probably untouched inside.

Kevin made his way upstairs and walked over to the locker and with a little trepidation pulled the drawer open. He did not see anything initially and he was beginning to feel disappointed but then he noticed something nestling in the corner of the drawer. It was the little match box that had been sitting there untouched and ignored for years. Kevin retrieved the object which was still present in the little box. He exchanged a few final words with his mum about the objects. He thanked his mum for the tea and then rapidly made his way home. He would shortly get back to his mum regarding arranging a good time for her to come over and spend some more time with him and Jane.

Kevin was now becoming excited about showing Jane his mum's extracted implant and the mini-report he had picked up regarding Jane's removed object. After some small talk they sat down together. Jane was now recovering well from her surgery and the pain and stiffness of her neck were minimal. Kevin told Jane about the object that had been removed from his mum's neck when he was a teenager. He showed Jane the written report on the object removed from her neck. Then he produced both objects and lay them side by side on the coffee table. They examined them as closely as they could. They were identical. Kevin felt amazed. He looked at Jane's face and she was horrified. How could this be? What did it mean?

CHAPTER 6

Alive In your Dreams

With the passing of time, the problem with Jane's neck receded into memory. Her recovery had been very good indeed. She was able to rotate her head and move it up and down with normal freedom and range of movement. All the movements were pain-free. Jane had attended appointments in the outpatients department at the hospital and after a couple of visits had been discharged. There was little to remind her of the operation on her neck except for a small area of scar tissue which was barely visible.

Daily life had resumed its usual routines and Kevin and Jane continued their occupational careers. There was stability in their predictable daily routine. Both Kevin and Jane received reasonable monthly salaries paid directly by 'giro' into their joint bank account. Jane did the household budgeting. She organised their finances well and her occasional indulgent shopping expeditions were very infrequent. Jane also managed to keep Kevin under financial constraint as he was prone to making sudden on the spot purchases which were not always value for money decisions. The couple were able to make small regular savings and they did not go short of daily life requirements. They did not lead an extravagant life but continued to get breaks from daily routine by visiting the cinema and eating out. The food at Mohinder's Indian restaurant had become addictive and the couple had become regular diners. Sometimes they had take-outs delivered to their home and Mohinder would be sure to include a few free extra spicy surprises with the deliveries. He was a shrewd business person and liked to have satisfied repeat customers who would refer others to his establishment.

Sylvie was a regular visitor at the couple's home. She was not a person who was easy to get to know intimately. Sylvie had quickly warmed to Jane and her daughter-in-law had become one of her few close confidantes. Sylvie would chat with her about all manner of things and even helped the couple out with household shopping. Sometimes she undertook domestic tidying up at times when Kevin and Jane were under workload pressure or when Jane was on a late work rota. Kevin and Jane visited Sylvie at her home too but Sylvie seemed to prefer getting out of her own house and having a change of environment.

Sylvie had been quite concerned about Jane when she had her neck problem and surgery. She was extremely relieved when it was all over and the problem resolved successfully. After Jane came home to recuperate she had made herself freely available to help the couple out. She was aware that it was not a good idea for an 'in-law' to be pushy or to exert any undue influence or interference. However, Jane was always grateful for her help and Sylvie did not feel that she was 'overdoing things'. Kevin had no qualms about his mum helping out and the three of them enjoyed a close familial relationship. Indeed, although Jane pined for her deceased mum, she generally suppressed her feelings. If she could not have her own mum in her life, her husband's helpful mum would make a good substitute. Of course, no-one could replace her real mum in her affections but Sylvie never outwardly showed any wish to assume this position. Sylvie's helpful actions allowed the relationship between her and her daughter-in-law to blossom.

Sylvie came over to Kevin and Jane to share an evening meal. The couple had given her a spare door key for her exclusive use. She was free to come and go as she pleased. Sylvie had pre-arranged her visit and offered to cook the meal as a little treat for her son and daughter-in-law. She did not mind cooking and did not profess to be a great 'chef' but she had always been very patient as a cook and meticulous with ingredients for a healthy balanced diet. She carefully monitored cooking times and her food was always tasty and fresh. Jane would get a break by not having to come in from work and cook food and nor would she have to reheat anything she had previously made and stored in the freezer. The microwave would not be required to heat up any TV dinners or ready-made meals on this occasion. They were not on the menu. Hot, freshly cooked and ready to serve food would make a treat. Kevin loved Jane's cooking but there was always something special about a meal made by his mum. Perhaps it triggered childhood memories of some of his favourite dishes of yesteryear.

The roast chicken and potatoes tasted great. They were accompanied by carrots and cauliflower. Hot chicken gravy was included in a gravy bowl and sat on the tablecloth in front of Kevin. He took a more than ample share for himself. The meal was concluded and Kevin made short work of the washing up. Fairy Liquid degreased the plates and they were left in the sink drainer to dry. The threesome retired to the lounge to chat. After an hour or more they found room to nibble some After Eight mint chocolates while Jane made some instant coffee for them all.

The conversation moved on to the topic of Emma. Jane had reached a point where she was able to recount good memories of times spent with her mum. At one time she would have quickly been in tears talking about her deceased mother but time had softened the cutting edge of her grief.

Nevertheless, Kevin thought he could detect a slight tearful welling up in Jane's eyes but no tears rolled down her cheeks. The conversation continued along a much more personalised route than normal. In fact, Kevin began to fear that some taboo areas might encroach into what was normally light-hearted chit chat about daily events. Jane's memories seemed to lead her conversation into the past including a few revelations about the dad she barely had known.

This line of talk eventually encouraged Jane to think about her own curiosity regarding Kevin's childhood and she referred to Kevin's dad. Kevin immediately felt uncomfortable. This was a topic his mum had never discussed. He looked sideways at his mum with some trepidation. Sylvie brushed the matter off as she had done numerous times over the years saying that there was nothing to tell and it was all so long ago. Kevin did feel the atmosphere around the table go slightly cold. Of course he was curious about his paternal ancestry but since childhood he had learned to avoid this topic. He felt that what he had never known was never missed. This had been a psychological tactic he had adopted all his life adopted so that he would not have to confront any possible unpleasant issues about his father. As for Jane, she could not see what all the secrecy was about. What could be so awful that it could not be revealed? Kevin had a right to know about his father and knowing nothing did not seem right. Jane did not want to argue with Sylvie or push her on the subject but she resolved to have a chat with Kevin about the topic when they were on their own.

The conversation moved forwards to another area of consternation. Jane brought up the topic of the 'implant' that had been removed from her neck. In due course Kevin produced the two implants. They really looked identical. They were two pristine mini-pyramids. Sylvie had always claimed to have no idea what the object was. She could not say how it was possible for it to have found its way into her neck and become embedded in her thyroid gland.

Kevin could now detect some aloofness in his mother's tone of voice. Her defensive barriers were being raised. Why was that? Kevin had always shown great curiosity with respect to this object and the discovery of another similar one in Jane's neck was amazing. This opened up the doors to wild speculation but nothing could really explain how similar objects could end up in both his mum's and wife's necks. As for Jane, she was very uneasy about it. She found it worrying if not a little scary. It was just so weird. It was something most curious and Jane felt there had to be a logical explanation. She would really like an answer. It was apparent that Sylvie was not going to be of any help in solving the mystery. Jane did find it a little strange that Sylvie did not seem to show much curiosity in this matter. She rather blandly accepted the anomaly with just minor interest and a lack of concern. There was no bemusement and not even any discussions about a lack of understanding with respect to what these objects were or how they had entered the neck.

Kevin noticed that his mum was beginning to fidget and look a little uncomfortable. Now was a good time to drop his mum home in the car. Kevin and Jane thanked Sylvie for her efforts cooking them all a lovely evening meal. She did seem pleased to hear these words of appreciation. Kevin thought that perhaps he could lighten the atmosphere even further by making some silly jokes and comments to cause a little laughter. He began making some idiotic suggestions about the implants being put in place by a man from Mars and then suggested that he too probably had one in his own neck. Jane did not find his remarks particularly funny. Kevin could be such an idiot sometimes. As for Sylvie, she did not smile but fixed her gaze directly into Kevin's eyes. Kevin found this slightly offputting. He thought he better distract his mum's direct eye contact so he thrust his right arm towards his neck and said he would find his implant. He placed his hand over a minor bump he had always had under his skin at the side of his neck. His fingers pushed down with considerable pressure. "Ouch" exclaimed Kevin. "That hurt. I must have a spot just there." Jane managed a slight smile. Sylvie fixed Kevin with a blank expression. Kevin felt his mum's gaze had a sorrowful look about it. Oh well, his mum had always had slightly eccentric behaviours. It was time to take her home.

Sylvie had recently turned sixty five. Throughout her life, Kevin had always been the 'apple of her eye'. Nothing had changed to alter this feeling. She had done her best to look after Kevin to her best ability as a child and had supported him in his education at school and onwards through University. The domestic stability had enabled Kevin to progress positively through his life. Sylvie was proud of her son's achievements and she more than approved of his choice for a wife. For his part, Kevin loved his mum and it was only in relatively recent times that he had gained sufficient insight and reached a certain level of maturity to understand the personal sacrifices she had made on his behalf. He knew that on occasion he had been over indulged and spoilt. Still, it had not been easy spending ones time as an only-child. Most of his life Kevin had taken his mum for granted and it came as a great shock when she had been taken ill many years previously.

Kevin was not someone who liked to dwell on issues of mortality. He lived mostly in the present but on occasions tried to look into the future and consider his life route and where it may lead. Similarly, he did not, on the whole, dwell in the past. What had passed by was gone. He knew it was sensible to learn from events in the past and not repeat mistakes and also not to waste time trying to change past things or getting stuck with historical baggage on his shoulders.

The whole concept of the passage of time seemed a rather

odd one to Kevin. It was almost an enigma. It would be good to catch time in his hand and manipulate it. Bending time and the events therein according to his thoughts would be so powerful a proposition. His adult mindset had been moulded into a 'scientific default mode' but from time to time he would dream away from this outlook at a tangent. Some of his imaginary trips had been full of weird imagery since his childhood. Normally in the waking state only snippets of such dreams remained.

At the present time in his life a few things had recently started to bother Kevin. He sometimes had strange thoughts about time being some kind of continuum. Past, present and future were all somehow interlinked. The passage of time was not just a 'linear' event. It was flexible, reversible and changeable and different versions of it ran parallel with each other. These ideas were not really comprehensible and Kevin wondered why they flashed through his mind. He thought it might relate to his scientific and mostly logical way of thinking about things being affected by the more repressed artistic and imaginative side to his personality.

Kevin was quite an avid reader. He took a small interest in daily world news and politics but this did not play a big part in his interests. If he was in the right mood he would listen to various genres of music but he would like to read and watch documentaries on television. He had taught himself some aspects of history in this way and also read and watched quite a lot of science fiction and paranormal stories. He also rather liked movies in these areas along with action and adventure stories. This personality profile seemed to fit rather well with the slightly weird thoughts and dreams that Kevin experienced now and again. Nowadays they were getting into his head more frequently and they were becoming more vivid. In fact, these ideas and thoughts were more like flashbacks rather than dreams.

His ideas about the passage and nature of time somehow had a connection with the apparently implanted objects removed from the necks of his mother and his wife. He did not know what these objects were nor what they were for but the worrying thing was that they seemed strangely familiar to him. The tiny pyramids seemed remote from his thoughts about temporal issues but Kevin felt that there was something he knew about these objects that was locked away behind closed doors somewhere in his head. If it were possible to drift through time the relevance of a mini metallic pyramid in one's neck could hardly have any significance. Or could it?

Kevin also had very brief moments of lucidity about things he had dreamed about or unusual events in his life but any enlightening thoughts were fleeting. He had recently had quick mental imagery of times in his past when, on a couple of different occasions, he had seen door handles turn and rattle. He felt that something happened after this but he did not know what. It was the same thing when he recalled the day he was going to work and had fallen off his bike. He again felt something else happened shortly afterwards but his memory was suppressed.

Kevin had been processing thoughts about odd past life events more and more frequently in an effort to recall them more clearly. A new idea suddenly jumped into his conscious thoughts. What if these were not real-memories at all? Maybe they were 'screen memories' designed to mask some other events that might be too shocking for him to deal with in a normal conscious state. Such false memories would be, in a certain sense, protective of his sanity. The idea of screen memories entering Kevin's mind only served to increase his confusion about the undesirable thoughts and memories which popped in and out of his mind.

Now that Sylvie had reached sixty five, Kevin felt that a physical milestone had been reached in her life. Kevin was pleased his mum was still in relatively good health. The feeling that life was about to change pervaded his thoughts. These thoughts nagged at him but he did not share these concerns with either Jane or his mum.

He began to become aware that his mum's life, as well as his own, was passing by. For the first time in his life, Kevin began to wonder about his mum's husband. He had always assumed his mum had been married to his father. She referred to herself as Mrs Powell. How did he know if this was really true? How could he know if Sylvie had really been married? What if his dad was someone she had a one night fling with? Maybe his dad had wanted to have contact with him and his mother had prevented this. Why had his mum been so evasive over the years about his father?

Kevin began asking himself why he was suddenly getting these thoughts about his dad after all the years of not knowing and not really caring. There were many unanswered questions. He strived for answers to these questions that had suddenly emerged into his *psyche*. He did not really know who he was. His unknown paternal roots had begun to take on a sudden importance that had never concerned him before. It occurred to him that should his mum pass away he would never find out the truth. Kevin concluded that the ageing of his mum and the onset of her sixty fifth birthday must have been the reason he had started to think about his paternal background. He considered sitting his mum down to talk to her about his dad. He knew she would change the subject or walk away. Perhaps he should be more 'forceful' and insist on answers.

Kevin went to bed that evening with his thoughts a little scrambled by the things he had been thinking about earlier on. He was thirty five and a well balanced individual with a good job, beautiful wife and lovely home. He was about to undergo an experience which would leave a permanent mark on his soul. In fact, he would not be sure whether it was something he had really experienced at all. It might have been an illusion or screen memory, or just a nightmare. Whatever the incident was called, it was bizarre and disturbing.

Kevin had been feeling unusually tired so he had left Jane downstairs watching a soap opera on television. He had popped up to the bedroom to have a quick snooze. 'Forty winks' and he would feel more awake. He slipped off his shoes and lay flat on his back staring at the ceiling. His eyelids felt heavy and he began to 'nod off'. He was reawakened with a jolt when he heard the door rattle as if someone was trying to get in without turning the handle. "Jane! Is that you?" He tried to mouth the words but his lips felt frozen. Oh no! He was not going to have another one of those stupid dreamlike experiences. He knew he had gone through this kind of thing in the past but could not recall the specifics. Anyway, he knew it was a dream and it would soon be over. He saw the door handle start to rotate. It always did that and then stopped. This time the door very slowly began to open. Surely this was not the way his recurring dream was meant to go. Was there a shadowy figure entering the room? Yes there was. It was surrounded by a white light. There was mist behind the figure and nothing of the house landing could be seen. Where was Jane? Did she not know there was a stranger in the house? Fear began to grip his mind. A feeling of dread suggested something very bad was about to unfold but nothing happened at all for some time. Kevin wanted to get off the bed and get up. It was a losing battle. All he could do was watch and stare ahead.

Everything seemed to be occurring in slow motion. He could move his arms a little bit but the flexing and straightening of his limbs was so slow it was like watching a snail traverse its way along the garden path. The experience was terrifying yet it was fascinating. Kevin felt that he might have enjoyed this curious dream had he not been so frightened. Anyway, he knew it would not be long and Jane would be joining him in bed. She would waken him out of this stupor with a kiss like a female princess awakening a male sleeping beauty.

Kevin waited for the dream to stop. He still lay on his back but peered at the figure standing motionless in the space where the bedroom door had opened. Kevin was not sure that the figure was actually standing. It seemed to be floating motionless above the floor. Kevin realised it was floating towards him, a few centimetres at a time. It was definitely getting closer and heading towards the bottom of the bed where his feet remained static and stretched out.

The figure slowly drifted forwards. This was very strange. It resembled a bird and quite a large one. Kevin imagined he heard a hooting sound. What was going on? There it was again. The object floated slowly into clear focus. It was clearly a bird but not just any old bird. It was a beautiful owl.

As it approached the end of the bed Kevin began to be able to make out some details. This surprised Kevin as dreams did not normally include minute visual information about things that were being fantasised. Kevin was able to focus his eyes on the figure but was still unable to liberate his body from the frozen grip that enveloped it.

Kevin and the owl faced each other eye to eye. He felt as if a contest of willpower was being fought out in an eye to eye duel. All at once the owl disappeared. He began to be able to distinguish new features. The figure was now a man. Well, it was not exactly a man. It was some kind of humanoid. In fact, it seemed somehow to be human but 'different'. The figure emanated benevolence. Kevin's fear subsided but he still wanted to wake up and move away. The figure stood at the end of the bed and looked down at Kevin and neither made any further movement nor uttered any sound.

Kevin stared intently at this bedroom visitor. He had a head. It was a rather large head, Kevin thought. No hair was on the head. He was bald. The man almost resembled a giant unborn foetus. The eyes were dark and slanted. There was a small narrow nose and very small lips. Kevin could not make out any ears on the sides of the head though a tiny orifice was present on each side of the head. The skin appeared iridescent and kept varying in shades of bluish-grey in the kind of way that a chameleon reflexly alters its colour when placed on different backgrounds for camouflage against predators. In the case of the figure, no particular details were visible behind him other than the white light and swirling mist.

The torso was long and thin and covered by light blue tightly fitting material. It might have been some kind of uniform. Perhaps it was some kind of 'spacesuit'. Who could tell what it was? This material extended downwards covering two thin legs. No external genitalia were visible. The arms were free and not enclosed by any kind of clothing material. They were very long and spindly and reached beyond the knee. The figure was humanlike but had an insectoid quality about it. The fingers were extremely long and slender. Kevin noticed that each hand had four jointed digits including a thumb. There seemed to be a bony stub which looked as if another ancestral finger had once been present at that juncture with the wrist but was missing.

Kevin's background biological knowledge 'kicked-in'. Animals had developed specialisations in certain habitats as adaptations for survival or obtaining food. This resulted in bodily changes. Perhaps the reduction in the number of fingers on the hand of this bedroom visitor related to this. Darwinian theory accounted for such anatomical change by a process of evolution.

It worried Kevin that he felt he had seen this entity before and had interacted with him on previous occasions but it was impossible to rationalise the situation. Kevin knew he was in a predicament. The logical and 'scientific' part of his brain was not of any help to him at this moment. He could not wake up and remove himself from this vivid dream.

Kevin was now becoming desperate. He wanted the creature to disappear. Surely all he had to do was wake himself up and Jane would be the next thing he would see in his line of vision. He began to make frantic efforts to move and get off the bed. He strained at his muscles with all his willpower. Again, as earlier, his arms made very slow and weak bending and straightening movements. He thought that perhaps his toes had twitched. He remained able to move his eyes around though and his blink reflexes remained intact.

Some unpleasant thoughts crossed Kevin's mind. Was he insane? This was a possibility he had to seriously consider. Was he hallucinating? He had never taken any mind altering drugs in his life so they were not an issue. Perhaps something he had eaten or drunk earlier had been 'spiked' with a chemical agent. It seemed unlikely but maybe the situation he was witnessing and experiencing was actually real. In that case was this an alien abduction? Did the creature mean him harm? Perhaps the figure wanted to communicate something. The figure did have a ghostlike quality to it so maybe this was a paranormal event.

No answers were forthcoming. The manlike creature just stood there at the foot of the bed. His gaze seemed to be fixed on Kevin. Time was without meaning. Kevin could not tell if five minutes or five hours had passed in this situation. Now and again the creature seemed to blink but there were no distinct eyelids to make this ocular movement clear.

Kevin began to sweat. Beads of sweat ran down his brow. He almost felt like crying but he knew this would not assist him. He tried to shout at the creature to frighten it but his lips just quivered and his dry tongue was irresponsive. He made a massive effort to roll over on one side but he remained laying prone on his back. Kevin decided to give up. It was inevitable that he was going to die.

Kevin's eyes closed. He then began to get certain thoughts in his head like those he had contemplated on a Friday evening years ago when similar strange things had happened to him though the memories of this previous experience had been largely erased. Did he exist? Had he ever existed? Who am I? What am I? What is this place? Kevin's hold on reality had gone.

"Keeeeevin!" He heard a voice in his head. "Keeeevin… Keeevin… Keevin… Kevin." The voice in his head continued.

"Yes Dad, it's me" said Kevin. Who was he talking to? Was he having an imaginary thought conversation with a father he had never known? Kevin's mind was becoming alert. He knew he had been through this situation before. Kevin felt strange. It was rather like he had a split personality. Yes, he was Kevin Powell but he was also someone else. In fact, it was more like something else rather than somebody else.

Kevin could not understand the way he felt nor the direction in which his mind was taking him. Strange and random thoughts entered his head. Kevin felt that these thoughts were entering his mind by some kind of telepathic transfer from the creature that still stood over him at the end of the bed. "Remember… remember… remember… your knowledge." These thoughts were clearly in Kevin's head but he had no clue as to what knowledge he was supposed to remember. This thought seemed to trigger a response. "Wormhole… the portal." What was this to do with him? Kevin had read about these topics but they held no significance for him. They were areas of conjecture if not pure fiction. Scientific evaluation of these things was very limited to say the least. A sharp 'loud' thought entered his head as if to not only disagree with him about the topics being areas of fiction but to reprimand him for having such misguided thoughts. The term 'Einstein-Rosen bridges' filled his head. This was a theoretical spacetime anomaly he had seen discussed in a television documentary. Kevin decided he did not wish to think about such things any further.

The creature was moving. Unfortunately it was not retreating backwards through the bedroom door. It was floating in a most unnatural way to the side of the bed. The movement was extremely slow but it was perceptible. Kevin's fear was suppressed though he knew he ought to be petrified. Perhaps the creature itself was somehow calming him down. It now occupied the space next to the bed on Kevin's right hand side. From this view he was able to estimate the creature's height at about four feet.

Further thoughts began to enter Kevin's mind while he once again observed the physical form of the creature with its thin body and slender arms and legs. "Low gravity... low gravity... muscles wasted." This suggestion made Kevin think hard. The suggestion was almost sarcastic. Perhaps it was not sarcastic, it was almost witty, or maybe it was simply a statement of fact. Perhaps the creature existed somewhere in a gravity field lower than the Earth where large muscles and heavy bones would not be needed to move around. Maybe the normal principles of evolution applied to this creature. Perhaps its ancestors had developed in a low gravity environment and over time had adapted to those surroundings. The thought that this creature like all others was subject to the usual laws of nature further reassured Kevin. He pondered on this but could take the thought no further.

The creature slowly raised its left arm as if to reveal something. Nothing was visible in the bedroom at all except the area of the open bedroom door which led out onto the landing but it was still bright and misty in that area. The only thing that Kevin could make out in the room other than the mysterious creature was the bedroom mirror. It was relatively new and full length. It had been purchased as a Christmas gift by Sylvie for Jane. Jane always liked to check she was dressed properly for her job before she left home in the mornings to go to work and a long mirror was just the thing.

Kevin watched as the creature beckoned him with an arm movement to approach the mirror. Kevin felt strength return to his muscles though they did not seem to have their usual power. He managed to roll out of bed on his right side and stand. He considered trying to run away or maybe attacking the intruder but decided to go along with his uninvited guest's wishes. Kevin moved closer to the mirror but realised he was not walking. He was floating with his feet just off the bedroom carpet. His body movement was extremely slow and his mind seemed to be controlling his directional locomotion.

The strange figure watched Kevin move slowly towards the bedroom mirror. Kevin could feel the gaze of this strange being piercing him. He felt like he was being observed in order to see how he was going to react. It was akin to being a laboratory rat or guinea pig. Kevin now faced the mirror full on. He was not sure if his feet were in contact with the ground or whether they were somehow still floating above the carpet. There were no sensations coming from the soles of his feet to suggest they were in contact with anything.

Kevin looked intently into the mirror. It was very dark. He could make out a dim reflection of something but he could not see anything with clarity. While Kevin faced the mirror the unwelcome companion remained motionless to his left side. He was just a mere foot or two away.

Suddenly the mirror seemed to brighten. His reflection stared straight back at him. However, what Kevin saw in the mirror was for sure not Kevin Powell. As he looked at himself he could see the same creature that had invaded his bedroom. The large bald head, the long arms and legs, slender fingers, dark slanted eyes and so on were all there. "Aaaaargh!" Kevin

155

tried his best to scream but his vocal cords would not work. Had he become the creature? Had he been the creature all along? Maybe there had never been a strange being in his room other than himself. He tried to turn his head. He could not see the other entity. The other being was either out of his line of sight or he was all alone. Kevin wondered if he had undergone some kind of metamorphosis into a new life form. Kevin was transfixed by his image. The question then arose as to what to do next. He did not want to spend the rest of his life staring into a mirror, monster or not. At this point the 'changed Kevin' vanished and he looked like his normal self once again. The experience had been fleeting and had only lasted for seconds. However, to Kevin it seemed that a considerable time had passed by.

Thoughts once again began to form in Kevin's mind. He was not sure if he was generating these thoughts himself or if there was an external source. "Neck... neck." Kevin gingerly and carefully raised his right hand to his neck. He found the small bump in his skin that had been present for as long as he could remember. He gently pressed on the area with his fingertips. The area felt slightly warm and he could feel very small vibrations. As he pressed down he felt tiny pinpricks rather like very mild electrical shocks. He exerted more pressure and as he did so new knowledge came flooding into his brain. Perhaps this knowledge was not new but had long been hidden in the deep recesses of his mind.

As the moments passed Kevin's brain seemed to fill with a new set of memories. He was still aware of his present life. He knew about his mum, his childhood, his wife and his marriage but there was a new component to all of this. He did not understand everything he perceived.

Kevin maintained the pressure on his neck. He noticed that if he lightened the pressure his clarity of thought became reduced. He began to speculate that he might have one of the pyramid shaped implants in his neck like those extracted from his mum and his wife. He would like to know one day how these objects had found their way into the tissues of his loved-ones. As for now, did he also have an implant buried in his neck? What was its purpose? Who had put it there? He spent a few minutes struggling with these questions in his head and then the thought came into his mind that maybe the entity that had been or still was present in his bedroom had something to do with it. Just what was the connection to this creature and himself? Why had he thought such a being was his dad?

There was plenty of confusion in Kevin's mind. His brain could only absorb a certain amount of information in a certain time. His mind was overflowing. Kevin felt the area in his neck vibrating. More thoughts appeared in his brain. It was beginning to appear to Kevin that, assuming he did have one of those implants, one of its functions at least involved communication or thought transfer. Maybe it could exert control over his body by an outside agency. Goodness knows what else it might do.

"Come!" The thought in his head caused Kevin to make an effort to turn away from the mirror and his body slowly turned itself 180 degrees to his left. The creature was still there. Kevin was independent physically from this other life-form but not mentally free. The being now had its back to Kevin. It drifted towards the illuminated open bedroom doorway. Kevin knew that he had to follow.

Kevin passed through the doorway and the hall landing was nowhere to be seen. He was in a different place. He appeared to be in a woodland setting. It was still night-time but there was very little light coming from the half moon because there were cloudy skies. The canopy cut out a lot of the overhead view. Nevertheless the stars peeked out of the night sky from time to time as the clouds passed by. In fact, the surroundings seemed quite familiar. He was not certain but

Kevin suspected that he was in the woodland where he had spent pleasant hours years ago courting Jane. He thought he could detect a few glints of reflected light coming from the pond that he knew so well. The amusing idea crossed his mind that perhaps he had been brought here after all these years to retrieve the missing boot that had got stuck in the boggy ground. He almost managed a smile at this fond memory.

Kevin could not see the being that had led him to this place but he could feel his presence nearby. There was a dim light forming a funnel shape that passed through the trees in front of him. It was like a tunnel passing through the trees where the tree trunks, branches and shrubs did not intrude. Kevin thought it resembled a passageway but had no idea where it led. He noted that everything within this 'tunnel' was very still. Whereas around the tunnel a light breeze caused rustling of the leaves and plants there was no movement from within the tunnel itself and no noise.

Kevin stood for some time and then he noticed movement. A small group of people were travelling through this tunnel. They were not making their way on foot but appeared to be slowly floating along just off the ground. No-one was talking. They all stared directly ahead with expressionless faces. They passed across Kevin's viewing position just a yard or so in front of him. They did not turn their faces to acknowledge him or anything else for that matter. Kevin tried to speak out to greet them but he was unable to vocalise any sounds. The group drifted past him as if he did not exist. Kevin counted them as they passed by... one... two... three. In all there were seven normal looking human beings moving in single file in one direction with one of the group trailing a short distance behind the rest. The leading pair of people of this group were two young children, one being a boy and the other a girl. He reckoned they were aged about five or six. The people seemed to be in different states of dress or undress. Pyjamas were present on one child… a lady was wearing just knickers and a bra… a man was wearing a tuxedo.

The sight now seemed like a slightly familiar one that he had observed before but he could not recall the time or location. Where did the tunnel lead and what happened at the end of it? Kevin was still unable to understand not only what was happening but why it was happening. A voice in his head kept repeating the word "implant."

The group of people drifted along. Behind the two leading children were a couple of young people, a man and woman. What would anyone want with children and young adults? The female was in a state of semi-undress in her underclothes. She looked like she had been disturbed and removed from whatever she had been doing rather quickly and unexpectedly. Following the two young adults was a pair of middle aged people. This included the man wearing a tuxedo and a woman wearing a nightdress.

Thoughts involuntarily flooded Kevin's mind. "Fertile… breeders… implants." Kevin began to utilise his scientific knowledge and work experience. He knew about genetic manipulations, genetic engineering and selective breeding. Kevin was finally beginning to glimpse some kind of meaning to everything that was happening to him. He felt that everything he was experiencing was all somehow linked to genetic tinkering, adaptation and survival. Somehow he was part of it all. A programme was proceeding before his eyes. He was not sure exactly what role he was playing in this event.

Another figure followed behind the others. It was an older female. She seemed rather out of place compared to the rest. Kevin recognised his mum. She appeared to be at her current age of sixty five as he remembered her. He recognised the clothes she was wearing. He had seen them just the other day. Kevin was aghast! Oh no! How could this be? Of everything that he had experienced, this just could not be real. It was also completely unacceptable. He still could not speak but in his desperation to vocalise a slight gurgling sound emerged from his throat. Thoughts immediately appeared in his mind as if to try and calm him down. "Sylvie... Sylvie... love... safe." Kevin knew he had to follow his mum along the tunnel and see what destination lay ahead.

Kevin drifted along behind his mother. The tunnel continued in a straight line deep into the woods. It felt to Kevin that he had travelled for half a mile or so. The group finally reached a termination point. The seven people in front of him stood in a queue, one behind the other, all facing forwards towards something. His mum was at the rear of the others. Kevin felt helpless. He loved his mum and did not want her to suffer any harm. He didn't want her to be part of some bizarre experiment or abduction. Apparently, he did not have any choice in the matter.

In front of the group lay a pyramid. It was some twelve feet in height and tapered at the top. It appeared to be made of metallic material. Kevin noted that it had a remarkable similarity in its appearance to the tiny implants that he had seen extracted from his mum and his wife. This object was much bigger. The side facing closest to him made a huge triangular shape. The surface suddenly seemed to melt away before his eyes revealing some kind of entrance passage to a place on the inside that he could only glimpse. It did not look like the local woodland.

As the 'doorway' opened the space it had occupied became filled with pulsating flashing lights. The colours alternated in sequence. Red... green... blue... red... green... blue. He had seen such imagery in his past dreams. A faint humming noise also emanated from the object. The source of the sound was not apparent but it did seem to be generating from the region around the entrance to the inside of this object.

The group of seven people floated forwards and passed inside the object. As they moved inside through the 'doorway' they disappeared from view. When it came to Kevin's mum's turn to enter he felt he wanted to warn her or stop her but she just continued on her way and followed the others inside and was gone from view.

Kevin was uncertain as to what he was supposed to do now. Should he also enter the object? He did not know what it was. As he pondered the decision to enter or not he noticed that the entity which had impacted his life was drifting along the woodland tunnel towards the entrance to the object. This entity had been behind Kevin out of his view but now it accelerated past him. On reaching the entrance it stopped with its rear facing Kevin. This creature now once again resembled an owl. He felt that he knew this creature. It was not a creature at all. It was a living person. It was not a person in the everyday meaning of the word but somehow Kevin knew this being very well. It was very strange but he loved him. He wanted to call him 'dad'. 'Dad' entered fully into the pyramid and was lost to sight.

Kevin moved tentatively forwards towards the pyramid-like object. He placed both hands on the edges of the triangular entrance supporting himself in such a way that he could look inside without going all the way into the interior. He was wary of entering. He decided it was 'sufficient' to push his head through the entrance space and see what he could make out on the other side. He ignored the sequential flashing coloured lights and humming sounds and with a sudden jerk pushed his head inside.

The scene was incredible. The view was not confined to the expected 3D space relating to the dimensions of the pyramid. He was looking across a field of grass except it was not like any grass he had ever seen before. It appeared to have the texture and dimensions of a turfed garden lawn but this grass was a vivid blue-green colour and coarse looking. The landscape was flat. No hills or geographical features were visible. About thirty yards in front of him was a building of some kind. It had the appearance of a translucent dome. One area within this dome had an extra clarity at ground level and Kevin assumed this was a doorway or entrance into the structure. He thought he could make out some movement inside this building and he could see people inside, presumably the ones including his mum that had mysteriously floated along the woodland 'tunnel'.

Kevin looked around and tried to make sense of what he could see. He felt the view was somehow 'futuristic' in nature. What he could see did not resemble the world that he grew up in. Maybe the pyramid was a stargate and had transferred individuals passing through it to a far distant alien world. However, Kevin kept receiving a mental impression that the scene in front of him was at the same geographical location on planet Earth as his local woodland but viewed either in a different dimensional plane or many years into the future. He favoured the latter hypothesis but had no evidence to support any kind of conjecture. If it was the latter case, he could not 'feel' how far into the future this landscape existed. Nevertheless, he could tell it was not hundreds of years ahead in time, it was more like thousands of years. If this was the case, then the pyramidal structure he was peering into was some kind of time portal.

Kevin peered upwards. The sky was quite dark. He could not tell if this was a daytime or night-time view in this strange place. The sky was nearly devoid of stars and he could not make out any recognisable constellations. He knew that there was a theory that the Universe was expanding and the stars were moving away from each other. One day the night sky would reveal no stars, assuming the Earth itself would survive that long. Would there be anybody left to survey the heavens in the far future? Was he seeing something that conformed to this future scenario?

There were no clouds in the sky. An orb glowed overhead.

It was much larger than the sun in terms of its familiarity to Kevin yet it seemed to be a sunlike object. This sun was not a brilliant and blinding yellow colour. It was round and a colour that Kevin could only describe to himself as blood red. Its light was faint and did not dazzle the eyesight. It was possible to look directly at it without shielding the eyes. Perhaps this aerial object was the same terrestrial sun he had always known but it had evolved into some other state.

Kevin's curiosity got the better of him. He carefully pushed one leg through the opening while keeping the rest of his body outside. It felt lighter in weight. Kevin withdrew his leg from inside the pyramid. He bent over and inserted an arm. He examined the blue-green 'grass'. He tried to make a scientific guess as to what it could be. He had a good botanical knowledge and speculated on the nature of this plant.

Normal green plants on Earth made their food in the form of starchy material by photosynthesis. They utilised the green pigment chlorophyll which in 'higher' green plants like shrubs, flowers, trees and grasses stored starch in structures called chloroplasts within the living cells. Chlorophyll absorbed sunlight and used this radiant energy in a complex series of reactions involving carbon dioxide and water to generate starchy carbohydrate food. Oxygen was a by-product of the process and was released into the atmosphere used in the respiratory mechanisms of animals and people.

The grasslike plants Kevin observed did not appear to contain the green pigment chlorophyll. The strength of the overhead 'sunlight' was also rather meagre and of poor quality in terms of conventional plant nutrition utilising photosynthesis. There was also a complete absence of wind. No air movements caused any swaying of the 'grass'. Everything was silent. The air did apparently contain sufficient oxygen to breathe but seemed very 'thin'.

The plant material reminded Kevin of a primitive group

of plants back on the normal Earth he had been familiar with. These were called the *Cyanophyta*. The plants in this group were the cyanobacteria, more commonly called blue-green algae. They may have influenced the atmosphere of the ancient Earth by releasing gaseous oxygen into the environment. With the passage of time oxygen-breathing animals evolved and flourished so that biodiversity increased massively. Kevin speculated that the blue-green layer coating the landscape might have been purposely created by human genetic engineering.

Kevin stepped backwards and withdrew his hands from the edges of the pyramid. He needed a few moments to consider what he should do next. His head was no longer within the structure and the scene he had been viewing no longer had any clarity. He was standing in the tunnel-like illuminated region within the woodland facing the pyramidal obelisk. He pondered as to whether full bodily entry into the pyramid was a good idea or not. Kevin was sure his mum was inside, most likely in the translucent domed building he had seen. Could he rescue her? Maybe he would be harmed if he completely entered the pyramid. Perhaps he might become trapped inside. He needed to get back to his normal existence with Jane.

As Kevin pondered his situation it was as if his thoughts elicited a response. The 'doorway' into the pyramid disappeared. He now faced a solid looking triangular surface. The flashing red, green and blue lights had ceased occurring. The humming noise briefly increased in volume and was followed by a 'swoosh'. The pyramid was gone. He was standing somewhere within his local woodland. It was chilly and dark. The mysterious illuminated tunnel had disappeared. Kevin peered upwards into the sky. A bright moon shone its reflected light over the trees and stars twinkled in the heavens. Everything was back as it was supposed to be. He felt like the stars were twinkling just for him.

One star overhead was so bright. It was stationary but flashed and twinkled as if it was sending out a Morse code message. Kevin felt compelled to give the star a wave. He knew he had been in a similar situation in his life before. He had a clear recall of his ride in the funfair when he was eight years old. He had taken a ride in a lovely yellow rocket that he had caused to rise as high as it would go using the joy stick. His life since then had episodes of intermittent strange events over its time course. He wondered if strange things had happened to him before age eight. Maybe something had intervened in his life even before he had been born. Kevin felt like his memories were scrambled just as one might put an egg in a saucepan to beat and mix the yolk and white. He remembered various strange events but was not sure if they were real or not. He could certainly remember some incredible scenes. He wanted to get home. He desperately wanted to be in Jane's arms. Tomorrow he would check on his mum.

Kevin stumbled through the woods catching his clothes on the undergrowth and receiving many scratches. He spotted the little pond out of the corner of his eye and this gave him a landmark to head for. At around 3 am Kevin finally arrived at his front door. The lights blazed inside. He struggled with the door key but after some fiddling managed to get the street door open. He walked inside and was met by Jane. She was crying hysterically. "Kevin! Where have you been?"

"I have been so worried" she said. He entered the house and hugged his wife. Kevin was not sure what to say. He could hardly launch straight into the story of the pyramid and what he had seen inside. Kevin's clothes were tattered and his shoes were muddy. His skin had an odd tanned appearance as if exposed to ultraviolet radiation.

Jane ran Kevin a hot bath and put his dirty clothes to one side. She thought that throwing them away might be a more sensible idea than trying to wash them. Kevin was soon cleaned up and in bed drinking hot chocolate that Jane had made him. He could neither explain to Jane where he had been nor what he had experienced. Jane could see that Kevin was stressed and she realised he had undergone some kind of traumatic event. She thought explanations could wait. It was good to see her husband home safe and sound. Jane wondered whether he had suffered a mental problem and had wandered off. Anything might have happened to him.

The next morning was a Sunday so any concerns about work attendance were put on the backburner. Kevin lay in bed resting for some time and then joined Jane downstairs in the kitchen. Jane wanted to know what had happened the night before. It seemed the best thing to Kevin that he should tell Jane that something had compelled him to go into the woods and he had experienced some strange things. He knew this was not the way it had really happened but the full truthful version was too crazy to comprehend. The complete story was not going to go down well, not even with his wife. He thought of mentioning that he had discovered some unusual grass in the woods and would like to find some more so he could study it.

The most significant part of his experience related to his mum. He told Jane that he had a vision of his mother taking a walk in the woods and getting lost and he had developed an overwhelming desire to look for her. Jane reassuringly reminded Kevin that his mum was coming round about 3 pm that day so he would see her shortly. Jane told Kevin that he had been at home and told her he was going up to the bedroom to take a short snooze. He had vanished from the house without telling her a thing about where he was going or how long he would be away. Jane told him he had been away for so long she had considered reporting him missing to the police. She had wondered whether he might have had an accident or run off with another woman. She did in fact call the police but they told her that it was too early to start a missing person investigation. The desk Sergeant Peter Phillips said that Kevin would probably show up shortly and indicated that maybe he had been out and had too much to drink. The Sergeant did not know Kevin like she did and Jane found this attitude to be rather annoying. The officer did indicate that if Kevin did not turn up in due course then Jane was to recontact him and standard procedures would be set in motion. Her call was noted and logged.

Jane wondered whether Kevin needed a medical appraisal. If he continued wandering around again in future, a bad accident might befall him. Perhaps he was unwell or suffered from a delusional or sleep disorder. His job might also be put at risk. Jane's only concern was for her husband's well-being. Kevin had recently taken on some cutting edge genetic engineering tasks at his work place. He had become an expert in gene splicing and similar techniques. He was involved in studies investigating hybridisation and how newly combined traits in offspring could undergo genetic recombinations giving physical advantages. There were future possible benefits to mankind in the prevention and treatment of genetic illnesses both before and after birth. His company stood to benefit enormously in the financial sense if any breakthroughs were forthcoming.

Jane decided to allow the day to pass by without too much fuss. Although she had been distraught worrying about Kevin, he was now back home. He seemed unclear about what had happened to him. For his part, Kevin remained unforthcoming about the events of the previous night. The memories were vivid but ironically he did not think it appropriate to share them, not even with Jane.

Kevin wondered if he should talk to his mum about his memories. Maybe she would understand more fully what was going on. It was possible that she would remember moving

167

through the trees into a different 'realm' of existence. How could he start such a conversation? Jane could hardly participate in this discussion. Surely he could not really have observed his mother passing through a woodland illuminated tube?

The time moved past his mum's expected time of arrival. She had wanted to take some exercise and planned to go by foot to their house. She was late. Sylvie was now thirty five minutes overdue. Kevin was becoming concerned. His mum liked to be on time when meeting people. Kevin tried to phone her but there was no answer. She must be making her way to their house. Perhaps she had stopped off at a corner shop to buy something. Although she was a frequent visitor, Sylvie did not like to turn up empty handed. A box of Quality Street chocolates would be a fine gift, or some ginger biscuits.

At 4 pm Sylvie had still not arrived. Jane told Kevin not to worry and relax. She would get in the car and drive slowly towards her mother-in-law's home. More than likely she would see Sylvie on the way and she would stop and pick her up. Sylvie was nowhere to be seen. Jane arrived at her house. She knocked on the door and rang the doorbell. There was no response. The front and rear doors were locked and bolted. The curtains were almost closed and there was no sign of activity inside. No lights were on and no sound could be heard from indoors. Sylvie was clearly not at home. Jane suspected that she had driven past her. She might have gone into a shop just at the moment Jane drove along the road at her location. Jane felt sure that when she returned home she would find her mother-in-law in deep conversation with her husband.

Jane drove home, parked outside and went indoors. Kevin was alone and waiting impatiently for her. They were unsure what to do next. Time passed by and the wall clock reached 6 pm. Kevin and Jane anxiously decided to go to Sylvie's house again to see if she was there. Kevin had the door key. He had half expected to find his mum on the floor having been taken ill or having had some kind of accident. No, she was nowhere to be seen. The couple decided to go into the police station in case there were any reports of accidents or incidents.

They walked into the station which seemed very quiet and walked up to the desk officer. Jane introduced herself and Kevin and they explained their concerns. "I know you. I spoke to you recently about your missing husband. I am Sergeant Phillips." The Sergeant then looked Kevin in the eye and said "You are the 'missing' husband. I am glad you have turned up safely. Your wife was so worried about you." Jane was reassured by the police officer's calm manner. Kevin was not quite so content.

Sergeant Phillips explained that people often disappeared for all kinds of unexpected reasons. Invariably, they turned up sooner or later safely with a story to tell. He asked Kevin where he had been the night before. Kevin was rather cagey in his reply. "Oh I went out and unexpectedly got myself lost, it was just one of those things" said Kevin. The policeman suspected that alcohol was also something to do with it. He felt sorry for Jane. She seemed a nice lady and it was such a pity that Kevin, like many other men, preferred to drink to the point of becoming senseless rather than spend time at home with their wives. Sergeant Phillips turned to them both and again said it was too early to take any action. Their visit had been logged. He was confident that Sylvie would soon turn up or be in contact. If they had not heard anything in another day or so they were welcome to get back to him. They could ask to speak to 'Peter' but should he not be there his colleague Constable Hickman would assist them.

A day went past and after work the couple revisited the police station. A different officer was at the desk and they assumed that this was Constable Hickman. The officer consulted the log and after hearing the story again and asking a few questions he said he would start investigations going into Sylvie's whereabouts. He told them not to worry.

The following weekend there was still no news about Sylvie. Kevin had heard nothing from his mum. He had gone back to her house and nothing had been moved or was out of place. A few bills lay on the floor below the letterbox. His mum's mail was being delivered but not opened or read.

Kevin and Jane returned once again to the police station. They were now very worried. There had been no reports of any emergency admissions in any local hospitals. Sergeant Phillips was once again on duty. He asked the couple to enter a small 'interrogation' room and take a seat. He sat opposite them and fixed them both with a stern look. Kevin and Jane did not on this occasion feel any warmth emanating from the policeman. After a considerable delay he spoke. He addressed them in a very informal and monotone voice.

Sergeant Phillips explained that on the previous weekend a young couple had been walking around the local woods in the early hours of Sunday morning. They were a courting couple and had been in the vicinity of the local pond. They had been seeking some privacy for their kissing and cuddling. They had noticed a faint glow some distance away between the trees which extended deep into the woodland. They could see what looked like a group of people moving along an illuminated route. A woman passed by heading for this illuminated area. They hid behind a tree because they did not want to reveal themselves being only partially dressed following their amorous activities. Following police enquiries into the whereabouts of a missing local person (Sylvie), they had contacted the police. They recognised the woman in the woods in the early hours as Mrs Powell. She was well known in the local village.

Jane was shocked to hear that her mother-in-law had been

wandering round the woods in the dark. Whatever had possessed her to do such a thing? Kevin was not quite as surprised as Jane. He believed he had not dreamed the recent events and confirmation of the presence of his mum in the woodland was not surprising. The failure of Kevin to look shocked or surprised elicited a response from Sergeant Phillips.

"You don't seem too surprised sir" Sergeant Phillips said. "I have some further information for you." The couple had again hidden behind the tree. The police officer told them that following on behind the passage of Mrs Powell through the trees came a man. They both caught a glimpse of his face. They did not know what to make of all the activity going on at that unearthly time but decided it was their public duty to come forwards. They had gone into the police station regarding their identification of Mrs Powell.

Some while later, the couple observed a bright flash of light rise vertically into the sky from in between the trees about a mile away. A bright light briefly shone at a high altitude and glittered in the sky rather like when a rocket firework explodes and bursts into colours. Something overhead briefly twinkled red, green and blue before it faded away from sight but this was much too big to be a firework. They could not think of any logical connection between this visual display and the passage of people including Mrs Powell through the wood. A police search of the area had revealed nothing.

Sergeant Phillips leaned towards Kevin and made direct eye contact. He spoke in a gruff voice. "Were you wandering in the woods at the same time your mother disappeared? Your wife reported you missing during the same time period. Did you do something to your mother?" Kevin replied that he was was confused about when he had last been in the woods but he definitely did not do anything to his mother. He had not spoken to nor interacted with his mother on the occasion in question. He said he loved his mum and there was no motive for him to do her any harm. Jane was horrified by the idea that Kevin may have done something harmful to his mum.

"I am going to get to the bottom of this matter" said Sergeant Phillips. "I am going to step up our searches and enquiries and ask for more resources. I do not wish to further worry you but I am going to get the sniffer dogs involved and get them to search for any signs of digging that could indicate a shallow grave. I will also get a frogman to take a look in the village woodland pond. It is quite deep in places. I think it would be a prudent idea for you to remain in the local area Mr Powell and ensure that you are contactable. There may be more questions and you may be required to help us further with our enquiries."

Kevin sat with his head in his hands. He was sure that he was not the cause of his mum's disappearance. Whatever had happened was out of his control. Jane sat speechless. Tears welled up in her eyes. Life was taking an unpleasant turn. She was very fond of her mother-in-law and she was missing. It was not possible to say what had happened to her. Here she was in a police station with a police officer implying that her adored husband might be implicit in doing some malevolent deed to his own mother. Things could not get worse. As for Kevin, his mum was alive in his dreams.

CHAPTER 7

Overloading the Mind: Gone So Soon?

During the next three weeks there was no significant news regarding Sylvie's whereabouts. The police had searched the local woodland but found nothing that was of any help to their investigations. The police dogs did not indicate anything out of the ordinary to their handlers. It was unknown why Mrs Powell left her home and had gone wandering around the woods. Perhaps the young witnesses had misidentified her. They did not have any motive to lie and make up a story about whom they had seen. Where was Mrs Powell?

Sergeant Phillips was suspicious of Kevin. It occurred to him that maybe Kevin had been drunk and had been stumbling around the woods in an alcoholic stupor. Another possibility was that Kevin might have had a secret liaison with another woman and wanted to keep this secret affair from his wife. A third possibility was that Kevin had been meeting people to supply or receive illicit drugs or stolen items. There was no evidence for any of these things. Kevin had denied any wrong doing. There was no obvious reason why Kevin would want to harm his mother. There was a missing part to the jigsaw.

Kevin made a number of visits to the police station. He was interviewed under caution. The police decided there was insufficient evidence to arrest or charge Kevin with any malpractice. There was not even a dead body to provide any clue to the mystery. Mrs Powell seemed to have completely vanished. Since her disappearance, investigations revealed that no financial transactions had transpired either into or out of her accounts. Phone records came to a sudden halt and no calls were showing. A few bills remained unpaid and mail had accumulated within the house and had not been touched. Hospital records showed no patients resembling Sylvie's appearance or with her name reporting for emergency treatment or being admitted as an inpatient.

Life in the Powell home was sombre. As for Kevin, he had retained memories of what he thought he had seen, heard and experienced. However, he did question his own sanity. If he found it hard to accept what was in his mind himself, what was the point of trying to explain it to the police? They would never believe him. He might be referred to a police psychiatrist. He would end up in a police prison psychiatric hospital. He did not know the fate of his mum.

Kevin recalled memories which, although vivid, had a dreamlike quality about them. He could remember looking across a field of blue-green grass and viewing a translucent dome shaped building. People were inside it. He was sure his mum was one of those present. What had happened to her? Was she alive or dead? He did not know the answers and he felt helpless and distraught. He had taken some holiday time owing him and was off work. He needed time to reflect on everything that had befallen him.

Jane in the meantime was very low spirited. Nothing had diminished her love for Kevin. The whole situation caused her great grief. She was very worried about Kevin. His explanations about where he had been and what he was doing when Sylvie vanished far from satisfied her. Jane's concerns were mainly focussed around the possibility that Kevin had developed some mental issues. Maybe he had suffered a nervous breakdown. She hoped if this was the case that she was not a factor on the onset of this. Jane had made Kevin visit their GP and have a medical assessment. There was no evidence of any clinical problem. There were some areas of memory and recall which Kevin claimed were rather vague but the doctor felt this was mainly due to a reluctance of Kevin to talk about certain details or events. It was not in the medical remit to try and 'force' patients to speak. It was possible that something traumatic had occurred to Kevin but he had shown no willingness to delve into any issue with the doctor.

Jane believed that whatever the explanation of what had happened to cause Sylvie's disappearance, it was not caused by Kevin. She knew Kevin would not be involved in any 'wrong-doing'. All she could do was to 'be there' for Kevin and act as a 'listening board' in the event that he wanted to talk about things. Jane could see that Kevin's stress over his mum's disappearance was genuine and heartfelt.

Jane managed to continue attending work. It was very hard for her with so many negative thoughts on her mind and unsolved issues remaining. On the other hand, her work came as a welcome distraction to all the things that bothered her. She maintained her interest in foetal development and after-birth healthcare. Kevin had always encouraged her to be active in this field and keep herself up to date on issues relating to birthing techniques and child development. Kevin's work especially in the area of genetics and foetal health and development complemented her own interests.

At this unfortunate time, however, Jane felt that even Kevin did not appreciate the extent of her own grief which had overwhelmed her since Sylvie had gone missing. Kevin was mainly caught up in his own thoughts and worries. Normally he would share his emotions with Jane. On this occasion he seemed to be hiding and bottling up his feelings. Jane assumed he did not want to burden her with his sorrow and so was keeping a lot of his thoughts to himself. While this was true to an extent, she had no idea of the memories filling Kevin's brain regarding what he had been through. After all, even had Kevin told Jane the full story, even she would think he had 'flipped' his mind. An extra problem for Jane was that she herself was not sure how to handle her own grief. She had been very fond of Sylvie and her disappearance was not 'fair'. It was not an appropriate way for her 'replacement mum' to exit from her life. Jane herself shed many secret tears over her missing mother-in-law.

Kevin had time to himself while he was absent from work. He contemplated his life story. The childhood years had been happy ones even with no father in the house. His mum had provided and looked after him. He now felt rather guilty for taking her for granted. The shock of his mum becoming unwell and requiring surgery remained a significant time in his life. His mind wandered through his teenage years and the days he had spent with Jane and how a loving bond had grown between them. His student days had been hard work but rewarding but the day of his marriage to Jane was probably the highlight of his life. He remembered Jane's mum Emma and her death in far away Australia. That event had badly traumatised his wife. Now he was thinking about the possible death of his own mother.

The events of the fateful early morning persisted in Kevin's mind. Did he really engage in communications with a father he had never known? What had he seen when he peered through the pyramid device? Did he glimpse another reality? Had he viewed a futuristic Earth? There were so many questions. All the events seemed very real. The humming sound, the flashing coloured lights, the oddly coloured grass, the starless sky and peculiar sun all felt familiar. Kevin's mind mulled the images over and over.

Kevin's meetings with the police were less than friendly.

He felt they would like to 'pin something on him' but they just did not have proof or evidence that he had undertaken a criminal act. Kevin felt they should have been more sympathetic to his situation. The police had given Jane the option of attending a counselling service but she had respectfully declined. Kevin felt that he was very peripheral to this support offer and he was more of a 'suspect' who was getting away with a misdemeanour rather than a victim of unpleasant circumstances. He accepted this as his mum was the real victim in this matter. He was no nearer knowing what had happened to her.

As time moved on Kevin gradually became more and more disillusioned with the police and their dealings with him. He even found Jane to be slightly indifferent to him though he could see that at a conscious level she was trying to be supportive and cheerful. Kevin began to feel somewhat socially isolated. Feelings of resentment grew within him. He did not resent Jane but he felt that she was not revealing her internalised doubts and worries to him and these were reducing her normal warmth. She was somewhat 'tetchy' he thought and less tactile than normal. The police were not showing the professional attitude that he felt was required from them. It was his mum that was missing. He needed kindness and reassurance from the police force. Kevin's frustration was growing. His mind was filling up with more and more emotional thoughts. He started to wonder if he could cope. Why had he been exposed to the experiences that had befallen him? What was the point of it all?

Kevin's mind was filled to the brim. He wanted to know what role he had played in his mum's disappearance, if any. Kevin had plenty of time to continue thinking in this way. He was not at work. Perhaps he should return to his employment. Kevin's mind filled to a point where he felt his brain was going to explode. He felt he was mentally reaching a point of no return. As his mind reached this 'saturation point' he suddenly felt different as if a light switch had been turned on. All the troubling thoughts vanished from his mind. His thoughts entered a new mental paradigm, a new way of thinking. Messages started appearing in his head. He had experienced such 'transmissions' before, especially on the occasion his mum had gone missing. Thoughts in his mind addressed him.

"Keeeeevin!" He heard a voice in his head. "Keeeevin... Keeevin... Keevin... Kevin." The mental sounds became more lucid and precise. "It will soon be over. Your task approaches." Kevin was slightly taken aback by this revelation. What would soon be over? What task was being referred to? Kevin did not mind if his present situation would somehow resolve itself. He was feeling more than mentally stressed. Perhaps he was supposed to kill himself? That would end his predicament. Kevin immediately rejected the idea. Yes, this was a very bad situation and he felt vulnerable and pressured but suicide... no way... that was not an option. Besides, if he was destined to fulfil some unknown task, suicide was hardly going to help him achieve anything. It would be great if his current situation would soon be over but how this could be accomplished was totally unclear.

Kevin decided to speak out loud. "I don't understand. What must I do?" After a short delay a response filled his head. It was not the kind of answer he had expected.

"Gain knowledge! Learn! Prepare!" Kevin had no idea what this meant. The voice in his mind stopped.

Jane and Kevin were able to continue with their relationship but Jane felt Kevin had undergone a slight personality change. Jane found it hard to put her finger on the change. He often appeared to be in deep thought. He sometimes stared blankly through Jane as if she was not there until she nudged him and then he would return to his normal self. Jane had no idea that Kevin's brain was filling with information from some external source. Even Kevin felt that the information he was receiving was overloading the mind.

As time passed, Kevin became increasingly introspective. He became very inwardly thinking and preoccupied with internalised ideas. At the beginning of this retroflection, his minded meandered through genetic information. Most of this knowledge was already known to him. He had obtained this knowledge during his studies or acquired it over the course of his employment. He felt like his mind was 'ticking over' with a purposeful outcome, rather like revising prior to taking an exam. He did not know what the outcome was going to be but his mind led him not only through information but to possible uses and applications of it.

Kevin's deliberations regarding information centred on DNA. He mulled over information about it in his head. This complex molecule encoded genetic instructions in all Earthly animals and plants. They stored most of their DNA in long thin structures called chromosomes located in the nucleus. DNA provided a template of instructions for development and function by way of the genes on chromosomes which controlled vital characteristics. Kevin knewthat the human genome had been documented and this somehow had relevance to the as yet unknown task which he believed would befall him to undertake.

Kevin then began pondering the field of genetic engineering. This area related to his employment and research work. Genetic engineering involved making changes to genetic make up. Genetic modification required biotechnology to manipulate the genome. As Kevin continued to think about this, his mind seemed to open up to various means of achieving this far in advance of anything he had previously read or learned at work. Genes could be inserted or removed. New DNA could be added by copying DNA sequences by 'cloning' samples or by artificial DNA synthesis. Various enzymes could act as a 'molecular scissors' to remove DNA. Individual genes could be targeted. New characteristics would result from such work. Kevin felt that this work would be required of him. He had an expertise that increasingly revealed itself to him above and beyond his previous knowledge. Yes, all the odd events that he had gone through related to this. Kevin's mind related to making human genetic changes. This would throw up ethical and moral dilemmas. His current thoughts encompassed images of people living in a changed futuristic world requiring genetic enhancement in order to survive. He had glimpsed just such a world on the occasion of his mum's disappearance.

Genetic selection and breeding might also be undertaken to produce a class of 'superhumans' for greater intelligence or other 'designer' features. The rights and wrongs of this could be debated but if any changes or enhancements aided survival then perhaps these were justified.

The doubts Kevin had briefly considered about undertaking genetic manipulations vanished though Kevin did not know whether this was due to a conscious decision of his own or whether it had been induced by an external source. Techniques of 'gene-splicing' were well understood by him and it was relatively easy to 'cut up' a section of DNA and splice fragments together. Why should he not use his knowledge and skills to benefit individuals yet to be born?

It occurred to Kevin that genetically modifying humans to improve future viability may have already been done in the distant past, thousands of years ago. He had read theories held by some people that the human race had been modified by ancient aliens that had descended from the stars. Races such as the Annunaki and other 'Gods' were documented in ancient texts and biblical writings. Perhaps it had all happened before.

However, a vestige of caution remained in Kevin's mind. He was aware of the belief in eugenics held by some people.

This idea encouraged the selective breeding of human populations with desired traits. People with undesirable traits might not be allowed to have children. In some extreme historical circumstances, such populations had experienced mass extermination and attempted genocide.

"Would you like a cup of tea?" Jane asked.

"What?" Kevin enquired.

"You were snoozing and dreaming out loud. You were mumbling. I thought I'd better wake you. It's only 9 pm, too early to sleep" said Jane.

"Oh! Sorry! Yes, I'd love a cup of tea. I was thinking about... things" said Kevin.

"I know this is a difficult time for you Kev. It is hard for me too. I miss your mum and am so worried because we don't know where she is or what happened to her" said Jane.

Kevin looked his wife in the eye and spoke in a surprisingly reassuring tone. "I get a feeling that she is alive and ok... she is fine."

"How would you know? Is there something you are not telling me?" asked Jane.

Kevin felt defensive. "I hope you are not implying that I had anything to do with my mum's disappearance. Put it this way. If I did know something about what happened to her there was absolutely nothing I could have done about it."

"Kevin, I wouldn't like it if you kept any secrets from me."

Kevin gave Jane a hug. "Look Jane, I really love you. If there was anything I could tell you that you would believe to clarify the situation I would do so." Kevin felt that this statement was truthful. It was not meant to mislead Jane and he tried not to blatantly lie about his whereabouts when his mum went missing. He did not like to lie to Jane.

Jane brought them both a freshly brewed cup of tea. They sipped the hot brew for a short while in silence. Then Jane spoke. "Kevin! Tell me again! I want to know the truth no matter how bad it might be. What were you doing away from home in the early hours? Were you sleep walking?"

"I have been over this with you before" said Kevin. "Look! I know it is crazy but I can't explain it. All I know is that I was at home and somehow I found myself in the woods. I don't know how I got there. I did not go there to meet anybody. I am very sure that I did not do anything to my mother. Why would I? I did not have any conversation with her."

Jane replied… "Kevin, if you know where your mum is would you take me to her?" These words uttered by Jane would come back to haunt her. If she had been able to envisage future events she would have wished that she had kept her mouth closed.

"I hope we can all be together again in the future" said Kevin.

Tears began to flow down Jane's cheeks. Kevin's answer was strange. He did not seem to be quite the same as she had always known. It was hard to pinpoint exactly what was different. Maybe his personality and attitude had altered. He was more analytical and less intuitive in his behaviour. His sense of fun had diminished. He spent so much of his time in deep thought. Despite Kevin sounding very truthful when answering her questions she could still not completely discard the possibility from her mind that he had been lying to her. Kevin's account of his whereabouts and subsequent events had so many 'holes' in it. She was surprised he had not been arrested and charged by the police for his mum's disappearance. Perhaps it still might happen. Maybe Sylvie's body might suddenly turn up. Jane knew that despite everything she was still in love with Kevin but she needed some personal space and time on her own.

"Kevin, I am going up to bed. I want to think things through in my mind. I am going to sleep in the spare bedroom tonight. Please don't disturb me" said Jane.

"Good night" said Kevin. "I understand how you feel. You must do what you think is best. Try to relax and sleep" said Kevin.

Jane looked at Kevin and with tears streaming down her face said "Goodnight. I still love you, you know."

"Love you too" replied Kevin.

Jane had retired to the bedroom. Kevin felt isolated in his own home. Tears rolled down Kevin's face but no-one was there to see it. He sat in a large armchair and feared for his marriage. He had believed Jane when she said she still loved him but sitting alone in a chair had not been the way he had foreseen his future panning out. His wife was becoming estranged from him. His mum had disappeared in a strange dreamlike episode which he felt was a true depiction of reality but one which would be believed by nobody. Even his mother-in-law had died and he now had no-one to share his innermost thoughts with.

Kevin intended to follow his wife up to bed but he would have to sleep in the matrimonial bed by himself. However, Kevin's mind drifted off and soon he was snoozing in the armchair. In his slumbers he remembered his earlier thoughts which perused facts about DNA and issues relating to genetic engineering. Although he appeared to be asleep he again began to wonder exactly what task was destined for him to perform. Maybe after all it was all a figment of his imagination. "Gain knowledge! Learn! Prepare!" He had received the same thought impression earlier and now it was back in his head. It kept repeating itself. "What do you want me to learn?" mumbled Kevin.

New information instantly started to enter his head. It was like a dam wall had burst open and the flowing torrent of water was racing through his mind in an information overload. Kevin felt that he was receiving a mentally transmitted 'education'. He had known about DNA and its related issues already but what was coming into his head now was totally new or only known to him in outline. Once again, he could feel his mind overloading. He feared it might 'burst'. Sleep was no barrier to this information intrusion, if anything it made it more expansive and compelling. He felt he needed a bigger head with a larger brain to retain the information he was receiving, like those of the creature he had seen in his bedroom.

Kevin felt that he was being re-educated. He did not know what this new knowledge was for but he suspected it was relevant to something he would be required to do. As well as information about human genetic manipulation it included knowledge about binary codes. Computer processing instructions used two digits, zero and one. The system could be used to encode data. Numeric values could be represented by varying combinations of zero and one or 'off' and 'on'.

Other types of information began to 'imprint' into Kevin's mind. He began to feel his viability and 'rights' as an individual were being violated. He had not requested this knowledge. Where exactly was it coming from? It was as if a computer was downloading directly into his brain. Kevin thought that the implant he suspected had been placed in his neck without his agreement or prior knowledge had something to do with what was happening. Kevin tried to resist and ordered his mind to relax and 'blank out'. It did not help. Kevin decided to try a different tactic. He would try and distract his mind by thinking about other thoughts and memories. His wedding night with Jane should do the trick.

However, new information continued to flood into Kevin's brain. He realised there was nothing he could do to stop it. He absorbed information which was completely out of his previous intellectual remit or knowledge. He learned about specialised theories of science known as General Relativity and the principles of quantum mechanics. The Universe had formed billions of years ago in an event which was some kind of massive explosion or Big Bang. Residual background noise supported this idea rather than the Steady State Universe idea in which the Universe had always existed. According to ideas about General Relativity based on Einstein's proposals, the Universe at the Big Bang was a singularity. He learned about gravitational and spacetime singularities. One type of singularity might be found inside a black hole. The latter was due to a star collapsing. Matter would be drawn inescapably into this 'structure' and even light could not escape. Such a black hole had an 'event horizon'. The event horizon was a point of no return. Gravitational pull was so strong at this point that escape was impossible. Light emitted from beyond the event horizon would not be able to reach any outside observer. Black holes were able to stretch the fabric of spacetime.

Kevin's mind began to reel with the unrelenting downloading of knowledge but it would not stop. Objects cannot accelerate to the speed of light within spacetime. Kevin acquired the concept that a spaceship could traverse vast distances by contracting space in front of it and expanding space behind it. Advanced engine propulsion technology could achieve this and allowed faster-than-light travel. Technologies allowed the creation of wormholes using a pair of singularities. A section of spacetime fabric could make a direct connection with another allowing travel between the two coordinates. Kevin felt that he might go insane. He was struggling to grasp what he was being told. His knowledge was fast becoming the proverbial mountain from the molehill. Suddenly he understood concepts of interstellar travel and even intergalactic travel. Related to these and associated with them were time travel and interdimensional travel. His knowledge grew of matter-antimatter universes, parallel universes, multiverses and interdimensional existences. All these phenomena were interlinked. His 'education' continued and he began to conceive further new concepts.

His 'lesson' moved on to an understanding of stargates. Such devices allowed rapid travel between far distant locations. Even intergalactic transfers were possible. A pair of stargates could artificially generate an interconnecting wormhole. Providing this was stable, individuals could move through them to specific locations.

All the time Kevin had been processing these messages and information he had been sitting in the large downstairs armchair. He did not get a chance to go up and sleep in the nice comfortable bed upstairs as he had dropped off to sleep while sitting upright in the chair. He had been tossing around and shifting about as he had been getting somewhat uncomfortable as his muscles objected to being kept in a restrained posture. The remnants of the tea that Jane had made earlier had long since gone cold. Suddenly, Kevin sat bolt upright. His eyes were open and his pupils dilated. His mouth opened wide exposing his teeth as if he were about to be given an oral examination by his dentist.

Kevin knew he was sitting upright but at the same time he knew he was not awake. He stared straight ahead with a zombie-like expression. The thoughts in his mind became more intense as if someone was now shouting at him. The thoughts became very compelling. He felt he was about to learn something particularly important that he needed to remember. As information entered his mind his eyes closed and opened not in the usual blink reflex manner but more like a machine with flashing lights receiving data input. Had Jane seen her husband at this moment she would have been very scared but fortunately she was fast asleep in the second bedroom upstairs.

Kevin's mind focussed on portal technology. Portals could either occur naturally or were artificially induced. The latter behaved as advanced technological doorways. An object or person passing through the gateway could enter a distant location separated by spacetime. The transfer was instantaneous.

A portal might link to a different area within the same Universe or some other plane of existence. The main thing that stuck firmly in Kevin's mind was the revelation that a portal could connect with a parallel world. This would enable interdimensional transfers. Portals could also connect with the past or the future. Kevin's grasp of advanced technology grew and he now understood that such portals could work by using artificially generated wormholes.

Kevin woke up and looked around the room. It was now the early hours of the morning and he decided he better get himself up to his bed while there was still time to get some good quality sleep. He reckoned he must have been snoring and that had woken him up. However, he could recall all the new information that had been fed into his brain. It had become established in his long term memory. He now possessed a futuristic technological database in his head.

Kevin made his way up to bed and removed his shoes and although he was still dressed went straight under the duvet. The experience he had just been through had drained him mentally and to some extent physically. While his head lay on the pillow and while waiting for sleep to overtake him, he contemplated his odd life experiences which were starting to make some kind of sense. Perhaps the pyramid shaped object he had seen in the woods when his mum disappeared was an artificial portal. Anyone passing into it might jump into a different dimension and occupy the future.

Kevin's conscious mind could function no further. He just wanted to sleep. He hoped that he could now go into a long and deep slumber without further disturbance. Sleep did indeed take place but within two hours Kevin's mind was stirring again. He switched between deep sleep, dreaming and wakefulness. In his waking moments he felt that the process of expanding his mind with new knowledge was being accomplished in a harsh manner. Why did this have to happen to him? His human brain was struggling to cope.

He had been trying to get to grips with ideas about portals before his fatigued mind had finally been merciful to him and allowed him to sleep. Kevin's exhausted mind began to function. His mind returned to the concept of portals and progressed into the realm of the multiverse. The perceived human Universe as currently experienced was misleading. There were alternate Universes. Space, time, matter and energy could exist in a parallel Universe. It was possible for life in such parallel dimensions to exist in alternate realities but what intrigued Kevin was the idea of alternate timelines. Historical events had many alternative pathways to choose from.

Kevin's brain wanted to further understand the science behind the exotic images and facts he had been exposed to. This thought triggered an unpleasant response. Whereas Kevin had felt his mind had previously been swamped with information, now a true floodgate opened. Torrents of information came hurrying into his mind with a frightening speed. His brain now understood the intricate workings of the Hadron collider. This research tool accelerated particles such as protons to a high kinetic energy and collided them. By-products were various fundamental subatomic particles which quickly decayed.

A multitude of particle types entered Kevin's brain and became embedded in the form of new long term memory synaptic connections. His mind absorbed knowledge of fundamental fermions and matter particles like quarks and leptons and antimatter equivalents. Force particle types became familiar to him including bosons and the Higgs boson. Some composite particles were made up of two or more components. Strongly interacting composite particles were the hadrons. Composite fermions were called baryons and composite bosons were mesons. Photons that form light energy existed both as particles and in wave form. This information flow was arriving in his head from some advanced unknown exotic source. Kevin's neural circuitry was at breaking point... baryons, hyperons, gluons, muons, gravitons, tachyons and many more. The knowledge download was akin to mental torture.

Kevin's mind wrestled with the bombardment of information entering his head. Knowledge was the key to understanding existence and enabled the development of exotic advanced technology. Faster-than-light travel, time travel and interdimensional jumps all depended on grasping this knowledge.

String theory put particle knowledge into a form which was vital for its mastering and utilisation for technological purposes. A strongly embedded thought in Kevin's mind reverberated and told him that string theory was the bedrock of human advancement. All the particles that make up matter were composed of strings which vibrated at different frequencies so determining various features of matter. String theory largely explained all the types of observed elementary particles. String theory could incorporate gravity. It provided a 'theory of everything'. However, even the exotic sources teaching Kevin seemed offered other versions of this. These ideas were not at odds with the concept of interstellar and temporal travel and the existence of other dimensions. The observed Universe existed in three space dimensions and one time dimension. Six or more further dimensions formed the multiverse. However, Kevin was aware of other possibilities such as the existence of eleven dimensions. Clearly nature still had some secrets left to uncover or be clarified.

The next thing Kevin knew was that he was sitting up in bed. He was screaming. He screamed and screamed and screamed. He leaped out of bed and in his confused haste fell heavily against the bedside locker. Blood dripped from a wound to his temple. He lay face down on the bedroom carpet. He continued screaming but then had to stop because he became hoarse. His throat was parched. A throbbing headache filled his head and his vision was blurred. Mentally he felt totally confused. He had a bad sense of foreboding. He knew some 'final task' was approaching. Somehow his life as Kevin Powell was coming to an end. It might not be the end of his existence but rather some kind of transition was going to occur. He could sense it. He felt apprehensive and afraid. Worst of all, Kevin was very scared for Jane's future.

At that precise moment Jane came rushing into the bedroom. She found Kevin still prone, face down on the bedroom floor. He was weeping. Jane helped Kevin to his feet and sat him on the bed. She raced into the bathroom to get the green First Aid box with its huge white cross on it. She dabbed the blood away with some cotton wool soaked in diluted antiseptic. The cut on Kevin's temple had bled quite a lot but was not as bad as it might have been. Jane decided it was clean and did not need any stitches. She applied an iodised plaster over the wound.

"Whatever happened? You frightened me. I heard you screaming and fall" said Jane.

Kevin gathered himself together and regained his composure. "I was thinking about a lot of things. My head was bursting. I could not take any more" Kevin replied.

"My poor baby! Oh Kev, I am so sorry. It's all my fault. I should never have gone off to sleep in the spare room. I should be with you whatever happens in our life. I will never do it again. Please forgive me" said Jane.

"There is nothing to forgive. I am so sorry to have

frightened you. I know I have not been myself recently. I have a lot of things on my mind." Jane knew that Kevin was badly stressed regarding the whereabouts of his missing mum. She believed him when he said he did not know how or why he had ended up in the local woods. Kevin was not well. He needed her love and support. She had done the wrong thing by going off to sleep in the spare bedroom on her own, leaving Kevin to his own devices alone in the armchair downstairs.

They had tea and some digestive biscuits and then retired back to bed, together. Kevin felt somewhat better except for an unpleasant throbbing headache. At least his clarity of thought had returned. The new information he had received was still in his head. He had indeed received an uninvited 'education'. This new information was not at the forefront of his mind. Just as the brain stores long term distant memories that sometimes resurface out of the blue, all his newly found knowledge was somewhere deeply buried and stored in his cerebral cortex but it was available if and when required.

Kevin and Jane cuddled up together in their bed. The lights were dim. "You know I will always love you" said Jane.

"I love you too. You know I would never allow any harm to come to you" replied Kevin.

"I know that."

"If something bad were to happen to either of us, you know it would be something out of my control. I could never consciously do anything harmful to you. I love you so much. If I ever did anything you did not approve of, I hope you would forgive me" continued Kevin.

Jane momentarily wondered if Kevin was referring to something relating to Sylvie but she did not want to hold on to the thought and let it go. "I have no regrets marrying you Kevin. You are a good person. You are perfect for me."

Kevin did not want to lose Jane. He did not feel like she would leave him yet something in his mind continued to tell him that things were going to change. He did not know when or how this would occur. Perhaps his insecurities were showing through. He also felt that at some point, in due course, he would not have to worry anymore about police enquiries. The link between this and his future life with Jane was not apparent. It was a shame his mum was not around to talk to about the overloading of his mind with so many thoughts. She was gone too soon.

Kevin's current thoughts about his life were stopped in their tracks. He felt Jane's soft lips on his. Their tongues intertwined and skipped round each other. Kevin became aware that Jane had placed her hand on his thigh. His breathing quickened. He had a wonderful wife and he never wanted anything to change. He lived in the moment. The future was on the backburner. Kevin was becoming aroused. Their kisses continued and Kevin fondled his wife's breasts. His hand slid along the inside of Jane's thigh. "Mind your head" whispered Jane, "do not bash that cut." This comment seemed to energise Kevin. A moment later he was upon his wife. A long period of passionate lovemaking followed.

CHAPTER 8

Reverse Engineering the Mind

Jane made her way home. In her hand she clutched a white paper bag. Her grip on the bag was very tight due to both anxiety and trepidation. At the same time, she had an underlying feeling of excitement. She had decided to walk back from the pharmacy instead of using the car. That would give her some extra thinking time. Anyway, the exercise would be beneficial. She would not tell Kevin about her news even though she could hardly contain herself. She needed to be sure. Confirmation was required. Jane's heart rate was raised by the time she stepped through the front door.

Both Kevin and Jane had reached thirty six years of age. This would be a special moment in their lives. Things would never be the same again. Jane's thoughts moved on to the two mothers. She wished her mum was around. Emma would have been so proud. As for Sylvie, she was still missing. The police could find no clue to her whereabouts. There was no firm evidence of any malpractice, she had simply disappeared. Of course the presence of Kevin in the area where his mum had last been seen clearly pointed the finger of suspicion at him but he could not be taken into custody for just being in the same vicinity. Sylvie would have been sixty six by now but there was no indication of whether she was dead or alive.

Kevin was not at home when Jane entered the house. That was perfect. She did not want him to be there, not yet. When she was sure, he would be the first to know. She decided not to rush. It was best that she compose herself. Another ten minutes would not matter. She would have an instant coffee and a snack. It was a good time to indulge herself. Her life was about to change. A lot of hard work lay ahead of her in the not too distant future and this was a good time to spoil herself.

Jane headed straight for the kitchen. A teaspoon of Nescafe granules quickly found their way into her personalised drinking mug. One spoon of sugar joined the coffee granules. The kettle was soon bubbling and steaming and the boiling water was poured straight into the mug. A little milk was added to take the edge off the strong colour and dilute the brew. Vigorous stirring followed. Jane then had to make an important decision. The choice was between a ginger biscuit or a piece of cake. She decided against the 'cookie' and cut herself a large chunk of chocolate gateaux. She opened her mouth widely and bit into a large chunk. The cake was delicious. Dark chocolate plus a few wisps of cream covered her lips. It was not long before the coffee and cake were gone. She would not be able to distract herself from what she had to do for much longer. The excuses she had given herself for delaying were running out.

Jane picked up the paper bag she had brought home and emptied the contents. The main object of her interest lay in a small light blue box. She opened the lid and removed the items inside. She eyed them and reached for the printed information sheet. It was quite long but she read it all the way through twice. She picked up the other contents which included a small plastic container, pipette for withdrawing liquid and a vial of chemicals. Jane headed up the stairs, onto the landing and entered the bathroom. She placed a small volume of urine in a small tube and added several drops from the chemicals vial. Some kits were more expensive and the results were instantaneous but the one she had bought would suffice. However, she had to wait three minutes. Waiting for anything to happen felt like an eternity but just before the time was up as, a brown ring appeared in the liquid contained within the little tube. Jane smiled and she felt so happy. This was a wondrous event. Kevin would be 'over the moon'. She was pregnant. Jane's mind raced into maternal mode. A name would need to be chosen. She would have to make a list of possible names. No, she would make two lists, one for boys and one for girls. She did not mind if it was a boy or a girl.

Jane returned downstairs and sat down in the armchair in the living room. Her mind continued with thoughts in 'baby mode'. What about clothes? A whole new wardrobe would be required. Jane asked herself whether she would use modern disposable nappies or not? Yes, she did not want to bother herself with extra washing and laundry. She also considered if she should breastfeed or not? She was still undecided about this. They would have to get a baby cot but at last they would make proper use of the spare bedroom. Perhaps the walls should be appropriately decorated. Jane then considered her job. She would take maternity leave. Maybe Kevin would be granted a certain amount of paternity leave too. It would help out a little bit. Kevin would make such a good dad. Jane then wondered what would happen when it came to returning to work. How would they cope with nursery attendance? How would they manage school drop offs and picking up? Emma and Sylvie were not around to help out. Jane decided that the best thing was not to look too far into the future. She didn't propose to worry about anything at this point. She just wanted to bathe in the good news and enjoy the moment. Jane heard Kevin enter the house through the street door. She would not tell him her news straight away. She decided to wait until the 'right moment'. They greeted each other with a hug and a kiss.

Kevin had been at a garage to pick up their car. It had been in the garage for a few days. Something had been wrong with the gearbox. It felt sticky when changing from one gear to another. He had been concerned in case a new gearbox would be required. Fitting a brand new one would be an expensive job. Luckily, the mechanic had managed to sort out the problem without the need to get another gearbox. While the car was in the garage, Kevin had also decided to get the brake pads checked and to get some small scratches in the paint work covered up. He was not sure if these had been made on purpose by somebody with a key or whether they had got there some other way. In any event, they were fairly superficial and mainly had rubbed out with special wax and a little careful 'touch up' paint had finished the cosmetic improvement. He had been phoned to say the car was ready to pick up but when he got to the garage he found that the adjustment to the brake pads was only just being completed. He decided not to make a fuss but waited patiently for thirty minutes before getting the go ahead to pay and take his car keys back so he could drive home. Despite the short delay, the garage had done a good job.

Jane restrained from saying anything to Kevin about her news for a considerable time. In the evening they were both relaxed and had been watching a movie on television. It was a comedy and they both felt in a good frame of mind. Jane thought this would be a good time to say something to Kevin.

She suddenly felt nervous. There was the hollow feeling of 'butterflies' in the pit of her stomach. From out of the blue various reservations and doubts came to mind. What if Kevin did not like the news she was about to impart? Maybe he would not feel he was ready to be a father. She worried that he might see the upheaval a child would bring to their everyday life as a threat to their marriage. He might say they could not afford to have a child. Maybe as the pregnancy progressed he might no longer find her attractive. He might even see the baby as a rival in some way and be jealous.

Jane told herself to 'stop being stupid'. It was time. She went over to Kevin and hugged him. "That's nice" he said. "What did I do to deserve that?" Jane looked him in the eye. She did not speak but she smiled. She lowered her right hand onto her stomach area and she rubbed it gently with slow circular movements.

Kevin was unusually slow on the uptake. "Have you got a tummy problem?" Jane slowly shook her head to indicate a negative reply. She was still smiling. After a short delay with no spoken response by Jane, Kevin was suddenly enlightened. "You don't mean... there is a little one in there." Jane nodded her confirmation. Kevin was overjoyed. He had a broad smile on his face. He hugged Jane and told her how much he loved her. She would have to be extra careful from now on, there were three of them to consider. They were going to be a 'proper' family. Kevin was overjoyed at the thought of fatherhood. Jane was very happy too. "When did you find out" asked Kevin?

"I only found out a couple of hours ago. I used a pregnancy test kit. I did not get my period this month. I wanted to be sure before I told you" said Jane.

Both of the couple were thrilled with the news of Jane's pregnancy. She informed her doctor and also became registered at her own place of work as a 'patient' and was assigned a midwife whom she did not know very well personally but Jane was satisfied with this. Kevin and Jane had frequent conversations about babies and childcare. Kevin particularly thought about schools and education. They discussed all the areas Jane had previously considered: names, nappies, baby clothes, cots, whether or not to breastfeed, bedroom decorations, childcare, parental leave from work and lots more.

Jane began her pre-natal check-ups and started the

recommended exercises which she did in fact know about already. A date was given for the expected arrival of the newborn. As for Kevin, he could not wait for the special event. In fact, he was so excited about the pregnancy and forthcoming birth that he could hardly contain himself. He knew that new potential fathers might have a degree of apprehension. After all, it was a lifelong care responsibility. New family dynamics impinged on the relationship with one's wife, work and on personal finances. Like most men were concerned, any worries were left at the back of the mind and the positive rewards of fatherhood were in the forefront.

Kevin felt no negativity or doubts about becoming a father whatsoever. In fact, he could not wait for Jane to 'get on with it'. He did come to realise that his thinking was a touch unusual, if not a little odd. His positivity to the forthcoming event was almost 'over the top'.

Kevin had retained the information that had been 'downloaded' into his mind a while ago. It did not bother him in his everyday life because it sat deep in his mind and did not express itself in any form on a daily basis. It just 'sat there' buried in his head. He did not need to make use of this information so he did not think about it. Although he was aware that he held a huge amount of new information in his brain, he was able to accept the idea consciously that he knew about a lot of things that others were totally ignorant of. He had no need to share his knowledge with others so he could keep it to himself. In any event, Kevin thought that even if he did try to share any of his newly found information, other people would not be able to understand it. They would probably just end up calling him a 'nutter'.

Kevin's mind suppressed most of what it had learned and kept this information away from his conscious thoughts. The coming arrival of his son or daughter was to be celebrated. As time moved along some of the buried information in his head resurfaced without revealing any specific details. Something reminded him that he would have a task to do which was very important. A life changing role would occur. He assumed that this referred to him becoming a father. Something nagged at Kevin from his subconscious mind. The 'life change' was much greater in scope than having a baby though this was part of it. There was no point worrying as the clarity of what it was all about was extremely vague. He would just continue to support Jane and enjoy the build up to the birth and when the time came it would hopefully become another high point in his life, perhaps the greatest one of all.

Jane continued to work as long as she felt physically able. She wanted to be eligible to apply for any benefits that might become available. She also wanted to continue working as close to full term as she could. Her workload was amended and was lighter than normal. Jane attended the required antenatal classes and persuaded Kevin to go to the classes aimed at first time dads.

Jane had, on the whole, quite a 'good' pregnancy. Some days she did suffer 'morning sickness' but it was not severe. Eating breakfast later than usual or snacking seemed to help her. She developed a passion for eating fresh tomatoes which lasted about five or six weeks. Kevin was continuously restocking and this left the local village store wondering about the sudden increased demand for tomatoes which frequently resulted in their stock running low. Jane was most assiduous with her diet. She was keen to keep her iron and calcium levels up. She ate more red meat than usual including liver which was not among her favourite foods. Fresh green leafy vegetables were also regulars on the Powell domestic menu, including cabbage, spinach and broccoli. Dairy foods were also high on the priority list but milk was frequently consumed and never in short supply.

A lot of spare time was taken up discussing names for the

baby. They were not sure whether or not to give the baby a middle name. They mused over the possibility of inserting the names Emma and Sylvie as middle names should the baby turn out to be a girl. After some debate they decided not to do this. Of course it would be respectful for the child to have names which reflected her grandmothers' but on the other hand in some way it might end up becoming a burden. She would be a person in her own right and should not have to carry with her the names of ancestors. She would be forever explaining to people that her middle name was that of her maternal and paternal grandmothers. Also, the two names did not somehow 'flow' well one after the other. In the end they decided to plump for a single modern and 'simple' name. This would make future form filling easy to do.

The two lists of boys' and girls' names grew. At one point Kevin suggested 'Kevin Junior' as a name. He quickly thought better of it. His 'ego' was overpowering his judgement. In any case, Jane was not too keen on the idea. They ended up with fifteen names… Peter, Michael, James, Robert, Brian, Graham, William, Keith, Johnathan, Albert, George, Owen, Charles, Samuel and David. This final list contained no new age innovations or exotic examples. It was relatively conservative.

The list of possible girls' names was much longer than that of boys'. Jane had listed about twenty possibilities. Kevin insisted the list was too short. He told Jane that although he had been involved in choosing boys names, he was now certain that they were going to have a girl. After a while, Kevin became convinced that Jane was going to deliver a daughter. Jane did not know why he seemed so sure of himself. She had not undertaken any tests to indicate the sex of the baby. That was not quite correct. She had attended the clinic to have an ultrasound test to check that the foetus was developing normally. All had been well and the staff had asked Jane if she wanted to know the sex of her baby. She had replied negatively as she wanted it to be a wonderful surprise. She was sure that no-one had told Kevin.

The list of girls' names continued to increase. It was now more than twice the length of the boys' list. Kevin insisted that Jane continued to add further names to the list. She did not mind doing this and in fact she researched the origin and meaning of all the names on her list.

Kevin scanned the list of names by eye. His concentration was completely focussed on the girls' list. He told Jane that one name in particular was missing. "The name of our daughter is not here. Let's add it to the list" said Kevin.

Jane chuckled as she assumed Kevin was joking. "Oh yes, of course Kevin."

Kevin turned and walked quickly to the table in their small study area. "I'll be back in a moment." Kevin quickly returned pen in hand. He wrote something down on the list of girls' names.

"Show me" said Jane. The name 'Amy' was written in capital letters and twice the size of the other names on the list. "It's a nice name but let's wait and see" said Jane. "I have some other names in mind as possibilities. My mind has been juggling some quite different alternatives. I was thinking about the name Rebecca. Then I decided I like the name Hayley. Yesterday I was trying to think of a name with a bit of Eastern influence and the name Jade came into my mind." Kevin grinned 'knowingly' at Jane. He mouthed the name Amy.

Jane's abdomen began to show evidence of pregnancy. The first signs were almost imperceptible. Kevin referred to the expanded region as Jane's 'bump'. The morning sickness had gone along with her desire to eat tomatoes. However, as the bump grew in size, Jane's mobility gradually slowed down. She could still walk but from time to time had a degree of backache. Her lower back was very tender in the lumbar region. Kevin was very supportive and helped Jane a lot. He took on the roles of housekeeper, cook and laundry worker.

He was also Jane's personal chauffeur and drove her anywhere she wished to go. Kevin liked to feel the baby moving inside Jane's belly. He placed his hand on her skin and felt for the movements. Sometimes he talked to his developing offspring and even sang to it. Jane thought this was very cute behaviour. She was not quite so content when Kevin spoke to the developing baby through her abdominal wall and called the baby Amy. They had not mutually agreed a name yet. In fact, they did not even know if they were having a girl or boy.

Jane grew in bulk. Her breasts enlarged and became slightly pendulous. They were beginning to express small quantities of milky exudate. Jane was becoming keener on breastfeeding. She knew that the early mammary secretions contained colostrum. This fluid contained antibodies and conferred a degree of passive immunity on the newly born infant. Breastfeeding would confer immunity on her offspring unlike man-made baby milk.

Jane discussed her pregnant state with Kevin. She had gained considerable medical information during her training and employment as a midwife. She reminded Kevin about her having a 'show'. The amniotic waters would often burst prior to the birthing process. Labour might start slowly but the myometrial uterine muscle contractions would gradually increase in frequency and strength. Kevin must be ready to take her by car to the hospital as soon as any indications of birth began. Jane had packed a bag with a nightdress, toothpaste and brush, clean underclothes and so on. It sat close to the front door ready to grab and go.

Kevin was very interested to hear all the information relating to birth imparted to him by Jane. However, his head was already filled with huge magnitudes of information pertaining to the origin of the Universe, spacetime, the nature of matter, energy, time and dimensional travel. He could hardly discuss this knowledge with Jane but he was content to add her miniscule snippets of biological information to his mental 'database'.

Jane at the age of thirty six was about to become a mother for the first time. This was truly a momentous and life-changing event. Things would never be the same. Jane was a little nervous of the actual birth process. She was not looking forward to the pain but she felt that she could cope with it. She wanted Kevin to be present at the birth and hold her hand. This would build the bond between him and the baby and his calm manner would keep her emotions and misgivings in check. Overall though, she would cherish her memories of natural childbirth for the rest of her life. Jane was certainly right in her idea that the birth would be life changing.

It was a Monday evening and it was dark. The sky was clear and the stars twinkled. The moon was full and bathed the local houses and streets in a glow as the sun's light reflected off its surface and made its way to the Earth. Jane was in the kitchen making herself a warm milky chocolate drink. Kevin was upstairs taking a shower. They had eaten about two hours previously. That evening they decided to get a take-out Chinese meal and have it delivered directly to their home. Neither of them had felt like doing any cooking and there was nothing in the fridge or freezer worth heating up. The meal delivered included dim sum dumplings for Kevin and wonton soup for Jane, as starters. They both shared chow mein noodles and Szechuan style roast chicken. The delivery came with chilli oil for Kevin, barbecue sauce for Jane and a packet of free prawn crackers.

They had enjoyed the meal. Jane was virtually full term and her abdomen was extremely swollen. On the whole, she had been eating a healthy diet throughout the pregnancy. Chinese food was not her usual fayre and now she would enjoy a calcium rich milky drink which her unborn child would make use of. It was almost amusing. As Jane took the first few sips of her drink things began to happen. She was not sure she was going to have time to finish her drink.

"Kevin! It's starting" said Jane.

"Stay calm! Stay calm" shouted Kevin from the bathroom. He tried to give his voice a reassuring tone to mask his own anxious feelings. "The baby won't come for a while" he continued. "I am getting dressed right now. I'll be down with you in a moment." Kevin found Jane still standing in the kitchen. She had a mug of hot chocolate in her left hand while the right hand was supporting her body weight as she leaned against the kitchen bar. Kevin removed the drinking mug from Jane's hand and placed it in the washing up bowl in the sink. He kissed Jane and said "Let's go."

Jane experienced a mild contraction and knew that these would gradually get stronger and come more often. Her time had almost come. It was her destiny to give birth. Even as a little girl while she played with baby dolls, she wondered if she would have her own real baby one day, when she was 'big'. Jane grimaced at Kevin as she felt a birth pang but then smiled. "I love you" she said.

"I love you too. Never forget that" said Kevin.

Kevin took Jane's arm and supported her as they slowly made their way to the car waiting outside their front door. He buckled Jane safely into the seat by clicking the seat belt shut. He quickly returned to the house and retrieved the waiting bags Jane had placed near the street door especially for this moment. Kevin turned off all of the house lights leaving the property in darkness. This was unusual as normally they would leave some house lights on to deter burglars from entering. Kevin also bolted the back door and double bolted the street door and turned off all the heating as if the house was going to be permanently vacated. Jane did not notice any of this. She sat in the passenger seat of the car and had both eyes closed. Her right hand gently rested on her abdomen. It would not be too long now. Her mind was fully engaged with her imminent childbirth.

Kevin sat in the driver's seat and closed his door. He turned the ignition key and the engine burst into life. Jane was very relieved to hear the sound of the engine. She had been worried as to whether the car might break down at just the wrong moment. All was well and Kevin pulled gently away to start their visit to the hospital. He had alerted the maternity unit by phone just before he had exited the house. The hospital staff would be expecting them to arrive soon. It was not a particularly long drive and Kevin knew the way extremely well.

"Kevin" enquired Jane, "where are we going?"

"We are going to have our baby" said Kevin.

"This is not the usual route to the hospital" said Jane. "Are you taking a shortcut?" asked Jane.

"Don't worry! Stay calm! We will soon be there" replied Kevin. Jane closed her eyes again and allowed Kevin to continue on the journey. She could feel movements inside her and the occasional contraction.

After ten minutes Kevin said "we are there." However, the hospital was nowhere to be seen. Jane peered out of the passenger window. The car was parked close to the local woodland. The entry into the woods was nearby and she could see the moonlight reflecting off the surface of the pond which had been a feature of the early days of her courtship.

"Kevin, please take me straight to the hospital. There is no time for this" said Jane.

"Trust me" said Kevin. "I want you to take a little walk with me."

"This is not funny" said Jane.

"Please come with me" repeated Kevin.

"I don't know what this is all about but after I go with you, please promise me you will help me have my baby" said Jane.

"I can absolutely guarantee that" replied Kevin. "Now come with me."

Kevin took Jane's arm and gently supported her as she removed herself from the passenger seat. He closed the car door and gently led Jane a relatively short distance past the pond to the start of the line of trees, undergrowth and woodland pathways. Jane had been holding her abdomen and feeling confused. Why had Kevin brought her here?

Jane looked at Kevin and smiled broadly. She could hear an owl hooting. She thought she could see an owl a little further ahead along a narrow pathway through the trees. "How wonderful" said Jane.

"Yes" said Kevin. "I have been here before in the dark. I like the company of owls. I expect my mum saw them on the evening she disappeared. She would have liked them." The owl that Jane had glimpsed silently took off. Actually, she was not quite sure what it was. It looked somewhat different to any owl she had seen before. The 'owl' seemed to hover in the air and then very slowly began to move along the woodland path.

"Let's follow it" said Jane. "I do not want to lose it." Kevin released his supportive grip from Jane's arm. She stood upright apparently oblivious of the impending birth. Her expression had become fixed and her demeanour statuesque and immobile. Her eyes were wide open and her pupils fully dilated to a diameter of 8 mm. She did not blink at all. Kevin, on the other hand, was fully mobile. He looked perfectly 'normal' to the naked eye. He was so happy to be here in the woods with his pregnant wife. He was sure now that this night was going to be the greatest experience of his whole life.

Kevin was in the woodland where he had spent pleasant hours years ago with Jane. He could detect glimmering light reflecting from the pond that he knew so well. He smiled at the fond memories in his mind's eye. Kevin now knew what had led him to this place and he was very excited.

Kevin could feel the presence of a third party nearby. He could see movement along the path ahead of them but Jane's eyes focussed on what she saw as an unusual owl. Just ahead of them a dim light formed a funnel shape through the trees. This tunnel cut through the undergrowth and no plant material intruded within the interior. Kevin had experienced this tubelike passageway before. It did not hold any fear or mystery to him anymore. They entered the tunnel several yards behind the 'owl'. There was no noise from within the tunnel. There was silence. The air was completely still. No air currents or breeze ruffled their hair yet the trees and bushes outside this illuminated zone swayed in the wind. The air had a stale quality to it.

Jane's face remained fixed and her eyes remained wide open and she maintained a big toothy open mouthed smile. Her eyeballs did not move within her eye sockets but continued to fix on the 'owl' ahead of her. From time to time she thought she could hear it hoot and this reassured her and gave her confidence in what she was looking at and where she was going. Both of Jane's arms hung loosely by her sides. Her mind was far distant from concerns over childbirth. She was spellbound by the hooting and moving 'owl' not far ahead of her. Jane wanted to know where it was going. She had never seen such an appealing creature. It was definitely taking her somewhere.

Kevin stood a short distance behind Jane. They were not making their way on foot anymore but slowly floated along just off the ground. They did not speak or otherwise communicate with each other. Kevin tried to speak to Jane but was unable to vocalise any sounds. He tried to reach forward to touch her on the shoulder but was unable to do so. For her part, Jane did not acknowledge Kevin's presence at all.

Kevin knew he had been inside this tunnel before. He had been there during his early childhood and again on the night his mum had vanished from daily life. In fact, his mum had traversed this journey along with other people he did not know. He had watched them move along with his mum being at the very back of the group. They had passed inside an object through a 'doorway' and disappeared from sight. He had a good idea what lay at the end of the tunnel but was not completely sure about the place beyond its termination. He had peered through the doorway into a different physical reality but not entered properly into it.

Kevin drifted along behind his wife. The tunnel continued in a straight line through the woods for some considerable distance. In front of them lay a pyramid like structure. It appeared the same as he remembered it. It narrowed to a point at the top and Kevin reckoned it stood about twelve feet high corresponding to his previous height estimate. Its metallic nature and shape reminded him once again of the miniature implants which had been removed from his mother's and wife's necks.

They came to the end of the illuminated tunnel. The side facing closest to them was triangular in shape. On the previous occasion when he had seen his mother about to enter the object, he had wanted to stop her. This time was different. Jane remained motionless in front of the pyramid. Kevin had no fears for her. She was going to have his baby shortly, as he had promised her. He did still love Jane but her role as a birth-mother was only a small part of a much bigger jigsaw. Kevin was very keen for Jane to enter the pyramid. The surface of the pyramid immediately in front of them became hazy and then disappeared completely. An entrance doorway had opened up.

The space within the opening became filled with bright and flashing coloured lights. Each light filled the space in turn and persisted for about one second before being replaced by another. The colours alternated in a sequence Kevin had seen before. Initially the flashing had started with red which was replaced by green. The green in turn was replaced by blue. After that the sequence started again. There was also a background hum which seemed to originate just on the other side of this doorway. Kevin now knew that this was not just a simple 'doorway'. It was, in fact, a portal. It led to a totally different reality. Kevin had no reservations about passing through it.

Kevin was behind Jane. In front of her she could still see the 'owl' in close proximity. However, she could not focus sharply on it. It seemed to be gently vibrating and the edges were blurred. The 'owl' proceeded to enter the pyramid and disappeared from sight. Jane could hear hooting beyond the coloured flashing lights. She felt unsure as to how to proceed with the 'owl' having gone from her view. However, she moved ahead and passed beyond the lights in order to continue following the 'owl'. Kevin, unlike Jane, did not see an owl pass through the opening of the portal. His view was different. The object that Jane was following was in fact the same 'creature' that Kevin had seen in the past. It had first appeared as a bedroom visitor and he had called it 'dad'. Kevin followed on behind Jane, immediately behind her.

For a moment, Jane vanished from Kevin's view as she passed inside the structure. Kevin moved past the flashing lights at the opening of the portal and entered the realm beyond. As he emerged on the other side, the humming sound ceased and the woodland view was gone. Ahead of him was a strange but amazing landscape. He could see Jane moving through this new environment. As far as she was concerned, she felt she had to carry on following the 'owl'. It held some great importance to her but she did not know what it was. However, it had a magnetic quality which attracted her and she continued to move along behind the 'owl'. She was oblivious of her surroundings and not only was Kevin not in her thoughts but neither were the considerations of impending childbirth.

The view seemed familiar to Kevin. He had seen and

experienced this place before. However, this time Kevin took his time to fully absorb everything his senses would allow. He needed to fully activate his awareness of the surroundings before he proceeded any further. There were no physical constraints imposed by the apparent external dimensions of the pyramid. On the previous occasion he had been here he had only taken a quick view. He decided to take a few moments to orientate himself to the conditions.

Everything appeared to be the same as he had encountered before. He remained motionless and fully surveyed the scene. The land was flat and he could see to the distant horizon since no hills were present which would have obstructed his view. No bird or animal sounds could be heard. In fact, there was total silence. There was no wind in this place unlike in the woodland he had left not long before. The air was completely still. Below his feet and stretching out into the distance was the coarse blue-green grass on which he had spent time postulating its origin and nature. It was as if a vast blue-green carpet had been unfurled and rolled out to cover the land. There was no sign of any other plant life. No trees, shrubs, flowers or even weeds were visible. The air had a somewhat stale quality to it. Once again he was aware of a sulphur like odour, perhaps the faint odour of hydrogen sulphide. The air also felt in some way 'thin'. The oxygen level was reduced, resembling the anoxic conditions found near the summit of some mountain ranges. However, he was able to breathe satisfactorily.

As Kevin moved along, further environmental differences became apparent. His 'floating along' movement related to the low gravity. His body felt distinctly lighter than usual. There was a strong resemblance to the weightless conditions found on space stations in orbit. The body frame here did not require bulky bones and muscles in the rarefied atmosphere.

The level of illumination was extremely low. The light

intensity had the hue of those dull heavily clouded days when everything takes on a miserable feel. However, there was a red tinge about the view when looking straight ahead as if peering through a thin, faint, red and transparent plastic sheet. It was difficult to ascertain the source of what light there was. However, an aerial view revealed a red orb. This sun had clearly seen better days. It was a burnt out shadow of its former glory. It did not have a blinding glare. It had a dull blood red colour which resembled an eye badly infected by conjunctivitis. The sun stood out against a very dark sky. There were no clouds to obscure the view. The sky was very nearly starless except for an odd twinkle here and there. Astronomers would not have much to see as far as star-gazing was concerned in this place.

Kevin looked around him. He had seen this view before but this time the scene appeared 'normal'. It was how things ought to look. In front of him was a building. It was a large dome. It resembled a very large round plastic ball which had been cut in half along its diameter and placed face down on the ground. The surface of this structure was smooth. No windows were visible. It had a translucent quality and nothing could be seen clearly inside. There was a slight internal glow. There was clearly some kind of illumination within the structure. Kevin had glimpsed this building before. He was sure the small group of people he had previously seen moving through the woods and into the portal had terminated their journey within the confines of the domed building. His mum was included in this group.

While Kevin had been 'taking in' his surroundings, Jane had continued following the owl. Jane was still visible but was now some distance ahead of Kevin and rapidly approaching the building. Just as she was about to come into contact with the structure the area ahead of her changed subtly in appearance and seemed to briefly become transparent and

Jane passed through the surface layer to the inside. Kevin's mind suddenly reverted back to Jane and her physical state. He was pleased that she had gone inside the building. He felt that the air quality in there would be better suited for Jane's respiration compared to outside. A long exposure to the external atmosphere was potentially harmful and might also damage the unborn child. He also knew that the atmosphere in this place lacked an ozone layer and various cosmic rays and particles could penetrate all the way down to the ground. Jane was much safer inside the building. He decided it was time to join her and he drifted off in the direction of the dome.

Kevin arrived at the structure and an entrance opened in the same way as it had done for Jane. He entered and found Jane motionless a couple of yards in front of him. He found he could not vocalise any sounds. It was as if someone had turned a switch and locked his vocal chords. The key to unlock them lay elsewhere. There was no sign of any other people or entities. Kevin wondered if at one time his mum had been in just the same place as Jane.

Kevin looked round and overhead the rounded roof of the dome could be seen. It somehow exuded a faint glow sufficient to illuminate the inside with a pale white light. Directly in front of Jane was a barrier or wall such that it was not possible to continue moving ahead in a straight line. It was only possible to turn either left or right. Both the passageways followed the rounded contours of the dome. Jane still had no apparent conscious awareness of either her surroundings or her body making final preparations for childbirth. For the time being her mind had removed all traces of her former life with Kevin. She had lost sight of the 'owl' she had doggedly been following but thought she could hear it hooting. She turned in the direction of the sound and began to move along the 'corridor' to her left. It was not long before she was out of Kevin's view. The vision and sounds of the 'owl' had protected

Jane from any conscious feelings of fear and stress in her situation. They had made for effective 'screen memories' distracting Jane's mind from her reality.

Kevin was inclined to follow Jane but he thought he heard his name whispered from the other direction so he decided he better take a look along the right hand corridor. He would catch up with Jane shortly but first he would have a look along the right hand passageway. Kevin made his way along the narrow corridor. There was not enough room for more than one person to travel next to each other. The corridor resembled a narrow tube with a low roof and was very claustrophobic.

Without warning the corridor came to an abrupt end and opened out into a surprisingly large rectangular room. This surprised Kevin as it was something he had not been expecting. The room was brightly lit with a diffuse white light though it was hard to make out exactly where the light was coming from. Kevin gazed into the room and even he could hardly believe what he was seeing. His mind had been forcibly educated with all kinds of knowledge and information and many suppressed memories had also surfaced. Nothing had quite prepared him for this. Clearly, the newly acquired information he had been given did not include everything he needed to know.

The room had three sides, one to the left, one to the right and one directly facing. There was no other obvious exit or entry place other than the way he had entered. Standing upright against the walls were very large rectangular vats. They were all about seven feet high and three to four feet across. Kevin thought they resembled home fish tanks standing on end. Their similarity to an aquarium placed upright was striking. However, the content of these vessels was astounding.

Kevin counted the vessels as he was curious to know how many were there. There were thirty embedded into the wall to the left, thirty in the wall to the right and forty on the facing

213

wall. Kevin observed that these containers were vats containing liquid. The liquid was viscous and reminded Kevin of melting jelly. It did not look watery but resembled a syrup. Bubbles of gas rose from the bottom and moved upwards through the liquefied contents very much like air bubbles blowing through the water from an air stone in a fish tank. Except for just a couple of vats that were empty on the facing wall, the contents of the containers enclosed people within the syrupy liquid. All these people were alive and in an upright vertical orientation as if standing. Somehow they were not drowning in the fluid and it was maintaining their vital processes. The people faced front-on to Kevin and many were pushed up hard against the perspex-like walls of the container. Some made continuous movements with their arms as if they were trying to swim. All of them had wide open mouths. Their eyes were also open but Kevin did not think they were focussed on him, it was more like they were looking through him at some imaginary scene in the distance.

Kevin decided he would take a close up look. He entered fully into the room and approached the vats on the left hand wall. Kevin stood directly in front of each vat, one at a time, immediately facing the occupant. The liquid content of all the vats on this left hand wall was emerald green in colour. The to and fro movements of the people inside the vats reminded Kevin of an aquatic turtle or a fish swimming up against the glass wall of its fish tank. All the people in the green liquid were male and they were all stark naked. Strangely, they all appeared to be about the same age which Kevin estimated as early to mid-thirties. None of the men had any sign of beard growth as if they had taken or been given a close shave just before entering the vat. Also, no pubic hair was evident. The genitals of these men appeared intact and their bodies in general looked toned and without any sign of excess weight. What was intriguing was the fact that

214

the men represented probably all the races of planet Earth's modern *Homo sapiens* species. There were Caucasion and white people of European, Nordic and Mediterranean extraction plus subcontinental brown skinned Asian types, black dark skinned individuals, Orientals and Mongoloids, eastern Asians, Pacific Islanders, Red Indians and Aboriginals.

On the occasion in the past when Kevin had seen a group of people including his mum heading towards the portal, they had clearly been at different stages of their life. Some were still children and there were young and more mature adults. Kevin did not know if any of the people in the vats were in the group he had seen entering the portal on the previous occasion but it was a puzzle as to why they should all appear to be the same age. Perhaps they had journeyed through spacetime via a wormhole which in some way influenced their arrival at the destination such that they appeared at a similar stage of development age wise. Kevin crossed the room to observe the vats on the opposite wall.

Kevin stood in front of each vat. He moved slowly down the line pausing briefly at each container to look inside. The vats contained a variation of the liquid contents he had just observed across the room. Although the syrupy fluid contents appeared to be similar to that in the previous vats, its colour was pink. Kevin assumed the colour difference related to differing needs of nourishment and support for the people in these vats since they contained females. All the vats along this wall contained naked women. Just like the men in the vats opposite, the women were animated within their vessels and made extensive arm movements while pressed again the wall of their containers. They did not fix their gaze on Kevin but stared wide eyed beyond him as if they were observing something interesting on a distant horizon. As with the men, the encased women were from a wide range of humankind. There were individuals from a diverse range of races and skin colours.

As Kevin moved from vat to vat it became very obvious that some of the women were about to give birth as their abdomens were extremely swollen. He wondered if the syrupy fluid maintained them in some kind of 'stasis' so that they did not actually give birth while immersed in the liquid medium. Maybe the birth process started when the women were removed from the liquid so that their progeny could arrive at a convenient moment. It was not clear why this was desirable nor who was controlling it. Moving along the row of vats Kevin observed that some females appeared to be in an early stage of pregnancy while others did not appear to be pregnant at all, although he thought a few of them looked as if they might have given birth very recently. Although it was difficult to be sure, as with the males, he estimated their age range to be in the thirties.

Kevin came to the final vat on the right hand wall and faced the figure in the container. He stared at the nude figure making rapid 'swimming movements' directly in front of him. His attempts at eye contact were not successful. "Noooooo!" Kevin's initial reaction was horror. It just could not be. Kevin was unable to vocalise much in the way of audible sound but in his mind he was yelling. He was separated by thin transparent vat wall material from his mum. He was overwhelmed with emotion. The shock took time to sink in and Kevin's mind raced on a rollercoaster ride. He experienced joy to see his mother still alive but then pity and anger at her plight. Frustratingly, no communication occurred between Sylvie and her son. For a fleeting moment, Kevin thought his mum smiled at him but it was just wishful thinking. Her arms flailed around pointlessly in the bubbly gas currents passing through her fluidic chamber.

Kevin felt helpless. He considered trying to break open the vat to release his mother. Even if he were to succeed, it might be a risky thing to do. He did not know the physiological relationship of his mother to the fluid she was immersed in and it was possible her extraction from it might prove fatal. After a while of gathering his thoughts together he realised that his mum's physical appearance was quite youthful. Like the others in the vats, he guessed her age to be mid-thirties. This did not make sense chronologically, of course. Sylvie had disappeared when she was sixty five. She had been missing for some time and by now she should be sixty six years old. This was clearly not the case as far as the maternal image before him was concerned. Whatever the temporal effect had been on the other people in the vats, it had clearly affected his mum too. Perhaps even the children he had previously seen entering the pyramidal portal were among the individuals held in 'captivity' now as adults for a purpose yet to be fulfilled. Maybe his mother had already been used for some activity and was now in 'storage'.

Kevin did not like the experience of finding vats with trapped humans. Presumably they were taken away from their everyday lives against their will or knowledge, or at least were unable consciously to avoid ending up where they were. The vats reminded Kevin of oversized goldfish bowls. What would be the fate of these people? Kevin was not sure what to do about his mum. She seemed to be in a stable environment. For the time being, she should stay where she was until he knew more about what was going on. He decided to take a look at the content of the remaining vats which had been located along the facing wall he had seen on entering the room.

The first five or six vats contained the syrupy fluid and gaseous bubbles but no people were in them. Perhaps they were waiting to be filled. The fluid medium in these vats seemed to have the same viscosity as the others but again the colour of it was different. These vats contained an orange substance and as he moved from container to container Kevin suspected that this related to their content. These vats contained children and babies.

Some of the babies were very tiny. They looked like they had just been born. Kevin wondered how they could survive and flourish without access to milk. The orange fluid must have provided nourishment as well as supplying oxygen and somehow taking away wastes. The next ten or so vats contained boys and girls he thought of as toddlers. They must have been about a year old. The appearance of these young children and babies was indistinguishable from 'normal' children and infants. They looked like normal humans but were of varying racial groups reflecting the diversity of the adults in the vats along the side walls. This suggested some kind of consideration of genetic factors had been relevant to whatever was going on.

Kevin moved slowly along the remaining vats. The contents of these were very different to what he had just been observing. All the vats contained children but not in the form he was familiar with. They resembled the creature he had once called 'dad'. Kevin felt they were aged about ten and had not yet achieved puberty.

All the children were naked and there was no evidence of sexual maturation. The group did however consist of a mixture of males and females. Male sex organs distinguished them from the females but their facial features and bodily forms were very similar. The children were about four feet tall. The skin had a uniform grey sheen. Kevin recalled that the 'dad' creature he had seen in his bedroom had been covered with light blue tightly fitting material. Perhaps this clothing had been protective and was required during the visitation but in this place was not essential.

Kevin closely observed the heads. Several of both the boys and girls were completely bald. Some of them had crops of hair which swayed in the fluid baths and these varied in colour, length and texture. The hair types ranged from blonde and fine to coarse and black with various other shades in-between. The heads themselves were unusually large.

The most striking thing about these children was their eyes. They had a hypnotic effect and made Kevin feel uncomfortable if he tried to stare directly into them. The eyes wrapped round the side of the head at an angle and were almond shaped and slanted. The eyes were pitch black and he could not see any eyelids. The eyes apparently did not require eyelid reflexes to cover and protect them against injury from dust or particles nor was there any need to distribute a moist lubricating film of tears across the surface. The eyes themselves did make occasional quick movements which resembled blinking perhaps reflecting a useful function from yesteryear which was no longer necessary.

The arms and legs were long and slender compared to the length of the body. The arms in particular stretched below the level of the narrow hips. The fingers and toes were also long and thin and each hand and foot had four digits. The thumb appeared to be opposable so that a gripping movement was probably possible. On closer observation, Kevin thought he could make out the stump of a fifth digit. Perhaps there was once an extra finger or toe which had reduced and been lost over time.

No nose was in view on the face and no eyebrows were present. There were two very tiny holes or openings where perhaps a nose had once existed in their ancestry. Also, there were no lips or proper mouth visible. There was a tiny slit which perhaps had once served as a mouth. The mouth slits did open more widely from time to time like a fish sucking in water but Kevin could not see any teeth and there was no evidence of a tongue. If these children were able to communicate with others either now or later in their lives it would not be by conventional speech and a different mechanism would be necessary.

Kevin speculated about the presence of adult humans from a mix of human races filling the vats in the room. They were all at an age of sexual maturity and in good health in so as far as their current appearance indicated. This even applied to his mother. The babies and young children appeared 'normal' but the older children looked 'different'. It occurred to Kevin that if all these young persons were maintained in the vats perhaps for years, as they matured their anatomy and physiology might slowly change as they developed and they gradually became less human looking in the conventional sense. It was not clear what might happen to these children once they became sexually mature and entered adulthood. Maybe there was some kind of 'release programme' setting them free from their containers into the environment though what the point of all this might be was unknown.

Kevin was deep in thought about the children in front of him. They may have evolved into their present form over a long time period of evolution. Possibly this process had been artificially accelerated or modified. Kevin was very knowledgeable about genetic engineering and the manipulation of genes. Programmes of gene splicing, cloning and selective breeding might produce a population of children containing a mixture of pre-existing genetic traits and newly introduced ones. Such children were unknown from his younger days but maybe in this place their genetic make up and physical features gave them some kind of advantage.

Kevin looked at these children. He felt sure they were human but not like anything seen before. Kevin had knowledge of various paranormal stories. Among these he had read about UFO experiences and watched recordings, documentaries and movies. Claimed historical events included crash-retrievals, reverse engineering, governmental conspiracies, humans contacted by aliens and abductions. Most of these reports were due to misidentification or were hoaxes. There had been so many stories about different types of beings being observed from little green men to tall blondes, reptilians and greys. The latter did, however, show a resemblance to the children in the vats. Kevin did not think they were alien in any way. They were more like an alternative version of humans living in a different reality or a far distant future altered form of mankind.

Kevin's thoughts finally returned to Jane. She was about to have a baby. It was his baby and he needed to find Jane and assist her. There was nothing he could do to change his mum's situation so he left the room with the vats and retraced his journey back along the passageway and moved down the route Jane had taken earlier.

CHAPTER 9

Harvesting a Genetic Crop

Kevin followed the corridor along the rounded wall of the domed building. Unlike his previous journey along the corridor which opened into the single room filled with the vats, this was different. The corridor he was in now made a sharp right angle turn inwards towards the centre of the domed structure. As he moved along there were openings both to the left and to the right. These openings led to either empty rooms or to further corridors. It became apparent to Kevin that this building was much more complex than he had thought. It was akin to a beehive and Kevin felt like he was inside a three dimensional maze. There were upper floors and levels but what was on them eluded his gaze and kept their secrets from him.

The corridor Kevin had been following came to an abrupt end. It was not a dead end. It divided into two openings rather like facing a Y-junction. He could either go left or right. Which one should he choose? There was no indication of what lay ahead in either of them. Any choice he made would be arbitrary. He wanted to find Jane. That was his priority.

Many questions were still unanswered and he wanted to know exactly what this place was and why it existed. He chose the right hand route and continued on his way. The corridor came to a termination which resembled a very small round room with just enough space for him to enter. It looked somewhat like an expanded bubble or a ping pong ball. The walls in this rounded room looked more solid and whiter than those in the corridor. There was very little space inside this room but he decided to enter. There was a very claustrophobic feel to the surroundings and barely enough room to turn round. The overhead ceiling was no more than a couple of inches above his head. Kevin considered returning the way he had just come and he turned to go back. The entrance he had come through was gone. He was trapped in the tiny round bubble.

Kevin rotated 360 degrees and felt the walls for an exit but there was none. He was inside a ball-like cavity with white walls. He was a living ship-in-the-bottle. There was not enough room to stretch his arms out fully. The ceiling curved over his head and descended in an arc just in front of his face.

The walls suddenly changed to a sunflower yellow colour. He peered ahead and a hazy scene slowly formed. This grew in clarity and it soon became crystal clear. He felt like he was the sole viewer in his own private cinema. He viewed a scene all around him and it was in three dimensions. The ceiling, walls and floor were no longer visible. He was part of the scene he was viewing. However, he was sure he was only an observer, not a participant. He could see himself in the scene in front of him.

Kevin relived a snapshot of a previous time in his life. He observed himself as if he was watching a movie. There was a dreamlike quality to the view. The initial scene showed him riding his bicycle. He was riding along a country lane and his face looked like he was in deep thought. He seemed to be looking up at something which was not visible in view. He was distracted from the cycling and was not taking care where he was riding. The inevitable happened: he crashed and had gone into a ditch. Kevin could remember the occasion very well.

Kevin was viewing a time gone by when he was twenty-five. Jane was the same age. It was a Friday night and now he saw himself in his bedroom. Jane was with him. She was in bed, asleep. He was unable to move. They were not alone, there was an entity with them. It was the 'dad' creature. Jane was standing. She looked so sexy in her white nightdress. Jane was not moving. She stood motionless and had a blank facial expression. He could see and hear himself crying out "Jane." He was trying to warn her that something odd was happening and attempting to wake her up. Kevin could see himself moving towards Jane. He lifted her and lay her down on the bed. Kevin saw himself bending over Jane. He was doing something to her neck. Was he trying to strangle her? No, he was making cutting movements with his arms and hands as if he was doing surgery or a dissection. He had instruments in his hands.

Kevin continued to observe the scene from his younger days. He felt like he was physically there but could not do anything to intervene. He loved Jane then and still did. As he watched a scenario developed. He realised that what he was hearing and seeing was something that had already happened to him and Jane but it had been erased from his mind. He observed before him a scene that he now fully remembered. His conscious mind had now shaken off some kind of memory block. The bedroom event from the past he was watching seemed to have a connection to the present situation. Kevin watched and listened to a repeat of a previous verbal exchange with Jane. It was almost as if he was watching an old movie that was repeated on Christmas television programmes every year.

"Kevin! Kevin!" Jane was screaming.

"Quiet" said Kevin, "the neighbours will hear you."

"What are you doing? Why are you doing this to me? Stop it!" shouted Jane.

"You should be grateful" whispered Kevin, "especially with your interest in child development."

"Have you lost your mind?" asked Jane.

"Our future baby will love us for this" said Kevin.

Jane was pleading with him. "You are hurting me. Leave me alone." She tried desperately to push Kevin away. "My neck is so sore. Please Kevin, stop. You know I love you with all my heart."

Kevin could see that Jane's desperation had a profound effect on him. Poor Jane! How could he have been so callous and insensitive? Kevin continued to observe the scene. The view before him moved ahead like when someone flicks the pages of a book, skipping some of the story. Kevin could now see the next morning. Jane appeared to be fine and it was a pleasant Saturday. There were signs of a puncture wound in Jane's neck. She laughed it off as a love bite. Kevin wished he could relive the life with Jane he had now left but he knew his destiny was about to be fulfilled. He could not escape his fate and nor could Jane. However, the observation of his past was very nostalgic. The 'viewing' skipped onward through the day and Kevin saw himself and Jane enter the Indian restaurant and meeting the manager Mohinder. Kevin recalled that he had felt unwell in the restaurant and been troubled by the overhead light but had felt better after they changed tables.

The viewing stopped abruptly without warning or explanation. It was over. Kevin was still inside the small space of the ball-like room. The walls were once again white. He was enclosed by the curved ceiling and barely had room to turn round. He felt entombed and trapped. Time passed and nothing changed. There was no visible way out. Any escape route was not evident. The bright yellow colour that had preceded his viewing had gone. The room was featureless. He had time to ponder what he had witnessed. He had time to reflect.

Kevin waited helplessly for something to happen. After a

short time the surrounding walls once again turned a bright-yellow colour. He knew that something further was going to be revealed to him. Once more he peered ahead and could see a hazy scene. At first he thought he was going to get a 'repeat showing' of the bedroom events he had just witnessed. It was not long before he realised that what was unfolding before him this time was a different version of what he had just witnessed.

Kevin again could see himself riding his bicycle. He had crashed. He watched himself looking skywards. Above his head was a dark starless sky with a rouge orb. The grass had a blue-green colouration. He was outside the domed building. Kevin felt he had been told something during this visit but he still did not know what it was. Kevin then saw himself once again in his bedroom.

Jane was in their bed. She was fast asleep. Kevin saw himself moving around the room restlessly. He was speaking to somebody. Nobody else was visible in the room. He had previously seen in the earlier 'viewing' of this bedroom event the 'dad' entity but this time he did not see anything. If there was another person present he could not see it this time. Perhaps he was talking to himself? He was quite animated in his conversation.

Kevin saw himself standing next to the bed staring at his sleeping wife. He stood watching her for some fifteen minutes. He was motionless as if in a dream state. Kevin then heard himself shout out "Jane." He knew he had wanted to see if she would wake up. He had given Jane a sleep inducing drug before she went to bed. He had put it in her drink. It would not harm her but she was in a semi-comatose state.

Kevin watched himself pick Jane up from the bed. She was fast asleep and oblivious of him. She was in her white nightdress. Her facial expression was blank and unchanging, reflecting her drugged state. He watched as he saw himself carefully carry Jane out of the bedroom and down the stairs. He opened the street door and unlocked the car. He gently placed Jane in the passenger seat. He returned to the house and calmly locked the front door. He started the engine of the car and drove away. No-one had seen them.

Kevin watched as their car pulled up at the local woodland area. He saw himself stop the engine and turn off the car lights. He watched as he removed Jane from the passenger seat. She had no idea what was happening to her. Kevin carried her into the woodland. The pond water glistened to his left as he walked with Jane deeper into the undergrowth. He followed a path between the trees. Once they were deep inside the wood Kevin saw the now familiar tunnel of white light. He entered the tunnel and carried Jane along until they arrived at the pyramid. Kevin watched as the coloured lights flashed and the doorway hummed and he saw himself step through the portal into the landscape he now knew well. He watched as he carried Jane to the same building in which he was now currently located. He entered the domed building still holding his wife in his arms.

They entered the building but it was not clear exactly where he had taken Jane or which route he had followed. The next thing that Kevin viewed was a transparent horizontal table. It was something like a surgical table in a hospital theatre. The table itself had a glass like quality. There was no obvious means of support. The table seemed to be hovering or floating. It seemed surprisingly stable as it had no supporting legs to hold it up. Kevin could see Jane lying on her back upon the table. She was still wearing her white nightdress. He was standing next to the table.

The scene in front of Kevin continued as if a camera was sweeping round a view of the room. This was a very big room indeed. There were many of the transparent floating tables in view. Kevin estimated he could see about fifty of them. No-one was present except himself and Jane. The room was full of instruments. They had a medical or surgical look about them. Some complex devices descended from the ceiling and some were suspended near the tables but there was no electrical wiring or supporting cabling in sight.

As Kevin watched, the table with Jane's prostrate torso rotated and tipped over but she did not fall off or change position. There did not seem to be any gravitational pull to cause her to fall towards the ground. The side and back of Jane's neck was now exposed to him. He could see that he held an implement in his hand. It was a tool which resembled a toy laser beam. This object was much more powerful than a toy. A red beam shot out of the end of the device onto Jane's neck and began to make a small puncture through the skin and into the deeper tissue below.

This seemed to partially wake Jane from her unaware state. Perhaps the pain of the probing beam had stimulated her enough to start waking up. Kevin observed his own face. He could see that he was shocked. He had not been expecting any response from Jane. Kevin felt he had not intended to hurt or scare his wife.

Kevin watched himself and he could see Jane mouthing his name. She was calling for him. He saw himself reply to Jane. He was not sure if it was an audible reply or a thought response but he knew he had communicated with Jane. He could see the concerned look on his own face. He wanted to keep Jane calm and reassure her. Kevin watched as he saw himself tell Jane to remain quiet. She was clearly disoriented and he had told her not to disturb their neighbours as a way of distracting her from what was happening. He watched as he helped Jane to relax and go back to sleep. However, before he took any further action, Jane 'spoke'. Jane told Kevin to stop doing whatever it was that he was up to. She did not like it and had no idea why he was tampering with her body.

Kevin watched as he tried to distract Jane's thoughts away

from her neck and the place they were in. He was telling her about her interests and knowledge of child development and about how their own future baby would benefit from what he was doing. Of course at that time Jane was not pregnant and even in a semi-comatose state she was not worrying about a developing foetus or an unborn child. She continued to resist going back to sleep and appeared to be in some pain in her neck region. At that point Jane managed to partially turn her head towards Kevin and mouthed the words "I love you." Jane could no longer resist the effects of the drug she had consumed and she relapsed into a deep sleep.

Kevin watched himself restart the surgical procedure on Jane's neck. He did not see any remorse or pity on his own face. It seemed he had a task to do and he had carried on with it relentlessly and without remorse. Kevin did not like what he saw himself doing. He now felt so sorry for his wife. She loved him so much. Even while in a state of trauma, she had told him she loved him. He would never find a partner like his Jane again in this or any other lifetime.

The scene within the room continued. Jane lay in front of him and once again he saw himself using the laserlike probe. The red pencil-thin beam cut into her tissue. Kevin watched as he then picked up a thin pyramid shaped wirelike device. This was pushed deep into the puncture that had just been made. Kevin noted that when it was fully inserted there was a small red glow from the 'wire' which stopped after a moment. The 'wire' was then withdrawn. Kevin knew what was being done. He was watching himself insert a tiny metallic implant into Jane's neck. He remembered that later this was removed by hospital surgery and retrieved from the region of her cervical neck vertebrae and discs. Kevin still did not know the purpose of the implant but he now did realise that it was himself that had put it into his wife's body.

Kevin's thoughts were momentarily distracted from the

scene in front of him. He began to think about the implant removed from his mum's neck when she had thyroid surgery. Had he inserted the implant into her neck? Surely this was impossible? His childhood memory did not have had any recollection of such a thing. Someone else must have been responsible. Maybe it was his illusive father that Sylvie would never talk to Kevin about. Perhaps it was the 'dad' creature. Kevin was now not sure if such an entity did or did not actually exist. If he did exist, was he the same father that had been married to his mum? He had seen Sylvie in a vat of syrup. What would become of her? What would become of Jane? What would become of his yet-to-be-born baby? What would become of him? There were so many questions still needing answers.

The device utilising a red beam was replaced by another similar looking tool. He watched himself guide a yellow beam onto Jane's neck where the surgery had been done. It was some kind of cauterisation procedure. Perhaps it reduced inflammation, prevented pathogen invasion into the wound and aided healing.

When this was completed the table turned back to its original position. Jane was now lying flat on the table's surface with her face orientated upwards. Kevin observed himself pick up Jane and he carried her away from the table and across the room. The view then jumped ahead in time. He saw himself leaving the pyramidal portal and carrying Jane through the dimly illuminated tunnel in the woodland. When he emerged from the end of the open aperture at the entrance to this tunnel into the woodland, the tunnel disappeared. It was nowhere to be seen. Kevin carried his wife past the pond now on his right hand side. It was still dark. Their car was parked in the same place as he had left it. He put Jane back in the passenger seat and drove home.

When they got back he observed himself carry Jane up the

stairs and lay her down on the matrimonial bed. She was still deeply asleep. Kevin noticed that the wall clock indicated an hour difference from the time that he had first seen himself leave the house with Jane in his arms. There was an hour of missing time. Jane slept on until the morning and had no recall of what had happened to her. She passed the next day perfectly normally and enjoyed the curry at the restaurant in the evening. Although her neck was sore from Kevin's 'love-bite' it was not until later in her life that she would require surgery relating to neck problems.

The 'viewing' now came to an end. Kevin realised that both he and Jane's minds had been manipulated. He had been given 'screen memories' which masked the real original bedroom experiences. Perhaps at that time he was not meant to know the truth of what had really transpired. He was sure that the events he had just been watching represented what had really happened. Removal of conscious memory had affected both him and Jane. This had enabled Jane and himself to continue with their daily lives untroubled by strange dreams. The pregnant Jane of later years who followed the hooting 'owl' had succumbed to screen memories and memory loss aimed at distracting her from her surroundings.

Kevin had to get himself out of the tiny space in which he was confined. He was once again enclosed by white walls in a spherical space which gave him very little room to move. He had to find a way of continuing his search for Jane. She was still missing. The white wall to his left side faded away leaving just enough room for him to exit. He proceeded back along the corridor and reached the location of the Y-junction. He turned and followed the left hand pathway that Jane must have taken earlier.

Kevin moved along the corridor. He could see some distance ahead to an opening into what appeared to be a large room. As he moved towards it he came across another small entrance to his right. It led to a small spherical room that looked identical to the one he had just left where he had been shown viewings of forgotten events in his life. He paused at the point of entry. Should he continue ahead in search of Jane or should he enter the tiny room? Maybe if he entered the small space it would reveal where she was? Curiosity clouded his judgement and he entered the claustrophobic space. Again the walls and ceiling had a white colour and he felt once more like a goldfish in a very small round bowl. There was barely any space to manoeuvre his body and in moments the entrance he had passed through was gone.

For a short while nothing happened and Kevin felt he may have made an error in judgement by entering this enclosed space. He was trapped. However, after perhaps three or four minutes, the white walls and ceiling once again changed colour to a very bright yellow. He knew something was going to be revealed to him but he hoped it would not be a repeat of the scene where he crashed his bike followed by what had happened in the bedroom. The walls and ceiling faded from view but what he observed over the next ten minutes or so were totally unexpected.

He could see an Earthly place. It did not look like the world he had left behind in the woodland. There were many people in the view and primitive looking buildings. Kevin could also see people holding clay tablets on which there was writing which he could not understand. The buildings formed part of a very old city in the geographical region of Iraq but the place was not known by this name. It was Mesopotamia. He was observing an ancient long gone civilization. He was seeing a snapshot of Sumeria some 6000 years BC. Walking among the people were individuals who looked different to the others. They were very tall and had elongated skulls. Their origin was from an unkown world. These people were worshipped as gods. These unusual individuals were assisted by smaller beings who resembled the creature he had called dad. They had blue-grey skin, bald heads and large slanted black eyes were undertaking some kind of genetic experiment on the people.

The view before Kevin now shifted. It seemed that he was viewing the Earth which had changed in space and time. He could see the extraordinary pyramids of ancient Peru and Egypt. The scene then focussed on a huge Egyptian pyramid. Kevin knew it was the Great Pyramid of Giza around 2500 BC. The local populace had received some kind of external help in its construction.

Now he was viewing another place and time. The people in the scene were being helped in astronomical observations and complex calendar production by 'outsiders'. It was the Mayan civilization in about 500 AD. The people were making hieroglyphic records and producing artefacts to record what they were experiencing. Some of these artefacts had survived at the site of Calakmul in Mexico.

All at once the viewing ceased. Kevin was once again encased within the white walled spherical room. An opening appeared in the wall behind him and he backed out into the corridor. A mental explanation of what he had seen gradually came into Kevin's mind. People from the future had created the building he was currently inside. They clearly had knowledge of Earth's ancient history and had travelled back to the past. They were 'sliders' who were able to manipulate space and time. In doing so they had influenced mankind. They had helped impart scientific and astronomical knowledge and had aided civilizations to make complex buildings and develop highly organised social societies. Much more than this, they had an ongoing historical role in moulding human development and technological advancement. This had been done by genetic manipulation and DNA engineering techniques. As far as Kevin personally was concerned, they had also shown him a view of his own past life with Jane and his involvement in things he had done that until recently he could not recall. However, Kevin still felt that there was still much more to be revealed.

The people in this current time and place had travelled back in time and influenced his and Jane's lives. This seemed to be the explanation which fitted everything he knew. His mum was also present in this future place. Had his mum's life been manipulated too? Did his mum's husband, his dad, have a part to play in what was going on? Jane was here with him somewhere in the building and she was about to have his child. What was going to happen to his wife and child and what role did he have to play? Why were they here in the future at all? Kevin had some answers but there were plenty more questions to be resolved. In due course, all would be revealed.

Kevin once more went in search of his wife. He passed along the long corridor and entered the big room in front of him. He had seen this room before. It was the place he thought of as similar to a hospital surgical facility. Numerous floating horizontal tables lay before him unsupported by any visible base or legs. He had once inserted an implant into Jane's neck in this place. Jane had been twenty five at the time. Now she lay before him once again. This time she was moments away from giving birth. Jane was now thirty six.

CHAPTER 10

A Novel Parturition

Jane lay horizontally on her back, facing upwards. She was on one of the numerous transparent tables that packed the room she was in. She was completely naked and her bulbous abdomen was her prominent feature. Kevin observed his wife who was unaware that he was present despite her eyes being open. Jane at this point did not observe her surroundings at all but she was not unconscious. In her mind's eye she was observing the 'owl'. It was so beautiful. She had caught up with it and now it hovered just in front of her face. It had a short curved beak and long brown feathers tipped with white. She was captivated by its eyes. They were so dark and fascinating. They mesmerised her. She felt she could peer into the dark pool behind the ocular extremities into a world beyond, a world where the 'owl' kept its soul. Its hooting sounds made her feel calm and tranquil. Her very existence was wondrous because the 'owl' was protecting her. Jane remained prone and motionless.

A spiral device above Jane emitted a green light. It looked like it could have been made by a 'mad artist' with an extremely imaginative design for a spotlight. Her whole body was scanned and bathed by the light. Kevin knew that all was well. There were no complications. A vaginal delivery could proceed. The illumination disappeared. Kevin was confident that he had more than sufficient knowledge and skills to monitor and support the birth. Jane's own midwifery background training was primitive compared to what he now knew. His wife would have been impressed if she had been given his knowledge.

Jane had been having regular uterine contractions every six minutes for some time. Each uterine contraction had been lasting around sixty seconds. In her present state, Jane was unaware of this and felt no pain. Jane's cervix increased in dilation from 6 cm to 10 cm. The labour process had been ongoing for some eight hours. The frequency of contractions increased to once every four minutes. The amniotic membranes had already ruptured.

The table on which Jane lay tilted from horizontal to about a thirty degree angle. The downward inclination of her lower abdomen would make it easier to help the baby remove itself from Jane's body.

The 'owl' vanished from Jane's sight. There were no further hooting sounds. 'Screen memories' had been masking Jane's reality keeping her distracted and calm but now they had been removed. Her awareness of the surroundings returned. "Kevin! Is that you?"

"Hello love" said Kevin.

"You look kind of strange, Kev. What is happening?"

"Take it easy" said Kevin, "you are about to have our baby." Contraction pains then stabbed at Jane's abdomen. She moaned in pain. "Everything is fine. You are having a natural childbirth" said Kevin.

Labour pain struck Jane once again. The pain was severe. She screamed in agony. "I am confused. I don't know where I am. I can't remember anything about the last day or two. I am in such pain."

"It will be over soon" said Kevin. He grasped Jane's legs with a firm grip and pushed them wide apart. Jane screamed once again.

Jane's cervix was now fully dilated. The increased pressure within the uterus initiated in Jane a desire to 'push'. The head of the baby had descended. Jane began panting in just the same way as she had trained other women to do in the past. She had no painkillers. Analgesia did not exist in this place. There would be no epidural or 'gas and air'. The head passed through the expanded neck of the uterus and through the pelvis. Jane screamed. Then she screamed again. She could see Kevin calmly observing the proceedings. He was strangely remote. He did not seem to be supporting her. He was neither comforting her nor encouraging her. He even looked rather strange in his general physical appearance but Jane did not have the concentration to focus on this. She did, however, wonder what kind of 'hospital' she was in. Where were the staff? Why was Kevin alone with her? The instruments she could see above and beside her looked strange and unfamiliar. She was beginning to feel a little fear. However, there was little time available to panic, the pangs of childbirth were all-consuming.

The head of her baby was now at the vaginal orifice. Kevin viewed this 'crowning' stage with delight but made no effort to communicate with his wife. Jane panted frequently and pushed hard. The baby was expelled from her body. Jane gave a final scream.

Kevin held his new born daughter. It was not long before the infant took her first breaths. Kevin had a small clip like implement and after a short delay of a minute or two he used this to clamp the umbilical cord. He then used a pencil like device which emitted a narrow thermal beam to cut through the umbilical cord. This action was painless. Within ten minutes the afterbirth separated from the uterine wall and was expelled.

Kevin cradled the new born child in his arms and smiled. He placed her in his outstretched arms and raised them vertically with the baby over his head. He inclined his head backwards, rolled his eyes and his larynx emitted a high pitch noise. "Raaaaaaaargh!"

Jane looked on helplessly. What had happened to Kevin? He was almost dehumanised in his behaviour. "Stop it! Give me my baby. Please stop it" yelled Jane. Kevin moved away from Jane's table. She remained in the same inclined position as if she were glued to its surface. He placed his daughter on a small table behind Jane and out of her reach. She could hear the baby crying but could not see her. The infant was enveloped by blue light which radiated downwards from a circular overhead device. Membranous debris and blood from the infant was removed and after just thirty seconds of exposure the baby had been 'cleaned up' and the light was gone. "What are you doing? Bring my baby to me."

Kevin returned to Jane's side. "Congratulations Jane! We have a daughter. You performed very well."

"What do you mean performed? I don't understand what is happening. Where is our baby? What have you done with her?" asked Jane in a desperate voice.

"Amy is being prepared now. She is fine."

"Kevin! Have you lost your mind?" Jane was now screaming at her husband. She did not have much strength left after her physical efforts giving birth and her voice was hoarse. Jane implored her husband to bring her daughter. She wanted to hold her. She needed to see her face close up. Tears began to flow down Jane's cheeks.

"It is your turn now, Jane. You also need to be prepared. I will clean you up in a moment. I have something I need to do. It won't take long. I will be back in a few moments." Kevin picked up the placenta and took it to one of the free tables adjacent to Jane. He applied a suction like device to it. The device removed blood and other material and transferred it into a round container for storage. Kevin was delighted with the extracted sample. The sample contained stem cells. He knew that these non-specialised cells had the ability to develop into various tissues and could also guard against a range of potential diseases. The cells would be specially grown and the direction of their differentiation into specialised tissues guided by genetic manipulation. Their use had many potential benefits for children developing in this place including his daughter, Amy.

Kevin returned to Jane. She was still in contact with the sloping table. A shower like nozzle began to spew pink syrupy liquid over Jane's head. It covered her hair and then poured over her face and into her mouth and nostrils. Jane tried to resist but could not move her body off the sloping table. The syrup gushed down Jane's body and on reaching the floor was vented away through some drainage grids. Jane believed she would suffocate or drown in the thick matrix that enveloped her but was surprised that her breathing was able to continue. The slowly flowing molten gel cleared away the physical signs of childbirth on Jane's naked body and she became totally encased by the material which by now had covered her. Like a jelly setting, it became more viscous but was still liquid enough for Jane to make small bodily movements. She was no longer able to speak. At this point she was still able to hear Kevin.

"You have been prepared now Jane. Your stasis chamber is waiting for you. You have been an excellent baby vessel. I congratulate you on the quality of your eggs. I would like you to know that when I told you that I loved you, it was genuine. I still do love you and I hold you in great esteem. Our daughter has a very important part to play in this world and she will be well cared for."

Jane's clarity of thought now diminished. She had understood what Kevin had told her but the shock and implications of his words did not seem profound. The absence of her offspring was known to Jane but she no longer felt the normal maternal bond. Her daughter had been taken away but this was merely a fact. It was not a cause for concern, especially as her daughter was going to fulfil some useful function. She herself still had a further useful contribution to make to something which she did not yet know about. It was not long ago that she had a husband whose name had been Kevin. He had loved her. This was wonderful. She had been so lucky. Not only this, but her body had made great eggs. What more could a woman ask for? Jane's mind became increasingly hazy and her thoughts obtuse. The pink syrup had done its job. She was ready for storage. Jane heard Kevin's voice for the final time. "Goodbye Jane" it said.

Kevin turned his attention to baby Amy. She lay on the table behind the one where Jane had given birth. She was crying and her tiny arms and legs were waving and kicking. Amy was hungry. Kevin would soon provide her with nutrition but first there was something he had to do. He had done this job before. This task was not always done on babies. Jane had the same procedure done to her when she was already mature. However, in this case, the availability of Amy was convenient and the insertion of an implant would go un-noticed by Amy and would not be remembered.

The table supporting Amy's tiny body rotated and tipped sideways. She was held in place by an unseen force with her neck exposed to her father. Kevin held a device he had used in the past on Jane. It really did not look like a surgical implement and a child would have gravitated to it for use as a toy instrument. This was no toy. A laser like thin beam shot out of its end. The beam was bright red and impinged itself on Amy's neck. She had already been crying with hunger but now the baby began to wail. The beam singed her skin with a stinging pain. A tiny puncture wound opened up and deepened into a cavity in the young tissues. Kevin by no means intended to intentionally hurt his child but he knew this job had to be done and there would be no lasting damage. The pain would not last very long and it would soon all be over. Kevin mouthed reassuring words to his baby to try and soothe her. These words did little in the way of having a calming effect. Speed was of the essence. Amy was clearly an unhappy newborn infant. Kevin continued with his task.

Kevin took away the pencil like laser and turned it off. It was now time for the wire like probe he had skilfully wielded in the past on his wife. Kevin inserted the probe through the puncture hole and lowered it deeply into the underlying cavity in the neck tissue. The wire glowed bright red and Kevin immediately removed the probe. He had successfully inserted a tiny pyramid shaped metallic implant in baby Amy's neck.

Kevin now held another pencil like tool that also looked as if it belonged in a child's toy box. He shone a yellow beam onto the region of the puncture wound and its immediate surroundings. He was now confident that the pain would quickly go and the wound would rapidly heal without the risk of any infection.

The table rotated back to its original horizontal position and then tilted so that Amy lay on her back at a thirty degrees downward incline. She now lay in a similar position to that in which her mother had been placed a short time before. Kevin attempted to communicate with the frightened and hungry baby. "You are a very brave child. I can already see fine qualities in you. You do not need to worry. I can make you even more perfect with the cells I have obtained from the placenta. The DNA will be manipulated and given to you for your benefit. You do not yet know what I am talking about but one day you will understand. I will ensure you have the best genes and you will survive and live a full and active life."

Kevin continued to address the crying baby. "It is time now to put you in stasis. You will grow and develop but we will meet again. There is much for both of us to look forward to." Amy still lay on the sloping table. The nozzle on the overhead structure resembling a shower head began to pour out the thick syrupy liquid. This time it had an orange colour, the same as Kevin had observed in the vats in the other room which contained babies and children. It did not take long before the small body was completely immersed. Amy carried on moving her arms and legs. Her respiratory movements continued untroubled. Kevin knew that his baby was safe. Her wastes would be absorbed into the fluid and she was enveloped in a sterile protective nutrient medium. She could develop and mature while confined in the liquefied jelly and her genetic make up could be altered to remove any flaws or unwanted traits.

The horizontal tables on which Jane and Amy lay began moving under Kevin's thought control. They passed out of the entrance way of the large room and into the external corridor. Jane and Amy were encased by thick gel. They were like whole pieces of fruit trapped within a semi-fluid jelly. Indeed, they had been subject to an advanced moulding mechanism which although it had entrapped them continued to maintain their life support. Amy still moved her arms and legs but her movements were slowed down by the viscous substance surrounding her body. Her mouth made crying movements but no sounds were audible. As for Jane, she also made occasional movements of her head, shoulders, arms, hips and legs. It was as if she was slightly uncomfortable in bed and was wriggling to change her body position. Jane's mind was vacant. Her eyes detected the illumination within the room and the optic nerves continued to send electrical messages to her brain's visual cortex. No images visualised by her. Similarly, her auditory nerve continued to function normally. The impulses passed from her inner ear to her brain but she registered only silence in her mind.

The two tables floated along slowly and made their way

242

towards one of the rooms that Kevin had previously visited. It was ironic that Jane was now within touching distance of her baby daughter. She could not see or hear her, nor hold her and put her to her breast. Jane would have loved cradling and talking to her offspring but now the possibility of any mother-baby bonding was non-existent. Kevin delayed following the moving tables carrying his family and purely observed their departure. There were no feelings of remorse, regret or pity. His mental outlook was now moulded into a totally new perspective of events and existence.

Kevin was very happy for several reasons. He had assisted the birthing process and had been able to follow up with procedures to encase his wife and child in nutrient protective mediums. Jane was undamaged and would be available for future as yet unknown purposes. His baby was a very valuable product. She would be of great value in this place at a later time. She would be stored for some time and then, like himself, would fulfil her future destiny. The stem cells he had collected from the placenta would be genetically engineered and inserted into Amy so her genetic makeup would be adaptive and give her great survival value. He was very proud that this had been accomplished. He was pleased he had managed to successfully extract viable cells.

Jane had been a great human subject for his work. Her own employment, training and personal attributes made her an excellent choice for his task. Her physical and mental traits were perfect. Kevin was pleased with himself because he knew that he had been selected and given the responsibility of carrying out the task he had performed and he had done this more than admirably well. There was a breeding programme which could go ahead due to his efforts. He had managed to insert the implant into Amy while she was still young. This would maximise control and monitoring.

Kevin had not quite lost his humanity. He was not evil,

rather he now saw things a different way. It was somewhat like religions. Two people might strongly believe in God but each followed their own religious practices convinced that their way was the correct one. Two animals might view the same object but one might see it in colour and the other in black and white. This reflected the way that Kevin now perceived everything around him and all the events that had occurred. He also now had great knowledge. He remembered that his knowledge had once been limited but new information had poured into his head as if by a massive database download. He did recall that he had felt his brain was going to burst and had not enjoyed the experience but finally he had been very grateful to gain such an increased understanding of complex universal laws and nature.

Kevin still recalled his love for Jane. She had made him very happy. She had supported and looked after him. They shared good and bad times together. She made him laugh. Kevin reflected on the nature of love. What was love? It was a feeling initiated by complex neurochemicals in the brain and electromagnetic processes. It was not a tangible object that could be touched. It was also a fleeting event. Love was ephemeral. The concept of 'love' had improved the quality of his past life and helped him to proceed with his recently completed task.

Kevin did not have a cynical viewpoint about love and his feelings and attitude towards Jane. He knew that in his younger days he would not have agreed with the way he saw life now. His current perceptions would have been anathema to him. The same applied to his apparent disloyalty and callousness to his wife. He did not feel disloyal or callous in any way. Jane had played a vital role in a very important event. In fact, he did retain some residual pride in her bravery and fortitude. He had not harmed Jane and she would, after a phase of 'deactivation', be ready to perform further important functions in the future. She would become a member of a group of both men and women who now remained in stasis in the storage vats he had seen earlier. Jane would be joining them shortly. Her past love for Kevin reinforced the quality of her storage. He would ensure that she was monitored and maintained in good condition.

Kevin had not forgotten his mum. She was already in stasis in a storage vat. Time travel via an interdimensional portal had allowed his mother to exist in a healthy younger adult form in this place. He was glad that she was alive and safely stored. Like Jane, she would be able to play a further role in this new time and location. His feelings towards his mother were much the same as for his wife. Sylvie had been a good mother and had protected, fed and educated him. She had loved him. Once again his current viewpoint on love had a totally different hue compared to his former life. The instinctive bonding between humans aided survival and his mother had been very effective in this respect. Kevin still had no knowledge of how or when the implant had been put into her neck. It had been done by someone else. Maybe it was his absent father that was responsible. Perhaps Sylvie had known all along what would happen later in her life or in his life and did not like to share her knowledge of future events with her son.

Amy would be the apple of his eye. In his old daily role he would have spoiled her rotten. His tiny baby daughter was gorgeous. She had been chosen for such a very important role along with a few other babies and children that existed in safety in the storage vats. Amy would be nurtured here and her physical and mental faculties would develop. At the appropriate time she would be transferred through the portal and spend much of her life with her dad. There would be no point telling Amy about her unusual background. She would not comprehend the situation and only stress and apprehension would come of it. It would be best to nurture her and allow her to live her life. The old style Kevin would love her as a dad until such times as it became necessary for her to perform her role as a fertile adult female.

By the time Kevin followed the route taken by the floating tables and entered the room with the vats, the stasis procedure had already been completed. He first proceeded to the vat which contained his baby daughter. Amy floated in the syrupy gel and drifted up and down. There were clearly strong currents passing through the orange matrix. Bubbles streamed upwards from the bottom of the container to the top.

Amy no longer seemed to be crying nor did she attempt to do so. Her mouth was slightly ajar and the syrupy 'goo' was visible inside the buccal cavity. Her eyes were half open and her gaze fixed. However, she was very active. Her arms and legs flailed around in all directions as she was wafted around in the fluidic currents and gas bubbles. Kevin could see her chest rise and fall as she made breathing movements despite her lungs and airways being filled with the orange medium. Kevin retained enough humanity to feel that he was a proud father. Amy was an excellent specimen as a female infant and he had helped generate her. She had well developed healthy physical features and she should also have potentially useful psychological traits programmed into her DNA. She might not need a lot of genetic modification. He preferred that genetic changes would not be made unless it was really necessary but on the other hand there should be no hesitation modifying here genes where they needed 'fixing'.

Kevin continued watching Amy for a long time. He was fascinated by her. He liked the way she moved around the vat and the patterns she made in the fluid. It was akin to watching a goldfish moving about in a bowl. He was transfixed by the view. Kevin knew he would have to move away in a while but this view was the fruition of his work. His main life task had been completed and he was in no hurry to move on. Round and round and up and down, Amy moved about as if she were part of a circus act like an acrobat doing flips. Every now and again she rotated fully in a 'head over heels' movement. Kevin smiled at the scene. His mind was rather vacant and he did not think about events past, present or future. He was enjoying the view. There were other babies and children in vats nearby similarly engaged with the orange fluid but Kevin only took brief glances at them as his visual field was centred on his own daughter.

After an inordinate amount of time had passed by, Kevin decided he would move across to the right hand wall with respect to the entrance to the room. This wall contained the vats of adult naked females. Kevin did not have blatant sexual desire but he retained a residual attraction towards the women. Many of them were what he would once have called 'pretty'. All of them were attractive. Their bodies seemed to be making sexual gyrations and thrusts. They were pushed about by the strong current flows within the chambers and their skeletal muscles made involuntary reflex contractions.

Kevin positioned himself directly in front of the tanks. He was interested to make eye to eye contact with the adult occupants. As on the previous occasion he had been here, although the women had their eyes fully open, they appeared to look right through Kevin. There were no signals from any of them to acknowledge that they were aware of his presence. Their eyes did not blink and stared vacantly ahead. Most of the figures were pushed tightly up against the facing container wall. Their arms and legs moved around in the pink fluid as if they were trying to swim. It even appeared that some of the inmates were waving at him but this was not the case, rather the movements were due to changes of fluid current flow and random muscle contractions.

Kevin paused to take a closer look at the occupants

compared to his viewing on the previous occasion when he had entered this room. The women all appeared to be at a stage of physical maturity at which they had the potential to breed or at least generate viable ova. They were so very varied in their racial origins. Some of the women had an African or Aboriginal appearance and possessed coarse hair and very dark ebony skin. Others had fine features with silky soft long hair and looked very much like stereotypical 'Scandanavian' blue eyed blondes. There were also redheads and brunettes. Several vats contained brown skinned sub-continental looking women with long black hair. There were also numerous oriental ladies with narrow eyes and small physique commonly seen in some Japanese and Filipina women.

All the women were attractive and appeared to be healthy and fit. Kevin noted that the stature of individuals varied regardless of their race. There were no outright obese people. All were relatively slim but some were very tall, slender and elegant looking while others were short and relatively stubby. They were not 'perfect' specimens by any means. He noticed that some of the women had breasts of unequal sizes. Some had lengthy extended nipples emanating from a large areola while others had inverted nipples. Some of the women had pubic hair growth while others were depilated. He was struck by the apparent quality and fresh supple appearance of the skin of all the women. No birth marks or blemishes could be seen. The nutrient medium was doing a good job. All these women could contribute to a repopulation programme and any imperfections could be altered by genetic manipulation. Kevin had observed these vats once before but now he was in search of Jane. He also wanted to check that his mum was still safely in stasis.

Kevin moved along the row of vats and soon found the objects of his search. He first located Sylvie. Kevin had got used to his mother's appearance as a mature lady in her mid-sixties. He had seen her moving along the woodland tunnel towards the portal which had transferred her to her destination within the domed building. Kevin observed his mother in her vat of pink fluid. She had undergone a time distortion so that she physically now had the appearance of a younger version of herself. She looked how Kevin remembered her from when she was in her thirties. Like all the rest of the enclosed people, Sylvie was naked. It was not common practice for a son to see his mother unclothed. However, Kevin's mindset no longer followed conventional social attitudes.

Kevin closely observed his mother. The fact that she was naked was neither here nor there. The key point was that she was in stasis and alive. This would enable her to either become sexually active again within the population or be a source of further reproductive egg cells. Sylvie was Kevin's mother but she was also a female reproductive resource. In his younger days Kevin had always accepted Sylvie as his mum. It was as simple as that. She was everything that a 'good mum' should be and she had nurtured her son magnificently. Now she was a potenital egg donor.

Like most children, Kevin had not thought of Sylvie as a 'sexual' woman. She was his mum. As a child he could not conceive of Sylvie having a romantic relationship with a man let alone having sexual intercourse with his father, whoever that might be. She was there to feed him and to take him to and from school. When he was upset he would go to his mum for reassurance. If he had a problem his mum would know what to do and his concerns would be gone in a flash.

Kevin's perception of Sylvie was now very different. He appreciated that his biological mother was a genetically-programmed female who had carried out her maternal instincts brilliantly and had done a great job of raising him. He was not exactly grateful as it was the way things were meant to be. Nevertheless, he felt that Sylvie had been a fortunate choice for his mother and now deserved her place in stasis so that she could further contribute to the gene pool.

Sylvie pushed up closely against the wall of the container. Kevin and his mum were separated only by inches. He engaged her open eyes but no recognition was forthcoming. It dawned on Kevin that his mum at this age was a good looking woman and sexually attractive, something he had never considered before. Indeed, such taboo thoughts had not remotely crossed his mind as a youngster. Kevin was pleased he had developed from her fertilised egg. There were numerous beautiful and attractive women in the adjacent storage vats but Kevin was happy that Sylvie was the source of his existence. He watched his mum's arms and legs gyrate for a few more moments before passing along the containers.

The blonde hair and blue eyes were still evident. He had found his Jane. She had been cleaned up. Now it was post-partum, her body could start to recover from its birthing efforts. Her abdomen showed a degree of swelling left over from the birth but this would soon reduce. There were no stretch marks and her skin appeared lubricated and clear. Jane had high cheek bones and her pretty face retained its attraction to Kevin.

Jane's body was pushed up hard against the vat wall. Her arms were outstretched vertically above her head. It was as if a lawless gunman had said 'hands up' and she had raised her arms in compliance. Kevin aligned his own arms along the container matching her position. An observer might have thought he was going to 'high five' her. Kevin pressed his face against the vat wall and his head was positioned face to face opposite Jane. The gap between them was so small. Kevin observed Jane's soft lips which he had once kissed so passionately. Their eyes met but eye contact was not maintained. Jane no longer knew who or what lay in front of her.

Kevin moved backwards so he could observe the complete torso. Jane had beautiful, pert, rounded breasts which he had once fondled with a mixture of awe and lust. He would never again mount his wife and make love to her. He had provided the male gametes to fertilise her and that is what counted the most. The pink fluid did not obscure her beauty.

Jane's muscles became more active and her arms flailed up and down in a sideways motion like a swimmer using their arms to speed up their rise to the surface from the bottom of a deep swimming pool. Jane's neck muscles tilted her head up and down and then rotated it left and right. Her eyeballs moved in their sockets fully exposing the whites of her eyes.

Kevin momentarily began to wonder if something was disturbing Jane. Had she become aware of his presence? Did she remember that she had not long given birth and her baby was missing? It was not possible, she was in stasis. Jane became more and more active and Kevin again wondered if his presence as a close observer had something to do with it. Her movements became increasingly exaggerated and almost frenetic. None of the other female 'inmates' was acting in such a kinetic manner.

Jane's eyes regained their normal position and her dilated pupils stared directly at Kevin's face. Her mouth opened and closed as if trying to speak. Her fists clenched and she appeared to strike the inside of the container's wall but her strength was far below that which could cause any damage. Her facial muscles became contorted as if she was in a rage and she suddenly twisted round so that Kevin was facing her bare back and buttocks. There followed a period of severe pelvic thrusts which were so intense that Kevin did consider the possibility that she might damage herself. This was very unusual.

Jane turned once more and faced front on to Kevin. Her body now relaxed and she floated gently in the fluid. It was like flotsam and jetsam caught in a marine rock pool drifting gently back and forth with the wave action. It almost appeared that her exertions had sent her off to sleep. Kevin had a feeling that she had been trying to communicate something to him but his logic told him that this was an illusion and could not have been the case.

It was time for Kevin to go. His immediate family were accounted for. He knew the whereabouts of his child, wife and mother. Now it was time to find his father. His mind was consumed by the thought that his father was nearby. At last he had the chance of meeting the dad he had never known. A compelling thought instructed him to leave the vats behind and leave the people to continue to thrive so that they could successfully achieve the condition their future activities depended on.

Kevin retraced his steps passing along the curved corridor of the domed building. He passed a number of rooms and side corridors and paused when he reached a small entrance way which looked a little different to the others. This entrance had a rectangular shape but was not very high. There was just enough room to squeeze his body through the opening but he would have to stoop slightly to gain entry. It seemed that this 'doorway' had been designed for individuals of a shorter height than the average human. Kevin momentarily hesitated, inhaled a deep breath and passed into the space behind the entrance.

Ahead of him, the floor rose. A flat elevated ramp led to a level above that in which Kevin had been moving since he had entered the domed building. Kevin passed up the ramp and found himself on a narrow ledge that followed the curvature of the building. Looking upwards he could see the top of the structure but various ledges criss-crossed above him between himself and the domed ceiling. Some of the ledges led to square, rectangular or round enclosed areas which he assumed were rooms designed for various unknown purposes. The complexity of structures above him reminded Kevin of a maze but the space around him was in three dimensions and vast.

Kevin continued moving along the ledge. To his left was the translucent curved wall of the building. To his right there was a drop down to the ground level. Only flat surfaces were visible below him which he assumed were the tops of rooms and corridors on the ground floor. There was no guard rail on the right hand side and the ledge was only wide enough for two people to pass by or walk side by side. However, it would be very easy to slip and fall over the side. Since the pull of gravity in the building, as in the outside environment, seemed lower than normal, his movements were somewhat slowed down and there would be more time to react should he slip.

The journey around the perimeter of the building took Kevin some distance before an area of interest appeared in the curved wall. A small section of the wall was not the usual whitish hue but rather a faint 'wishy-washy' yellow. Kevin approached this area and touched the wall but it seemed to have the same texture as the rest of the wall. He contemplated as to why this small area should have a different appearance but nothing came to mind. After a few minutes touching and examining the wall Kevin was making the decision to move on. He decided to try one last thing. He turned and positioned himself face on to the wall. Kevin then placed both of his hands on the curved yellow surface. The colouration immediately disappeared and the wall in front of him became completely transparent.

Kevin had a clear view of the outside environment. The landscape was flat and covered by the blue-green grass. This continued to the horizon and no buildings, animals or other plants were visible. Overhead the sky had its now familiar appearance and was very dark and cloudless. A faint reddish light gave a low intensity illumination to the scene. The light emanated from an orb in the heavens which Kevin confidently believed to be a vision of the future sun. This star could be viewed directly without dazzle or risk of blinding. The red colour was extremely pronounced and once again reminded Kevin of the colour of fresh blood. There were some starlike twinkles in the background darkness but they were few and far between. Kevin had never before taken the time to behold the view and fully take in the scene. He realised for the first time that in its own way this view was rather beautiful even though it was so different to the 'normal' sky at night.

Kevin surveyed the scene in all directions and he focussed his eyes directly ahead of him. He realised that the scene was not totally desolate or barren. In the distance he could just make out a triangular structure. He had not noticed it before because of the low level of illumination. This object had started to flash sequential light bursts. They followed red, green and blue alternating sequential light patterns. The increased illumination had drawn Kevin's attention to the pyramid. He knew that the time portal had become active. Kevin continued to observe the area patiently in the expectation of seeing 'something'.

Kevin was not to be disappointed. Within a few minutes he could see some objects heading towards him across the blue-green grass heading for the domed building. The distant pyramid's lights stopped flashing so Kevin assumed that whatever or whoever had passed through the portal were on their way but now it was 'closed'. A line of figures slowly approached. They moved in single file but the space between them was uneven. Some followed closely behind others while others straggled backwards with gaps of up to about five or six yards between them and the figure in front.

Kevin watched intently as the figures came nearer and nearer. As the distance reduced he could see that leading the group was an object which to all intents and purposes resembled an 'owl'. It floated along at head height in front of the column of what was now apparent as a row of people. The 'owl' moved to the wall of the building where it stopped and hovered in mid air. Kevin could only just make it out as it was partially obscured by the curvature of the remaining translucent wall. He could see it below him and to his right and he heard faint sounds like an owl hooting.

The sight and sounds of the 'owl' seemed to be triggering some kind of reflex 'following response'. The 'owl' waited until the queue of people caught up with each other and then it disappeared into the domed building with the people following behind.

Kevin took a quick count of the number of people he could see and he estimated that there were about fifty individuals. He estimated that about twenty were adult males who looked like they were aged in their early thirties and another twenty or so were females of about the same age. The remaining ten consisted of a mixture of boys and girls. They were quite young children. Kevin estimated their age to be about eight. They reminded him of some of his earliest and clearest childhood memories at home with his mum Sylvie when he was about the same age.

Kevin also noted from their attire that the people appeared to have varied ethnicities and cultural backgrounds. They were clearly of different racial groups and Kevin felt that they represented most of the variants of modern human beings referred to by scientists as *Homo sapiens*. The genetic make-ups of these individuals would provide a good variety of genes from within the human gene pool which were expressed in their very varied physical statures and features. Kevin knew that these people were heading for stasis in the vats. The syrupy medium awaited them.

Kevin had not noticed many spare or empty storage vats in the room he had visited where he had located his family and others. Presumably the 'owl' would oversee some kind of preparation process which would then be followed by the insertion of the naked people into vats containing the correct syrupy medium. They would then be stored safely until it was their turn to provide genetic material for manipulation. No doubt there were several if not many other rooms which contained storage vats in addition to the room which he had entered.

The last of the people disappeared from sight into the building. The outside scene was now devoid of movement and the pyramid was barely visible as no lights were flashing to give away its location. Kevin continued along the ledge following the curved wall which had its usual translucent appearance. Kevin began to wonder what was happening to the people who had just entered the building. He carried on moving for about fifteen minutes and by now he was wondering if the ledge would lead to anything of significance or maybe even come to a dead end. The ledge did eventually come to a termination point but led through an opening into a roofed-over expansion, rather like a small closet or under-stairs cupboard found in a house. Kevin did not wish to reverse the long journey he had already made so he moved gingerly into the little room and stepped through an opening on the other side.

As Kevin emerged from the little room he came into a very large facility. This huge room was rather like the one he had seen previously but was much bigger. 'Medical' instruments were in abundance and there were hundreds of 'floating' tables. However, Kevin could not see the full view in front of him. Facing him at head height was the 'owl'. It hovered and looked directly into his eyes. Kevin did not feel fear. He felt that the 'owl' was benevolent and would not harm him. On the contrary, Kevin felt as if he was consumed by love.

The 'owl' stared at Kevin. He began to feel there was a

paternal connection to this creature but it was a bird. It had large round eyes with black pupils, a curved beak and long claws. The bird hovered before him motionless with fully outstretched wings. The view did not make sense and seemed bizarre and unreal. He felt he was not viewing what really was before him. Perhaps his perception of the world had been altered. As these thoughts passed through Kevin's mind the 'owl' turned and moved into the room and Kevin followed on behind.

The 'owl' approached what looked like a solid doorway within the room. It was rectangular and the 'door frame' was bounded by silvery metallic looking material. The 'door' looked very thin and Kevin moved his head to look around the 'door' and he could see the long room extending behind it. However, he could not see anything through or beyond the 'door'. Filling the space between the metallic frames was solid-looking silvery material. It resembled the sliding doors that open into elevators at train stations, high buildings and shopping malls.

The 'owl' continued moving towards the silvery solid 'doorway' and Kevin felt that the 'owl' was not looking where it was going and might harm itself. It reached the 'door' and 'melted' into it and disappeared. There was no sound of any collision. Kevin assumed that the 'owl' had passed right through the solid looking material and out the other side but he could not see anything through this opaque material. Kevin decided he would try and follow. He moved directly towards the silvery material but made no physical contact whatsoever. He emerged on the other side.

It quickly became clear that the 'doorway' was a technological wonder. It was a transfiguration device. It caused a distortion of physical appearance and Kevin assumed it could be programmed to alter the physicality of the subject. The device was able to change the anatomical reality to an observer and enabled a sophisticated form of disguise imagery. A subject could take on a different reality to viewers It could change the appearance into other pre-programmed formats such as the floating and hooting 'owl'. This could be done for various reasons. It might give the viewer an agreeable view of the subject and have a calming influence. It could also induce false memories and such screen memories could minimise and suppress any real memories which might be stressful, traumatic or needed to be hidden.

Kevin realised that the new human arrivals were already under some kind of influence and control. They would be further processed by being passed through this 'doorway' device before being inserted into the storage vats. This would continue altering their brain's neural pathways and synaptic connections so that their psychological state and thoughts were appropriate for being maintained in the storage medium. Clearly their everyday memories and emotions were removed by this process but Kevin did not know if the effects were temporary or permanent. Baby Amy, Jane and Sylvie had gone through the mind programming process before their placement in storage. Kevin knew all this because of telepathic thoughts placed in his head.

Kevin remained still and looked ahead at the being directly in front and facing him. He no longer visualised an 'owl'. No sound was made but clear telepathic thoughts entered Kevin's head. "I am your father" the being said. The thoughts in Kevin's mind were loud and clear.

"Are you an EBE (extra-terrestrial biological entity)?" This was a momentous occasion for Kevin. Although he possessed a huge understanding of nature, technology and scientific theories and facts acquired by a 'download' into his mind, he did still not have all the information regarding his whereabouts, origins and purpose. Kevin's dad informed him that full revelation would soon be given to him.

Kevin's dad had a physical form that he had glimpsed before. His head was bulbous and bald. The eyes were slanted and dark. Small holes were present where there should have been external ears. The mouth was a narrow slit with thin almost non-existent lips. Tiny openings were present in a very small thin nose. The skin had a shimmery blue-grey colour which covered a slender frame little more than four feet high. The torso was enclosed by pale blue tight clothing which could have been a uniform. No visual indication of male reproductive organs was evident.

The futuristic version of humankind represented by Kevin's dad was an evolved form of mankind known as *Homo sapiens futuralis*.

Kevin's dad made a sweeping movement of his arm as if inviting Kevin to view the room over to his left side. Kevin could see all the newly arrived people standing shoulder to shoulder next to each other in a neat line. None of the people blinked. They were all upright and motionless and stared blankly ahead. All their clothes had been removed and were nowhere to be seen. The people showed no sign of awareness of their surroundings. Their naked bodies showed no visible signs of fear or discomfort and only the slight movements of their rib cages indicated that they were alive and breathing. All the men were lined up next to each other followed by all the women. Beyond these were the stationary, staring children.

Kevin noticed that one or two of the females looked as if they were pregnant. They were at a stage of pre-birth just as Jane had been when she arrived at the domed building. He assumed they would give birth and both they and their offspring would subsequently be placed into the vats. His father would carry out surgical procedures on the babies and the adults before storage to ensure they were all fitted with neck implants. There were more than enough floating tables in the room for neck implant procedures to accommodate the number of people present. Kevin wondered how many people in total were kept in stasis. Was it tens, hundreds or thousands? This was something he did not know. He was also unsure what the ultimate fate of these children and adults would be. Amy, Jane and Sylvie would, presumably, be a part of the same fate.

Kevin knew that he had surgically inserted an implant into both Jane and baby Amy. He looked at his father and he wondered if his dad had given Sylvie her neck implant which had been removed by hospital doctors when she had thyroid surgery. Had she known about her implant all along? Maybe she initially knew about it but the memory had been erased. Kevin believed that an implant was present in his own neck. When was it put there? Who had inserted it? He suspected it was done by his dad. He had some good guesses as to the functions of the implants but he would like a definitive explanation. Kevin's dad had already informed him that all would be revealed in due course. He needed to be patient a little longer.

Kevin now experienced a new feeling that although he had started his task in life, it was still incomplete. There were still important things left for him to do. A picture came into his mind but he was not sure if it had been placed in his head by his dad or if it was his own mind at work. He felt that he must go back in time and continue an old Earthly life. Amy was going to follow him back and he would have the responsibility of managing her upbringing in just the same way that Sylvie had overseen his. He still needed more clarity of thought and understanding in this and other areas of what was going on. He hoped his dad would help explain everything for him.

CHAPTER 11

Revelation

Kevin faced his father. He could communicate with his dad. It was not a conversation in the usual manner, rather it involved mutual thought transmissions. There was no requirement to vocalise sound waves. A focussed thought would generate its interpretation and meaning in his father's mind and vice versa. There was so much Kevin needed to know.

"Father! Who am I? What am I?"

Kevin's father replied. "You are Kevin Powell. You have always been Kevin Powell and you will remain Kevin Powell. You are my son. You knew your mother as Sylvie. She was my wife." This basic confirmation of facts was very reassuring. "You are human. Your biological age is now thirty six."

"I don't understand a lot of experiences I have had. I do not know what this place is" continued Kevin.

The forthcoming answer was not completely unexpected. "This is your home. It is the same place you left some time ago. It is many years into what you would understand as the future."

"It is confusing to me. It does not look like the home I remember but yet it is familiar to me. Why is this place so different? Why am I here? What is going to happen to the people you brought here? Do you know my mum is here and my wife and baby daughter?"

Kevin's dad responded to the questions. "There is much to explain. The information will be passed to you in sections so you will be able to grasp all the concepts of what you have observed and experienced."

Kevin's father continued. "This place is planet Earth. You are in exactly the same geographical area that you were familiar with as a child and later as an adult. The environment has changed many times over the aeons since the formation of the planet. In your terms, the Earth was formed some 6.5 billion years before your life as a child. The conditions for life were perfect in terms of its distance from the sun. Your scientists called this the Goldilocks zone. The plant and animal life which arose changed over and over again in adapting to new conditions of heat, cold, wet and dry and so on. Many species died out and became extinct. In this place I am ensuring that it does not happen here and now."

"Father! This place does not look anything like the world I grew up in."

Kevin's dad responded to the comment. "It is thousands of years into the future as you would perceive it. The sun that you knew has 'collapsed'. It began to emit huge solar flares. This lasted for centuries. Various charged solar particles battered the planet. The protective ancient ozone layer disappeared. Ultraviolet light also streamed down to the surface. Our scientists raced to find means of ensuring survival. However, most plants and animals became extinct. Humans were only able to save themselves using advanced technology and genetic engineering. Genetic manipulations resulted in anatomical changes in the survivors of the human population enabling the body to cope with the changing conditions. My anatomy, plus your physiology and biochemical metabolism are quite different to the people that lived on the bygone Earth." Kevin absorbed the information with acceptance and understanding.

Kevin's dad could see that his son was coping well with the explanation so he decided to continue. "In fact, this is your birthplace. Your mother Sylvie gave birth to you in this very room. As a young child, you were transferred back through spacetime to the world in which you grew up. This is part of my explanation to you which I will return to later if you so wish."

"I want to know everything" said Kevin using mental thought transference. "Please tell me more about this present world. You say it is my world."

His dad continued the explanation. "The sun is partially 'burnt-out'. It still emits enough light and heat for the limited survival of life. The blue-green plant material you have seen stretching across the landscape is genetically engineered and did not naturally evolve. Its genome contains a gene pool of combined ancient green grasses as you knew them and various primitive blue-green algae. The recombined genes gave rise to a hardy plant species. The wavelengths of light they are exposed to from the red sun are sufficient for the plant's photosynthesis. The cells store their own water and release carbon dioxide which chemically react together in a complex way using the low level light energy to make and store carbohydrate foods. There is nitrogen gas in the atmosphere which the plants 'fix' and build up proteins for growth and their very slow reproductive processes. No other plant matter lives here. The plants only release a limited amount of oxygen into the atmosphere. My lungs have adapted sufficiently to these reduced oxygen levels to enable my survival. The original human respiratory system can only function for a short time in this atmosphere but once a body is encased in a survival vat it can be stored safely indefinitely."

"I understand what you have told me so far" said Kevin. "However, there are many other physical differences in your bodily functioning and anatomy compared to what it was like on the past Earth."

"That is correct Kevin. My eyes are dark and adapted to the low light intensity of the illumination here. There is no requirement for eyelids as no protective responses are needed. There are no air currents here and there are no dust or other particles in the air to get into the eyes. Also, the eyes are sufficiently lubricated over the surface so as not to dry out and eyelid blinking to spread out moisture is not needed. I have referred to the lungs. The minimal nose and nasal orifices are quite sufficient for breathing. External ears no longer exist except as vestigial openings. There is nothing to hear, it is a silent world now. The brain has enlarged giving us increased intelligence, learning and memory functions. They also provide the means by which telepathic thought transfer can take place. The head has no need for hair as mechanical protection from objects is not needed."

"What about food? Why are your limbs like they are?" Kevin's father continued to patiently answer his son's questions.

"Food supply was a major problem for our scientists. There are no food animals or plant crops here. We learned how to synthesise our foods artificially. As time moved on, using genetic modification, we became able to internally make and regenerate nutrients from within our body. Waste chemicals were also recycled into useful compounds inside the body so there is no longer any requirement for excretory organs. Our mouths are barely functional for chewing or swallowing. On rare occasions we had to infuse depleting nutrients directly into our blood or by immersion in nutrient vats. Soluble foods would diffuse through the skin over the whole body surface."

"I want to know why your body is so slender. Another thing! You explained about the sun but why are there so few stars in the sky?"

"The gravity here is much lower now than it used to be

on the old Earth. You have noticed I am sure how easy it is to float along. Strong muscles and bulky skeletons have no uses here. It is easy to pick up objects without well developed muscles or skeletons. We still have an opposable thumb for gripping but one of our finger digits has disappeared and only four are now in use. As for the stars, we live in an expanding Universe. Since the Big Bang and generation of the cosmos, the stars have been flying away from each other and the furthest stars have escaped the pull of gravity from the centre of the Universe. The stars are receding and have become more distant. Now there are few left that are visible by eye."

"What about reproduction?" asked Kevin.

"That requires a long and intricate answer. It includes tasks that you have been involved in. It also involves the people you have seen stored in survival containers."

"Where are the other people like you?" asked Kevin.

For the first time Kevin's father was not immediately forthcoming with a reply. After a pause, he responded. "I think I should show you round this building now. I will return to your questions later."

Kevin followed his father past the numerous surgical tables to the very end of the long room. He entered a small exit route which had been partially obscured by some of the tables. Kevin's father beckoned to him to follow. They emerged onto a viewing platform. In front of them was an open area where the space was considerably more extensive than any of the rooms Kevin had seen so far. The scene resembled a warehouse. Packed in lines along the walls were vats containing people. Kevin observed vat after vat after vat. There were hundreds of them. No, that was a much too conservative estimate, there were thousands of them. If this arrangement continued along other as yet unseen areas above or maybe even in underground levels, the number of vats would be vast.

Inside each vat was either a man, woman or child enveloped by the now familiar viscous medium.

"Father! What is this all about? Who are all these people? Where have they come from? What are they doing here? What, if anything, do they have to do with me? I need to know my full purpose and my life story." Kevin's dad began a lengthy explanation which he hoped Kevin's mind would accept and understand.

"Kevin! This world is your world. You were born here. This is where you truly belong. Your childhood memories belong to an Earth which has long ago moved on and changed. You were taken through a time portal that you have seen as the pyramid like structure a short distance from this building. The machine causes a rift in space and time. It acts as an inter dimensional bridge connecting two realities. The machine warps the very fabric of spacetime. It is possible to move back and forth through time, from one era to another, via the portal. The ability to make time jumps and slips are a product of advanced technology enabled by the mental capacity of the people in Earth's future."

Kevin's dad continued. "You were not sent back in time alone. My wife Sylvie was an inhabitant of the Earth at the same time period as your childhood. She was taken into the future by me when she became pregnant. She gave birth here to a son and she was temporarily stored. The name of the baby was Kevin Powell. It was you. You were reared in one of the stasis vats in the same room in which you saw your mother currently stored. You were kept in stasis for some time. While you were here as a baby, it became necessary for me to make some genetic adjustments to you. You were subject to gene splicing and various selections of genetic engineering: gene deletions, insertions, translocations, inversions and duplications were performed. You are genetically enhanced, son. After a time I sent your mother back to live in the bygone

Earth and she took you with her. She was allowed to retain her memories of childbirth because she made an oath to never speak about her visit to the future and never to discuss me. Besides, no-one would have believed her if she said she had married, got pregnant, been taken to the future to give birth and after some years of storage returned to the past with her young son."

"I clearly had no choice in proceedings. I was just a baby. What about mum?" enquired Kevin.

"Sylvie had no free choice" continued Kevin's dad. "While she was here she had an implant placed in her neck by me. She was allowed a generous amount of free will but when it became necessary her mind was remotely controlled. The implant integrates with the neural synaptic network. Thought transfer from me generates new nervous connections by the stimulation and output of the implant. In this way, the recipient of the implant is subject to mind control. This is manifested in changed intentions, new emotions and thoughts, new activities and altered memory states. Advanced technology can induce false memories or protective screen memories, such as the 'owl' that you experienced. The effect of the implant device is a kind of nano-technology or micro-technology. Once it has been done there remains a level of control even should the device be removed, as with your mother and your wife. You have your own neck implant which is still present. Your one was put there by me. It was you that inserted an implant into your wife's neck using transmitted thought guidance on how to do it from me. You also have inserted one into my granddaughter Amy, your baby daughter. Implants have further uses. They can also be used to monitor DNA function in generating enzymes and proteins and assess how gene activity affects growth, anatomical and physiological development."

"This is beginning to become hard to accept yet I believe

you. Now I understand why mum would never talk about you. Even had she wanted to, you could have stopped her" said Kevin.

"I never had need to do any such thing" said his dad.

There were still so many loose ends that Kevin needed to tie together so he could make sense out of everything. "I suspected that I too had something in my neck" said Kevin.

His father continued to discuss the neck implant device. "Yes, it has been in your neck since you were a baby. I have been monitoring you but on the whole I have allowed you to choose your own life activities back on the old Earth. You had complete freedom of choice of your hobbies and interests, employment and choice of wife. There came a time when I had to begin to prepare you for a return to the future" said Kevin's dad.

"Yes!" said Kevin. "I know what you are referring to. I remember when vast amounts of information came pouring into my mind. I used to think of this as a mind download but I realise I was being educated. I received so much information above and beyond what I learned at school, college and in my job. I came to understand so many scientific and technological advances: spacetime, relativity, astronomy, advanced mathematics, fundamental atomic structure, historical anomalies dating back to antiquity and so much more."

Kevin's dad confirmed his son's ideas. "You are correct. The information that you received derived from me. Its source was my mind. I have a highly advanced mental capacity. I was able to impart a lot of my knowledge into your brain. You need to have this knowledge and understanding to survive in this place. Besides, you are going to assist me shortly. All will become clear in due course" said Kevin's dad.

"Father! There is still a lot I need to know. I have to know about the fate of my baby, my wife and mother, as well as myself. I still do not know what all the people in storage are here for. Where are the other people like you?" Kevin was desperate to get all the facts organised into an understandable picture. He did not want a half finished jigsaw puzzle of information in his mind. He wanted to have all the factual pieces and be able to fit them into an overall completed picture that he could fully understand. The puzzle was gradually getting solved but there were still many missing pieces.

"I did not wish to divulge all the information to you too quickly but you need to know how things are. Kevin, there are no other naturally evolved people here. I am the last survivor of natural evolution. I am the final and ultimate form of Earthly humanity. You see, this future Earth has an environment which is not conducive to the survival of life. There have been so many changes over the years. Let me list for you just some of the changes that have occurred in the planet's environment. They include the loss of the ozone layer, a change in the intensity of sunlight, penetration of microwaves and cosmic particles from outer space, oxygen depletion, temperature change, loss of freshwater, reduction of gravitational pull, lunar catastrophe, radioactive bombardment and magnetic pole reversal. Habitat destruction, pollution, overhunting and overfishing killed off wild creatures and plants that managed to adapt to these changes. Climate change wiped out any survivors."

"This is a disastrous history of the Earth, father" said Kevin. "I do not understand why everyone died except for you."

Kevin's dad continued with his explanation. The answer surprised Kevin. "Stasis technology was discovered too late. I was the first person to be stored. My mind was programmed with advanced technological knowledge and history of the world. I am responsible for all the individuals you have seen in storage. At one time there were others who would time-jump with me but eventually they became sick. They put me in stasis. When I awoke I was alone. My storage container opened after many years of containment. I was released from stasis into this world you see around us. No other people were here, I was alone. People existing here with me either died or escaped. Maybe they went back in time and never returned. This is something I do not know. However, on my release from stasis I continued my task of repopulating the world. I jumped back in time through the portal where I met and married your mother. You were born here. I have continued the task of repopulating this world alone. I have been able to jump back and forth in time to collect human specimens from many stages of Earth's history. The technological process enables me to maintain a constant biological age. Your daughter Amy will grow up on the old Earth looked after by you, son. She will return to become one of the new people to make this present Earth her home. She will bring her own baby with her."

Kevin responded to what he had learned. "This is a very difficult situation for me. I am not sure I approve of the destiny you have planned for my daughter. I would like to see the world repopulated with consenting and happy human beings. Many genetic manipulations have already been done so it is too late. However, I am uneasy about the forced removal of people from their lives and the changes made to them or their offspring."

Kevin's dad replied to his son's misgivings. "To me there is no ethical or moral right or wrong. It is a matter of choice. The fate of humanity is in the balance. The priority must be the continuation of the species. This is the logical outcome. It is the rational course to take. In any event, you will not be able to change the fate of your daughter. You will help me in the task which has befallen me. I maintain the control of your mind and body with your implant. You will nurture Amy and return with her when I decide. I do not act out of malice Kevin, you and Amy are very important."

Kevin pondered the remarks made by his father but his conscience led him to consider that what was happening might be wrong. He was very undecided. It seemed that his father had no qualms. He had no conscience or ethical concerns at all. He was very firm in his beliefs. He was not able to think in any other way.

"The issue is a complex one" said Kevin. "I am undecided as to whether intervention is the correct procedure. People are being removed from their lives and changed to serve another time in history. I am your pawn in this event. So too were my mother and my daughter. I am uncertain if the human withdrawals and modifications can be justified. Is there a 'greater good' to be achieved or not? Perhaps human beings do not have sufficient genetic potential to solve the problems of Earth's future."

Kevin's dad was confident in his reply. "The human species is quite flexible and mutating genes within the population allow variations to occur among people. Some individuals produced in the past were better able to adapt and survive than others in the changing environments that occurred over the years. At one time there were many other people alive similar to me. The planetary problem that developed was not only confined to people, it was about life on Earth in general. Our scientists were skilled in genetic therapies but the scale of the environmental changes eventually overwhelmed us. There were too many problems and difficult issues to solve even beyond our advanced technology. Our efforts to encourage adaptive genetic changes which would allow survival failed. The only plant survivor is the genetically engineered blue-green grass that abounds over the landscape outside this building. All animal life has become extinct. The responsibility of maintaining intelligent life in this world has fallen on me. I need you to help me fulfil my task. I wish to repopulate the world. The people who will be released will enjoy life and rebuild a future. They will be genetically different to me but this does not matter. They will be genetically altered for survival here."

"The people stored here in the vats are so mixed" said Kevin. "They did not ask to be brought into this time. Why were certain individuals chosen to come here but not others?"

Kevin's dad replied. "I am not going to argue an ethical or moral case. The fact is that this world, planet Earth, needs repopulating now or human life in any form will be gone forever. The people in the vats were chosen for their genetic make up. Their DNA was screened and deemed suitable for genetic engineering in our laboratories. They were brought here for the primary purpose of extracting their eggs and sperms. The DNA can be modified and fertilized eggs implanted into the womb. Adult females in their early thirties are a good age for foetal development to proceed through to term and successfully give birth. This process may be repeated over many generations until the babies become children genetically modified to survive outside. There are many individuals in stasis who are near the stage of release."

Kevin's dad was now in 'full flow' and was pouring out the information that Kevin had been desperate to know. "The adults in the storage vats come from countries all over the old Earth as it used to be. Having a wide range of racial types gives a good degree of genetic variation. The men are selected for their health and are living sperm banks. The women are baby breeders and egg donors. They will provide offspring to be genetically modified before release. There are thousands of people stored here. Kevin, they are not just people from your time back on Earth. People like me are sliders or time travellers. As I said, I am the last survivor. Previously sliders have gone back into the ancient historical times of Earth. We helped the people leave the stoneage behind them. We imparted

272

astronomic and scientific knowledge. We helped ancient peoples build temples and pyramids. Ancient cave paintings commemorated us and we are remembered on the hieroglyphs of the Sumerians, ancient Egyptians and Mayans. Biblical accounts and religious scripts recall our presence and even our flying craft. We were once called Jinns and our craft Vimanas. Old paintings of your old Earth era record strange flying craft and in your time there were ongoing reports of unidentified flying objects. We had the use of portal technology to slip from time zone to time zone and pass through interdimensional spacetime. Our craft could pass through enlarged portals and travel free from gravity at tremendous speeds, slipping in and out of different realities. Our vehicles were of many shapes at different times and travelled in outer space, the Earth's atmosphere and underwater. Now almost all of that technology is lost. What is left must be channelled through me. I have imparted as much as possible to you, Kevin. The new survivors being processed here will soon be released outside of this building into the environment and will begin their own new evolutionary path and eventually rediscover advanced technology."

"How did I come to be part of this overall historical situation?" asked Kevin.

"Kevin, you are my biological son. Sylvie was my true wife. I loved her but I had to get her to help me in my task. I told her the whole story. I trusted her with the truth. At first she thought I was joking. I persisted until she believed me. There came a time when I had to return to the future as I had tasks to fulfil. This meant I would have to leave your mother as a married woman without her partner. She promised me she would never reveal the truth. Nor would she discuss me, her husband, with others. There was never any requirement for me to influence her mind or her conversations. Your mother knew our offspring would help to save the future of planet Earth. Your offspring will be one of many who will breathe new intelligent life into our future sterile world."

After a short pause, Kevin's dad continued. "Your mother knew everything that was going to happen to her but she carried on a routine daily existence. Sylvie was a willing participant in everything that happened in her adult life. She realised that the survival of humans in the future was at stake. We married and had you as our offspring. Your mother chose to have a child and your mother loved you. I loved you too. Kevin, you are a hybrid human being, a cross between a future form of humankind which is me and an original Earth female of years gone by, your mother Sylvie. Sylvie remains here and is in perfect health, held in stasis at a fertile age. She may be required to make further egg donations. The future Earth is a sterile place. The people that lived here in the far future lost their emotions. They also lost their fertility and drive to reproduce. Their resistance and immunity to the environment reduced to the point where I have been left alone and am tasked with survival of mankind. I am alone Kevin, except for you and the people in the storage vats. Surely you see why you must assist me."

The enormity of the revelation dawned on Kevin but he was stoic in dealing with it. "What about my wife and my daughter?" asked Kevin.

"Your wife Jane is safely stored and in good health. She may also be chosen to donate more eggs in the future. Some of the stored adults as well as developed children will be released into the outside world if they have the genetic constitution for survival. As for your baby..." Kevin's dad hesitated.

"Tell me the truth" said Kevin.

His father continued. "She has an implant in her neck. You inserted it Kevin. I can control her thoughts and monitor her DNA and development. You will be returned to Earth at the same stage as when you lived there previously. You will return through the time portal and resume an everyday life. When your daughter Amy reaches childhood at age eight, she will also pass back in time through the portal and into your care. She will have undergone some genetic manipulations by that stage. You will care for Amy and nurture her into adulthood. She will in time marry and become pregnant. At that point she will be brought back here through the time portal and she will give birth. Her baby, your grandchild, my great grandchild, will be placed in stasis and genetically manipulated. If Amy's baby's characteristics are suitable, he or she may be released outside of this building as part of my programme to repopulate the planet. Your daughter may also be one of those set free."

"Father! What if I do not want that future for Amy and her baby?" asked Kevin.

"You will comply Kevin and so will Amy. Both of you already have neural implants and will not be able to resist mind control. You must play your part in repopulating the future world. Amy is a very important part of the process."

"My mother was very loyal to you" said Kevin. "She supported you in a great task. I am grateful to know I had parents who loved me. You have downloaded great knowledge into my mind father. There is far more information stored in my brain than I could have ever imagined on the old Earth. I know about wormholes, fundamental particles and spacetime. You have not widened my understanding of ethics, father. What is right remains right despite the noble aspirations of individuals. You have noble aspirations father and for that I commend you. However, I am inclined to think that perhaps the correct route would be to allow the Earth's future to take its natural course."

"This cannot be allowed to happen" said Kevin's dad. "Human life will disappear. There will be no intelligent life left on Earth."

"Perhaps that is the ultimate destiny of mankind" said Kevin. "Removing people from their lives and family to save the future world does not justify their removal from the bygone world in the past."

Kevin's father continued. "I stated before that a moral debate is not on my agenda. Mankind has always intervened to change events. The use of drugs and medications preserved the lives and reproductive gene flow of individuals that would otherwise have died. The use of machines like aircraft, sea-going vessels and spaceships moved humans to locations they could never otherwise have reached."

"It could be father that the benefit of having human existence in the galaxy is over. Perhaps it is time to say that humankind had a good run. Now it is over. My wife and daughter had their own destiny to be part of my family. Now they are part of your destiny. This is not right" said Kevin.

"You do not know the bigger picture" said his dad. "There is still much you do not comprehend. The history of the Earth could be changed unless we ensure it continues to have a future. You see, people from the future like me are not the only ones visiting the old Earth. People of my time developed time portals enabling us to travel between the Earth's ancient past and future. However, there are others who also have been visiting. The agendas of these visitors have been varied. Some had benevolent intentions, others had malevolent intentions though most were indifferent to humankind. Some species reached the Earth across interstellar space using wormhole leaps and sophisticated space engine drives to get round the problem of limitations of below light speed travel. Others used stargates to jump vast differences and teleportation technology. Still others used interdimensional portals to jump between parallel Universes."

Kevin's dad explained further. "The old Earth was subject to many agendas to alter the course of its history and future.

Individual humans were brought into the proximity of visitors who imparted their own influences. Some people believed they were in contact with strange beings who took them on wondrous travels and gave them profound philosophical messages. Other people thought they were being abducted. In certain cases, it was true. Humanity was being controlled by species with different agendas. Some visitors integrated into Earth society to exert their influence. A few people suspected a problem with groups of such controlling and powerful people. They were known as the Illuminati. Many species were glimpsed but their presence was debunked by governments seeking technological gains or advantages and by military conspiracies. There were so many visitors. Many appeared in ancient historical times. Others appeared or returned in later recorded history including greys, tall whites, Nordics, Reptilians and many more. Of course, among the 'visitors' were ourselves, humans from the future."

Kevin pondered the information he had received. He then responded. "It is clear that the history of planet Earth is complicated. The route of its history could have taken many turns for the better or worse. In the event it has moved to the here and now. This future Earth is nearly devoid of life. The visitors of the past have done whatever they have done but the Earth has become this desolate place. What exists now? There is an artificial lifeform of blue-green grass covering the landscape. You are a lone survivor of a race of humankind that has gone, father. The stasis vats are filled with people of all types taken away from their Earthly lives at different times in Earth's history. They are here to provide reproductive cells for you to generate hybrid babies that may begin a new life here. I can understand your good intent, father. I remain unconvinced that you are following a desirable goal. Maybe it was time for humankind to give way. You already have told me that there are other intelligent life forms in our galaxy, let alone the

Universe. My mother, according to you, had the same views and followed the same path as yourself by her own free will. As for me, I am unsure which pathway life here should follow. I am not sure that life should continue here at all. The people in the storage vats have left their own history behind them. You took them away from their lives. My own daughter is stored here in a vat. She did not ask to be stored here. I was a key player in her life by delivering her in this very building. My wife Jane did not ask me to deliver her child in the future Earth. You expect me to nurture my daughter's childhood and then remove her from everything she has known and bring her back here. This is a dilemma for me, father."

"There is no need for you to have concerns, Kevin. You must not distract your mind from the task at hand. You will comply with my wishes. Kevin, I am a mortal being. My life-span is limited. In due course I will be gone. There is no-one else here of my generation or my time to continue and complete the work I have started. I am going to send you back to the bygone Earth that you knew before. I will allow you to retain the memories of your mother Sylvie and your wife Jane. You will also know of your daughter's delivery in this future time and place and be aware of the implant and its functions that you placed in her neck. However, you will be unable to discuss the nature and whereabouts of your daughter's birth and origins. It will not be allowed for you to discuss such matters with Amy when she is grown. You will also be unable to impart any knowledge of your wife or your mother to Amy. I love you son but I cannot allow you to destroy all the progress that has been made with regard to ensuring a human presence on Earth in its far future."

"Father! I will resist your wishes. I accept your love and your understandable desire to seed the Earth with new humankind. However, I do not wish Amy to be part of the plan. From what you have told me about the nature of the surgical implants, neither Amy nor myself will be able to free ourselves from your mind control. It seems your agenda will be fulfilled and we will be forced to assist you. To that extent, I have told you my view."

Kevin then raised another issue. "Back on the old Earth I was under suspicion of killing my mother. The police were watching me. Sylvie disappeared in the local woods and I was seen in the locality. If I return to the same life, I may be imprisoned."

Kevin's dad replied. "I will return you to the same location but to a different time period on the old Earth. It will be a very similar time in terms of everyday technology and existence but just sufficiently ahead in the future such that it will be unrealistic for you to be questioned as a possible police suspect. The time of your return will be twenty years further ahead into the future on the bygone Earth compared to the last time you were seen in the locality. Your biological age will be thirty eight. You will collect Amy from the time portal. She will be eight years of age. Any genetic manipulations will have already been done to her and she will be in excellent health. She will, however, have no memory of an earlier childhood before the age of eight. This will be due to a fictional accident that she will believe happened to her on her eighth birthday. Her true memories will be obscured by 'screen memories' which will be very real to her but never actually happened. I will ensure that although she will remember a head trauma following a fictional fall in the street, she will be free of any concerns about this and have no pain or flashbacks."

Kevin addressed his father. "My child is in your care. I will not be present to see her early years of development. She will know me as her father at the age of eight but have no recollection of any earlier childhood life. She will become a 'better' genetic version of herself, designed according to your manipulations and blueprint. You have taken upon yourself great responsibilities. Jane would not have consented to this. I have not consented to this. Perhaps even my mother Sylvie who followed your plans so faithfully and loyally may not have agreed to your proposed outcome for your granddaughter."

Kevin's dad fixed his view directly on his son's visage. It was eye to eye contact, a face to face battle of wills. Kevin knew he would be unable to resist his father's wishes for long or continue to argue a different point of view or critical opinion. Kevin felt that in a fair battle of willpower, he could match his father or even overcome him. This was not a fair contest. Kevin could feel the implant in his neck vibrating. His desire to resist his father declined. It was in fact a surprising mental joust. Kevin had maintained his outlook and opinions much longer than his father had anticipated. He was proud of his son. Since the time of his sole survival Kevin's father had never questioned his task as the saviour of humankind. He bravely had shouldered the work alone and the survival of the species was dependent on him.

For a moment a flicker of conscience passed through Kevin's dad's enhanced brain. His mind was abundantly filled with facts and theories and knowledge and technology but the concept of right and wrong was buried deeply. This was an archaic emotional chemical imbalance of no relevance in the harsh reality of the future Earth. Kevin had not shared his everyday experiences in the future Earth. His son's views were moulded by a life in a different age with different values. He must not allow himself to be distracted from the work fate had prescribed for him.

"Kevin! You are done here. You will return to the Earth as you knew it before. Your life will continue in the style of those around you. You will retrieve Amy at the time she has been prepared to join you on the old Earth. Give her a good life until she is grown and pregnant, ready to come back here and donate her offspring to this world. You will obey me, son. Come!"

Kevin left the domed building behind him. Ahead of him, an 'owl' led him towards the pyramidal time portal. Kevin's thoughts and memories were not clear. His recalled experiences had been skewed to suit the agenda of his father. Some of his recollections were 'screen memories' masking his real experiences. He knew that he was leaving behind his daughter Amy and that his biological age was now thirty. He would not see his daughter for a further eight years. When he reached thirty eight he would seek her out and bring her home. She would be an eight year old and he would be a 'single' father. He would have to invent historical family stories to sort out her registration with a doctor, schooling and so on. However, he knew he could rely on his father to help provide him with certificates, documentation and ID which might be required in his life back on Earth with Amy. He would not be permitted to discuss his parents with Amy nor be able to talk with her about her mother, Jane. These would be 'no go' areas. Such conversations were forbidden. Kevin had no choice in such matters. Any wayward thoughts in his mind would be met by an immediate vibrating stimulus in his neck implant which triggered nervous impulses along inhibitory pathways in his brain, blocking such conscious thoughts from manifesting. Kevin's father was very efficient in his programming of implanted neural devices.

At the entry to the time portal, the 'owl' became stationary and turned, allowing Kevin space to pass by. Lights began to flash around the boundary of the gateway, red, green and blue. A humming sound resonated through the thin air. Kevin moved alongside and past the 'owl'. There was no communication. No thoughts entered Kevin's mind nor did he attempt to transmit any final message, not even a 'goodbye'. He did not turn to face the 'owl' but boldly passed into the portal and emerged into the woodland he had known so well back on the old Earth.

Kevin journeyed along the dimly illuminated tunnel and emerged between a clump of beech and oak trees. Under his feet the green grass was sodden with fallen rain. Ferns grew large in the shade of the taller trees. Their fronds were laden with spores ready for dispersal. Shrubs and bushes abounded. There was no sign of the old woodland pond.

As Kevin stepped out into the fresh air and breeze, his clarity of thought returned. This was not the same woodland he had known in his youth. He was in a different place. Where should he go? He followed a track that widened out into a much bigger path, clearly caused by the trampling of plants by the boots and shoes of walkers. It appeared to be early morning and the yellow sun was rising in the east. It was a beautiful sight to behold. Songbirds were in full flow and the dawn chorus was a wondrous symphony. Kevin was pleased to be back. He had not realised how much he had missed being here.

Kevin glanced at his wrist. A wrist watch was in place. It was showing 5-30 am. The air was warm already and wispy clouds were few and far between in the blue sky. It was a fine summer morning. A dog was barking in the distance. Kevin was now free of the trees and headed in the general direction of the barking dog. He crossed a cut down field of corn.

The open farmland surrounded him. The land he was traversing seemed to be arable. Various cash crops were in view. Fields of corn on the cob, potatoes and cabbages spread out before and around him. This was a good place. In the distance he could make out a thatched farmhouse with some outbuildings. A blue tractor was parked close by. As Kevin approached he could see that one of the buildings was a stable within which several horses were peering out over the half gates into a concrete court yard. An enclosed building contained low jumps. It seemed to be not just a farm but a riding school too.

Kevin slowly passed the buildings and down the courtyard to a small hutlike building. A sign over the entrance doorway said 'Farm Shop'. Various signs referred to the home made jams, wines and other goodies that could be obtained within. Sacks of potatoes were stacked onto rows of pallets. Free-range eggs were available and pure honey.

Just beyond the Farm Shop was the barking dog. When the dog saw Kevin approaching instead of growling and snarling as it might do to a stranger, the dog pricked its ears and started whimpering. Its tail wagged rapidly from side to side. Clearly, the dog not only recognised Kevin but knew him well. "Hello Bullet" said Kevin. Bullet stretched forwards to reach Kevin and received several pats on his head as a reward for his efforts. "Good boy" said Kevin. Bullet was a sizeable German Shepherd anchored to a wooden stake by a very long rope leash. "See you later" said Kevin.

Kevin continued on his way to a wooden gate which separated the property from a narrow country lane outside. On the gate was pinned a metallic plate saying Mitchell's Farm. The outside lane was not tarmac but rather a muddy track along the centre of which sprouted stunted grasses and weeds. This rural lane would not take regular or heavy traffic. It would only see an occasional tractor or haycart following its winding route. The daily delivery of post would have to arrive along this same track by van carrying the mail. The farm owner probably used a powerful Jeep or SUV to go to and from the farm but the lane would be treacherous in the winter. Kevin instinctively knew he had to turn right at the gate and he walked half a mile before seeing a person walking towards him.

The figure approached and was wearing clothes well-suited for working on the land. His feet were enclosed by heavy well used muddy boots. As he came near he waved his right arm in greeting and through a broad grin cheerily greeted Kevin. "How are you?" asked the farmer. "I hope you are enjoying your early morning walk, Kevin."

"Hello Mr Mitchell" said Kevin. "I am enjoying my stroll. I am well, thank you."

"Ooooh arr! Good to hear that. You know, there 'ave been some odd lights in the woods last night... frightened the 'orses, they did... mighty strange... some say there be ghosts in them trees at night."

"I doubt it" said Kevin.

"Well, there's been some strange goings on. Me old dear tells me she 'eard some humming sound last night but I was fast asleep. The old lady didn't have the heart to wake her old boy up. Ha ha!" Kevin observed Mr Mitchell. He was very friendly and good humoured. He had grey hair and a thick grey moustache. He must have been in his early seventies but seemed fit and active.

"I'm sure there's nothing to worry about" said Kevin.

"Must get on" said Mr Mitchell. "I was late getting my walk today and there are a lot of jobs to do. I have to feed and clear out the 'orses and get the shop open, not that I am expecting a big queue of customers."

"Take care" said Kevin. "Give my regards to your wife. We can chat longer next time." Mr Mitchell waved his hand in a gesture of departure and continued his way towards his farm. Kevin proceeded along the lane in the opposite direction.

Within five minutes the lane took a sharp left bend. On the outside of the bend was a small cottage with whitewashed walls and a thatched roof. Kevin found the door key in his pocket and inserted it into the lock. The old oak wooden door creaked open. Kevin was home. Kevin's father had inserted him into a secure if rather isolated old Earth domestic location. Kevin was aware that he did not have a job. He had no need to work. He was financially secure and had considerable investment bonds and savings. Perhaps he was not quite a 'playboy' but he was a free spirit. No tractor for him. A shiny white and red sports car was parked at the back of the cottage.

Kevin sat down in a large sofa and closed his eyes. He did not feel like watching television or hearing the news on the radio. He did not want to read any newspapers nor check his cell phone for messages, texts or emails. Even breakfast did not appeal to him. He just wanted to sleep. Kevin slipped into a deep sleep and after a while he went into rapid eye movement mode as he dreamed wild and crazy things. He thought he could see his mother floating in a vat of liquid. Then his mind jumped to an operating table. He had a wife. Why was his wife not with him? He loved his wife. What was he doing to his wife? He was placing something in her neck. His wife did not like this surgery. She wanted him to stop. The dream changed and his wife was pregnant. She was so happy. He was happy too. His wife had given him a beautiful daughter. Amy was his daughter. He had put something in Amy's neck. Poor Amy! His father had taken Amy away. She was in a vat of goo. Oh noooooo! Kevin screamed out loud. He awoke with a start, tears streaming down his cheeks.

Kevin's pulse raced. He would have to wait patiently to get to see his daughter again. His mind started to create a story for the local inhabitants and authorities to explain how he would come to have his eight year old daughter living with him. He was an unmarried batchelor. He had a girlfriend who had given birth to his child some years before. Unfortunately, this girl had recently been killed in a car accident. The girl had no family and he had been informed of the tragedy by a mutual friend. He did not want his daughter to be brought up by the local authority in a children's home so he had applied for guardianship and custody of his own daughter. He had demonstrated satisfactorily that he had the resources and time to look after her as a full time custodial parent. Custody of

285

Amy had been awarded to him. Yes, Kevin's story was coming together. By the time she was eight and Kevin's father released Amy into his care on the old Earth, the story would be refined and all the paperwork would be prepared and available, proving its veracity.

Kevin continued an everyday existence but he did not work or seek social company. He was very much a loner. He awaited the arrival of his daughter. His whole life would be changed by the event. Years passed until one dark night a light illuminated a long tunnel in the woodlands a few miles from Kevin's cottage. Kevin was there waiting in anticipation. Amy arrived in an entranced state. She accompanied her father along the tunnel, through the trees and across the fields of Mitchell's Farm. Kevin put his exhausted daughter straight to bed. The next morning Amy awoke as a beautiful and bright eight year old. She resembled her mum so much but had no memories of her mother. Her earlier childhood was a misty mixture of confused thoughts due to a bad fall when she hit her head. This had affected her memory but she remembered her 'screen memories' of growing up with her dad in his cottage. No-one would question her to check her dad's concocted story. "Morning Dad" she said.

CHAPTER 12

Disclosure

The handle on the door turned. The movement was so slow, it was almost imperceptible. Amy lay in her bed, sleep washing over her tired eyes. She just caught a glimpse of the rotation of the handle out of the corner of her eye. Who would be coming into her room at this time? It was just 5 am. A sliver of sunlight crept through the darkened room, filtering through the small gap between the heavy bedroom curtains. For sure, something had woken Amy from her slumbers. Did she really see the handle rotating and then turn back on itself to the closed position? She was not sure. Something had disturbed her sleep. Perhaps she had been dreaming but she could not clearly remember her dreams, they were quickly forgotten. No doubt she had imagined what she thought she had seen. She decided to forget about it and go back to sleep. It was warm and safe under the duvet. It was still too early in the morning to get up.

Amy decided that the best course of action in the circumstances was to roll over and snooze until being called downstairs for breakfast by her dad. This call would set in motion the daily routine of the bathroom chores, the toileting, the washing and the cleaning of teeth. Amy's dad loved to spoil her. He would help her to dress, brush her hair and make a hearty breakfast. She was only eight years old and an only child. She deserved a bit of spoiling.

The smell of a cooked breakfast hastened Amy's decision to remove herself from the bed. Amy made her way to the bathroom and carried out industriously all the hygiene activities her caring dad had taught her to do. These were now repeating automatic habits she would perform every morning that would benefit her for the rest of her life. Kevin wanted his daughter to grow up with all the best social habits which would lead to her becoming a good citizen and mother in later life. Amy's mum was absent. She knew absolutely nothing about her. Perhaps one day in the future she might develop a 'need to know more' desire but for the time being she was content with the love, support and attention of her dad. Today was a Saturday and life could follow a slow and lazy path.

Amy made her way downstairs still in her pyjamas. She hugged her dad and sat at the large oak dining room table. The wooden chairs were designed for larger bodily frames so Amy placed a cushion on the seat to raise herself to a suitable position to eat comfortably. "And how's my beautiful girl today?" asked Kevin. "Did you sleep well?"

Amy replied. "I am ok, Daddy. I did wake up early but I went back to sleep."

"Good! Enjoy your breakfast. I tell you what. The sun is out. After you've eaten, I'll take you over to the Mitchell Farm. Old Mr Mitchell will let you have a ride on one of his horses. What was the name of your favourite pony?"

"He's called Lad, Daddy. I love riding him. Thanks. I can't wait." Amy gulped down buttered toast with scrambled egg, bacon and tomatoes and quickly downed a cup of tea. The wares were quickly washed up, dried and put away and Amy was soon attired in her riding clothes and hard hat. She spent a very enjoyable couple of hours trekking around the farm and along the borders of the nearby woodland.

Amy spent a wonderful childhood with her dad. She lacked for nothing. Kevin did not work and he was content to drop off and pick up his daughter to and from school, by car. The nearest village school was almost three miles away and there was no local bus. It was often a source of amusement if not envy when Amy was dropped or picked up by her dad's shining sports car.

The 'village' itself was rather isolated. There was a small collection of local shops close together but even here the bus service only passed by and stopped on request once a day in each direction. Local transport was supplemented by pickups provided by the post van. The shops consisted of a grocery shop which doubled up as a post office and mini butcher. There was also a take-out fish and chips shop and a ladies hairdresser. There was a village community hall with a notice board outside with byelaws and messages from the local council. There were sufficient houses scattered around the rural vicinity to run a small village infant and junior school. The number of children had 'swollen' over the last few years following the completion of a small modern housing estate at the far end of the village.

There were numbers of strangers and visitors to the area which supported the local economy. These were mainly holiday anglers and their families who paid to stay in a nearby fishing complex where there was rather upmarket chalet and bungalow accommodation with free fishing for residents on any of three private lakes. These visitors were a saviour to the local pub as the Fox and Goose had previously been struggling to make ends meet. Their sumptuous evening dinner menu was a great attraction to visitors to the area. Other facilities such as the senior school, hospital, doctor and dentist lay a further mile past the village to the east.

Amy progressed well at school and was a popular child. Kevin allowed her to have friends over and sometimes allowed her to have 'sleep-overs' at the houses of her best friends. Kevin never mentioned his mum Sylvie or his wife Jane. Amy resisted any fleeting temptation to bring such matters up. Kevin busied himself with hobbies such as golf, fishing and writing short poems but his main interest in life was his daughter.

As Amy slowly progressed through her early childhood years, Kevin would tuck her into bed but instead of reading her classic children's bedtime stories he told her his own wild tales. He gave Amy vivid descriptions of strange places with amazing devices and technologies. He described strange landscapes with funny looking grass and cloudless dark starless skies where the sun hung low in the heavens with an odd blood red colour. Amy loved her dad's stories and couldn't get enough of them. She even went as far as saying that she wished she could visit such a wondrous place.

Kevin's description of the strange land was so vivid to Amy that she felt like her dad must have been a visitor. Some of his stories were crazy and made her laugh. She loved the story about the talking owl. This was one of her favourites. Her dad's imaginative bedtime tales would send her off to sleep happy and content. Sometimes she even dreamed that she was living in the strange land that her dad had described.

One night Kevin heard Amy talking in her sleep. He entered her bedroom to check that she was ok. Amy was sitting up in bed mumbling but still apparently in a state of semi-sleep. Kevin very softly asked his daughter if she was all right. Amy replied in a monotone voice which suggested she was not fully awake. She recounted how she had entered a dimly lit woodland tunnel and walked through it. She encountered what she thought was a gigantic triangular mirror. When flashing lights started to appear around the mirror and it started making strange sounds, she walked up to it to investigate and fell into it without hurting herself. She came out the other side and saw an owl. She followed the owl as far as an odd building where it stopped and spoke to her. It told her that it was her grandpa. When she told the owl not to be so silly it changed its appearance into a very odd looking man. Then she found herself back in her bed. Amy lay back and went into a deep slumber. Kevin pulled the bedcovers over her to stop her catching a chill and he left his daughter to catch up with her sleep.

The future was looking bright for Amy. The only thing missing was a mother figure. There was no feminine presence at home. It did strike Amy that it was slightly strange that her dad would never mention her mother. There was just not a single word ever spoken about her. Not a word! There was no point worrying about such things. Maybe there was something about talking of her mother that upset her dad. It was best to just leave that subject alone. Inevitably, the matter did sometimes cross Amy's mind especially as she aged and matured but the thoughts were rapidly dismissed.

The years passed by and Amy matured into a very attractive, energetic and personable teenager. Kevin looked at his daughter and thought how closely she resembled her mum. He sometimes thought that Amy had the right to know about her mother's life with him and how much she reminded him of his wife. Any desires to share his feelings and memories with his daughter were curbed immediately. Sometimes Kevin could feel tiny vibrations from the implant in his neck as it triggered into life neural pathways which would turn off his intentions of communicating information which might harm his father's repopulation programme and plans.

When Amy entered her late teenage years, Kevin began to feel the need to discuss the family history with his daughter with increasing frequency. His neck implant noticeably became active more often than ever. Kevin felt like a person picking up a phone call from a prankster or stalker. To begin with, calls were coming just once or twice a day. Now the calls were coming every hour, twenty four hours a day. Kevin hoped the implant might malfunction. He did not hold out much hope of this. Anyway, his father had told him that even if the implant was removed its latent effects would continue.

These thoughts reminded him about the neck problems that had occurred in his mum and his wife. Sylvie had experienced thyroid problems and needed surgery in her neck area during which her implant had been removed. Jane had problems with the vertebral discs in her neck and during the surgical procedures an implant was removed from her. Kevin wondered whether Amy might also at some point develop unpleasant signs and symptoms in her neck which might require surgery. Perhaps it was better for Amy if the implant in her neck was taken out sooner rather than later. He could feel the foreign body as a subcutaneous lump in his own neck. He wished it wasn't there.

Amy was now in her early twenties and employed as a nursery assistant in the village infant school. She had been strongly drawn towards working with young children. She was particularly interested in their social behaviours, interactions and development. One evening Amy returned home after work. She sat down on a large wooden sofa, put her head back and closed her eyes. It was time to take a short mental break, think about nothing and chill out following a day monitoring and playing with lots of noisy and naughty small children.

"Are you ok, Amy?" Kevin asked.

"I'm fine, Dad. I am a little tired. I had a busy day, today" she replied.

"Ok" said Kevin. "I just wanted to see if you felt all right." Kevin continued to question Amy. "I see you have got your head leaning back. You don't have any pain in your neck I hope."

Amy opened her eyes. It was nice of her dad to be concerned but his question was slightly odd. She looked at him with a puzzled expression. "I am just fine, Dad. Should I be expecting something to happen to my neck? Is there something I ought to know?" Amy smiled at her dad.

"No, of course not" said Kevin. "If you should get any pain or feel that something is not right, you must tell me straight away."

"Of course I will" said Amy.

"I love you" said Kevin.

"I love you too" said Amy. She closed her eyes and once again leaned her head back on the sofa exposing her neck to Kevin's view. Amy thought her dad was having 'one of those protective fatherly moments' and did not think any further about it. She went off to sleep and awoke an hour later just in time to eat the evening dinner that her dad had cooked for her.

Amy made an interesting life for herself. The local village and immediate surrounding areas were beautiful and peaceful but very socially isolated. Amy was very sociable and needed to have some fun in her life. She was also very independently minded. By the time she was in her late twenties by frugal budgeting she had built up a healthy pot of monetary savings from her regular employment payments. She supplemented her income by becoming an independent agent for a cosmetic company and had built a large clientele of lady customers in the surrounding towns eager to try new lipsticks, face creams, make ups and eye shadows. She had her own car and so could travel wherever she pleased whenever she wished and by sheer hard work had grown a substantial customer base within a 'patch' several miles around her home.

On one of her home visits to an elderly client, she was met at the front door by a young man about the same age as herself. He welcomed her inside and introduced himself as Jason. Amy felt an immediate attraction towards him. Jason had a warm smile and a very relaxed nature. He was well-spoken and had a great sense of humour. Following another home visit to Jason's mum, he asked Amy out on a date. Amy accepted and they had a fun filled evening together. It was not long before their dating appointments became more frequent and they became in regular contact with each other by phone, texts, emails and social media.

Eight months after their first meeting, Amy and Jason became engaged. Kevin was pleased. He approved of Jason who was very likeable and would make a fine son-in-law. Jason's mum was elderly and named Agnes. Her husband had passed away many years before and she lived in a small bungalow with Jason, her only child. Agnes liked Amy and thought of her as a 'good match' for her son. Jason did not have a typical nine-to-five job. Jason was a young naval officer and from time to time he would be called away to serve on his ship and fulfil his duties. Sometimes he would be away for a few weeks but at times of crises or when humane assistance was required somewhere in the world, he could be away for three months or more. Amy was not put off by the prospect of Jason 'going missing' from time to time, she had plenty of things to occupy her life.

Amy was approaching thirty when she married Jason. It was a great day enjoyed by all. It was a low key affair, however. Amy asked a few of her closest friends to join them as guests at the wedding ceremony held in a Registry Office several miles from her home. A small nearby hall was rented for the evening celebrations and buffet food and free drinks were available to guests.

Kevin invited a few local villagers to attend including Billy Mitchell. Mr and Mrs Mitchell owned the local farm and stables but were not in good health and so were unable to attend. Billy was their adult son and he was pleased to be invited to the ceremony and be present at the celebrations. He had been harbouring a few lustful desires of his own towards

Amy but being several years her junior he neither had the maturity nor the chat up skills to attract Amy. Nevertheless, he was pleased to see Amy looking so happy.

Kevin 'gave his daughter away' and wore a big smile all day long. He was very proud of her and felt that he was gaining Jason as a son rather than losing his daughter. Agnes also enjoyed the day. She was rather bent over and used a stick for support but joined in all the post wedding festivities and imbibed a surprising amount of lager. She was very vocal joining in songs provided by a local DJ and even 'hit' the dance floor when music was played with a good rhythm and beat. Agnes had invited several relatives and Jason asked some of his friends to attend. There was a pleasant atmosphere and at the end of the evening Amy hurriedly made a change of clothes and Jason whisked her away to a waiting taxi cab. They made a 'beeline' to the airport and flew away to the Maldives where they had a romantic week's honeymoon holiday in a five star hotel.

Amy and Jason had purchased a small two bedroom house on the still relatively new housing estate just at the far end of Amy's village. After the honeymoon was over they returned to their cosy little property. It was not too long before Jason's leave was over and he had to report back to his ship for duty. Amy was resigned to the fact that he might be away for some weeks. After a tearful goodbye on both their parts he was gone. Amy decided to spend the day with Kevin at her childhood home and made her way to the old cottage where she once lived.

Kevin was very pleased to have a day alone with his daughter to 'catch up' with news and chat. Amy also enjoyed having some special time on her own with her dad. Most of the day passed by. Pleasant memories were recalled and Amy's plans for the future were discussed. As the evening approached Amy asked her dad to sit down. "Listen Dad, I have something to tell you before I make my way home. It is good news. I am pregnant." Kevin was overjoyed.

"Do you want a boy or a girl?" asked Kevin.

"I really don't mind" said Amy. "I just hope the baby will be born healthy." Kevin hugged his daughter. Tears flowed down his cheeks.

"Why are you crying, Dad?" asked Amy. Kevin recalled the destiny of Amy and her child, as foretold to him by his dad in the future Earth. He remembered the storage vats and viscous fluid containing his mother, his wife and all the other people in stasis. Poor Amy did not know it but she herself had developed in one of these vats from the time of her birth until the age of eight. His coming grandchild had no future on the present Earth. He or she would inevitably be born in the future Earth and spend its childhood being given surgeries for genetic enhancements before being released into a barren future landscape as part of a repopulation experiment. The child would live its life according to the programming of the implant that would be surgically placed in the neck.

He would not be able to impart this depressing news to his daughter. The implant in Kevin's neck would see to that. Even if he could tell Amy the truth, she would not believe him. Even if she did, her own neck implant would overpower her freewill and she would do whatever was commanded of her.

Amy repeated her question." Why are you crying Dad?"

"Amy, you know I love you. I mean, do you *really* know how much I love you?" asked Kevin. "I love your unborn child already."

"Of course, Dad! You are so sweet. I know you would do anything for me. I think you are the best dad in the world."

"What if I were not the best dad in the world?" asked Kevin. "What if I were not the best dad in *this* world?"

Amy did not know what her dad was referring to. He

appeared to be both very happy and very sad at the same time. "What if all your plans for the future were to fall through? Say you knew that something bad lay ahead but you were powerless to do anything about it?"

Amy replied to her dad. "None of us can be sure what lies ahead of us in our lives. All we can do is our best. Love is the most important thing there is. It can overcome anything."

Kevin looked at his daughter. She was wise beyond her years. Yes, she was right. Love could overcome *anything*. "Amy! I have some things to tell you. It is hard for me to get the words out. I did not think I would be able to say anything at all. Love can overcome everything. I have something to tell you about your past… and your future."

Kevin felt the implant in his neck vibrating. Nerve impulses were jumping along the nerves from his neck into his head. He asked himself if he had the strength of willpower to overcome his dad's mind control. His emotional strength towards Amy would surely win over his dad's efforts. However, despite his determination to speak, he was unable to do so. His dad had won.

A moment later he felt as if someone had switched on a light in a darkened room. "Amy! You are going to have a son. I can feel it. He is going to grow up to be rich and famous and discover many new things of great importance to the world. He is going to love staring into the night sky and studying the stars and our beautiful yellow sun. You and Jason are going to be very proud of him. You are all going to live long and happy lives."

"That's awesome" said Amy. "You are a cool dad."

"That's not all" said Kevin. "Your mum's name was Jane. She was beautiful like you. I have a lot to tell you about her."

"Wow" said Amy. "This is one of the best moments of my life."

Kevin raised his eyes to the heavens. His mind transmitted a powerful thought. "Thanks, Dad!" Kevin's dad replied, planting some thoughts into Kevin's mind for the last time. "You were right son. I am fated to be the last of humankind. This is a great honour. All the people here in stasis will be restored to a life on the old Earth at appropriate historical times on completion of my final observations and research. Do not fear for Sylvie and Jane. They will relive full and wonderful lives. You are free. Your implant and that of your daughter are deactivated. I love you. Goodbye son."

Amy did not know why her dad was staring into the sky. He was crying and talking out loud. Nothing was visible except for an old owl which seemed to be circling round and round the roof of the house. "Goodbye, Dad! The future is now" said Kevin.

REVIEW OF UNEXPLAINED SIGHTINGS AND HISTORICAL EVENTS

Are We Alone?

What am I?

Where do I come from?

Who is out there?

Questions like the ones above have intrigued mankind since time immemorial. Irrefutable answers to these questions may never be found. From time to time evidence presents itself which is tantalisingly close to giving an insight into some of these mysteries. Even when evidence is found, it is open to different interpretations and criticism. Speculation as to the meaning or origin of a discovery or observation does not make the speculation factual. What one person believes to be an absolute truth may be nonsense to another. Facts may be skewed in a certain direction to suit a person's personal beliefs according to their age, culture, religious views, education, life-experience and so on. To a scientist, the sun may be a heavenly star emitting heat and light energy due to its core nuclear reactivity whereas to a tribesman in times long since gone by, it may be a God riding across the sky demanding religious worship.

Strange sights have been seen in the skies of the Earth dating back no doubt to times of pre-history. Some of these sights and encounters have been documented. In ancient times, they appear to have been recorded as hieroglyphics on temple and pyramid walls, perhaps even as cave wall paintings. Recently, anomalous photos, films, videos and cam recordings have captured many unexplained sights and sounds. People have tried to logically explain what has been observed while others have engaged in alternative explanations, debunking and misinformation.

Unexplained objects seen in the sky came to be called flying saucers or flying discs in the late 1940s. Later, the term UFO (Unidentified Flying Object) came into popular use by observers. The term UFO probably originated in 1951 following its use in an article by Edward J. Ruppelt of the United States Air Force (USAF). The study of such phenomena is now known as 'Ufology'. This term increased in popularity in the late 1950s. Ufologists investigate, document and analyse UFO reports. They also interview witnesses. Some consider Ufology to be a pseudo-science as it does not conform to all scientific parameters. Nevertheless, there are numerous 'serious' UFO groups and societies around the world.

Unexplained sightings have had characterisations ascribed to them. Various workers in the field of Ufology have produced ways of grouping anomalous objects into different categories. One of the most popular systems was developed in the 1970s by J Allen Hynek. This system groups observations into 'Close Encounters' (CE) which at the present time includes up to five types. CE of the first kind relate to observations of unfamiliar objects which do not appear to affect the environment. CE of the second type is where an object leaves some kind of physical evidence or trace. The typical kind of effect here would be damage to plants such as to leaves, stems, roots or flowers. The soil itself might show depressions, disturbance or other markings. Quite commonly, radiation or raised radioactive levels may be detected or measurements may indicate other electromagnetic anomalies. The third type of CE is where entities or occupants of a craft are reportedly seen. A CE of the fourth kind involves an observer who reports being forcibly abducted. Finally, a CE of the fifth kind is a situation in which humans initiate contact with EBE's (extra terrestrial biological entities) or alien intelligences.

Objects sighted in the skies come in all manner of shapes and sizes. Among these are glowing orbs, spirals, discs, cigar shapes, crescents, cubes, triangles and boomerangs. They have been reported to accelerate from a standstill to incredible velocity in just moments. They often fly at amazing speeds, make sharp turns, hover, change shape and colour, or appear and disappear. Observers sometimes refer to these UFOs as spaceships, flying saucers and flying discs. They are often suspected to come from other solar systems or galaxies. This supposes that faster than light speed travel is possible. The speed of light has been measured at 186,000 miles per second. Current theories based on work done by Albert Einstein and his equations relating to his Theory of Relativity suggest that it is impossible for an object to travel quicker than the speed of light. According to Special Relativity, it is the maximum speed at which matter in the Universe can travel. This includes massless particles including electromagnetic radiation such as light and gravitational waves in a vacuum. Even if it were possible to travel faster than light, it would take thousands of years to cross the galaxy or reach the nearest stars.

Interstellar and intergalactic visitors are not the only candidates for anomalous observations. Others include paranormal manifestations and religious events. Some explanations have putative scientific theories behind them which although speculative may in the future prove to be correct. One concept is that visitors can jump from a parallel Universe and are interdimensional. Indeed, there may be more than one parallel existence. In fact, numerous parallel Universes, or Multiverses as they are known, could exist. One version of this is a matter-antimatter Universe (which scientists believe would annihilate each other if they came into contact). A further plausible explanation for some or all of the anomalous observations of beings and crafts could be put down to time travellers. Temporal considerations are encompassed within the Theory of Relativity where time passes at differing rates as the speed of light is approached.

Various future technological advances may produce starship engines powered in novel ways which may be able to accelerate past the speed of light barrier. Proposed future engines include nuclear and fusion systems, antigravity technology, warp drives and theoretical 'Alcubierre' engine star drives. An Alcubierre star-engine is a speculative idea proposed by theoretical physics by which a spacecraft could achieve faster-than-light travel by contracting space in front of it and expanding space behind it. Exotic means of travel might also involve warping spacetime while passing through wormholes using Einstein-Rosen bridges. These are hypothetical shortcuts through spacetime rather like a tunnel with each end located at a different place in spacetime which might connect different Universes. There has also been speculation about craft and objects travelling through stargates, time portals and by teleportation. Some or several of these possibilities may account for the strange observations of anomalies experienced over the years.

The Universe

Life on Earth may be unique in the Universe. Space probes to other planets may in due course detect non-terrestrial life.

The definition of 'life' is perhaps suited to a specialist discourse on philosophy. There may be forms of life very different to the familiar carbon-based life forms on planet Earth. Scientists have speculated that silicon might form a chemical skeleton for life instead of carbon. Futuristic robotic and cybernetic advances may result in machines with the properties associated with life. Indeed, man and machine may one day become intertwined into one entity. The creation of life on Earth has been described by scientific theories and also by divine, religious and supernatural means. There are proposals that life on the Earth arose due to a process of 'panspermia'. The planet may have been 'seeded' with materials brought to it through space such as spores carried to Earth by comets.

In the vastness of the Universe it is hard to accept that life has only arisen on the Earth. The observations of strange beings and craft suggest that perhaps life does exist elsewhere in the Universe. A brief consideration is given next to exactly what the concept of a Universe includes.

The Universe represents a 'totality of existence'. It contains outer space with its planets, stars and galaxies. Also contained within the Universe are subatomic particles, matter and energy. The visible part is called the observable Universe.

One of the primary models for the formation of the Universe is called the Big Bang Theory. According to this, a very brief period of 'cosmic inflation' caused the Universe to reach a much larger size virtually instantaneously. In the early moments of creation there was an imbalance of matter over antimatter. The latter is a 'mirror image' of matter. Atomic neutrons, positively charged protons and negatively charged electrons have their counterparts in antimatter. These are anti-neutrons, negatively charged anti-protons and positively charged anti-electrons or positrons. As the Big Bang occurred, matter and antimatter mostly annihilated each other producing photons ('light particles') and other products including a huge release of energy. However, a small residue of matter survived which formed the observable Universe.

It is believed that the Universe is expanding at an increasing rate due to what has been dubbed 'dark energy'. (The Universe also is thought to contain unidentified material called 'dark matter'). The stars seem to be moving apart from each other at increasing speed despite the constraints of gravity. It is not known if the size of the Universe is finite or infinite. Only part of the Universe is visible due to limitations related to light speed as Einstein's theory suggests matter cannot travel faster than light. There may be an unknown non-observable Universe. The distance between Earth and the edge of the observable Universe is forty six billion light years. A light year is the distance that light travels in one year which is nearly six million, million miles. As mentioned, light travels at an incredible speed of 186,000 miles per second.

The solar system with its planets including the Earth orbiting the sun is located in a galaxy called the Milky Way. Galaxies or nebulae are enormous groups of stars and other material. Each one may have a 'black hole' at the centre which can absorb not only matter but also light. Galaxies occur in three main types: ellipticals, spirals and irregulars. The Milky Way is described as a 'disc shaped barred spiral galaxy'. The sun is just one of billions of stars in the Milky Way. The Milky Way is a galaxy about 100,000 light years in diameter. The nearest galaxy called Andromeda is located about 2.5 million light years away from the Milky Way. There may be more than one hundred billion galaxies in the observable Universe. Galaxies in deep space and their stars viewed with the Hubble space telescope are seen as they appeared thirteen billion years ago.

Cosmic microwave background radiation indicates that the Universe had a beginning and this supports the concept of the Big Bang theory. According to the Big Bang model, the age of the Universe has been estimated as 13.798 ± 0.037

billion years. However, a different view was given by Sir Fred Hoyle (24th June 1915–20th August 2001) who opposed the Big Bang theory. The Steady State theory suggests that the Universe has always existed and always will exist. However, this idea was put forward before the discovery of the cosmic microwave background radiation.

The fate of the Universe is unknown. One possibility is known as the Big Crunch. The Universe might contract and re-collapse. A black hole singularity might be formed. There could be a reformation of the Universe starting with another Big Bang. Perhaps there have been infinite numbers of repeating Big Bangs. Data suggests that the expansion speed of the Universe is not decreasing but increasing and it has been suggested that the Universe might eventually rip itself to shreds (the Big Rip).

The Nature of Reality

The subject of Ufology brings into question as to what is real or not. What is meant by 'reality'? A philosophical analysis is not attempted here but some considerations can be applied to the subject. The topic area in this book at its basic level relate to the observation of exotic entities and craft. Are such sightings real or imagined? There may be relevant psychological issues applicable to some observers. Genuine mistaken and misinterpreted observations may also have been made. Some of these, perhaps many of them, may be put down to hoaxes or fakes. However, these do not account for *all* unusual sound recordings and sightings seen on films, photos, videos and so on. Science and 'pseudo-science' may be used to look at these phenomena but these could relate to other areas. Explanations of unknown phenomena might also come from religion, divine acts, paranormal activities, occultism, temporal (time) slips and dimensional anomalies. All of these, some of them, or none at all may be responsible for documented cases. Strange observations have been reported by a huge mix of people from differing social groups in countries around the world. These include doctors, lawyers, pilots, police officers, military staff, politicians, farmers, teachers, tribes-people and children.

The notion that reality only occurs in our world with three spatial dimensions and one time dimension has been superseded by modern theoretical physics. String Theory (see the following section) predicts the reality of further dimensions. This has implications for at least some previously unexplained sightings and related events.

Physics and Theories

Albert Einstein (14th March 1879–18th April 1955) was a German-born theoretical physicist and philosopher. He fled Nazi Germany due to his Jewish origin as a refugee and became an American citizen in 1940. He is best known for his mass-energy equivalence formula $E = mc^2$ which incorporates the speed of light. Einstein's ideas which would lead to his famous equation were documented in 1905. The relationship between energy and mass was a new way of considering motion in the Universe and is referred to as Special Relativity. He developed the General Theory of Relativity alongside what is now called Quantum Mechanics. General Relativity provides a set of ten equations for measuring spacetime (Einstein's Field Equations) which can be used to account for or predict the past and future of the Universe. He received the Nobel Prize for Physics in 1921.

Einstein's theories predict that it is impossible for matter to move faster than the speed of light. This puts limitations on interstellar travel for mankind using conventional transport as it would take many lifetimes to reach the stars due to the vast distances involved. Many sceptics therefore cast scorn on sightings of UFOs or strange beings based on the fact that it would take too long for visitors to reach the Earth from such far away origins. There are some current ideas that might just make such visits possible using advanced technology which do not contradict the laws provided by Einstein's work. Time slows down as the speed of light is approached and there is speculation about possible time travel. The fabric of spacetime may be warped and jumps made through wormholes. There are also related ideas on stargates, portals, teleportation and exotic star drive engines which are discussed elsewhere in this book. So-called visitors might also have been present on Earth all the time or be interdimensional in nature. The familiar observable Universe has three spatial dimensions and the fourth temporal (time). However, this may be a flawed concept.

A complex model in Physics attempts to explain elementary particles, gravity, fundamental forces and forms of matter. This is known as String Theory. It is a version of a 'theory of everything'. String Theory was first proposed in the late 1960s. Theoretical detail is not attempted here but is just touched on. In String Theory, subatomic particles are replaced by one-dimensional objects called strings. An early version of the theory incorporated only the group of fundamental particles called bosons (see the section on Fundamental Particles). Later Superstring Theory included a connection with other elementary particles called fermions (see the section on Fundamental Particles). In the mid-1990s there was conjecture regarding eleven dimensional theory, now known as M-theory. Many theoretical physicists including Stephen Hawking support this idea: "M-theory is the only candidate for a complete theory of the Universe." However, some other prominent physicists have criticised the theory. An interesting aspect of String Theory is its prediction of extra dimensions. This opens up intriguing possibilities regarding explanations of unknown sightings of craft and entities.

A 'black hole' is a region of spacetime with a strong gravitational pull so powerful that no particle or electromagnetic radiation (including light) can escape from it. Approaching a black hole too closely would reach a point of no return. The boundary of the region from which escape would become impossible is called the 'event horizon'. Since the 1960s, theoretical considerations suggested black holes could be predicted by the ideas of General Relativity proposed by Albert Einstein. Black holes are thought to form when stars collapse at the end of their life cycle. They may absorb further stars or merge with other black holes. Supermassive black holes may exist at the centre of most galaxies including the core of the Milky Way. At the centre of a black hole General Relativity theory predicts a gravitational 'singularity'. The singular region is viewed by physicists as having 'infinite density'. Objects falling into a black hole would be carried to the singularity and be crushed to infinite density. The mass would be added to that of the black hole. The object would be torn apart in a process sometimes called 'spaghettification' or the 'noodle effect'.

There is a hypothetical possibility that certain types of black hole could act as a 'wormhole'. Entities might be enabled to pass through time to another Universe or across the Universe via wormholes. These represent a possible shortcut through spacetime. The term 'wormhole' was coined by an American physicist John Archibald Wheeler in 1957, though the German mathematician Hermann Weyl proposed the concept of wormhole theory in 1921. A wormhole resembles a tunnel with two ends. Each end is located at separate points of spacetime. Some wormholes could be crossed in both directions and have acquired the term 'traversable wormholes'.

Well known physicist Stephen Hawking has suggested that it might be possible to stabilize a traversable wormhole. While travelling through a wormhole, the speed of light would not be exceeded. This would comply with the concepts of Relativity implied from Einstein's work where faster-than-light speed is not possible.

Highly advanced beings with well developed technology might be able to utilise the concepts of the theory of General Relativity which does in fact predict that traversable wormholes might allow time travel. One end of the wormhole might be accelerated to a higher velocity relative to the other. Time would connect differently through the wormhole compared to outside it such that entities in their craft entering the accelerated wormhole mouth would exit the stationary one at an earlier point in time compared to its entry.

There are three basic properties of a black hole including mass, spin and charge. Once these three are known, the black hole can be specified as a particular type. A 'geometric property' of a black hole is that another group of dimensions exist attached to the one from the known Universe. This property exists in all black holes but is called an Einstein-Rosen Bridge for those black holes characterised as 'static' (Schwarzschild holes). Passage through this bridge and into another Universe is a mathematical possibility. It has been suggested that an object returning from the future would not return to its own Universe but to a parallel one.

Fundamental (Elementary) Particles

Matter is made from atoms. They are the smallest particles that cannot be divided by chemical reactions. An atom consists of a nucleus of neutrons and protons surrounded by orbiting electrons. Each type of atom corresponds to a specific chemical element and 118 elements have been discovered. Although atoms were once considered to be indivisible, in recent times they have been found to contain elementary or fundamental particles which have an unknown substructure. Protons and neutrons are made of quarks though electrons are considered to be fundamental particles. The knowledge of fundamental particles is rapidly expanding. A new area of scientific study has opened up to study and research these particles. This vast area of study is only considered here in outline.

The Large Hadron Collider (LHC) is located near Geneva in Switzerland. It was built by the European Organization for Nuclear Research (CERN) from 1998 to 2008. It allows scientists to reproduce the conditions that existed within a billionth of a second after the Big Bang. Different theories of particle physics like the 'Standard Model' can be investigated. The latter is the most successful theory of particle physics to date but does not fully account for experimental results and predictions relating to gravity, dark energy, dark matter, neutrino masses and matter-antimatter asymmetry. The LHC collides beams of high energy protons or ions at close to the speed of light in a long tunnel containing electromagnets and sensors. The first beam circulated through the collider on the 10th September, 2008. The experiments at the Large Hadron Collider sparked fears that the particle collisions might produce doomsday events. There were fears of the production of stable microscopic black holes. Some postulated that hypothetical particles called strangelets might be generated. Two commissioned safety reviews concluded that the experiments would not present any danger. The LHC was back in operation on 5th April 2015. 'Matter particles' and 'antimatter particles' include fermions (quarks, leptons, antiquarks, and antileptons). 'Force particles' determine the interactions among fermions which include bosons (gauge bosons and the Higgs boson). A theoretical elementary boson mediating gravitation has been postulated and has become known as a graviton, speculated to be massless. Experiments to detect gravitational waves as states of many gravitons are underway. Any particle containing two or more elementary particles is called a composite particle, such as hadrons. These occur in two groups including baryons (such as protons and neutrons, made of three quarks) and mesons (such as pions, made of one quark and one antiquark). Gluons are elementary particles that act as a strong binding force between quarks. A tachyon is a hypothetical particle that moves faster than light. Further details require reference to specialist sources and texts as this is an extremely complex topic.

During the 1930s, as well as neutrons (without charge), negatively charged electrons and positively charged protons were observed. Also known was the photon, the particle of electromagnetic radiation forming light. A paradox was found which is still not fully explained. Light appeared to exist not only in particulate form but also in waveform.

Speculation: Possible Anomalies and Advanced Theoretical Technologies

A stargate is a fictional device which perhaps could exist in reality under intelligent control by a species with advanced technological expertise. It is a form of portal (see below) which uses proposed Einstein-Rosen bridges allowing rapid travel between two distant locations. The device would allow near instantaneous interstellar travel within a galaxy and even intergalactic travel. Pairs of stargates might function by generating an artificial stable wormhole between them.

Portals may work using wormholes and provide a connection between two different locations (singularities). Temporal portals might allow transfers in time, either into the past or the future. Interdimensional portals might connect with a 'parallel world'. Portals have been claimed to have once occurred in ancient Egyptian and Mayan pyramids and temples. They have also been claimed to open up in the side of mountains in Peru and over the water in areas such as the so-called Bermuda Triangle including the Atlantic Ocean around Catalina Island, California. Other claims for the location of portals include the Antarctic where there is a purported entrance into a 'hollow Earth' and even in regions of the lunar and Martian landscapes.

Ufologists such as Jacques Vallée believed that unidentified flying objects (UFOs) and related events were visitations from other realities or dimensions. Such dimensions co-exist alongside known reality. Visitations of this sort may have been occurring from times before the dawn of recorded history. Observed entities with their craft entering the known reality via portals in ancient times may have been described as 'gods' or strange supernatural beings.

Hilary Evans suggested that the inter dimensional hypothesis can explain the ability of UFOs to appear and disappear both visually and on radar targets. These common observations of UFOs may correspond to them 'materializing' and 'dematerializing' when they enter or depart our own dimension. Another dimension into which UFOs move back and forth might well be more advanced in technological development. This might explain why certain UFOs exhibit features not yet invented at the time of their observation on the Earth. An example is the airships seen over the USA in the 1890s. Further examples are the ghost rockets over Scandinavia and speeding discs seen over the USA in the 1930s and 1940s.

In order to accept the possibility of life arriving in the known world, for example from other dimensions predicted by String Theory, the concept of a 'Multiverse' (or Meta-Universe) needs to be considered in more depth. The Universe as observed and experienced in everyday life may be just one of a finite or infinite group. The various Universes within the Multiverse are referred to as 'Parallel Universes' or 'Alternate Universes'. The term 'Multiverse' was coined in 1895 by an American philosopher and psychologist named William James. Supporters of the concept include Stephen Hawking, Michio Kaku and many others. However, there are also many well established scientists like Jim Baggott and Paul Davies who feel that the Multiverse debate is more philosophical than scientific.

An Alcubierre drive mentioned earlier is a theoretical type of starship engine which might manipulate the fabric of spacetime using large quantities of pure energy. It is based on a speculative idea related to a solution of Einstein's field equations in General Relativity. The idea was proposed by theoretical physicist Miguel Alcubierre in 1994. A spacecraft might be able to contract space in front of it and expand space behind it, resulting in effective faster-than-light travel. Objects cannot accelerate to the speed of light within normal spacetime but the Alcubierre drive gets around this as it would shift space around the object. The ship would ride a wave inside a region of flat space termed a warp bubble. The ship itself would not move within the bubble. Rather, it would be carried along as the region itself moved. The engine is consistent with General Relativity but might need exotic matter and huge amounts of 'negative energy' to power it and so might be impossible to construct. Other exotic modes of transport have also previously been mentioned including nuclear powered engines, matter-antimatter warp drives and antigravity systems.

An alternative system of transportation to those above is based on teleportation. An incredible claim has been made by a lawyer called Andrew Basiago. He insisted that he was enrolled in a secret U.S. Central Intelligence Agency (CIA) programme from a young age. The programme had 140 children and sixty adults. He claimed to have travelled in time and has photos as evidence such as being in a photograph together with President Lincoln at Gettysburg. He also claimed he has travelled to Mars. He said the group of travellers included President Barack Obama, known as Barry Soetoro at that time. As many as one hundred people may have worked on the teleportation programme called Project Pegasus. The technology was supposedly based on Nikola Tesla who had ideas regarding the use of free energy. Basiago claims there are secret underground cities on Mars with large numbers of people as part of Project Camelot in which the human genome will be sustained by the selected Martian colonists in the event of an Earthly catastrophe. It has been claimed that Laura Eisenhower, the great granddaughter of the President, was invited to join the secret U.S. colony. It has also been claimed that alien underground bases are found on Mars.

Ancient Astronauts

It is possible that mankind has been visited and influenced by species not of this Earth since times before recorded history. Indeed, some people believe that the transition from primitive stone age cave dwellers to societies with complex customs and sophisticated buildings only occurred because of extraterrestrial interference. It is possible that enhancement of the human species was artificially encouraged by what would nowadays be referred to as genetic engineering. Ancient temples and pyramids were built by transferring huge boulders and rocks miles to designated sites. How this was done remains controversial. Another anomaly is that precision cutting of stones and fitting them together probably required sophisticated tools and technology not available to mankind at that time. Advanced mathematical knowledge would also have been needed to calculate the angles of adjacent blocks and alignments to withstand the stress of the great weights of the building materials. Many ancient buildings were aligned to the movements of the sun, stars and moon. They appear to be ancient astronomical observatories but it is unclear how such knowledge was obtained.

Amazingly, archaic wall paintings in caves seem to reflect possible ancient alien visitations. Some pictures bizarrely resemble craft which these days are known as unidentified flying objects. Some cave paintings appear to show spacemen with helmets or creatures who do not come from Earth. Some people have interpreted cave paintings as illustrations of aircraft including rockets and planes. The so-called 'helicopter hieroglyphs' discovered at Abydos in Egypt have been suggested to depict flying craft.

It seems possible that alien visitors have been present on the Earth from the dawn of time. Human beings may have drawn and painted mysterious images on cave walls based on things they imagined, religious or cultural customs, pleas to spirits to give good hunting or heal the sick, or just as pure artwork. However, it is also possible that they recorded things that they actually saw.

Cave paintings which might have representations of aliens or UFOs have been found worldwide. For example, the Wandjina images found in Kimberley, Australia and rock drawings in Val Camonica, in Italy, depict creatures that resemble aliens as Ufologists would describe them today. Chhattisgarh is a state in Central India, the tenth largest state and the sixteenth most populated state of the nation. 10,000-year old rock paintings possibly depicting aliens and UFOs have been found in the Chhattisgarh region.

Various religious texts and scripts have accounts which imply a presence of ancient astronauts on the Earth. The Bible is one such source. In the Old Testament, Chapter one of the Book of Ezekiel, reference is made to a cloud emitting a bright light and a fire with four winged living creatures which moved back and forth. There were also four shiny objects which rose from the ground and could fly. The Book of Genesis, Chapter six verses one to four, refers to the sons of God marrying daughters of humans. "The Nephilim were on the Earth in those days." Hebrew scripture refers to the Elohim or God(s) and the Book of Enoch explains that the 'sons of God' were a group of 200 'angels' or 'Watchers'. They came down to planet Earth to breed with human females against the wishes of God. Their offspring were the above mentioned Nephilim, referred to by some sources as 'giants'. The 'Watchers' shared some of their knowledge and skills with mankind. In due course God created a Great Flood to destroy the Nephilim and the humans who were given knowledge by the 'Watchers' or 'fallen angels'. Noah was informed of the impending flood and built his famous Ark to survive. Some believe that the 'Watchers' were extraterrestrials who were observing or watching mankind on the Earth. Various other claims have been made regarding biblical accounts which are very controversial. A couple of examples include the suggestions that the Ark of the Covenant contained alien technology and that Jesus was an extraterrestrial.

References to potential off world visitors also come from religious sources other than the bible. According to the Hindu Ramayana (which dates to the fifth or fourth century BCE), Gods travel from place to place in flying vehicles called 'flying chariots', 'flying cars' or Vimanas. The Quran and other Islamic scriptures refer to supernatural creatures called the Jinn who inhabit an unseen other Universe.

The general concept of ancient astronauts was popularised by the writings of Erich von Däniken. Supporters of this hypothesis are too numerous to name in full but a few well-known individuals include Giorgio A. Tsoukalos, Zecharia Sitchin and David Icke. Many ancient structures on Earth such as Egyptian pyramids, Mayan temples, the stone heads of Easter Island and even Stonehenge in England may have required help from extraterrestrials to enable humans to build them. Humans may be descendants of ancient extraterrestrial beings or may have been created by manipulation of the gene pool.

The Sumerian civilization sprang up from the stoneage. There were four states making up ancient Mesopotamia (now Iraq) in about 4000 BC. Cuneiform writing on clay tablets has been discovered dating back 6000 years. Some ancient writing appears to record encounters with strange beings. The remains of a Queen called Puabi of the First Dynasty of the ancient city of Ur (ca. 2600 BCE) were found who had a large elongated skull like others found in Egypt and Peru. Some believe she was a member of a race of individuals with giant skeletons who may have been an extraterrestrial or a hybrid human. Some people have speculated that she was a member of a race called the Annunaki who may have had long lifespans and possibly were winged creatures that descended from the sky. It has been speculated that the origin of the Annunaki is the planet Nibiru which has also been designated as planet X. This planet may cross Earth's orbit every 3600 years between Mars and Jupiter. Professor Zecharia Sitchin interepreted Sumerian writing and studied stone glyphs. The Annunaki may have come to Earth with the intent of mining raw materials, especially gold. The Sumerians describe Planet X as being 30,000,000,000 miles away at its farthest point in orbit. The Sumerians produced depictions of humanoid figurines and had a surprising knowledge of the solar system. They also described 'android beings' and non-living 'helpers' who acted as if they were alive that flew their craft. Some believe that the Annunaki may have created grey alien 'Watchers' to monitor their genetic engineering experiments to produce humankind thousands of years ago.

The Great Pyramids of ancient Egypt present a challenging anomaly both to their means of construction and purpose.

Although used as burial sites for the Pharaohs they may have had other astronomical roles. It appears that some of the Egyptian pyramids are aligned with three stars found in the Orion constellation belt and strangely, these correspond to similar alignments that Mayan pyramids also have with Orion. The Mayan pyramids are found far away in Peru. The ancient Egyptian and Mayan civilizations were very unlikely to have been able to interact due to the geographical separation. Some believe that ancient astronauts once came to the Earth from star constellations such as Orion and also Syrius. They subsequently influenced the development of mankind.

One of the oldest relatively intact 'Seven Wonders of the Ancient World' is the Great Pyramid of Giza, sometimes called the Pyramid of Khufu or the Pyramid of Cheops. It is estimated to have taken up to twenty years to build around 2560 BC with a height of 146.5 metres (481 feet). The Great Pyramid was once covered by casing stones that formed a smooth outer surface though at the present time a more basic core is visible. There are various chambers and surrounding minor pyramids but this ancient pyramid is the only one in Egypt known to have both ascending and descending passages. The general theory of construction involves the dragging of huge quarry stones and lifting them into position. Some people theorise that there is no way the Egyptian civilization of that period was capable of designing and building such structures so that extraterrestrial expertise was needed. Individuals with elongated skulls similar to those mentioned above have been identified in ancient Egypt who resemble postulated extraterrestrials. Among the ancient rulers depicted are Pharaoh Akhenaten and Queen Nefertiti who ruled for seventeen years or so and died about 1336 BC to 1334 BC. The well known Tutankhamun or King Tut was the son of Akhenaten.

The Mayan civilization became established around 2000 BC to AD 250. Mayan temples and pyramids are remarkable examples of ancient sophisticated architecture. They frequently have numerous hieroglyphic texts with information about the culture. Some have detailed astronomical knowledge and a famous Mayan calendar. The calendar predicted that a cataclysmic world event would occur on 21st December 2012. This date was regarded as the end date of a 5126 year long cycle. The civilization was advanced in art, architecture, mathematical and astronomical systems and was highly developed between AD 250 and AD 900. The society and culture continued at least until Spanish explorers arrived.

The Peruvian archaeologist Julio Tello made an astounding discovery in 1928 in Paracas where he found buried remains with large elongated skulls. Over 300 skulls were found and dated at about 3000 years old. There are claims that DNA tests showed the remains are not human casting doubt on accepted human evolutionary lines. Some South American tribes used to put pressure on infants' skulls with wooden blocks in order to change their shape but this does not account for the extensive elongated skull observations. The craniums were 25% larger and 60% heavier than typical human skulls. The anomaly arises as to where these individuals came from. Many believe the Mayans were influenced by an extraterrestrial presence. Some claim further support for this idea following the Mexican government's release of documents and images of objects found at a site called Calakmul near the centre of the Yucatán Peninsula. Calakmul was the seat of what was called the 'Kingdom of the Serpent' and had a population of about 50,000 people. There are 6750 ancient structures identified at Calakmul including a large pyramid. It was rediscovered by aerial exploration in 1931 having been buried by jungle overgrowth. The demise of the Mayan civilization came in 1521 during the Spanish Conquest of the Yucatán when Conquistadors destructively raided the Mayan buildings.

The deserts of southern Peru are home to some fascinating

markings etched into the land known as the Nazca Lines. Many of these are straight lines hundreds of metres long which may have once led to religious temples. Some lines form stylized animals and humanoid figures which are best seen by aerial observation in aircraft. They are visible from outer space. It has been suggested that they may once have been runways for the spacecraft of extraterrestrial visitors. The Nazca people might have made the lines using simple tools and surveying equipment like wooden stakes and rope.

Unexplained and Strange Historical UFO Sightings and Similar Events (Pre-1940s)

Various strange events and sightings of unusual craft have been recorded in old historical reports and logs of the past. Some of these go back a long way into history. It seems that the frequent sightings made in the 1940s at the dawn of modern UFO studies was preceded by many intriguing earlier events. Some examples are given next.

Objects have been seen leaving and returning to English seas from as early as 1067 AD. However, a documented maritime event occurred in 1492 AD, at 10 pm on October 11th. Christopher Columbus was aboard the *Santa Maria* on his first famous voyage. The *Santa Maria* was one of three Spanish ships in the fleet. He was accompanied by the *Pinta* and *Niña*. While over a deep ravine in the Atlantic in an area which nowadays might be called the 'Bermuda Triangle', lights were seen flashing deep in the ocean. Columbus described "a small wax candle that rose and lifted up." The event was recorded in Columbus's log. It has been suggested that the sighting occurred offshore from an area in the vicinity of Watlings Island (San Salvador). Some explanations have been put forward which perhaps are unlikely. The light may have been caused by a night time Indian fishing canoe (high winds were operating at the time of the observation) or bioluminescent Protozoa (single celled organisms) on the rocks. The crew also reported seeing a bright, disc shaped object rise out of the ocean and fly into the sky and on a different occasion observed stars spinning in the sky. These observations may have been related to UFO (unidentified flying object) and/or USO (unidentified submerged object) sightings.

In 1561 at dawn on April 14th, a mass sighting of UFOs was seen in the sky over Nuremberg, Germany. The accounts of what was seen have been ascribed to an extraterrestrial aerial battle. It was described as "a very frightful spectacle." The events lasted for about an hour and an artist, Hans Glaser, drew a woodcut of it at the time. Hundreds of spheres, cylinders and numerous other odd shaped objects (including globes, blood red crosses and curved rods) moved overhead. The objects flew backwards and forwards across the sun and some fell to the ground, smoking. A strange substance now called Angel hair was observed falling through the air. The events were followed by the appearance of a long object that looked like a great black spear or triangle. Some proposed explanations include light refraction through ice crystals and observation of the sun at low viewing angles.

On August 12th 1883, Mexican astronomer José Bonilla was preparing to study sunspot activity at the recently opened Zacatecas Observatory. He observed more than 300 dark unknown objects crossing the view. He took several photographs by exposing wet plates. It was subsequently suggested that the objects were high flying geese. It was later suggested that the photos had captured pieces of a billion ton comet passing within a few hundred kilometres of the Earth. Some Ufologists interpret the objects as alien spacecraft. Bonilla is given the credit for taking the earliest photo of an unidentified flying object.

During 1896 and 1897, waves of phantom giant airship sightings generated reports across the United States. The reports spread from west to east. Sometimes these airships resembled dirigibles and human looking crew were seen. This was before the current technology of the time could account for the widespread use of such craft. Sometimes crew members in the airships waved at people on the ground and claimed they came from Mars.

In 1897, a strange UFO incident was reported in Aurora, Texas. A mysterious airship was reported to have collided with a farm windmill and crashed, killing the occupant. The dead pilot was unusual looking and described as being "not of this world" and a "Martian." The body was buried at the Aurora Cemetery and the site marked with a plaque. Pieces of wreckage were placed in the grave and in the damaged well below the windmill. A new owner subsequently sealed the well with a concrete slab saying the water was contaminated. Some people later claimed the incident was a hoax and the story a fabrication done to attract visitors to the town and generate revenue. In an investigation undertaken in 2008, the well was opened and water samples taken. A large amount of aluminium was present. A past owner had previously removed metallic pieces of debris from the well. Ground penetrating radar was used at the cemetery on an unmarked grave but the grave was in bad condition and nothing conclusive or significant was found.

On August 1st, 1904, a British cargo ship called *The Mohican* was en route to Philadelphia when it experienced a terrifying event. The account of what happened was given by Captain Urquhart and endorsed by the crew. A strange grey cloud rapidly approached from the southeast which seemed to resemble a large balloon. The hair on the sailors' heads and their beards stuck out like bristles. The ship came to a stop for thirty minutes and was enveloped in a strange vapour which glowed like phosphorus. Strange magnetic effects occurred. The needle of the compass revolved with the speed of an electric motor. Sailors were unable to lift pieces of steel from the decks which had become magnetized. It became difficult to talk or move but after a while the cloud moved off and everything went back to normal on the ship. Some believe that the events on that day were associated with UFO activity.

A brief mention is made of the Tunguska event. This was a large explosion that occurred on June 30th, 1908. The explosion was an airburst that happened at an altitude of three to six miles in the remote area of Podkamennaya near the Tunguska River in what is now Siberian Krasnoyarsk Krai, Russia. Estimates of the energy of the blast have varied but it has been put in the order of three to thirty megatons of TNT. The energy of the explosion was about 1000 times or more greater than that of the atomic bomb dropped on Hiroshima, Japan, during World War II. Something like eighty million trees over an area of 830 square miles were flattened but no human fatalities were reported. Mainstream suggestions are based on the theory that the explosion was caused by an asteroid, comet or meteor. In 2013, a research team led by Victor Kvasnytsya of the National Academy of Sciences of Ukraine suggested microscopic samples collected from the region indicated a meteor impact. There have been a variety of other theories put forward to try and explain what happened at Tunguska and these include the possibility of UFO activity or collision.

A famous event occurred near Fatima, a village seventy miles north of Lisbon, Portugal. In the spring of 1916, a group of children had encounters with a 'being of light', the Angel of Peace. He encouraged them to pray for peace (at the time of World War I). Three children were involved. These were Lucia dos Santos (aged ten) and her cousins Francisco (aged eight) and Jacinta (aged seven) Marto. On 13th May 1917, the three children were tending their flocks of sheep in an area called Cova da Iria when lightning like flashes occurred in the overhead blue sky. They then had a religious encounter with a "Lady from Heaven" clothed in brilliant light in which exchanges were related concerning prayer and peace. Among these was the urgent need for the Consecration of Russia to the Immaculate Heart of Mary. This figure was later purported to be the Holy Virgin Mary. The children had another encounter on 13th June 1917 with about fifty people in attendance. One witness heard a whooshing sound like "a rocket, a long way off" after Mary departed. The children had a further encounter on the 13th July, 1917. Lucia later revealed that Mary opened her hands and rays of light penetrated the earth revealing horrific visions of demons and hell. A three part secret was imparted. The first two parts of the secret only became publicly known in 1942 and the third part divulged by the Vatican in June 2000. On September 13th 1917, large crowds converged on Fatima and the children arrived around noon. There was a flash of light and Mary was seen again and conversed with Lucia. In due course a public miracle was proclaimed.

An estimated 70,000 pilgrims including the children assembled reciting the rosary in bad stormy and rainy weather conditions to witness a final promised appearance of the Lady in the Cova da Iria on October 13th, 1917. The black clouds parted and the sun became visible as a dull, grey disc that could be looked at directly. People in the crowd proclaimed that the sun "danced." Others saw the sun change colour, spin and lower itself to the earth. Heat from the descending sun dried people's wet clothes. This incident has been referred to as the Miracle of the Sun.

In later years some scientists and UFO researchers such as Jacques Vallée ascribed the apparitions and observations at Fatima to a UFO incident or some kind of Unidentified Aerial Phenomenon (UAP). A white substance fell from the sky during some of the Fatima incidents referred to as Angel hair. This has been associated with UFO incidents.

Francisco died on 4th April 1919, probably from influenza. Jacinta passed away from a chest condition in February 1920. In 1947, Lucia joined the Discalced Carmelite Order in a monastery in Coimbra, Portugal. She died at the age of ninety-seven on February 13th, 2005.

Recent History of UFO Sightings and Related Events (1940s Onwards)

Sightings of unusual aerial objects have been explained away over the years as divine events, misidentified conventional aircraft, stars, the planet Venus, swamp gas, flocks of birds, geological Earthlights, lenticular clouds, temperature inversions and other weather phenomena. It seems that the vast majority of sightings can be logically accounted for. However, there remains a small residue of sightings which defy explanation. The 'modern' age of UFO observations and history is popularly agreed to have begun in the 1940s.

In 1946, a wave of sightings of so-called Ghost Rockets occurred in the skies over Scandinavia and Sweden in particular. These UFOs resembled missiles in shape. Some of the rockets had wings while others did not. About 2000 sightings were reported and some of these gave radar returns. Reports often explained them away as meteor trails or Russian testing of wartime V1 and V2 rockets, though some people in the Swedish military considered them to have an extraterrestrial nature. These objects were unusual in that they often travelled slowly in formation, left no exhaust trail and emitted no noise. Rockets were sometimes seen to crash into lakes but left behind no debris though the lake bed might be left cratered or disturbed.

Richard Rankin had more than 7000 hours flying experience when he saw mystery craft high over Bakersfield, California, going "maybe 300 or 400 miles an hour" on June 23rd, 1947.

There were ten objects in formation flying north but when they returned heading south, there were only seven visible.

On June 24th 1947, one of the most celebrated events in UFO history occurred. Pilot Kenneth Arnold claimed that he saw nine, shiny unidentified flying objects flying past Mount Rainier in the Cascade Mountains at speeds estimated at about 1200 miles an hour. He was flying from Chehalis, Washington, to Yakima, Washington, in a Call Air A-2 plane on a business trip. Arnold described the objects as convex or crescent shapes flying in formation. He placed their distance as they flew past Rainier as about twenty five miles distant. The objects weaved and banked reflecting flashes of sunlight. He later likened their movement to saucers skipping on water. The phrase 'flying saucers' was born. The sightings received much attention by the press. The U.S. Air Force put the Arnold sighting down to a mirage.

On July 8th, 1947, it is claimed that a disc shaped object crashed at Roswell, New Mexico. This was a most controversial incident and some say there was a military cover-up and alien bodies were recovered. This is discussed more fully in the Crash-Retrieval section.

One of the first UFO cases in the United States to receive national publicity occurred from August to September 1951 over the city of Lubbock, Texas. The air force investigated observations of lights flying in formation over the town at speeds estimated at about 600 miles per hour and at 2000 feet high. The lights were initially ascribed to birds called plovers. The air force stated that an anonymous scientist had given this explanation but a realistic explanation was not provided. Carl Hart Jr managed to take some photos of the lights. The physics laboratory at Wright-Patterson Air Force Base in Ohio analysed the Hart photographs. The Lubbock Lights were investigated by Lieutenant Edward J. Ruppelt (the supervisor of the air force's Project Blue Book). He released a written statement to the press saying that the photos taken by Hart had not been proven to be a hoax.

In 1952, a series of events began which became known as the Washington Flap. Over a period from July 12th to July 29th, a fleet of UFOs in the form of white or orange balls of light flew over Washington DC and were not only seen visually but confirmed on radar. These objects moved at speeds up to 7000 mph, outran jet planes sent up to intercept them and made amazing ninety degree turns. Colonel John Samford explained the visual sightings away as misidentified aerial phenomena such as stars or meteors. The unknown radar targets were due to temperature inversions. These explanations were later disputed by many people. Samford claimed the observed targets posed no threat to national security. This incident took place during a period of the cold war when there was great suspicion regarding Soviet Union military activity. The sightings made front page newspaper headlines.

A very deep area of the Atlantic Ocean around Catalina Island, California, has generated many UFO (unidentified flying object) and USO (unidentified submerged object) reports. Such reports have been made since the 1950s and have continued until the present time. Objects have been observed by viewers from aircraft, the shoreline, boats and ships out at sea. Aerial objects have been seen to move at supersonic speeds and make rapid changes of direction. Some witnesses report seeing strange looking men disembarking from landed craft. Various types of object have also been observed to enter and leave the water. On February 5th, 1964, eleven passengers were rescued by the Coast Guard following an unexplained sinking of their yacht, the *Hattie D*. The yacht was struck or rammed by an unidentified 'metal object'.

Until recent times in the same region, there have also been frequent reports of lights moving rapidly under the sea. This area of the Southern California coast near the Topanga

Canyon is a UFO 'hotspot'. Witnesses described approximately 200 craft rising into the sky, one at a time. Many believe that there is an underwater UFO/USO base or portal in the Santa Catalina Channel. There have been similar UFO/USO reports since the 1990s coming from Puerto Rico near the tip of the so-called 'Bermuda Triangle'. Again, UFO/USO bases or portals have been suspected to be located in the area. Objects have been witnessed emerging from and returning to not only the sea but also freshwater lakes.

Some UFO sightings have been ascribed a biological appearance. Examples include shapes resembling an *Amoeba*, octopus, jellyfish and a cocoon. During 1948 in San Pablo, California, two witnesses including a retired U.S. army Colonel observed not only a grey rectangular UFO but also a fast travelling object that resembled a translucent *'Amoeba'* with a dark spot at the centre similar to how a living cell contains a dense nucleus. The arms of the *'Amoeba'* undulated. In 2008, a woman in Ohio saw a large orange, glowing object in the sky near her home which looked like an *'Amoeba'*. One case in 2009 resulted in damage to a 213-feet high wind turbine near Conisholme in Lincolnshire, England. Witnesses said the damage was caused by an object which had "tentacles of light" resembling an octopus. In 2009, a UK resident in Wimbledon described "a large bright pink jellyfish looking object surrounded by a pink haze." This object was seen to be hovering near electricity pylons. In the previous year of 2008, an Ohio truck driver with a background in military aviation, reported seeing a glowing yellow and white object near the Ohio River which resembled a 'cocoon'.

Objects in the sky may be explained all or in part by Trevor James Constable's 'Sky Critter Theory'. This claims that UFOs come from a parallel Universe, some being machines and others living creatures which live in the sky.

Such 'Bioforms' are invisible to normal sight but can be recorded by infrared film.

The existence of Bioforms or 'Floaters' occurring even in unlikely environments such as in the atmosphere of Jupiter, is not inconceivable. The well known astronomer Carl Sagan (born in 1934) pioneered such ideas in a new branch of biology termed 'exobiology'. Sagan also promoted the Search for Extra-Terrestrial Intelligence (SETI) and urged the scientific community to listen with radio telescopes for signals from potential intelligent extraterrestrial lifeforms.

The witnesses of some UFO-claimed sightings have sometimes been challenged as to their veracity or mental state. However, on Friday April 24th in 1964, Lonnie Zamora, a police Sergeant, had a close encounter with a strange object. This occurred in New Mexico at Socorro in the Middle Rio Grande Basin. Physical evidence was left behind. There was burned vegetation and a triangular area of glassy fused sand. Metal fragments were found on a broken rock and intriguingly, there were even impressions in the soil which suggested a landing. The case was investigated by astronomer Dr J. Allen Hynek. He could not find any satisfactory way of explaining the case away.

Sergeant Zamora heard a loud roar and saw a "bluish-orange" flame in the sky around 5-45 pm. He proceeded westwards in the direction of a dynamite shack he thought might have blown up. He came upon a shiny object "shaped like a letter O" made of something "like aluminium." It rested on "four legs." Zamora then caught a brief sight of two people in white coveralls beside the object. He lost sight of them but heard noises as if a hatch was being closed. The object subsequently lifted up off the ground with a roar and then flew off quickly, apparently without noise and leaving behind no smoke. Zamora returned to his car and radioed the Sheriff's office. He was quickly joined by Sergeant Chavez (though he did not see the object). Zamora sketched a picture of insignia he observed on the object. Several independent witnesses reported sightings in the same area at the same time as the purported landing. Some witnesses observed an "egg shaped craft" while others saw a bluish flame.

The following UFO incident is included as it is somewhat unusual and allegedly involved interaction with the public. It has come to be known as the Colares Flap and occurred on a Brazilian island in 1977. UFOs apparently attacked people with beams of 'radiation'. Victims suffered burns, puncture wounds and blood loss. Local people held night vigils, burnt fires, rattled pots and pans and set off fireworks in an effort to keep the unknown lights away. The government sent in an investigation team under a programme called Operation Saucer following requests for help by the mayor of the city. The operation was commanded by Captain Uyrangê Bolivar Soares Nogueira de Hollanda Lima who tried to calm the public and investigate the events. There was never any 'concrete proof' of the UFO attacks. His reports were classified as 'secret' for some time by the government. In 1997, Captain Uyrangê gave two researchers an account of his experiences. Three months after the interview, he was found dead, hanging by his belt. There has been speculation and controversy as to whether he committed suicide or if foul play was involved to 'stop him talking'.

In late December 1980, unexplained lights were observed near Rendlesham Forest in Suffolk, England. The incident that followed has been called 'Britain's Roswell'. At that time, RAF Woodbridge was twinned with RAF Bentwaters and used by the U.S. air force as a nuclear facility. Incidents occurred over two separate days starting on 26th December, 1980. A triangular shaped craft with flashing lights and enveloped by a yellow mist was seen to descend in the forest around 4 am. The craft moved through the trees and became stationary. Local farm animals were said to have gone into a state of fear and some cows stampeded. The object was approached by military staff Jim Penniston and John Burroughs. Sergeant Jim Penniston claimed he observed and photographed the craft for forty five minutes and actually touched it. Unknown hieroglyphics were seen on the craft. Small beings immersed in light were seen to emerge. Penniston claimed his mind became filled with the digits zero and one (which in later years became known as binary code). Eventually, the code in his memory was translated as an amazing message which referred to an area called High Brazil off the coast of Ireland. The date of origin of the message was 8100. It suggested that the occupants seen in the craft might have been time travellers. The watches of Penniston and Burroughs had been synchronised when they set out into the forest but after the object had lifted off and disappeared, their watches showed a time difference. It seemed time had moved at different speeds for the two men with a forty five minute difference. Burroughs memory of the incident was less clear but he did remember the craft taking off. After daybreak, servicemen returned to a small clearing near the eastern edge of the forest where the object had been located. They found three small impressions in a triangular pattern, reminiscent of holes made by a tripod of landing legs. They also found burn marks and broken branches on nearby trees.

The next evening, the base commander Ted Conrad was told that 'it' was back. Conrad was just about to present an after-dinner speech and asked his deputy, Lieutenant Colonel Charles Halt to sort out the matter. Halt (who was the Deputy Base Commander of USAF Bentwaters and Woodbridge), went out again with other military personnel to investigate a second landing. He made a famous voicetape recording as they cautiously approached the craft through the trees. The craft was metallic in appearance and triangular in shape. No windows were seen. It measured about two to three metres across the base. The craft illuminated the entire forest with a white light. There was a flashing red light on top and a bank of blue lights underneath. As the men got near, the craft levitated just above the ground and backed off. The craft was followed by the men for about an hour and it then took off at fantastic speed. Some sceptics put the viewing down to the planet Venus or Orford Ness Lighthouse. Halt believed that he had seen an extraterrestrial event (which was later covered up). Halt made a sworn affidavit to confirm what he saw. Files detailing Geiger counter readings taken at the scene of the forest landing were shown to experts by Nick Pope (a UK government official working in defence and studying UFO reports and sightings) in 1994. According to Pope, the figures were ten times above expected background levels.

Some amazing viewings occurred in the Hessdalen Valley in Norway in the early 1980s. Lights had been seen since the 1940s but around 1981 they were seen fifteen to twenty times a week. Research fieldwork was subsequently undertaken by UFO-Norge and UFO-Sweden since 1983. Lights were seen along the mountains passing over the tree tops in the municipality of Holtålen. The lights were bright and often white or yellow. They were seen floating above the ground but were sometimes recorded as moving at around 30,000 km/hr. They also appeared to land and move off. Suggestions were made that these lights consisted of 'ball lightning' but the lights were sometimes visible for over an hour which made ball lightning an unlikely explanation of the phenomena. Some people believed that the lights were hiding UFOs. In 2007, a University study group captured the phenomenon on film and obtained measurements which suggested that the lights were a form of plasma or charged particles. In 1998, the Hessdalen AMS (Automated Scientific Research Station) was built in the valley to monitor and make recordings of lights.

In 1987, a well known series of sightings began on November 11th. The events became known as the Gulf Breeze incident. The town is located in Florida, USA. Ed Walters, a building contractor, reported not only UFO sightings over a three week period but also took many clear photographs. He claimed to have seen a hovering, glowing object in his yard and that he was struck by a paralysing blue beam. He was told by voices in his head that he would not be harmed. World-wide publicity followed the case. However, it was later claimed that Walters had made a UFO model and fabricated the photos.

An incident occurred with many witnesses in the Soviet Union on September 27th, 1989. This is known as the Voronezh UFO incident. The story was reported by the publication TASS. A group of children observed a landed disc in a park. A 'three eyed alien' and a robot left the craft. The onlookers were terrified and frozen to the spot. The occupants departed but returned five minutes later and abducted a sixteen year old boy using a 'pistol tube' device. The craft was not only witnessed by the children but it was also seen by adults including a police officer.

In November 1989, a series of UFO sightings began called the 'Belgian Wave'. There were multiple witnesses including police officers. A large, silent, flat, triangular craft with lights underneath it moved slowly moved across Belgium at low altitude. At the end of March 1990, similar objects were tracked on radar and chased by two Belgian Air Force F-16 jet aircraft from Beauvechain Air Base. Photographs were taken and sightings made by an estimated 13,500 people on the ground. The craft made several sudden changes in acceleration and deceleration which would have been fatal to human pilots. Some people claim the observations were due to mass public delusions.

UFO sightings sometimes occur in 'waves' or 'flaps' as they occur a number of times over a period of time, such as the 'Belgian Wave' discussed above. Mexico has been exposed to long lasting unidentified flying object sightings. The first wave probably started shortly before the eclipse of July 11th 1991, when seventeen different people in four cities captured a shiny, hovering, unidentified craft, on videotape. Something unknown had been in the sky over Mexico and it was discussed during live television broadcasts lasting up to seven hours. A second wave of sightings on a daily basis started in the spring of 1992, especially in the volcanic zone south east of Mexico City. One enlarged police photograph showed an orange-coloured spherical object ringed by 'windows' emitting light. In May of 1992, journalist Junichi Yaoi and his crew from Nippon Television joined an investigation team on a small knoll known as Casita Blana near Atlixco at the foot of Mount Popocatepetl. A brilliant triangular shaped object was observed flying above the desert floor. A third wave of sightings occurred on January 1st, 1993. Several UFOs made a six hour appearance over Mexico City. They were observed by hundreds of people of all ages and the city virtually came to a standstill. The events were covered on television and in newspapers. Even the Mexican Air Force was put on standby. A fourth wave began in August 1994. Captain Fernando Mezquita and his copilot, Captain Carlos Corzo, were on a routine commercial flight from Acapulco to Mexico City when an unidentified object crossed their path at 12,000 feet. Over the following week, several more close encounters with disc shaped UFOs were reported by crew members of passenger airliners.

A brief mention is made of the Cosford incident that occurred in March 1993. Sightings initially occurred across the eastern counties of England. A UFO subsequently passed over RAF Cosford at high velocity at an altitude of about 1000 feet. Later that night, staff at RAF Shawbury saw a similar UFO. It moved slowly across the countryside towards the base at low speed around 40 mph, making a humming sound and firing a narrow beam of light back and forth across a field until disappearing at high speed. The object was not detected on radar. The incident is of significance because there were large numbers of witnesses including police officers and military staff. A police officer claimed the object looked like "two Concordes flying side by side and joined together" while other reports suggested a more triangular shape. Some people have tried to explain the sightings away as the debris from a Russian Cosmos Satellite re-entering the Earth from orbit.

A shocking and terrifying UFO sighting was made on September 16th in 1994. This occurred at Ariel Elementary School east of Harare in Ruwa, Zimbabwein, Zimbabwe. Sixty two children independently confirmed seeing a saucer shaped UFO and alien beings. Students ranged in age from five to twelve years and came from various races and ethnic backgrounds. Most of the children had no previous knowledge or conception of UFOs. The children independently described the same event and made similar drawings of what they saw (about thirty five sketches were done). A fleet of four UFOs was seen overhead and one of them landed near the school playground. A small grey 'man' with a thin neck, slitlike mouth, reduced nose and ears and huge rugby ball shaped black eyes left the top of the craft and approached the children. He was about three feet tall and wearing a tight, shiny black and silver one piece costume. The children were 'warned by thoughts' that humanity should take better care of the planet as it was being polluted. The children were terrified and traumatised by the event and ran to their teachers to escape. Investigations made at the time appear to show that the children were telling the truth and not making up a story. A follow up study was made sixteen years later. The children were now adults and scattered around the world. They all maintained that what they observed that day in school really happened.

In 1997, a well witnessed aerial sighting occurred which came to be known as 'The Phoenix Lights'. It occurred over Phoenix, Arizona, on March 13th. Lights were reported by thousands of people over a 300 mile area. There seems to have been two events. In one event, a triangular craft with lights passed silently over the state generating many calls to the police by the public. Witnesses claim to have observed an incredible aerial object. It was V shaped and the size of several football fields (estimated to be as large as a mile in diameter). The object blocked out the stars as it moved across the sky. After the sightings the governor, Fife Symington, made fun of the incident and brought out his aide on stage dressed in an alien costume. Later, he admitted that he also had seen something strange in the sky. In another event, stationary lights were seen high in the sky. Military officials and the Federal Aviation Administration claimed the sightings were caused by flares dropped by F-16 aircraft training at Luke Air Force Base. Witnesses claimed that three jets were seen heading west in the direction of the lights but this was denied by the military. The events received extensive television and press coverage.

Between 2007 and 2009, various reports of unknown aerial objects were reported across Turkey. They were witnessed by many people over several days and nights. Several videos showed lights, round, disc and cigar shaped objects which were flying, making turns and hovering over the sea off the coast of Istanbul. At least one film was reviewed by The Scientific and Technology Board of Turkey and TUG National Observatory. These organisations were unable to prove a hoax. Dr Roger Leir analysed some of the footage and declared that two alien occupants were visible within a craft.

On July 7th 2010, an unidentified flying object forced Xiaoshan Airport in Hangzhou, China, to cease operations in order to avoid a possible collision with aircraft. About eighteen flights were affected. A flight crew detected the object around 8-40 pm and notified the air traffic control department. Less than an hour before the airport closures, residents claimed they saw a flying object emitting red and white rays of light. The UFOs identity remains unsolved but sparked a lot of speculation.

The Helioviewer Project's aim is to enable exploration of the sun and its inner heliosphere. SOHO (Solar and Heliospheric Observatory) is a satellite built to study the sun from its core to the outer corona and was launched on December 2nd, 1995. There are twelve instruments on board SOHO. These communicate with large radio dishes around the world forming NASA's Deep Space Network. In April of 2012, a photo was released which was taken by NASA's sun-watching observatory. A strange object was seen which resembled a huge, metallic 'mothership'. The object seemed unaffected by the extreme heat or solar flares. NASA, after two other similar sightings of 'alien spaceships', debunked the claims amid accusations of 'brushing out' information from photos. A hovering pyramid shaped object and a gigantic cross shaped object have also been observed in close proximity to the sun and there was a report of some kind of beam being emitted into the sun from an object. It has also been claimed that objects have actually dived into the sun. It has been speculated that such exotic craft might be refuelling with Helium-3 or entering a portal or wormhole. On December 5th, 2014, an alleged UFO as big or bigger than the Earth itself was reported by UFO researcher Scott Waring, editor of *UFO Sightings Daily*. He noticed (from NASA Helioviewer pictures online) a giant triangular UFO leaving the sun which resulted in a massive solar explosion.

In 1947 the famous 'Roswell incident' occurred in New Mexico. An object crashed near a ranch. Debris was found by William Brazel, a foreman working on the homestead. Brazel contacted Sheriff Wilcox and he in turn contacted Major Jesse Marcel of the Roswell Army Air Field (RAAF). A 'man in plainclothes' accompanied Brazel back to the ranch where pieces of wreckage were picked up. The RAAF public information officer Walter Haut issued a press release stating that personnel from the field's 509th Operations Group had recovered a 'flying disc' which had crashed on a ranch near Roswell. Soon afterwards the military changed the story and the commanding General of the Eighth Air Force Roger Ramey said that a weather balloon had crashed. Debris (foil, rubber and wood) said to be from the crashed object was shown to the press. In the 1990s, the U.S. military published reports suggesting the wreckage came from a crashed Project Mogul balloon. Project Mogul used high altitude balloons with microphones to monitor Soviet nuclear testing.

In 1978, nuclear physicist and author Stanton T. Friedman interviewed Jesse Marcel and this raised the profile of the incident. The son of Jesse Marcel later claimed the wreckage had been switched. His dad had brought items home with foil that could not be burned or cut and sprang back into position if crumpled up. There were also hieroglyphic-type images on debris recovered from the crash.

Many believe that following the Roswell crash, a crashed disc was loaded onto a truck. Colonel William H. Blanchard ordered the object be flown to Fort Worth Army Air Field. A B29 bomber with wreckage continued to its final destination at Wright-Field (later Wright-Patterson) Air Force base in Dayton, Ohio. After landing, General Ramey took over and began a suspected cover up that continued for the rest of the century. Witnesses of the retrieval claimed they were threatened by the military to keep silent about what they had observed. A few witnesses also claimed to have seen alien bodies with large heads and abnormally-shaped, oversized eyes. A couple of these were purportedly still alive after the crash, one of which survived and was taken away.

A possible UFO crash-retrieval incident occurred on December 9th, 1965. A fireball dripping hot metal debris was seen passing rapidly across the skies in a number of USA States causing sonic booms. It eventually crashed in the woods at Kecksburg, Pennsylvania. Blue smoke was seen and the authorities were informed. Fire department and other members of the public reported seeing an 'acorn shaped' object with hieroglyphics around its base. The United States Army secured the area and ordered civilians away. The object was purportedly removed on a flatbed truck. The military later claimed they searched the woods and found absolutely nothing. The official explanation of the widely seen fireball was that it was a meteor. There was a lot of press speculation as to what the object may have been including a plane crash, an errant missile and a crashed Russian satellite. There was later speculation about the object being a time travelling Nazi device called Die Glocke, more commonly known as 'The Nazi Bell'.

Contactees and Abductees

Some people claim to be in contact with unknown or alien entities either telepathically and/or physically. Such 'contactees' tell stories of being taken aboard spaceships and flown to other planets where they witnessed great civilizations. They are often given messages for mankind. Commonly, these messages are warnings of future catastrophes or global conflict. Sometimes photos have been produced as evidence of contact but these are often controversial and suspected of being hoaxed. The frequency of contact claims increased in the 1950s as 'cold war' tensions grew and fears of nuclear destruction increased. This was often referred to as 'M.A.D' (Mutual Assured Destruction) and it haunted relationships between the West and the Soviet Eastern block countries. Some contactees became well known and were socially sought after and they often wrote interesting illustrated books. There are too many individuals claiming to be in contact with other-worldly beings to document all of them but some well-known examples are given below.

George Adamski (April 17th 1891–April 23rd 1965) was an American citizen of Polish descent who became well known in the 1950s. He claimed to have seen various mother ships and scout ships and taken flights in them to the moon and planets like Venus. He took many photos but many sceptics suggested they were faked. Adamski was the author of three books describing his meetings with human like 'space brothers' or Nordic aliens. He began giving his first UFO lectures in 1949 in Southern California. In 1952, Adamski went with some friends into the Colorado Desert. An object was seen hovering in the sky and Adamski left his friends at the main road. They observed him approach a 'Venusian' scout ship which had landed. He met with and communicated with a blonde haired being called Orthon who warned him of the dangers of nuclear war. Adamski met Orthon again in future encounters. In 1954, Desmond Leslie (who co-wrote a book with Adamski) said he witnessed several UFOs while with Adamski when visiting him in California. Adamski received a lot of publicity and in May 1959 he was contacted by officials at the palace of Queen Juliana of the Netherlands who went ahead with a private audience.

'Billy' Eduard Albert Meier was born on February 3rd 1937 in the town of Bülach, Switzerland. He produced numerous photographs of 'beamships', metallic samples, sound recordings and films as evidence to show that he was in contact with human like extraterrestrials called the Plejaren from a world called Erra. This world is located about eighty light years beyond the Pleiades in a dimension a fraction out of phase with known reality. Meier was particularly 'active' in the 1970s. He claimed his first extraterrestrial contacts occurred in 1942 and that he subsequently visited other worlds and galaxies. He also claimed to have had a number of meetings with variously named extraterrestrial men and women. His conversations were published in several books, mainly in German. After Meier's relationship with his wife Kalliope ended in 1997, she stated in an interview that the UFOs in the photos resembled models that Meier had made himself.

Many individuals claim to have been forcibly removed from their daily lives and taken aboard an alien spaceship. Quite commonly medical investigations were reported as being carried out by alien beings, some of which were painful. Many accounts described the removal of ova or sperms and even the presentation of hybrid children. It has been suggested that some kind of genetic manipulation of the human race is occurring. Some pregnant women may even have had their unborn foetus removed. It is quite common for 'abductees' to report periods of 'missing time' in their lives. Many abductees have suffered nightmares and only following sessions of regression hypnosis were able to recall what had happened to them. Quite often their experiences were masked by false 'screen memories'. Sometimes, strange objects or 'implants' have been removed and odd scars left on the body.

Antônio Vilas-Boas (1934-1991) was a twenty three year-old Brazilian farmer who claimed to have been abducted by extraterrestrials in 1957. While ploughing fields near São

Francisco de Sales, he saw a 'red star' which came nearer. It resembled an egg shaped craft. It came down in the field and extended three landing 'legs'. Boas decided to leave the area but his tractor engine died. He was seized by a five feet tall humanoid wearing grey coveralls and a helmet making noises like barks or yelps. Three further beings arrived and overcame Boas struggles. He was subsequently dragged into their craft. He was stripped naked and led into a semicircular room through a doorway with red symbols. Blood was taken from his chin. Gas was pumped into the room making him feel unwell. An attractive naked female humanoid joined him. She had a pointed chin, large blue catlike eyes, long white blonde hair and bright red underarm and pubic hair. They had sexual intercourse without any kissing though the female 'nipped' him on the chin. When it was over, the female smiled, rubbed her belly and gestured upwards. Boas assumed she was going to raise their child in space. Boas was allowed to dress and was shown round the craft. He tried to take a clock like device with him but was stopped from doing so. He was removed from the ship and the craft took off. He noticed that four hours had passed by. Boas suffered from nausea, weakness, loss of appetite, headaches and skin lesions. It appeared that Boas had been exposed to a large dose of radiation and was suffering from mild radiation sickness. Boas could recall details of his experience without hypnotic regression. This was some years before the famous Hill abduction in 1951 which popularised ideas of alien abduction. Antonio Vilas Boas later became a lawyer and married. The couple had four children. He maintained that his story was truthful for his entire life.

In 1961 Betty and Barney Hill claimed to have been abducted by extraterrestrials in a rural area of New Hampshire. Barney (1922–1969) was employed by the U.S. Postal Service and was an African-American. Betty (1919–2004) was a social worker of European extract. The Hills were driving back to their home in Portsmouth from a vacation in Niagara Falls and Montreal. At about 10-30 pm, Betty observed a moving bright light in the sky. The Hills claimed that they continued driving on an isolated section of route three and about a mile south of Indian Head an object rapidly descended towards their vehicle. Barney stopped in the middle of the highway. About eight to eleven humanoid figures wearing glossy black uniforms and black caps peered out of the craft's windows. The couple were frightened and Barney drove away at high speed. After hearing buzzing sounds they found they had travelled nearly thirty-five miles with no conscious memories of the journey. They noted damage to their clothes and marks on their car. Betty believed that Barney had turned off route three. Betty telephoned Pease Air Force Base to report their UFO encounter and they were subsequently interviewed. Betty began having a series of vivid dreams in which she and Barney walked up a ramp into a disc shaped metallic craft. The beings she encountered communicated by 'thought transfer'. Physical examinations were undertaken and they were told their memories would be blocked. Barney had similar dreams and later in an emotional hypnosis session recalled pulling off the road and driving into the woods where he encountered non-human figures who resembled the grey aliens of present day popular culture. The Hills were referred to Dr Benjamin Simon of Boston for regression hypnosis. Under hypnosis, they recalled various painful examinations including their genitals. Betty sketched a 'star map' she had seen on the ship. In 1968, Marjorie Fish deciphered the map as matching the double star system zeta reticuli. Barney died of a cerebral haemorrhage on February 25th 1969, at age forty six. Betty Hill passed away from cancer on October 17th 2004, at age eighty five.

Betty Andreasson Luca (a devout Christian) claimed she was abducted and taken before a 'Being of Light' where she experienced undisclosed religious ecstasy. In 1967 she was in her kitchen at South Ashburnham, Massachusetts, while her seven children, mother, and father were in the living room. The house lights went out and blinking orange/red lights appeared outside the pantry window. Five small humanoid creatures passed through the wooden door and entered the house. The floating grey beings were four to five feet tall and wore a coverall blue uniform adorned with a belt. They had pear shaped heads, wraparound eyes and diminutive noses and ears. They could communicate by telepathy. The beings radiated a friendly and reassuring aura when she became concerned for her family's well-being. Betty was taken on board a small craft which took off and merged with a larger parent craft. She was given a physical examination with equipment she did not recognise. During this abduction she interpreted the event as an angelic, religious awakening. She was returned home at 10-40 pm and recalled very limited memories of what happened. Her family seemed to have been in some kind of suspended animation. Betty responded to a local newspaper story about UFOs and contacted researcher Dr J Allen Hynek but her story was forgotten until an investigation in January 1977. A professional hypnotist and medical doctor investigated the case for twelve months. Under regression hypnosis by Dr Edlestien, Betty and also her eleven-year old daughter, confirmed her UFO experiences.

A sixteen year old boy Ted Davenport felt the need to go backpacking alone in June 1975. He subsequently went up the mountains near Alamogordo, New Mexico. He made camp but later saw two beings approaching his tent, after which he 'lost time'. He claimed to have been abducted and suffered several further similar multiple abductions. In 1990 he believed he was shown three alien-human hybrid girls who may have been his daughters from earlier abductions. He had noticed a weird 'knot' on the left side of his skull at the level of his ear since 1975 but in the early 2000s following an MRI scan, an implant 'device' was noted within a brain fissure.

Travis Walton was born on February 10th, 1953. He worked as a logger in the Apache-Sitgreaves National Forest in Arizona. In 1975, the twenty two year old Walton was employed by Mike Rogers who was contracted with the United States Forest Service. Walton in due course married Rogers's sister, Dana. The logging crew was composed of Ken Peterson, John Goulette, Steve Pierce, Allen Dallis and Dwayne Smith who lived in Snowflake, Arizona. Just after 6 pm on November 5th 1975, the crew finished work and got into Rogers's truck. As they drove homewards they saw a bright yellowish light behind a hill and shortly afterwards saw a large golden disc about twenty feet in diameter and eight feet high hovering above a clearing. Rogers stopped the truck and Walton ran towards the object despite the others shouting at him to come back. The disc shaped object started to make a noise, wobbled and emitted a blue-green light. Walton was struck by the beam and lifted off the ground with his arms and legs outstretched before his body fell limply to the ground. The crew sped off but at 7-30 pm Peterson called police to report one of their logging crew missing. Some of the group were in tears but Rogers insisted on returning to the scene immediately to search for Walton. The law enforcement officers became suspicious of foul play. They suspected an accident or homicide. If Walton was lost he might become a victim of hypothermia. Police and volunteers searched the area where Walton went missing but there was no sign of him. Police stepped up their search with helicopters, officers on horseback and jeeps.

In due course Walton returned after having gone missing for five days. His story made the news and received a lot of publicity. A medical examination revealed that Walton was in good health but two unusual features were noted. He had a small red spot at the right elbow that was consistent with a hypodermic injection but not near a vein. His urine revealed a lack of ketones. Ketone production should have been expected due to fat breakdown corresponding to starvation and his drop in body weight.

When he woke up in the UFO, Walton recalled he was on a reclining bed with an overhead bright light. The air was heavy. He was wet and in pain. Breathing was difficult. Three figures wearing orange jumpsuits were present. They resembled the now well documented grey aliens with foetal like large bald heads, dark eyes and small ears, noses and mouths. Walton threatened them and they withdrew. He entered a room and sat in a chair and pushed a lever. This caused stars to rotate around him as if in a planetarium. He then saw a human-looking being in blue coveralls and wearing a helmet. He followed the man down a steep ramp to a large hangar like room where he observed a number of disc shaped craft. The man took him to another room in which he encountered a woman and two men. The female placed a mask over his face and he passed out only to awake outside a fuel station in Heber, Arizona. A disc shaped craft hovered above the highway and quickly sped away. Walton stumbled to a public phone and called his brother-in-law, Grant Neff. He thought that only a few hours had passed but he had been missing for five days.

In due course Travis Walton underwent regression hypnosis by James A. Harder. Walton could only account for about two hours of his missing five days. Walton told Sheriff Gillespie that he was willing to take a polygraph test to support his account. Eventually a test was run by John J McCarthy of the Arizona Polygraph Laboratory. The results were contested and criticised but the examiner believed the events described by Walton to be hoaxed. Walton later took and passed two additional polygraph tests. A well known UFO debunker Philip J. Klass argued that Walton had a financial motive regarding the affair though others contested these views. In 1978, Walton published a book, *The Walton Experience*, in which he outlined his account of the events. In 1993, Walton's book was adapted into a film, *Fire in the Sky*. It was directed by Robert Lieberman. D. B. Sweeney played Travis Walton, Robert Patrick took the part of Mike Rogers and Scott MacDonald played Walton's brother, Dan Walton. Walton, Mike Rogers and Allen Dallis agreed to take further polygraph examinations conducted by Cy Gilson. Gilson concluded that all three men were truthful.

A brief mention is made next of what is known as the Allagash Abduction in the area of Maine that occurred in 1976. It is worthy of note because it is one of the few cases of 'multiple abduction'. It happened during a camping and fishing trip. Twins Jim Weiner and Jack Weiner along with Charles Foltz and Charles Rak claimed they were abducted by beings with four fingers and almond shaped eyes. They were taken on board a UFO and subjected to physical tests and probes. Interestingly, all the men gave similar accounts of the incident under regression hypnosis. The four men began their vacation and reached Eagle Lake by canoe. They decided to do some night fishing later on so they built a large campfire as a landmark they would be able to see from the water. A while later they observed a glowing orb about eighty feet in diameter hovering over the trees a couple of hundred yards away which was changing colour. Charlie Foltz signalled an SOS with his torch and the object silently moved toward the canoe across the tops of the trees. They desperately paddled towards the bank but were hit by a light beam from the craft after which they found themselves standing on the bank. Their glowing fire was gone and left as smouldering ashes which would have taken some hours to burn out. They did not know how the missing time had passed. The men had unpleasant dreams but it was not until around 1988 that they attended hypnotic sessions which suggested that they had been abducted. Skin and bodily fluid samples had been taken.

A fascinating abduction incident relates to Chilean army corporal Armando Valdés Garrido in 1977. He was on guard duty in the hills of Pampas Lluscuma in Northern Chile. The patrol included Garrido and seven colleagues. It was a cold night and the soldiers started a campfire in a military stables to keep warm. Two soldiers prevented the horses escaping. The soldiers noticed a powerful white light descending behind a hill. Shortly afterwards, an apparently different 'light' appeared at about 1640 feet away which became observable as a violet coloured oval craft. It was estimated to be about eighty two feet in diameter. Two luminous regions had flashing red 'beacons'. The soldiers opened fire but the object approached and illuminated them. At 4-15 am Garrido disappeared in a mist. Fifteen minutes later he reappeared accompanied by the sound of 'falling to ground'. He had sprouted substantial beard growth and his watch indicated that he had been gone for five days. The digital watch indicated the date of April 30th, 1977, five days into the future. In due course Garrido was taken for medical and psychiatric checkups.

Louis Whitley Strieber was born into a Catholic family in San Antonio, Texas, on June 13th, 1945. He became famous for various horror novels and his book Communion which related experiences with non-human entities. Strieber claimed he was abducted from his cabin by small beings referred to as 'visitors'. This occurred in upstate New York on the evening of December 26th, 1985. Since the 1987 publication of *Communion*, Strieber wrote four additional autobiographical books discussing his repeating experiences with the visitors, including *Transformation* in 1988. He claims the stories are real and not fictional. Streiber also claimed to have had anomalous childhood experiences. He did not put his experiences down to 'aliens', he did not know the origin of the visitors. He was tested for temporal lobe epilepsy and other brain disorders but no malfunctions were diagnosed. In the early hours of June 6th in 1998, he claimed he was visited in a Toronto hotel room by a man called Michael, referred to subsequently as the 'Master of the Key'. The stranger informed him that humans have an electron in front of their foreheads which was their soul. He also warned of forthcoming environmental problems. Strieber and his wife Anne made a cameo appearance in the 2009 movie *Race to Witch Mountain*.

An extremely controversial case of alleged alien abduction was the Manhattan incident. This case had some unique aspects to it. The abduction was reported as having taken place at about 3 am on November 30th, 1989. The subject of this abduction was Linda Cortile Napolitano. She claimed that small grey aliens floated her through a closed bedroom window into an overhead hovering UFO above her apartment. She recalled only part of the experience and sought help from researcher Budd Hopkins who used regression hypnosis in an attempt to bring out her hidden memories. She did remember entering the craft and lying on a table before having a medical examination.

It is what happened more than a year later that made this case so compelling. Hopkins received correspondence from two men called Richard and Dan who claimed to have witnessed the abduction. They were later revealed to be CIA agents. The two men were bodyguards of a senior diplomat from the United Nations who was on a visit to Manhattan. This diplomat was eventually identified as Javier Perez de Cuellar. The men said that he was shocked at viewing the abduction scene. Apparently they saw three entities accompanying Linda as she floated upwards into the UFO. Javier Perez de Cuellar was the former Secretary General of the United Nations. Cuellar corresponded with Hopkins and verified that he observed the abduction. Hopkins tried to get Cuellar to go public as it would open up the subject of abduction to serious scrutiny by the public and scientists. Cuellar apparently met privately with Hopkins but insisted on remaining anonymous.

Stan Romanek is an author and UFO enthusiast who claimed to have been abducted by a UFO in 2000. Since then he says he found strange bodily wounds and claims his body glowed under a 'black light'. He claims he has been able to communicate with aliens through a 'Ghost Box'. Intriguingly, he claims to have been returned from some abduction experiences in the wrong clothing including female garments. He even suspected that he had returned with a flannel gown which had belonged to a previous abductee, Betty Hill. In 2009, Romanek underwent hypnosis by Dr R. Leo Sprinkle. Dr Sprinkle had extensive experience with patients in alien abduction cases in his role as a psychologist. During hypnosis, Romanek wrote out the Drake Equation. This formula is used to estimate the number of planets in the galaxy that could harbour intelligent life. In 2008, Romanek appeared on the *Larry King Live* show and claimed to have recorded a video of an alien peering through his window. This has been called the 'Boo Video'. In May 2008 during an interview on Coast To Coast radio, it was suggested that Romanek take a lie detector test over the authenticity of the Boo Video and this was conducted later that year. He took the test but failed on the question "Is the Boo tape a hoax?" Romanek claimed this was due to a medical condition. In 2009 in an interview on ABC Primetime, Romanek said he had an alien implant in his leg which would provide evidence of his abductions. However, he later claimed it had disappeared when a medical examination was requested.

Thousands of people from around the world believe they have been abducted by alien beings and taken on board UFOs. Most cases emanate from the USA but by no means all of them. However, most abductees recount a similar story of what happened to them. Many abductees had no previous knowledge of UFOs or abduction cases. The question arises as to why people from various classes of society, differing jobs and from varied cultures all report similar experiences. Some phenomenon is clearly occurring be it real or psychological. Abductees are rarely diagnosed with medical or mental illness which accounts for their experiences. Neuroscientists and psychologists have claimed various causes for abduction experiences which include false (screen) memories, abnormal activity in the temporal lobes of the brain and sleep paralysis.

Betty and Barney Hill referred to earlier claimed to have undergone an abduction experience in 1961. After some time suffering with poor sleep and disturbing dreams, they were referred to a psychiatrist named Dr Benjamin Simon, from Boston. He hypnotically regressed the couple trying not to instill any clues from himself which might trigger false memories by suggestibility. The couple were regressed in separate sessions which were recorded on voicetape. They were asked about what they had seen both outside and inside the UFO. Dr Simon did not believe in UFOs but he did think the couple had seen 'something'. The couple may have been sharing Betty's dream experiences.

Dr David Jacobs, an American historian at Temple University, is well known in the field of Ufology for his research and books on the subject of alleged alien abductions and UFOs in American culture. Jacobs research includes hypnotic regression with alleged alien abductees. His research revealed that alien-human hybrids may be engaged in a covert programme to infiltrate human society. The end result might be that the Earth becomes taken over. These hybrids may have blended into human society and cannot be differentiated from normal humans.

Dr John E. Mack (October 4th 1929–September 27th 2004) was a prominent American psychiatrist, writer and professor at Harvard Medical School who became well known for studying spiritual changes following alleged alien abductions. He also interviewed many prominent political figures. He studied about 200 men and women who claimed to have repeating alien encounter experiences and abductions. His initial assumption was that these patients had mental illness but no pathologies came to light. He found many patients developed a heightened sense of spirituality and environmental awareness and concern. He was unable to fully account for the phenomena.

Budd Hopkins (June 15th 1931–August 21st 2011) was an American citizen not only well known as a painter and sculptor but was also a prominent figure in alien abduction phenomena and UFO research. In August 1964, Hopkins himself reported a daytime sighting of a dark, elliptical object off Cape Cod in Truro, Massachusetts.

Hopkins joined David M. Jacobs, history professor at Temple University, Philadelphia, and John Mack, psychiatry professor at Harvard University, Cambridge, Massachusetts, in designing a 'Roper Poll'. The aim was to discover the proportion of about 6000 respondents who might have experienced alien abductions. The poll results were released in 1991. Projected figures indicated that several million Americans claimed to have had alien abduction experiences.

Over the years, Hopkins interviewed and regressed numerous clients who related abduction experiences. Hopkins popularised the idea of alien abductions as genetic experimentation. He has been dubbed the 'father of the abduction movement'. Both men and women reported alien sexual encounter examinations. Abductees were frequently traumatised. Sometimes evidence for abduction was seen as marks and injuries on the skin. Many abductions may have been carried out for extraterrestrial eugenic purposes.

Alien Implants

Claims date back many years relating to victims of alien abductions finding physical anomalies within their bodies. Early reports referred to controlling earphones. Betty Andreasson claimed she had been abducted in 1967. A device was placed up her nose during this encounter. Ted Davenport following a claimed abduction in 1975 near Alamogordo, New Mexico, later had a MRI scan which revealed an object in a brain fissure. British abductee Mark Rowtly claimed he became unable to move in his bedroom and was subsequently abducted by three beings who surgically placed 'something' in his ear. There has been much speculation about the function of such implants including mind control, monitoring of movements, DNA evaluation, communication and many more.

Dr Roger K. Leir was a podiatric surgeon who was in private practice in Ventura County, California, for nearly fifty years. He was known as an investigator of alien implants and as a well known UFO investigator. Initially he was sceptical about the foreign objects found in his patients but he came to believe they were of extraterrestrial origins. He described how some objects moved during surgery. Dr Leir suggested they might send or receive radio signals. He performed about seventeen surgeries on alleged alien abductees. Anomalous objects were removed that were buried in deep tissue but surrounded by the skin of the host. Many of the objects he removed were sent to prestigious laboratories around the world for scientific study. One of the objects is said to have become invisible to X-rays following a pass in an X-ray diffraction device. Implanted objects were made of various materials but were often metallic or combinations of metal compounds. Some implants contained silicon and trace metals. Dr Leir passed away in March of 2014.

Dr John E. Mack (October 4th 1929–September 27th 2004) claimed to have examined a small wirelike object. It had come from the nose of a young woman who claimed to have been abducted. Dr Mack visited England for a conference but unfortunately suffered an untimely death when he was killed by a drunken driver in London. Dr Mack is discussed in more depth in the section above on Regression Hypnosis.

Psychological Aspects

So-called victims of alien abductions are often afraid of coming forward due to fear of ridicule or concerns over job prospects. The same applies to people who have seen strange craft or entities. Some people may even doubt their own sanity though most have shown no indications of mental illness. Sometimes regression hypnotic analysis (discussed above) opens the door to many suppressed memories. The question arises as to whether the experiences are real or imagined.

Michael Persinger worked as a cognitive neuroscience researcher at Laurentian University in Sudbury, Ontario. He used electrodes to stimulate various brain areas. Many subjects experienced near-death experiences, out-of-the-body experiences, alien abduction experiences and others. Abduction experiences may be related to states of sleep disturbance including 'sleep paralysis' or mild brain seizures. In a 'hypnagogic state', subjects were unable to move. They often felt some sort of presence, fear and were unable to speak or cry out. The issue of whether experiences and observations are real or imagined is still open to debate.

Philip J. Klass (November 8th 1919–August 9th 2005) was an American engineer and journalist He was also a zealous UFO debunker, known for his scepticism. He believed most observers were honest people that had seen something unusual (often at night) but were psychologically mistaken in their interpretation of what they saw. A few may have been hoaxers. An example of his debunking claims occurred when he noticed that some UFO incidents near Exeter in New Hampshire manifested near power lines and he ascribed the sightings to an unknown type of plasma or ball lightning. In 1966, Klass made a financial challenge that evolved into an offer to pay out a sum of money to anyone who could definitively prove the existence of a crashed alien spacecraft or extraterrestrial visitor. However, the party accepting this offer had to pay Klass $100 per year (for a maximum of ten years) each year that none of these things occurred.

Paul Devereux became well known for writing about hypothetical energy lines around the Earth called 'Ley lines'. He also assumed that observations of UFOs were down to people making psychological misinterpretations of what they saw and they also had psycho-social causes. He maintained that geological pressures and strains (especially where quartz occurs in the ground) gave rise to Earthlights or Earthquake lights which were mistaken for UFOs. This was quite common in the vicinity of volcanoes. The actual cause was piezo-electricity which is an electric charge that accumulates in certain solid materials such as crystals as a response to mechanical stress.

Some Miscelleneous Interesting Anomalies, Observations and Events

During World War II, Heinrich Himmler (7th October 1900–23rd May 1945) was Reichsführer of the Schutzstaffel (SS) and a military commander. He was a leading member of the Nazi Party and one of the people responsible for the Holocaust. Himmler was an advocate of an occult group. This Berlin group called itself The Luminous Lodge or The Vril Society. The group may have had links with 'Nazi UFOs'. Some members claimed that Hitler and Nazi Germany had made contact with an alien race. With alien cooperation, the Vril Society developed a number of flying disc prototypes. When the war was lost, the society allegedly retreated to a base in Antarctica. They then entered inside the 'hollow Earth' where they met leaders of an advanced race inhabiting the inner Earth.

Die Glocke or Nazi Bell was a purported top secret Nazi secret weapon or Wunderwaffe. It is associated with Nazi occultism, antigravity and free energy research. This device allegedly was developed at a facility not far from the Czech border known as Der Riese ("The Giant"). Die Glocke was supposedly a device made of metal about nine feet wide and fifteen feet high. It contained two counter rotating cylinders filled with a violet mercury like substance. It released dangerous radiation when activated and this caused several deaths. Die Glocke was sited in the ruined remnants of a concrete framework called 'The Henge'. There are claims that this device could undertake time travel and some say it was recovered in the Kecksburg UFO incident at Pennsylvania, USA, on December 9th, 1965. Italian Professor Giuseppe Belluzzo (once a government minister under Mussolini), claimed that various types of flying discs were designed in Germany and Italy as early as 1942.

During World War II, both allied and axis pilots were troubled by 'foo fighters'. These were orbs of light that followed aircraft and manoeuvred around them. Sometimes they caused electromagnetic disruption to control systems. They were considered by both sides as possible secret weapons. They could not be shot down and appeared to be intelligently controlled. Electrical discharge from the airplane wings called St. Elmo's Fire has been suggested as an explanation. Ball lightning was another possibility.

After the war, many leading German scientists were relocated to Russia and the USA. Many of these had worked on V1 and V2 rocket weapons, such as Wernher von Braun (March 23rd 1912–June 16th 1977). Scientists such as these contributed to later space age rocket science.

During the 1940s, troops from Nazi Germany set up a base in the Antarctic. Conspiracy theories suggest that Hitler was in some kind of loose alliance with aliens that had entry to the 'hollow Earth' through an opening or a portal in this region. It is certain that an American fleet did visit the region and entered into combat. Casualties were reported. It has been claimed that a 'threatening' UFO was seen emerging from and returning to the area and this is why there was no return by the fleet having left. 'Operation Highjump' (1946–1947) to the polar region was organised by Rear Admiral Richard E. Byrd Jr and led by Rear Admiral Richard H. Cruzen. This Task Force included 4700 men, thirteen ships and multiple aircraft.

Interestingly, in 1952, Britain's wartime Prime Minister Sir Winston Churchill sent the famous 'Churchill Memorandum' to Lord Cherwell, Secretary of State for Air. Churchill asked "What does all this stuff about flying saucers amount to? What can it mean? What is the truth? Let me have a report at your convenience." It was suggested that observations of flying saucers were due to astronomical or meteorological phenomena and mistaken identification of conventional aircraft, balloons and birds.

In 1953, Avro Canada announced that it was developing the VZ-9-AV Avrocar. This was a circular jet aircraft resembling a flying disc. It was hoped to fly the craft at a speed of 1500 mph but there were many problems with stability.

German engineer Georg Klein claimed that such designs had previously been developed by the Third Reich.

During the second World War, about three months after the Japanese attack on Pearl Harbour, an unusual event took place from the 24th February to 25th February, 1942. This involved an anti-aircraft artillery barrage over the city of Los Angeles, California. The incident is commonly called the Battle of Los Angeles or the Great Los Angeles Air Raid. The events which unfolded appear to be military 'false alarm' responses to a Japanese aerial attack. During the incident, air raid sirens sounded, there was a total blackout and air raid wardens rushed to their posts. Buildings and vehicles were damaged as an indirect result of the firing and falling shell fragments. A few deaths were also recorded. Some people claim that the aerial targets seen were UFOs.

During the late 1940s and in the 1950s, UFO sightings became more common. The 'contactee' movement grew with more and more people claiming to have direct links to alien visitors. Corresponding to this were popularised UFO conventions. In the 1950s, a number of conventions were organised by George Van Tassel. A popular location was at Giant Rock near a town called Landers in the Mojave Desert, California. In 1959, there were over 10,000 attendees. Restaurants, speakers and stalls were organised. Some guests arrived by plane and the conventions attracted celebrities like Howard Hughes. Back in 1953, Van Tassel held meditation sessions in the rooms beneath the rock. He claimed he could communicate with extraterrestrials and that a craft from Venus had landed near the rock. The occupants revealed technology to him which could aid healing processes. This resulted in Van Tassel trying to build a healing device called the 'Integratron' but he passed away in 1978 before it could be completed.

An interesting event occurred in 1954 about three years before the launch of Sputnik 1 from the Soviet Union. Major

Donald E. Keyhoe's statement about a satellite (possibly two) orbiting the Earth was picked up and published in various newspapers. The White Sands government research facility in New Mexico tried to determine what exactly this object(s) was. The Pentagon had defence concerns as to what the object(s) could be and who had done the launching. Artificial satellites were generally launched west to east following the Earth's orbit but one of these objects in particular did not move west to east but travelled along polar orbits. It also moved at an unusually fast speed. This satellite was called the Black Knight. There have been suggestions that this object has relevance to reports from Nikola Tesla who claimed to have picked up a repeating radio signal in 1899 coming from space. Some believe that the Black Knight is of alien origin and might be approximately 13,000 years old. The Black Knight satellite should not be confused with the Keyhole satellite. The latter is an American reconnaissance and spy satellite first launched in December 1976. It used an electro-optical digital imaging technology. Later updated versions are believed to resemble the Hubble space telescope in size and shape.

The Dogon are a tribal group living in Mali, West Africa. They are well known for their religious traditions and masked dances. Researchers investigating the Dogon reported that they seemed to possess advanced astronomical knowledge. Around 1930, French anthropologists heard legends from the Dogon priests which had been passed down through many generations. The Dogon spoke of a visitation by a race called the Nommos from the Sirius Star System. They were aquatic humanoid creatures, similar to mermaids, who descended from the heavens in a large boat with accompanying wind and noise. These visitors may have passed on some of their knowledge to the tribe. The Dogon believed that the brightest star in the sky, Sirius A, had a companion star. Artefacts over 400 years old depicted the orbits of these stars. The tribe had no instruments to view virtually invisible stars. In 1970, new powerful telescopes were used to observe Sirius and they identified a companion star, Sirius B. Sirius was indeed a binary system. The Dogon also appeared to know of the rings of Saturn and the moons of Jupiter.

A rather unusual event occurred in 1964. A fireman named Jim Templeton (13th February 1920–27th November 2011) took a famous photo on Burgh Marsh near Burgh-by-Sands, England. The picture of his five year old daughter Elizabeth came back from the developer Kodak showing what appeared to be a spaceman in the background. Tests confirmed that the photograph was likely to be genuine. Templeton claimed no-one else was in view when the photo was taken. The picture was taken to the police in Carlisle who examined it. The story became worldwide news. Templeton claimed after the photograph was published that he was visited and questioned by two men in black clothes who said they were from the government. However, they refused to show any identification. Templeton's picture became known as the Solway Firth Spaceman photo.

A fleeting mention is made here on what became called 'The Great North East Blackout' which occurred on Tuesday, November 9th, 1965. There was a significant disruption in the supply of electricity affecting parts of Ontario in Canada and several states in the USA covering an area of 80,000 square miles. Thirty million people or more were left without electricity for up to thirteen hours. The failure was probably caused by maintenance personnel who apparently set a protective relay incorrectly. However, some people believe the power loss was caused by a UFO. Sightings of UFOs had been made near Syracuse in Onondaga County, New York, prior to the blackout. The *New York Times* covered the story of these sightings and published a photo showing an apparent UFO on November 19th. The blackout connection was brought in front of Congress and Dr James E. McDonald, a top Ufologist of that time, testified regarding possible electromagnetic effects of UFOs. President Lyndon B. Johnson was at his Texas ranch at the time of the blackout. He was recovering from an operation to remove his gall bladder and a kidney stone and heard of the blackout while away from the ranch on his car radio. The President phoned Buford Ellington (the Director of the Office of Emergency Planning who was responsible for dealing with the blackout). Interestingly, he also phoned Robert McNamara, his Secretary of Defence. This suggests possible concerns over a 'UFO threat'.

So-called 'Star Children' were described in the 1960s having a maturity and wisdom beyond their years. They had telepathic abilities, clairvoyance and healing powers. They often described seeing "Beings of Light" or angels. Star Children had recollections of encounters with extraterrestrial beings and sometimes having been on alien spaceships. The concept of so-called 'Indigo Children' developed in the 1970s. They are alleged to have a blue indigo coloured aura that some people say they can see around them. These children also possessed special and sometimes supernatural abilities like telepathy. Such children had a high IQ, were empathetic, curious, strong willed, had great spirituality and a sense of purpose and entitlement. They were sometimes considered strange by their peers. The children may be the next stage in human evolution.

In 2001, heavy downpours of red blood coloured rain fell on the southern Indian state of Kerala. It was initially thought that the rains were coloured by fallout from a meteor burst but light microscope studies concluded that the rains had been coloured by airborne algal spores. In 2006, the coloured rains of Kerala gained publicity when the media reported a controversial claim that the coloured particles in the rainwater were extraterrestrial cells. Red rains were also reported in 2012 falling on eastern and north-central provinces of Sri Lanka.

A brief mention is made next relating to 'star jelly'. This is a gelatinous material which has been found as a coating on grass and leaves. On occasions it has been found in quite large clumps. Various colours have been reported but it seems to be non-toxic material. A range of terrestrial origins have been ascribed to star jelly including frog spawn, slime moulds and blue-green algae such as *Nostoc*. It has been seen to fall from the sky sometimes when meteor showers are in progress. An article in a paranormal magazine suggested that star jelly had an extraterrestrial origin referred to as "cellular organic matter" existing as "pre-stellar molecular clouds" floating through space.

'Angel hair' is a fibrous substance associated with UFO sightings. It resembles a spider's cobweb and quickly disappears after forming. Some theorise that it becomes created by ionized air 'sleeting off' the electromagnetic field that surrounds some UFOs. Angel hair formed during sightings at various locations in New Zealand and Australia during and beyond the 1950s. It was also seen at Oloron in France in 1952, Venice in Italy in 1954 and Évora in Portugal in 1959. Another occurrence was in Polonnaruwa in Sri Lanka on October 20th, 2014. Older instances were reported during the Miracle at Fatima during September and October 1917 and in 1561 during a celestial phenomenon over Nuremberg (discussed elsewhere in this book).

A very strange and unusual event took place at 5-10 pm on 26th November 1977 which most people assume was a hoax though this was never proven. A Southern Television broadcast in England was interrupted for about six minutes. A voice accompanied by buzzing and humming sounds overpowered the UHF audio signal of the early evening news being read by Andrew Gardner. The speaker claimed his voice was that of

Asteron (though some reports refer to Vrillon) of the Ashtar Galactic Command, who claimed to be an authorised representative of the Intergalactic Mission. The speaker said that the world was entering the period of Aquarius and evil Earth weapons had to be destroyed. There was only a short time for people to learn to live together in peace or else leave the galaxy. The incident caused some local alarm and was reported around the world.

An uncopyrighted treatise called the Blue Planet Project was published in the 1990s by an anonymous author which was supposedly government property. It was based on a researcher or scientist named Jefferson Souza whose actual existence is uncertain. It has been claimed that he attended a UFO conference, possibly the International UFO Congress held in Tucson Arizona in May 1991. Souza purportedly had information disclosing details of corporate companies developing gravity assisted technology helicopters and having involvement with cattle mutilations (see later section). Souza was supposedly beaten up and put on a flight to New York and his documents forcibly taken away by four MIB (Men in Black). MIB are also discussed further in another section of the book. Jefferson Souza subsequently 'went missing' or into hiding. Some believe he suffered foul play, injury or worse, though some online posts have claimed to have originated from Souza.

A strange unidentified underwater sound heard in 1997 is mentioned very briefly. It had ultra low frequency and was extremely powerful. This sound has become known as the 'Bloop'. It was detected by the U.S. National Oceanic and Atmospheric Administration (NOAA). The sound was heard several times from a remote region of the South Pacific Ocean west of the tip of South America. The sound did not appear to be manmade or of geological origin. One suggestion ascribed it to an icequake. The audio profile, however, resembled that of a living creature but was several times louder than the loudest recorded animal, the blue whale. There has been speculation as to whether the sound came from some exotic creature, possibly of alien origin.

Around 2009, Indian scientists claimed there were bacteria in the stratosphere which were resistant to ultraviolet light originating from outer space. Normally the ozone layer protects life on Earth against such radiation but there have been concerns regarding ozone depletion over the years. Three new species of bacteria claimed not to be found on Earth were discovered in samples collected through a balloon sent up to the stratosphere. The implication is that these bacteria might be alien in origin though this is disputed by various astrobiologists including a group in Washington.

In 2009 in the area of Trondheim, Norway, a spiral was seen in the night sky. It consisted of a blue beam of light with a grey spiral emanating from one end. There was initial speculation that it was a meteor. It was later suggested to be a failed Russian Bulava missile test. UFO enthusiasts speculated that the aerial lights might be evidence of extraterrestrial activity or a wormhole or portal opening up.

The Ararat anomaly is an object located near the summit of Mount Ararat, Turkey, at about 15,500 feet high, on a steep slope. Some proclaim it is the remains of Noah's Ark. It was originally observed during a U.S. Air Force aerial reconnaissance mission in 1949. Biblical Genesis 8:4 says that the Ark landed on "the mountains of Ararat" and, besides the religious connection, some believe this gives the object some kind of association with UFO activity.

In 2011, a strange rock like formation was discovered by a diving team on the Swedish ship *Ocean X*. The anomaly was discovered by Peter Lindberg and Dennis Åsberg. A 200 feet (sixty metre) structure was seen resting on a pillar of rock which appeared to have a staircase leading to a hole. The sea bed behind the rock was disturbed and looked like in the past an object had crashed and gauged out the sea bed, leaving a 980 feet (300 metre) 'runway'. A while after the 'object' was discovered a second smaller object was found nearby. These objects are referred to as the 'Baltic Sea Anomaly'. Various suggestions have been given as to the nature of the objects including a submarine turret, sunken fishing gear or ancient crashed flying saucers. Rock samples have been analysed and sonar images taken but geologists disagree as to whether the chemical nature of the rock formed naturally or unnaturally.

Strange Artefacts

The Piri Reis map is a world map compiled in 1513 by an Ottoman admiral and cartographer of which about one third survives. It was found in 1929 and drawn on gazelle skin. The map shows the western coasts of Europe and North Africa, the coast of Brazil, the eastern coast of South America and the northern coast of Antarctica. It claims to have used Columbus's lost maps as a source. The accurate map was drawn of the Antarctic 300 years before it was discovered with coastline below the ice which would have been impossible to chart as the last time it was free of an ice covering was about 40,000 BC. There has been a lot of speculation as to which civilization would have had a sufficient advanced technology to carry out the mapping and the possibility has been raised of extraterrestrial involvement.

Excavations of a 2000 year old village near Baghdad in 1936 revealed a surprising discovery. This was a small pot made of bright yellow clay found to be a couple of thousand years old. It contained a cylinder made of copper soldered with a lead-tin alloy. The bottom was sealed and insulated from a suspended central iron rod showing signs of acidic corrosion. This ancient Baghdad battery generated a voltage when filled with grape juice. It appears that electric batteries were used 1800 years before their modern invention by Alessandro Volta in 1799. There is speculation that the knowledge to produce such technology may have been passed on to the Persian population by an extraterrestrial source.

In 1938 the so-named Dropa stones (up to 716 of them) were found in the mountains of Bayan Kara-Ula, on the borders of China and Tibet. Some people claim they date back 12,000 years. In 1958, the stones were passed to Tsum Um Nui in China to study. These objects are discs with a central hole. Grooves in them were visible with a magnifying glass. It was suggested that these grooves were tiny hieroglyphs. Tsum Um Nui claimed later in 1962 that these told of a spacecraft crash landing on the Earth. People called the Dropa were marooned and had to adapt to living on the Earth. However, they were often hunted and killed by local tribal people called the Han because they were ugly yellow faced people with bulging heads and weakly developed bodies. They had to resort to hiding away in caves.

The Voynich manuscript is illustrated and handwritten in an unknown writing system. It is made of vellum and dates from early fifteenth century northern Italy. A Polish book dealer called Wilfrid Voynich purchased it in 1912. There are about 240 pages but some seem to be missing. Most of the pages have illustrations. Professor Stephen Bax from the University of Bedford claims some success interpreting the images including the term for Taurus. Mediaeval herbs (possibly medicinal in nature) and other plants are depicted with a picture of seven stars which may be the Pleiades constellation. The issue is whether the script is alien or not.

Klerksdorp spheres are small objects collected by miners from three billion year old deposits near Ottosdal in South Africa. Their diameter varies between 0.5 cm to 10 cm. Some are flattened spheres and others are disc shaped. Some people claim they are artefacts manufactured by intelligent entities. However, geologists have concluded that the spheres were formed by natural processes in volcanic ashes and sediments and were not manufactured.

A brief mention is made here of stone spheres discovered in the Diquis Delta of Costa Rica in the 1930s. Large numbers were found which varied in size. The smallest were just a few centimetres in diameter but some went over two metres and weighed up to sixteen tons. Some authors have suggested an extraterrestrial origin for these objects but it is perhaps more likely that they are monolithic sculptures made by humans. Estimates of their age have been suggested by some people to range from 200 BC to AD 800.

Thirteen crystal skulls have been found in parts of Mexico, Central America and South America. These quartz skulls were found near the ancient ruins of Mayan and Aztec civilizations. They have been ascribed with great knowledge, magical powers and healing properties. Some people believe they have inter-dimensional communication properties. Of the thirteen original skulls, twelve have been identified in various collections and the remaining one may be a 'backup' containing the collective knowledge within all the skulls. Some of the skulls may be between 5000 and 36,000 years old. It is surprising that the skulls were not damaged during their construction. There have been many ideas put forward as to the origin of these skulls including an extraterrestrial hypothesis, though there are claims that the skulls are modern or fakes. Some people believe that each skull derives from different planets including the Earth. There has been research done to investigate their electrical properties and effect on people. There have been claims the skulls contain secret coded images and information and some people report that they glow in the dark.

Some very old artefacts are mentioned next which either date from Biblical times or are described in the Bible. Some believe these artefacts may have come into being with the help of extraterrestrial influences or could have been associated with such activities. The first artefact is the Copper Scroll. This is one of 981 texts discovered between 1946 and 1956 at Khirbet Qumran. This is an archaeological site on the West Bank near the Israeli settlement and kibbutz at Kalya. These texts are a part of those commonly known as the Dead Sea Scrolls. Scrolls generally were written on either parchment or papyrus but these were made of thin sheets of rolled up copper. The writing appears to be a treasure map indicating more than sixty different locations where gold and silver was said to be buried or hidden.

The second artefact is called the Shamir. King Solomon is said to have used it in the building of the First Temple in Jerusalem. It was deemed that tools used for war or bloodshed must not be used to cut and shape materials. Stone, wood and metal were affected by being 'shown to the Shamir'. The Shamir may also have been used to engrave gemstones. Some descriptions of the Shamir refer to it as a green stone which was stored for safety wrapped in wool and kept in a lead container. However, translation from Hebrew of the word Shamir refers to it as a 'worm'.

According to the Old Testament of the Bible, an army which carried the Ark of the Covenant before it would be invincible. It could level mountains and lay waste large areas of land. It has been speculated that the Ark was a device acting as some kind of an alien communicator and a weapon. The device was used to communicate with 'God' but which might in fact have been alien entities. The Ark was lethal if touched. It is believed the object was overlain with gold plates which may have had positive and negative charges so that the device acted like a capacitor and stored electrical charge. The Ark may have caused death by electrocution if touched (unless 'special clothes' were worn). It had the appearance of an ornate gold chest. The 'holiest' part of the Ark was called the 'oracle'. Audible orders to Israel from 'God' emanated from here, made via Moses. The Ark apparently generated an electrical field which could be focussed and fired. A 'fire' emerged from the Ark preceded by a 'glow' called the 'Glory of the Lord'. Sometimes a cloudy dangerous gas formed (possibly ozone) which was best avoided. The Israelites carried the Ark seven times round the city of Jericho during a siege while the priests blew rams horns until the walls collapsed. The Ark was temporarily taken by the Philistines but they suffered numerous diseases and deaths so it was returned. When at rest, the Ark was placed in its 'Holy of Holies' which perhaps enabled it to restore its charge.

NASA, Astronaut Reports, Lunar and Martian Bases and Anomalies

NASA is an abbreviation for the National Aeronautics and Space Administration. As well as being responsible for the American space programme, it has interests in aspects of aeronautics and aerospace research. It was set up in 1958 with the support of President Dwight D. Eisenhower. A number of well known space missions have been organised by NASA. A few of these include the Mercury Project, Gemini Programme, Apollo Programme, Skylab, Space Shuttle and International Space Station. The Orion Multi-Purpose Crew Vehicle and other projects have followed its predecessors.

Various anomalies old and more recent have not been fully explained by NASA. An example is the observation of lights emanating from the lunar surface. Since around 1821, trained and amateur astronomers have observed instances of illumination or reflection on the moon. A repeating source is the Earth facing Aristarchus crater. On October 13th, 1959, E.H. Rowe in Devon, United Kingdom, described a light which was "brilliantly white in colour." He also observed a short lasting "bright reddish-amber glow in or near Aristarchus." During the time between October 29th and November 27th 1963, further observations of lights were seen by the Lowell Observatory, north of a crater called Herodotus. Two groups of bright red lights were reported. Speculation arose as to the possibility of radioactive gases such as radon-222 escaping from below ground.

In recent times, NASA has been accused of airbrushing out features it does not want to disclose to the general public. This includes objects and structures on the surface of both the Moon and Mars. Similar accusations are aimed at editing voice messages between Earth controllers and astronauts, as well as tampering with films taken of anomalous objects in space.

Donna Hare (formerly Tietze) was a female slide technician who received numerous prestigious space awards from NASA for her space programme work (including the Apollo missions) making illustrations of lunar surface features, landing sites, launch sites and so on. During a Disclosure Project press conference, Hare claimed that NASA covered-up and erased anomalies such as UFOs from satellite photos. Sergeant Karl Wolfe came forward to reveal that he saw NASA photos being altered to erase lunar surface anomalies filmed from the Lunar Orbiter. An officer at Langley Air Force Base allegedly told him that a base on the dark side of the moon must be erased from film.

Claims have been made that during NASA's lunar and Martian exploration studies, undisclosed objects and buildings have been revealed. Photos and video evidence may exist, for example from the Apollo programme, as well as from various space ventures made from the Soviet Union. Richard

Hoagland believed that NASA retouch and alter materials before they are published in public catalogues and files.

There have been claims that alien bases are present on the moon. A huge triangular anomaly (spotted on Google's map of the moon) had rows of seven bright dots along its edge. This feature has been ascribed to a possible alien base or UFO. Such observations have been suggested as the reason why no further trips to the moon have taken place since the 1960s nor any attempt to establish lunar bases. NASA is a civilian agency. However, some NASA programmes are funded by defence budgets. Astronauts are most likely to be subject to military security regulations and under strict orders not to discuss their sightings overtly. It does seem likely that The National Security Agency screens all films made by astronauts and probably radio communications too.

In December 2013, the Chang'e 3 mission put China's first lunar rover down on the moon. A Chinese moon probe (Chang'e 5 T1) returned to Earth in 2014 after testing technology for a lunar sampling project. The country has aspirations of putting people on the moon in the 2020s. There have been claims that the programme may have been abandoned possibly because of encounters with extraterrestrial craft or entities.

It remains an unanswered question at the time of writing as to whether life currently exists on Mars or did exist there in the past. Water is required for life to exist as far as is known at the present time. There is evidence for the presence of frozen water on Mars. It seems at one time Mars had flowing rivers and seas but these have dried up and evaporated. Mars has also lost many components of its atmosphere to outer space perhaps due to the lack of an extensive magnetic field as on the Earth. It has been speculated that Mars once had a molten core and planetary magnetic field which may have been largely lost due to an ancient collision with an asteroid or comet. Scattered areas of magnetic field activity now exist across the Martian surface.

During 2014, NASA reported on surveys by the Curiosity and Opportunity rovers, searching for evidence of ancient life. Various claimed anomalies have been observed including a 'coffin' found by Will Farrar on an image taken by the Curiosity rover. The object is claimed to be 3.2 feet across and 1.5 feet wide. Astronomer Joe White from Bristol UK claimed footage from NASA's Curiosity rover revealed a 'pistol' lying on the Martian surface. NASA's archives have also shown a possible 'fossilised iguana' and about fifteen further animals. A certain Mr Warring claims he has observed "a rock that moved four times in four photos and which vanished on the fifth." One particular area of Mars which has caught public attention is known as Cydonia. It is here that the famous 'Face on Mars' is located. This geological feature has been ascribed to extraterrestrial activity or a lost Martian civilization.

There are various 'outlandish' claims regarding teleportation programmes between the Earth and Mars and vice versa. Undergound cities of human colonists have been claimed to exist as well as an extraterrestrial presence. An ex-naval infantryman using the pseudonym 'Captain Kaye' claimed he spent seventeen years on Mars protecting five human colonies from indigenous species. He claimed to have served in a secret 'space fleet'. This was run by a multi-national organisation called the Earth Defence Force. This organisation apparently recruits military personnel from various countries including the USA, Russia and China.

Another 'outlandish report' is included here for information and interest. After the Apollo 11 moon trip in 1969, further missions were carried out until 1972. Apollo 17 was the last mission to undertake a lunar trip. NASA planned three more missions. These were Apollo 18, Apollo 19 and Apollo 20. Due to issues relating to budget expenditure problems, the astronauts had to be directed to other projects and the missions were cancelled. A lot of hardware was left over and unused. An example is the Apollo 19 command service module (CSM) on display at the Kennedy Space Centre.

In April 2007, an individual named William Rutledge claimed to have been an astronaut. He said that NASA's Apollo 14 mission flew over a polar region of the Moon and observed spaceships and ancient cities apparently abandoned for hundreds of years. Structures were seen resembling oddly-shaped, towering buildings. His video footage also purportedly revealed views from Apollo 20. This was supposedly a secret joint American-Soviet space mission dating from August 1976.

An Italian freelance writer (Luca Scantamburlo) subsequently obtained an interview with Rutledge. He said that he and his crew on Apollo 20 landed near the Delporte Crater in order to investigate an observed 'cigar shaped' mothership. It was estimated to have been abandoned for some 1.5 million years. The astronauts found two alien bodies and captured one of them on 16 mm film. There is amazing footage of a claimed corpse of an alien girl lying in the cabin. This girl has been nicknamed 'Mona Lisa' and had six fingers, hair, but no nostrils. She was apparently retrieved and brought back to Earth.

The term 'bogey' has been used in various communications between astronauts and mission control to indicate unidentified objects in space. Anomalous objects have been seen by a variety of astronauts and also by Soviet cosmonauts. Astronaut Walter Schirra aboard Mercury 8 may have used the code name 'Santa Claus' to indicate that he observed flying saucers. James Lovell on the Apollo 8 command module in 1968 travelled out from behind the moon and stated "please be informed that there is a Santa Claus."

Gordon Cooper was born in 1927. He was an American aerospace engineer, test pilot and air force pilot. Cooper piloted the longest and final Mercury spaceflight in 1963 and in 1965 flew as Command Pilot of Gemini 5. He claimed to have seen a UFO while flying over West Germany in 1951. He also claimed to have photographed a "strange looking, saucer like aircraft" that did not make a sound either on landing or take-off in 1957 while assigned to Edwards Air Force Base in California. According to Cooper, the U.S. government covered up information about UFOs. He quoted President Harry Truman who said on April 4th, 1950 "I can assure you that flying saucers, given that they exist, are not constructed by any power on Earth." Cooper referred to hundreds of observations and reports made by military (and civil) pilots and radar or visual ground sightings.

Dr Edgar Mitchell was born in 1930 and became the astronaut who was the pilot of the Apollo 14 Lunar Module and the sixth person to walk on the Moon. He believed UFOs came from other planets and that government officials had been in contact with extraterrestrials but covered up the meetings. Around 1996, Mitchell claimed that alien bodies were recovered from the flying saucer crash at Roswell, New Mexico, in 1947 and subsequently studied. UFOs had provided "sonic engineering secrets" to the U.S. government. In 2004, he stated that briefing U.S. Presidents in such matters after John F. Kennedy had ceased. It seems that even U.S. Presidents may now be out of the loop for 'need to know' secret groups such as Majestic 12 (see section on Government Projects, Military Files, Investigations, Misinformation and Cover ups).

NASA Astronaut Neil Armstrong indicated that humans were warned to stay off the moon. It has been claimed that at a site called Luna on the far side of the moon, some kind of mining operation was going on. Motherships and smaller scout ships allegedly were based there. Some believe that both Neil Armstrong and Edwin 'Buzz' Aldrin saw UFOs shortly after their historic landing on the Moon in Apollo 11 on 21st

July, 1969. Maurice Chatelain was the former chief of NASA Communications Systems. In 1969 he apparently confirmed that Armstrong observed two UFOs on the rim of a crater. However, the issue was not discussed openly at NASA. The UFOs may have been filmed by Buzz Aldrin from within the module. It is claimed that Maurice Chatelain confirmed that some of Apollo 11's radio transmissions were interrupted in order to hide the news from the public.

Military Reports

Military pilots are trained observers and are not easily confused by sightings in the sky. However, there are numerous examples of military pilots seeing and reporting anomalous aircraft. In some cases, planes have been buzzed by UFOs which can easily out-manoeuvre conventional aircraft and speed away from them. Some early encounters of UFOs with military craft occurred during World War II. Both Allied and Axis pilots had their planes followed by mysterious orbs they called 'foo fighters' (see the section on Some Miscelleneous Interesting Anomalies, Observations and Events). There even have been fatalities related to military encounters with UFOs such as the loss of Captain Thomas F. Mantell in 1948 while chasing an unknown craft (see section on Missing Pilots and Aircraft).

An amazing sequence of events occurred during Operation Mainbrace (14th–25th September, 1952). This was a large-scale NATO exercise to simulate a Soviet invasion of Western Europe. It was carried out during the height of the 'cold war'.

On 19th September 1952 at about 11 am, a silver disc-shaped object followed a Gloster Meteor jet aircraft returning to RAF Topcliffe. It was also seen by ground observers. Witnesses say the object then hovered and rotated before quickly flying away towards the west.

On October 21st 1952, flight instructor Flight Lieutenant Michael Swiney took off in a Meteor jet from Little Rissington, Gloucestershire, with trainee Royal Navy Lieutenant David Crofts. At 15,000 feet they encountered three stationary whitish circular or saucer shaped objects. The objects quickly vanished. They had been detected as radar 'blips' but disappeared at 600-1000 mph off the coast of Kent towards the English Channel. A pair of Meteors on twenty four hour Quick Reaction Alert (QRA) duty at RAF Tangmere, Sussex, followed the radar blips but could not make physical contact with the targets. Swiney and Crofts later made drawings of the three UFOs.

A radar and visual UFO sighting was made over Tehran in Iran on the 19th September, 1976. There had been reports of a light brighter and bigger than a star in the sky. F-4 Phantom II jet fighters were scrambled from Shahrokhi Air Force Base in Hamadan but developed problems with instrumentation, communications and weapons systems failure when they tried to intercept the object. The object disappeared from view but some later accounts suggest there might have been a landing.

The Shaitan Mazar incident occurred on August 28th, 1991. An object was detected on radar screens in Turkmenistan at 21,500 feet with a speed of 600 mph. Mangishlak Base sent a 'friend or foe' warning but there was no reply. The commanding officer at nearby Kaputsin aerodrome confirmed they had also detected the UFO and said it was not one of their aircraft. A total of four Mig-29 fighter planes from various bases were scrambled to investigate. The pilots reported seeing a gigantic metallic grey coloured object 2000 feet long and 360 feet in diameter over the Aral Sea. The planes' electrical systems failed and they could not fire warning shots so they had to return to base. Radar operators continued to monitor the UFO which flew off in a zigzag pattern at 4200 mph. The object disappeared from radar screens as it went over Lake Issyk-Kul not far from the border between Kyrgyzstan and Kazakhstan.

At the end of September there were reports of a crashed object in the Tien Shan Mountains of Central Asia. The locality is called Shaitan Mazar (the Devil's Grave). An investigative expedition was sent to the area consisting of experienced mountain climbers and members of the Russian UFO group SAKKUFON. The team leader was researcher Anton Bogatov. Rumours suggested that the local villagers suffered burns. They also reported watches stopping and unusually high levels of static electricity. The team had to turn back due to harsh weather conditions but there are claims that military forces located the crash site in November 1991 and found the remains of a crashed UFO. A military helicopter supposedly attempted to hoist part of the UFO aboard but crashed. Everyone on the helicopter died.

Pilot Reports

There are innumerable reports of civil and military pilots observing UFOs. Planes have been 'buzzed' and followed. UFOs have circled around aircraft in flight and headed directly head on but swerved away at the last moment. There are numerous recordings between pilots and control towers. Sometimes the encroaching UFOs have been observed on radar returns but not always. They may show up visibly without any radar confirmation. It has commonly been the case that pilots are unwilling to make official reports or logs for fear of ridicule and losing their jobs. A few examples have been selected from the records to illustrate pilot reports.

On October 1st 1948, in the skies over Fargo, North Dakota, a twenty five year old pilot with the North Dakota

National Guard named George F. Gorman was supposedly involved in a dogfight with a UFO. He was flying a P-51 Mustang. The object appeared in the west as a blinking light though no air traffic was reported at the location. He chased the object at about 400 mph. The object out-turned and out-sped the Mustang. Gorman reported that human pilots could not withstand the turns and speed made by the object and remain conscious. A check of Gorman's Mustang after landing showed that it measured more radioactivity than planes which had not flown for several days. This generated speculation that the object Gorman chased had been 'atomic powered'. It was later concluded that either Gorman had become disoriented and was chasing the planet Jupiter or the object was a lighted weather balloon.

There was a UFO incident involving Japan Air Lines flight 1628 on November 17th, 1986. A Boeing 747 cargo aircraft flown by Captain Kenju Terauchi was en route from Paris to Narita, Tokyo, with a cargo of Beaujolais wine. At 5-11 pm over eastern Alaska, the crew witnessed two unidentified objects ascending to accompany them. They had glowing arrays of thrusters which illuminated the aircraft's cabin and caused the captain to feel heat on his face. Although each object had a square shape, the captain felt that the objects would appear cylindrical if viewed from another angle. These two craft departed but another larger disc shaped object began following them. Captain Terauchi believed he could perceive the outline of an enormous spaceship on his port side. It was "twice the size of an aircraft carrier." According to Captain Terauchi, the movements of the craft showed a disregard for inertia and flew as if there was no such thing as gravity. Anchorage Air Traffic Control allowed the Boeing to change course but the object followed them. The object was not seen by two planes which approached JAL 1628 to confirm its presence. In due course, JAL 1628 arrived safely in Anchorage.

The captain maintained that the objects the crew had seen were UFOs. JAL grounded the captain for talking to the press and moved him to a desk job though he was reinstated as a pilot some years later. The Federal Aviation Administration (FAA) presented voicetape and radar data to a group of government officials the next day. All present were told that the incident was secret. The meeting "never took place." Some considered the sighting to be a stealth bomber. On March 5th, 1987, following three months of investigations, the FAA formally released their conclusions at a press conference. They accepted the descriptions given by the crew but were "unable to support what they saw."

On April 23rd 2007, Captain Ray Bowyer was taking passengers on a forty five minute flight on an eighty mile journey from Southampton on the southern coast of England south westwards to Alderney in the Channel Islands, a mere ten miles away from France. The plane was a BN2a Mk3 Trislander aircraft. The flight route took the plane towards two large stationary airborne craft which resembled flattened discs pointed at each end and emitting brilliant yellow light. The objects were estimated to be up to a mile across. Another pilot near Sark twenty five miles to the south confirmed the presence of one object. Jersey Air Traffic Control said there was no air traffic in the reported position though a faint primary return radar signal was obtained. Captain Bowyer made drawings of the two objects in his Air Safety Report. The encounter lasted for fifteen minutes.

Missing Pilots and Aircraft

On 7th January 1948, Godman Field at Fort Knox, Kentucky, received a report of a strange aerial craft in the area of Maysville. The object was round and about 300 feet in diameter.

Sometimes it hovered but it also descended towards the ground and then rose steeply to 10,000 feet. It flew at speeds in excess of 500 miles per hour. Four P-51 Mustangs of C Flight 165th Fighter Squadron, Kentucky Air National Guard, approached the object. One plane was flown by twenty five year old Captain Thomas F. Mantell (born on the 30th June, 1922) who had been honoured for his actions in the Battle of Normandy during World War II. Some claim that Mantell proclaimed over the radio that the object looked metallic and was of tremendous size. Mantell continued to climb without an oxygen mask and it has been suggested that after reaching 25,000 feet he passed out due to hypoxia. His plane spiralled downwards and crashed on a farm south of Franklin. Mantell's dead body was removed from the Mustang's wreckage by firemen. An Air Force Major who was interviewed by reporters following Mantell's crash stated that the planes had been chasing planet Venus. Some suggested that the object was a misidentified U.S. Navy Skyhook weather balloon. There was also speculation that Mantell had been shot down by the UFO.

Frederick Valentich was twenty five when he disappeared. He was taking a 125 mile training flight in a Cessna 182L. The incident occurred in the area of the Bass Strait in Australia, on the 21st October, 1978. He radioed Melbourne air traffic control to say there was an unknown lit aircraft about 1000 feet above him which was hovering over him and circling his aircraft. His engine began 'rough idling'. He radioed that the object "was not an aircraft." Metallic scraping sounds were heard and then Frederick Valentich disappeared without a trace. Search and rescue crews were immediately dispatched to the area by air and sea but no debris was found. After four days the search was abandoned. There was speculation that Valentich became disorientated after seeing his lights reflected in the water or he may have been flying upside down. Others believe he was abducted in his aircraft.

A very strange incident occurred five years later. The Soviet army allegedly recovered an odd metallic capsule on the Russian-Chinese border. It contained a message in Valentich's handwriting saying he had been captured by aliens from the Pleiades. In exchange for not ageing, he was trained as a pilot for their space cargo ship to export tons of oxygen out of Earth's atmosphere. Twelve years later in the Spanish Canary Islands, it was claimed that Frederick Valentich suddenly reappeared and had not aged. He spoke to people and showed his passport. He claimed he was a member of a group of humans who had been 'recruited' by extraterrestrials.

Government Projects, Military Files, Investigations, Misinformation and Coverups

Harry S. Truman (May 8th 1884–December 26th 1972) was the thirty third President of the United States (1945–53). President Harry Truman was the first President to have to deal with UFO phenomena publicly. In 1946 he set up the Central Intelligence Group, which became the Central Intelligence Agency in 1947. President Truman commissioned a study in 1949 into the 'foo fighters' (unidentified lighted orbs that plagued both sides during World War II). General Robert B. Landry, the Air Force Aide, claimed that Truman asked for a briefing about UFOs every three months. It is believed that the military gave only oral briefings for secrecy purposes. There may have been governmental concerns throughout the 1940s about alien activity especially after the alleged well-known Roswell crash in 1947.

Operation Paperclip was a programme initiative of the Office of Strategic Services (OSS). After World War II, many scientists, technicians and engineers working for Nazi Germany escaped retribution by being transferred to work mainly in the

USA but also in some other countries. Some 1500 or so individuals subsequently began work for new governments in the west. This occurred during the period of the cold war and the USA tried to obtain the expertise of the Germans while preventing it from falling into the hands of the Soviets. The Soviet Union had its own similar missions and operations such as Operation Osoaviakhim and the so-called 'trophy brigades' programme were undertaken. President Harry Truman ordered Operation Paperclip in August 1945 but it excluded anyone found "to have been a member of the Nazi Party." However, it is believed that fictitious employment and political biographies were produced for key individuals and Nazi Party memberships and regime affiliations were 'whitewashed'. Among the individuals recruited in this way were rocket scientists Wernher von Braun, Kurt H. Debus and Arthur Rudolph, plus the physician Hubertus Strughold. The American space and missile programmes gained considerable impetus from the knowledge of such individuals.

In 1970, Wernher Von Braun became NASA's associate administrator. Interestingly, according to Clark C. McClelland, Von Braun confirmed to him that the 1947 Roswell crash of an alien craft had occurred. Von Braun related that the spacecraft was not metallic but was made from aluminium-coloured, skinlike, biological material. The craft was surprisingly bare inside and had little in the way of instrumentation. Alien bodies had been found and temporarily kept in a medical tent near the crashed craft. The beings were small, frail and of reptilian nature.

In 1952, the appearance of UFOs over the White House caused Truman to give the order that flying saucers be shot down. Prominent scientists like Albert Einstein protested in the interest of future intergalactic peace and self preservation. The order was withdrawn. Around this time, many secret groups and projects were set up. Project Red Light and Project

Blue Team were concerned with disc retrieval and recoveries. Project Delta was concerned with security matters and there was the formation of the secret Majestic 12 (Magic 12 or MJ 12) committee of scientists, military people and government officials. There also came into being the mysterious reports of the Men in Black. Some of these issues are discussed more fully later in this section.

James Forrestal (February 15th, 1892–May 22nd, 1949) was the last Cabinet level United States Secretary of the Navy and the first United States Secretary of Defence. He was appointed by President Harry S. Truman in 1947. After some years he resigned and by March 31st 1949, he was out of a job. In 1949, suffering from exhaustion and depression, he entered psychiatric treatment at the National Naval Medical Centre in Bethesda, Maryland. Forrestal seemed to be recovering. However, in the early morning hours of May 22nd, his body was found on a third floor roof below the sixteenth floor kitchen across the hall from his room. Although the death appeared to be a suicide, many believed his demise was a homicide. Some felt his death prevented any public disclosures regarding UFOs.

In 1952, the Central Intelligence Agency (CIA) reviewed military investigations into UFOs following multiple sightings over Washington D.C. This resulted in the formation of a committee called the Robertson Panel in 1953. A report was produced which concluded that UFOs were not a direct threat to national security. Most, if not all, UFO sightings were due to misidentifications. The public needed to be educated in order to avoid swamping Air Defence systems with reports and an eye needed to be kept on civilian UFO groups. The Robertson Panel's report was contained within a larger internal CIA document written by F C. Durant. This wider document is called the 'Durant Report'. CIA officials came to the conclusion that no further consideration of the UFO subject was warranted other than monitoring sightings.

The first Director of the U.S. Federal Bureau of Investigation (FBI) was John Edgar Hoover (January 1st 1895–May 2nd 1972). He was initially the director of the Bureau of Investigation in 1924 and later in 1935 was involved in the formation of the upgraded Federal Bureau of Investigation. Hoover built the FBI into an efficient crime-fighting agency, centralized fingerprint files and encouraged the use of forensic laboratories. He also closely monitored communist individuals and groups to safeguard the national interest. He later became a secretive and controversial figure. There were claims that he exceeded the jurisdiction of the FBI. President Harry S. Truman felt Hoover was using the FBI as his private secret police force. He felt Hoover had his eyes on becoming President of the USA and congressmen and senators were afraid of him. President Truman did not like the way Hoover operated and kept him 'outside the loop' in various areas including the area of UFOs. Truman met directly with Hoover only once in his Presidential period.

In an FBI document released under the Freedom of Information Act, a handwritten memo by J. Edgar Hoover complained that the U.S. Army 'grabbed' crashed discs before the FBI could have it for 'cursory examination'. The information suggested that the U.S. government knew of the existence of extraterrestial vehicles and crashed UFOs that had been recovered by the army in 1947. The document suggested that Hoover would not allow the FBI to conduct investigations into UFO phenomena until they were given full access to recovered discs which had been prevented by the army. It is believed that Hoover received a memo dated March 22nd, 1950. It was sent by an FBI Washington field office chief Guy Hottel informing him of the Roswell New Mexico crashed craft and alien retrieval. However, the story was not considered to be worth investigating.

The government in the USA began an official programme to study UFOs. It was called Project Sign. This continued through most of 1948 and was undertaken by United States Air Force staff. Kenneth Arnold had reported flying discs in 1947 over Mount Rainier in Washington State travelling at speeds in excess of 1000 mph. On 7th July 1947 at about 10 am, a series of close encounters occurred in and near the restricted airspace near Muroc Army Air Base (now Edwards Air Force Base). Military aircraft could not intercept mystery disc shaped craft which seemed to move under intelligent control and they moved in ways which would kill a human pilot. Military personnel were told not to publicly discuss flying saucers without permission. Lieutenant General Nathan F. Twining at Wright-Patterson Air Force Base analysed the reports and decided they were real and not fictional and that the craft were not of domestic origin. There was some concern that the unusual aircraft sighted may have been made by the Soviet Union. In December 1947, General Curtis Le May requested an update on flying saucer investigations and recommended that a project be formally established to investigate the flying saucer phenomenon. Project Sign was born.

The project's personnel including director Robert Sneider supported an extraterrestrial hypothesis to explain unusual sightings. An 'Estimate of the Situation' was produced to argue this opinion. However, this opinion was eventually rejected by high ranked officers. Project Sign was dissolved and replaced by Project Grudge. The final report of Project Sign was published in early 1949. It stated that while some UFOs appeared to be misidentified aircraft, there was not enough data to determine the origin of most sightings. Project Sign was first disclosed to the public in 1956. It was described in a book called *The Report on Unidentified Flying Objects* by retired Air Force Captain Edward J. Ruppelt. It was not until 1961 that the full files were declassified.

Project Grudge succeeded Project Sign in February 1949. However, instead of unbiased evaluations, reports were based on the premise that UFOs could not exist. It did not matter what was heard or seen. Project Grudge operated under a debunking directive. Some UFO 'explanations' defied logic or even common sense. Project Grudge during its tenure issued only one formal report in August 1949.

Project Blue Book was set up to determine if UFOs were a threat to national security and to scientifically analyse data pertaining to UFOs. Project Grudge was replaced by Project Blue Book in March 1952. Captain Edward J. Ruppelt was the first person placed in charge of the project. He officially coined the term 'Unidentified Flying Object' to replace older terms like 'flying saucer' and 'flying disc'. Ruppelt tried to alleviate the stigma and ridicule associated with UFO witnesses and ordered and developed a standard questionnaire. Astronomer Dr J Allen Hynek (who created the categories of 'close encounters' still used) was the scientific consultant. After the 'reign' of Ruppelt ended in August 1953, the number of staff was reduced and many believe the work was no longer carried out very seriously. The activity under its auspices ceased in January 1970 by which time it had made 12,618 UFO reports. Most UFO observations were said to be misidentifications of natural phenomena but a tiny proportion could not be explained.

When the United States government ceased officially studying UFO sightings, most other governments of the world followed suit. Whether this has been the case in reality has been a matter for conjecture. However, France still maintained 'GEIPAN' (formerly known as 'GEPAN' during 1977–1988) and 'SEPRA' (1988–2004), a unit under the French Space Agency 'CNES'.

The many UFO reports around 1952 were noted by both the U.S. Air Force and Central Intelligence Agency (CIA). It concerned them because a hostile nation might cause mass public panic and hysteria by using false UFO reports. Enquiries into the UFO phenomenon may have been undertaken by the CIA. In January 1953, the CIA helped to set up the Robertson Panel under Dr Howard P. Robertson, a physicist. The Robertson Panel first met on January 14th, 1953. The panel dismissed and debunked UFO reports. Assurances were given that UFOs offered no threat to national security.

The Condon Committee was established in 1966 as a neutral scientific research group. The reports of the committee became very controversial. Some members accused director Edward U. Condon of bias. The Condon Committee eventually concluded that there was nothing extraordinary about UFOs. Only a tiny minority of cases were unexplained. The report also suggested that further research was unlikely to yield significant results.

Many believe that the alleged Roswell crash of an alien craft in 1947 was 'covered up'. A secret group was allegedly set up by U.S. President Harry S. Truman to facilitate recovery, investigation and studies of alien spacecraft. This 'above top secret' organisation is known as the Majestic 12 or MJ-12 (sometimes Magic-12). The group consisted of specially selected individuals including scientists, military officers and government officials. Documents (which might be real or faked) alluding to the Majestic 12, were found in the 1980s including briefing papers describing 'Operation Majestic Twelve'. Stanton T. Friedman and others claimed to have been sent anonymous messages from declassified files in the National Archives that enabled the discovery of a memo in 1985. It allegedly was sent by General Nathan Twining to President Eisenhower's assistant Robert Cutler in 1985 and referred to Majestic 12. There were later claims that the document was forged and a hoax.

Witnesses of many UFO or entity sightings have frequently been visited after the event by unusual looking individuals dressed completely in black clothes (usually suits) and often shading their eyes with dark sunglasses. These figures have become known as Men in Black (MIB). They enquire as to what the witnesses saw and have often been described as being aggressive and unfriendly. Sometimes witnesses have been threatened by the MIB to keep quiet about what they observed. They also do not reveal any ID but may claim to be government agents. Some witnesses have felt that the MIB are themselves of alien origin.

Harold Dahl worked on a harbour patrol boat. He told a story (later retracted) about UFO sightings he had in 1947. He originally claimed to have observed six doughnut shaped objects in the sky which dropped metallic debris onto his boat. This occurred near Maury Island in Puget Sound. He was later visited by MIB and threatened.

Albert K. Bender served in the United States Air Force during World War II and worked at a factory in Bridgeport, Connecticut. He undertook research into UFOs and founded an organisation called the International Flying Saucers Bureau and *The Space Review* magazine. In 1953, he received a visit from three MIB and following their warning did not release an unpublished report.

Presidents of the USA and UFOs

Presidents of the USA have had direct or indirect involvement with the phenomenon of UFO sightings and alleged contacts with exotic entities since at least the late 1940s. It seems likely that any knowledge has quickly been hidden from public view. Conspiracy groups maintain that records have been covered up and there are many above top secret files. Even many documents retrieved under the Freedom of Information Act have had all or most of their written reports blacked out on the grounds of national security. There is an assumption that revelation and disclosure of information would cause public panic and the institutions of government and commerce would crumble if it became known that there were living forces that could not be controlled by terrestrial governments. There might also be rioting as religious beliefs become unravelled. If free energy became available, there would be a great collapse of industries like coal and oil and associated vested interests. Perhaps there is exotically acquired military or technological information that the USA does not want to share with rival nations.

Presidential candidates have been wary of talking about personal sightings and experiences in case their political career should become damaged. Admission opens the door to ridicule or being labelled as a 'nut'. It is unclear as to what extent U.S. Presidents have been fully or partially briefed in the area of UFOs and alien contacts. Several incoming Presidential candidates promised to open the files and let knowledge out into the public domain. However, it seems that once a President is in place he then will not or cannot make any disclosures. The change of mind seems to follow secret briefings by organisations like the CIA. One thing for sure is that no President to date has openly admitted that aliens exist or concede that there has been contact. Crashed craft have never publicly been admitted to originate from other worlds, dimensions, galaxies or times. The government to date maintains total denial.

Truman: Harry S. Truman (May 8th 1884–December 26th 1972) was the thirty third President of the United States (1945–53). President Truman was the first U.S. President to have to formally deal with issues regarding UFOs. In UFO conspiracy theories, Majestic 12 (or MJ 12/Magic 12) is the code name of an alleged secret committee set up in 1947 by the President. The group consisted of scientists, military leaders, and government officials. The aim of the organisation was to facilitate the recovery and investigation of alien spacecraft. 'Leaked' secret government documents about this committee circulated in 1984. The FBI declared the documents to be "completely bogus." Truman is believed at one point to have ordered UFOs to be shot down after a number of appearances over the capital but this order was soon withdrawn.

Eisenhower: Dwight D. Eisenhower (October 14th 1890–March 28th 1969) was the thirty fourth President of the United States from 1953 to 1961. 'Ike' was a five star General who was in command of the Allied armies in Europe during the second world war. It has been claimed that he had three meetings with extraterrestrials. Races encountered included a group resembling humans, humanoid tall whites with bald heads and another group with reptilian features. On the night and early hours of February 20th–21st 1954, while on a 'vacation' to Palm Springs, California, President Dwight Eisenhower went missing. It was said he needed urgent dental treatment. Later, witnesses alleged that he was taken to Edwards Air force base (previously called Muroc Airfield) for a secret meeting. The initial meeting was with human looking Nordic entities. Apparently, no agreement was forthcoming in the areas of exchange of advanced technological assistance and nuclear weapons. The aliens were more interested in human spiritual development.

According to Timothy Good, another meeting in 1954 at the remote Holloman Air Force base in New Mexico was the location of an agreement with a different race of aliens known as the 'greys'. This race claimed they came from a planet orbiting a red star in the Constellation of Orion (Betelgeuse). Their planet was dying and at some future time they would not be able to survive there. The agreement included no interference by the aliens regarding human matters and no interference by humans with alien affairs. The aliens would aid human technological advancement and not sign any further treaties with other nations. However, the aliens would periodically abduct humans for medical examinations and monitoring. The humans would not be harmed and would be returned without memory of what had happened to them. Majestic 12 (supposedly set up by President Harry S. Truman) would be given a list of abductees and contactees. Later reports from whistleblowers said that the grey extraterrestrials were not trustworthy. They neither supplied lists nor returned all abductees.

Whistleblower Phil Schneider (mentioned elsewhere in this book) claimed that the Eisenhower administration entered into the treaty but it was never ratified as required by the constitution. Colonel Phillip Corso was a highly decorated officer in Eisenhower's National Security Council. In his memoirs, he alluded to a treaty signed by the Eisenhower administration with extraterrestrials.

Kennedy: John Fitzgerald Kennedy (May 29th 1917– November 22nd 1963), commonly known as Jack Kennedy or JFK, served as the thirty fifth President of the United States from January 1961. He was assassinated in November 1963. The Apollo programme was conceived early in 1960, during the Eisenhower administration. On November 21st, 1962, in a cabinet meeting with NASA administrators, Kennedy justified the costs and explained that the Moonshot was important for reasons of international prestige and military importance. President Kennedy requested the CIA give him highly confidential documents about UFOs just ten days before his assassination. In another memo, sent to NASA, he expressed his desire for cooperation with the former Soviet Union in outer space activities. A report suggested that Kennedy sighted a UFO in 1963. This was on a boating trip off Hyannisport off Cape Cod. He purportedly saw a disc shaped object, about sixty feet in diameter. It hovered above the water for forty seconds. The craft produced a low pitched humming sound before flying straight up into the air.

Johnson: Lyndon Baines Johnson (August 27th 1908–January 22nd 1973) was referred to as LBJ. He was the thirty sixth President of the United States (1963–1969). He had previously served as the Vice President (1961–1963). Kennedy had appointed Vice President Johnson as chairman of the U.S. Space Council. Johnson was a strong supporter of the U.S. space programme and had worked for the creation of NASA in the Senate. During Johnson's administration, NASA conducted the Gemini manned space programme. The Saturn V rocket was developed. On January 27th 1967, a shocking event occurred. The entire crew of Apollo 1 was killed in a cabin fire during a test on the launch pad.

Nixon: Richard Milhous Nixon (January 9th 1913–April 22nd 1994) was the thirty seventh President of the United States, serving from 1969 to 1974. He had also served as Vice President from 1953 to 1961. He was the only President to have resigned the office. Various UFO stories and space developments occurred during Nixon's tenure. He presided over the first manned lunar landings in July 1969. Nixon stated that the Apollo 11 mission was the "greatest week in the history of the world since Creation."

Ford: Gerald 'Jerry' Ford Jr (July 14th 1913–December 26th 2006) was the thirty eighth President of the United States from 1974 to 1977. He had previously served as Vice President from 1973 to 1974 under President Richard Nixon. It seems that the President had concerns over UFOs but it is unknown how this may or may not have affected any policies or actions. Before he became President, Gerald Ford was a Representative of Michigan in the U.S. Senate. In 1966, Michigan experienced numerous UFO sightings amid reports of weird dancing lights. There was discontent and furore which Ford was well aware of.

Carter: James Earl 'Jimmy' Carter Jr (born October 1st, 1924) served as the thirty ninth President of the United States from 1977 to 1981. In 1969, future U.S. President Jimmy Carter saw a UFO. He was standing outside the Leary Lion's Club in Leary, Georgia. Four years passed before a report was filed in 1973. He described it being "as bright as the moon." In response to a question, Governor Carter as he was at that time, said that he saw the UFO in October of 1969 and it was about thirty degrees above the horizon in the sky to the west. The UFO was watched for an estimated twelve minutes and changed in brightness, size and colour. It moved towards and away from him and varied through blue and red. It did not look solid. He made two reports to UFO study organisations including Mufon. Carter promised to make information about UFOs public after he became President but it is alleged following CIA briefings he decided against disclosure. A former Defence Intelligence Agency official Daniel Sheehan claimed that President Carter's attempts to obtain UFO information was thwarted by military and intelligence staff.

Reagan: Ronald Wilson Reagan (February 6th 1911–June 5th 2004) was an American actor and politician who became the fortieth President of the United States (1981–1989). President Reagan is said to have had two UFO sightings. One was when he was Governor of California and another was over Bakersfield, California, in 1974. Reagan and his wife Nancy were due to attend a Hollywood dinner party but arrived thirty minutes late due to the sighting along the coastline. Actress and comedienne Lucille Ball who was at the event overheard the Reagan's explanation and documented it in a book called *Lucy in the Afternoon*. Reagan told the story to Norman C. Miller of the *Wall Street Journal*. Reagan was in a plane and observed a zigzagging white light which he asked the pilot named Bill Paynter to follow. The light suddenly shot upwards into the heavens and disappeared.

President Reagan made a famous speech to the United Nations General Assembly on September 21st, 1987. His words were as follows. "Perhaps we need some outside universal threat, to make us recognize this common bond. I occasionally think about how quickly our differences worldwide would vanish, if we were facing an alien threat from outside this world. And yet I ask you, is not an alien force already among us?"

Bush the 'Elder': George Herbert Walker Bush (born June 12th, 1924) served as the forty first President of the United States from 1989 to 1993. He had previously served as Vice President (1981-1989). President George Bush had experienced a year as Director of the Central Intelligence Agency. He was the head of the entire United States Intelligence Community for President Ford. He was in charge of giving intelligence briefings to Jimmy Carter. This was during his transition to the Presidency. Many UFO commentators feel that George Bush was the best qualified President to have been given knowledge about UFOs and alien entities. He was a key figure for potential disclosure but has maintained confidentiality to the frustration of many UFO followers.

Clinton: William Jefferson 'Bill' Clinton (born August 19th, 1946) served from 1993 to 2001 as the forty second President of the United States. Clinton proclaimed that he did not have information about UFOs but would like to find out. There are records from the Clinton Office of Science and Technology Policy related to UFOs and extraterrestrial intelligence. It has been suggested that President Clinton was pressured to reopen super-secret government files on some baffling UFO incidents. The man who wanted the secrecy ended and information put out in public view was billionaire and philanthropist Laurance S. Rockerfeller. However, it seems that Clinton was not able to progress this information to

Rockerfeller. He may (or may not) have been kept out of the loop by elite groups on a 'need to know' basis and it was deemed that the President did not need to know.

Bush 'Junior': George Walker Bush (born July 6th, 1946) served as the forty third President of the United States from 2001 to 2009. President George W. Bush observed a UFO from the White House on November 20th, 2003. Radar from the Federal Aviation Administration (FAA) and the North American Aerospace Defence Command (NORAD) detected an unknown radar target within restricted airspace around 9 am. Preparations were started to evacuate the White House. NORAD (a combined organisation of the United States and Canada providing air sovereignty and defence) scrambled two fighter aircraft. However, the target vanished. A similar event occurred on April 27th, 2005. A UFO was recorded on radar at 10-40 am heading towards the White House at about 120 mph. President Bush was quickly escorted to an underground bunker below the White House. Black Hawk and police helicopters were scrambled but the object disappeared.

Another sighting occurred in Texas on January 8th, 2006. Witnesses in Stephenville saw a large silent illuminated craft headed directly toward President Bush's Crawford Ranch being chased by jet aircraft. President Bush had promised to reveal information on UFOs. Vice President Dick Cheney paid a visit to Roswell and many thought it was a sign of a positive move towards disclosure of UFO information. However, no reference was made to extraterrestrials or crashed craft. Bush was not open to UFO disclosure. For example, John E L Tenney who cofounded M.A.I.N (the Michigan Anomalous Information Network) along with others found his efforts to get George Bush to talk about UFOs unproductive.

Obama: Barack Hussein Obama (born August 4th, 1961) is the forty fourth President of the United States and the first African-American to hold the office. A UFO was captured on film on the occasion of President Obama's inauguration by a cameraman broadcasting the scene live for CNN. A disc shaped object flew across the Washington Monument as the camera zoomed out to show the huge crowd. The administration contends that it has no knowledge of UFOs or alien visitors.

Secret Military Bases, Reverse Engineering and Black Ops

The National Investigations Committee On Aerial Phenomena (or NICAP) was a civilian unidentified flying object research group. It was active and well followed in the United States from the 1950s to the 1980s. Donald Keyhoe (June 20th 1897–November 29th 1988) was a naval aviator and UFO researcher. He became NICAP director and appeared on CBS television in 1958. He was prepared to comment on UFOs but there was insistence on a degree of censorship. During the television broadcast, not only were his statements censored but the sound was subsequently cut for reasons relating to 'security standards'. Conspiracy theorists claim that he was prevented from disclosing unauthorised military information. Both before and after this incident, there has been much speculation about government coverups and secret military bases relating to UFOs. Many of these bases are purportedly deep underground facilities with many levels. Some are even said to have alien occupants who experiment on humans, possibly with governmental approval, in exchange for exotic technical information which could be used for new methods of propulsion or warfare. Efforts are supposedly made by people who work in such bases on projects to reverse engineer alien crashed vehicles.

Wright-Patterson Air Force Base is located east of Dayton, Ohio. It was established in 1948. The base has links with possible extraterrestrial history. Although unexplained sightings have never been attributed to any extraterrestrial sources, there were 701 residual unexplained cases documented by the 1969 Foreign Technology Division. There is a widely held view that following the purported crash in 1947 at Roswell, New Mexico, debris and alien bodies were taken to Wright-Field Air Base, as it was called back in 1947. Military sources claimed the debris came from a downed weather balloon. Controversial evidence does not clarify if a crashed alien craft came down at Roswell or not. Even if this crash did involve an alien craft, the evidence does not clear up the issue as to whether Major Jesse Marcel and his team collected debris along with alien bodies (who had small grey bodies with big heads and large almond shaped dark eyes without eyelids). Between two and five deceased extraterrestrials were claimed to have been witnessed. Some reports say that four corpses were transported to Wright-Field from Roswell Army Field in a C-54 cargo plane while the fifth body was taken to Lowry Field's air force mortuary. It is claimed that there was a heavily guarded hangar known as the 'Blue Room' or Hangar 18 at the Wright-Patterson base which contained a damaged disc shaped craft and wreckage. A refrigerated unit purportedly contained alien bodies. Some claim that one alien survived the crash and lived on at the Wright-Patterson base.

In the 1960s, Senator Barry Goldwater of Arizona was keenly interested to investigate the truth or mythology regarding UFOs. He visited the base and asked General Curtis Le May to allow him to view Hangar 18. His request was denied and this produced a lot of public comment.

The Roswell incident of 1947 is discussed more fully in the section on 'Crashes and Retrievals'. However, in more general terms, the 1940s was the time period when there were increased UFO sightings in the USA including the area of New Mexico. Some believe this was related to the Manhattan Project which was a research and development project that produced the first atomic bombs and subsequently tested them. The project was under the direction of Major General Leslie Groves from 1942 to 1946. Though Groves was the director and was affiliated to the United States Army Corps of Engineers, it was the physicist J Robert Oppenheimer who actually designed the bombs. He was the scientific director of the Los Alamos National Laboratory. Los Alamos is a town in Los Alamos County, New Mexico. Another well known member of the Manhattan Project was a colleague of Oppenheimer named Edward Teller who later became known as the 'the father of the hydrogen bomb'. He was a proponent of the use of nuclear energy including its use to disrupt any asteroid or comet encroaching upon the Earth.

Holloman Air Force Base is also located in New Mexico about ten miles west of Alamogordo. This base purportedly was the location of meetings between President D. Eisenhower and alien visitors in 1954 (see the section on Presidents of the USA and UFOs). Alamogordo is well known for its connection with the Trinity test, the first explosion of an atomic bomb. The United States Army detonated the device on July 16th, 1945. This was part of the Manhattan Project. The test was conducted at The White Sands Proving Ground on the Alamogordo Bombing and Gunnery Range, thirty five miles south east of Socorro, New Mexico. Alamogordo is the economic centre of Otero County in south-central New Mexico and the city closest to Holloman Air Force Base. Many believe the detonation of these atomic devices attracted alien observers to the area in UFOs.

Various cases have been reported where UFOs have intervened and allegedly been captured on film disrupting missile test flights. An example was witnessed by Captain Salas on March 16th 1967, at Malmstrom Air Force Base in Montana. This site is where Minuteman nuclear missiles were housed. He reported that a UFO hovered over the base and up to ten Minuteman missiles shut down. Similar events occurred about a week later at a nearby site and a launched missile was inactivated by a 'beam' emanating from the UFO which caused it to crash.

Cases have been reported in the USA and the Soviet Union where UFOs affected the control of nuclear missiles at military bases. One example might have led to another world war on October 4th, 1982. Soviet military staff reported the incident about ten years after the alleged event. A large UFO 'as tall as a five storey house' was reported hovering for about an hour above a Soviet nuclear missile base by Vladimir Matveyev and a further 1000 or so officers and soldiers. It was seen about a mile and a half from the base in the town of Byelokoroviche, Ukraine. A number of R-12 nuclear missiles activated without any countdown sequence or procedure and without any instructions from Moscow. Captain Valery Polykhaev and Captain Kovalenko reported seeing two brightly illuminated objects. They were about three to four miles high. These objects were shaped like a 'Christmas tree decoration' but changed from an elliptical shape to a straight line. The objects were about two miles apart from each other. A further viewing occurred around 8 pm when a ball of light appeared to break off and flew towards the ground. Other officers reported seeing unidentified objects on the road to Byelokoroviche. This was between 7-30 pm and 9 pm that night. One of the soldiers reported an electromagnetic effect of some kind which affected the car radio and an object hovering above the village of Usovo. This village gave its name to this event which became known as the Usovo Incident.

Major M. Davidovich Kataman was in charge of computerised control panels for the long range missiles at the base but could not directly see the hovering UFO as he was in a silo bunker. He later reported to Moscow stating that he observed "the spontaneous lumination of all the displays on the control panels for the missiles." It appeared that an unknown 'third party' was putting in the launch codes to activate the missiles. No computer or machine defects could be found. Perhaps the hovering UFO emitted some kind of powerful electromagnetic pulse into the bunker which activated the missiles' launch control sequence. Fortunately, the UFO disappeared and the controls returned to manual control before the missiles were launched.

A facility which is commonly subject to documentaries and conspiracy articles is known as Area 51. It is located in a remote region of the Nevada Desert called Groom Lake and is part of Edwards Air Force Base. Various other names are given to this facility but it is commonly nicknamed Dreamland. The air space over the base is restricted and there is an enforceable 'exclusion box'. This area is within the Nellis Air Force Range. Various fighter and interceptor aircraft are rumoured to be stationed in the region including the F-16 Fighting Falcon. No public access is allowed and security is monitored by cameras, motion sensors and military observation vehicles. Posted warning noticeboards regarding no entry are prominent and refer to the risk of lethal action on unauthorised entry. Workers and military staff are transported to the base by a fleet of passenger aircraft termed 'Janet'. The planes operate on behalf of the United States Air Force, commonly travelling to and from McCarran International Airport.

It is believed that the base at Area 51 is involved in the development and testing of experimental aircraft and weapons systems. Information referring to research at Area 51 is classified as top secret or even higher. Numerous UFO sightings have been observed near and over the site. For that reason, the nearby small town of Rachel is popular with tourists. The local road to the south of Rachel in the vicinity is named the 'Extraterrestrial Highway'.

Around 1962, the Lockheed A-12 was developed as a reconnaissance aircraft built for the Central Intelligence Agency (CIA). The CIA also chose Groom Lake in 1955 as the testing area which helped to develop the well known high altitude spy plane called the Lockheed U-2 which flew photographic missions over the Soviet Union during the cold war. The pilot, Gary Powers (August 17th 1929–August 1st 1977) was shot down while flying a reconnaissance mission over Soviet Union airspace in 1960 sparking a serious international crisis. Drones not requiring pilots were subsequently developed. There may also be links to the development of low radar visibility stealth aircraft such as the F-117 Nighthawk (1981–2008).

Various claims have been made regarding clandestine activities at Area 51 as UFO sightings became increasingly common during the 1950s and 1960s. The manufacture of 'human-made' UFOs has been claimed to occur within this facility. This supposedly has been enabled by the examination and back engineering of retrieved crashed alien spacecraft. Some believe that original or manufactured materials from a crashed craft at Roswell, New Mexico in 1947, was incorporated into such UFOs. Some also claim that living and deceased occupants of crashed alien craft have been studied at Area 51 and even meetings and mutually agreed deals have been struck with alien entities.

In a televised speech of March 23rd 1983, President Ronald Reagan asked the American public for support regarding the defence budget he had submitted to Congress for a 'Star Wars' initiative. Star Wars or the Strategic Defence Initiative (SDI) programme would use energy weapons which may have been developed at Area 51. Initially the system was designed as a defence shield against Soviet Inter-Continental Ballistic Missiles (ICBM's) but later suggestions intimate that the laser-like or particle weapons were to protect the Earth from incoming hostile UFOs entering the Earth from orbit. Further claims regarding activities at Area 51 relate to the development of time travel, teleportation and weather control. Further speculation has arisen as to the control of the facility by a one-world government group and/or the Majestic 12 organisation mentioned elsewhere in this book. Area 51 has also been linked to the Aurora Programme involving exotic futuristic propulsion systems. The Aurora was a rumoured mid-1980s American reconnaissance aircraft which officially was never built. However, many people believe it was developed secretly and has flown.

There are many claims of extensive underground facilities at Groom Lake or nearby Papoose Lake. The latter is often called the S4 location (see the section on J-rod). Multilevels of facilities have been claimed with an extensive underground railroad. An alien presence has also been claimed. Only officials with extra high clearance can access prohibited areas as they are above top secret. For example, there may be COSMIC and ULTRA clearance levels. Some other claimed clearance levels are: UMBRA, STELLAR, G2-7Z and TRIAD. There may also be UMT (Universal Military Training) and UMS (Universal Military Service). Further clearance levels include ASTRAL and SUB-ASTRAL. UMBRA is higher than ULTRA.

Another well publicised alleged secret military facility is the Dulce Base. It is said to be located below the Archuleta Mesa in New Mexico, USA. The base is said to consist of a deep maze of underground rooms and laboratories at different depths accessible by 'stepped escalators', one level at a time. Each level has massive security checks and systems in place. Businessman Paul Bennewitz in 1979 claimed to have intercepted alien communications from this area. This led to speculation about the presence of a base. This was supported by people such as the UFO researcher John Lear in 1990.

There have been claims of an alien presence and experiments on abducted humans at the site. There have also been claims of a military exchange of fire between aliens and Delta Force soldiers. Casualties and deaths were said to have occurred on both sides. The purported involvement of engineer Phil Schneider in this firefight is documented in the Whistleblowers and Hackers section of this book.

A military base not as well known as some of the others mentioned is a top secret United States run facility called Pine Gap near Alice Springs in Australia. There are in fact two other bases in Australia. One of these is at Nurranger, near Woomera in South Australia, while the other is in New South Wales. The Pine Gap facility is the largest of the three and is located in the Northern Territory on the slopes of the MacDonnell Range. The base is sometimes called the 'Joint Defence Space Research Facility'. The entrances to the base are very difficult to detect from above ground and the facility is an underground network of many levels. The original declared aim of the base was scientific research into space defence technology. It is now widely believed to be concerned with research into electromagnetic propulsion technology.

There is much speculation regarding Pine Gap but it is believed to have a five mile deep drilling hole. It has been speculated that this has a cable system having a role as an antenna which can recharge batteries of submarines in the Indian and Pacific Oceans. The facility may also have a role in monitoring spy satellites. Some claim powerful computers linked to others around the world hold personal details of huge numbers of private citizens of many countries. As far as extraterrestrials are concerned, disc shaped craft have been seen in the vicinity and some believe grey alien guests at the base are involved in technological exchanges. There is whistleblower evidence from former Command Sergeant Major Bob Dean and scientist Arthur Neumann that Pine

Gap is a major underground human-extraterrestrial liaison base operated by both U.S. military intelligence personnel and extraterrestrial personnel. Allegedly, the Anzus Security Treaty was signed on September 1st 1951 between Australia, New Zealand and the United States. This relates to a mutual agreement refusing to disclose the extraterrestrial and UFO presence at Pine Gap. The Pine Gap facility is sometimes called the Australian Area 51.

A brief mention is made here near the conclusion of this section of 'Black Ops'. Black Operations are covert operations carried out by a government, a government agency, or a military organisation. Black Ops are clandestine and not attributable to the party carrying it out. They involve a significant degree of deception to conceal who is behind the operation. They may shift blame or attention elsewhere ('false flag' operations). Examples of agencies believed by some people to have been involved in such activities include the Federal Bureau of Investigation (FBI), Central Intelligence Agency (CIA), Mossad, MI6, MSS plus several more organisations from various nations.

Black Ops have for a long time been suspected of having a role in UFO and extraterrestrial cases and activities. Dark unmarked helicopters have been seen accompanying UFOs and observed at craft crash sites. Unmarked military jets have also been seen trying to follow or intercept UFOs. Various military groups have turned up at crash-retrieval sites without any insignia. Some believe the mysterious Men in Black who turn up to question witnesses of UFO sightings may be part of such operations. There is thought to also be a 'Black Budget'. Considerable sums of government money in the USA have 'gone missing' and are unaccounted for. It is believed by some that a lot of secret expenditure has been diverted to military and research establishments. Research products related to novel propulsion technologies, eavesdropping systems and weaponry may be funded in this way. These have been linked directly or indirectly to extraterrestrial cooperation or involvement. Examples may be the production of manmade antigravity flying saucers, outer space defence systems such as SDI (Star Wars) and HAARP ionosphere studies. Some other possible areas include nanotechnology, cybernetics and robotics.

Project Moon Dust was a covert project carried out by the United States Air Force during the cold war. It operated out of the Air Force Missile Development Centre at Holloman Air Force Base. The project attempted to exploit the discovery of Soviet hardware when it fell into American hands. It also purportedly was to take and examine retrieved terrestrial and other crashed aerial and space objects back to Wright-Patterson Air Force Base. Perhaps material of non-terrestrial origin might have been included in the programme.

Whistleblowers and Hackers

Gary McKinnon was born on 10th February 1966. He worked as a Scottish systems administrator. He came into the glare of public view after he was accused of hacking United States military and NASA computers in 2002. He argued he was seeking information of potential use to the public. The USA applied to have McKinnon extradited and put on trial. The potential prison sentence was up to a lengthy seventy years if found guilty. In August 2008, McKinnon was diagnosed with Asperger's Syndrome and depression. His mother claimed he was suicidal and would not survive life in prison. A series of legal proceedings followed in Britain. In 2012, the British Home Secretary Theresa May decided to withdraw the extradition order. McKinnon was interviewed by the BBC and public media. He claimed there was suppressed knowledge of free energy kept secret to protect the interests of large companies and industries such as the oil industry. He also claimed extraterrestrial UFOs had been captured and back-engineered and there was knowledge of antigravity propulsion. Another controversial claim was that work was done at the Johnson Space Centre Building number 8 where NASA air-brushed UFO photos taken on space missions. He also claimed to have viewed cigar shaped non-Earthly looking objects in the atmosphere. Perhaps the most startling claim of all is that he said he had seen files which listed the names and ranks of 'non-terrestrial officers' in the U.S. military.

Paul Theodore Hellyer was born on the 6th August 1923 on a farm in Canada near Waterford, Ontario. He had a distinguished career in areas such as politics, engineering, writing and in military service. Hellyer became Minister of National Defence after the 1963 election victory as part of the Liberal Government. He announced that he believed in the existence of UFOs in September 2005 and claimed that he had personally seen a UFO. Hellyer opposed the weaponisation of space and suggested that the United States military were preparing weapons which could be used against aliens. In 2007, newspaper reports indicated that he demanded world governments disclose alien technology to help solve problems associated with climate change. In 2010, Hellyer accused Professor Stephen Hawking of spreading misinformation with respect to alien threats. Hawking felt that human contact with aliens might result in invasion and loss of resources. In 2013, Paul Hellyer was a guest speaker at the Citizen Hearing on Disclosure held in Washington DC on 29th April–3rd May. He proclaimed that aliens live among the human population and a couple were working closely with the government of the United States. He also claimed there were at least four species of alien that had been visiting planet Earth for millennia and they had different agendas.

Charles Hall was formerly a United States Air Force airman stationed at Nellis Air Force Base in Nevada who reported his interactions with the Tall Whites star race living there in 1967. He claimed that they did not abduct humans and that he had observed craft which routinely travelled faster than the speed of light. He speculated that the first formal interactions between the Tall Whites and the United States government took place during the 1940s or very early 1950s. Hall believed that Tall Whites have been coming to Earth for at least three thousand years. Hall claimed that the Tall Whites live underground in the mountains in the remote Nevada desert, their main base being immediately to the east of Area 53 (i.e. Area 54). Areas 53 and 54 and the western parts of the Desert south west of Game Range form part of a region known as Dreamland. According to Hall, the Tall Whites were only willing to exchange technology with the U.S. Military if it was to their advantage to do so. He believes the aliens have had meetings with government and military officials as well as the CIA.

Philip (Phil) Schneider was born on April 23rd 1947 at Bethesda Navy Hospital. His father Oscar was a navy Captain who was involved in Operation Crossroads testing nuclear weapons in the Pacific area. He may also have been involved with a well known incident popularly known as the 'Philadelphia Experiment'. Phil claimed to be an ex-government structural engineer. He claimed he was involved in building underground military bases. He went on lecture tours and in 1954 claimed the federal government under the Eisenhower administration formed a treaty with extraterrestrials called the Greada Treaty. In exchange for novel technology, the government allowed grey aliens a degree of freedom to implant and abduct humans. In 1979, Phil was employed in building work deep underground at the military Dulce base in New Mexico. He had Level one government clearance. His work involved being lowered down deep holes to check the rock samples and recommend explosives. He claimed workers accidentally opened a large artificial cavern acting as a base for grey aliens where experiments were being done on human subjects. A panic occurred in which sixty seven workers and blue beret military personnel were killed. Phil said he would have died but was saved and taken away from the area by a soldier. However, he was struck by an alien beam device which blew off two fingers. Philip Schneider died of a stroke in 1996 though some claim he was murdered.

Phil Schneider also claimed to have met a human looking alien with six fingers called Valiant Thor from Venus who worked with the U.S. government in the 1950s. He left the Earth in a spaceship on March 16th 1960 after warning humans to change their ways. He had an internal anatomy somewhat different to humans, an IQ over 1200 and lifespan of about 490 years. Some people believe Valiant Thor had meetings with Presidents Dwight D. Eisenhower and Richard Nixon.

Alien Contact and SETI

The search for extraterrestrial intelligence (SETI) includes a number of activities seeking intelligent extraterrestrial life. Scientific methodology is used to seek transmissions from civilizations on other worlds. Electromagnetic radiation arriving on Earth is scrutinised. Activity has been carried out at Harvard University, the University of California, Berkeley and the SETI Institute. In 1995, the United States federal government ceased funding SETI projects. More recently, private funding has been used. Carl Sagan in 1982 helped to restore a reduced government financial input. In 1986, the University of California, Berkeley, began using the Arecibo radio telescope. In March 2014, an all-sky survey started. Private individuals can become involved with SETI research by downloading the Berkeley Open Infrastructure for Network Computing (BOINC) software programme. This is attached to the SETI@home project. The programme runs as a background process using idle computer power.

The SETI organisation has a 'post detection protocol' which it is meant to follow if extraterrestrial life is confirmed. Some people, including Steven M. Greer, have expressed cynical views about disclosure to the public. There are many governmental, political and military agendas involved as well as any possible effects on social behaviour and religious beliefs.

On August 15th 1977, Jerry R. Ehman detected a strong narrowband radio signal. He was working on a SETI project based at the Big Ear radio telescope which was located at the Ohio State University. The signal was detected for seventy two seconds. Ehman circled the signal on the computer printout and wrote the comment "Wow!" This signal, now known as the 'Wow signal', was never repeated and not verified as coming from an extraterrestrial source by SETI.

Another candidate for extraterrestrial contact is radio source SHGb02+14a. It was discovered in March 2003 by SETI@home. However, it was a very weak signal and came from an area where no stars have been observed within 1000 light years from the Earth. The source emanated from a region between the constellations Pisces and Aries.

Underwater Submerged Objects (USOs)

UFOs (unidentified flying objects) have from time to time been witnessed both diving into and emerging from the sea, freshwater lakes and rivers. Such objects are now referred to as USOs (unidentified submerged objects). Many USOs have been observed and documented. Some of these are described elsewhere in this book including observations made by Columbus on his voyages in 1492, various sightings made in the Catalina Island region of California and the Baltic Sea Anomaly.

The steamship *RADUGA* was on a trip in the Red Sea in August 1965. A strange sight was observed a couple of miles away. A sixty metre diameter fiery sphere emerged from below the surface of the water and rose to a height of 150 metres above the sea, accompanied by a huge spout of water. It hovered over the water and illuminated it before disappearing.

A well known case occurred at Shag Harbour in October 1967. Shag Harbour is a fishing village in Nova Scotia, Canada. About eleven witnesses saw an illuminated flying object enter the water in the area of the Gulf of Maine with a loud bang. Some witnesses claim the object floated for a time about 980 feet from the shore. Reports were rapidly sent to the police and military. A rescue or recovery mission was started as it was assumed a plane had come down. Fishing boats and later divers took part in the search. No missing aircraft were reported and no debris was found. The incident received attention in the press and was investigated by the Condon Committee. This was an organisation funded by the United States Air Force from 1966 to 1968 set up to study unidentified flying objects.

A similar phenomenon to the *RADUGA* steamship occurred in December 1977 which was observed near Novy Georgy Island by the crew of a fishing trawler called the *VASILY KISELEV*. A doughnut shaped object emerged from below the surface and then rose vertically to an altitude of about five kilometres. The object then hovered over the area for about three hours. The diameter of the object was estimated at about 500 metres. It seemed to affect the ship's instrumentation as its radar equipment stopped working.

Crop Circles

Crop circles are patterns made in fields of vegetation such as cereals like wheat. They often form overnight though they do occur in the daytime on occasions. They have been reported in various countries but many formations have been in England. Reports of ring like patterns in mushrooms date back to 1686 and were called 'fairy rings'. Several well documented cases of flattened crops occurred in Canada and Australia in the 1960s. Other cases were reported in the USA, Soviet Union, Japan and several other countries. Quite a number of crop circles have appeared in Wiltshire in areas near Stonehenge, Avebury and Silbury Hill in the UK. Other examples were discovered in Hampshire. In the late 1970s, Doug Bower and Dave Chorley claimed to have produced hoax crop circles at various locations around England. It is likely that some if not all crop circles are manmade. One end of a rope may be tied to an anchorage point and the other end attached to a board used to crush the plants. Crop circle formation has also been put down to natural weather vortex phenomena, paranormal events, magnetic field changes and animal activities. There is another body of opinion that believes crop circles are of extraterrestrial origin and are caused by an interaction between the plants and nearby UFOs. Crop circle formation was investigated in depth by Pat Delgado and Colin Andrews. Pat has now passed away in Winchester, Hampshire, England at age ninety, after losing a battle with cancer.

Over the years the basic crop circle pattern has evolved into surprisingly complex and intricate patterns called pictograms. These appeared in the 1990s. Geometric shapes were followed by animals such as whales, dolphins and insects. Astronomy related glyphs followed including galaxies, asteroid belts and planetary orbits. Many people believe that crop formations carry a symbolically encoded message but these are open to criticism and different interpretations.

Two new crop formations were reported near the Chilbolton radio telescope in Hampshire. This interesting event occurred on Tuesday 21st August, 2001. The content was made up of 'pixel-like' units. Seen from the air, one resembled a 'human face'. The other was rather similar to a radio transmission sent from the Arecibo radio telescope located in Puerto Rico, in 1974. The latter was sent from SETI (the Search for Extra-Terrestrial Intelligence). Researcher Wayne Herschel has suggested the face resembles the Egyptian Sphinx or Inca god Viracocha. There is also some resemblance to the famous face feature found on Mars.

The Arecibo telescope was the world's largest radio-telescope and sent a binary coded message (zeroes and ones) out into the heavens on November 16th, 1974. The images included content from the well known astronomer Carl Sagan. It was pulsed in the direction of a globular star cluster M13. This is 25,000 light years away and contains 300,000 stars in the constellation of Hercules. The images included a representation of human civilization, mathematical numbers, the DNA double helix, the atomic numbers of the primary elements for life on Earth, simplified representations of human body form including height and population, the solar system including the sun and nine planets (indicating that humans live on planet three, Earth) and the image of the Arecibo radio dish instrument. The message received in the crop field had about nine differences to the transmitted message from Earth. These included the addition of the element silicon. The body shape had an alien like humanoid appearance. There were also differences in height and population numbers. There were differences in the Solar System chart and the third planet from the sun was not the only one 'highlighted', the fourth and fifth were emphasised as well. Intriguingly, the radio-transmitter device had a more complex appearance than the terrestrial Arecibo Earth system.

In 2002, a 'crop circle' with a 'malevolent' face resembling well known postulated alien 'greys' from zeta reticuli appeared. A code was deciphered by Paul Vigay and a message recorded which read as follows. "Beware the bearers of false gifts & their broken promises. Much pain but still time. There is good out there. We oppose deception. Conduit closing."

The McPherson Tapes

This film shows the final moments of a Connecticut family named the Van Heeses before they are abducted by extraterrestrials. The film took the format of a genuine 1983 home video recording. A remake in 1998 involves a teenager in Lake County, Montana, who makes a home movie of his McPherson family's Thanksgiving dinner. Unexpectedly, after sighting a landed UFO and being struck by a 'ray gun' weapon, they are attacked. After a gun battle, an automated camera in their cabin shows the family being abducted by extraterrestrials. They are never seen or heard from again.

The film caused confusion and controversy among viewers, many of whom believed it portrayed real events and there is still a measure of debate as to the reality or not of the footage.

Mutilations

For some time, a phenomenon has been occurring relating to 'mutilation'. Most commonly, various cattle mutilations have occurred on farms and ranches. Other mutilated species have also been documented including sheep, horses, goats, rabbits and several other types of farm animals and domestic pets. The bodies of the animals appear to be drained of blood. Commonly, various body parts have been excised with surgical precision. Such parts include the genitals and rectum. Other parts removed are the eye, ear, tongue and jaw. A range of suggestions have been put forward as to the cause of these mutilations. One possible cause includes predators like coyotes etc but surprisingly, on the whole, no footprints or tracks have been found near the carcasses. In some cases, tripod like indentations have been observed on the ground nearby suggestive of some kind of 'landing gear'. Other suggestions given to explain mutilations include decomposition and decay, government and military research groups, human cruelty, cult groups and cryptid creatures like the chupacabra. There is also a common suspicion that these strange mutilations were carried out by extraterrestrials. UFOs have supposedly been seen suspending cattle in the air which have subsequently been dropped from height back to the ground.

Although cattle mutilations were reported in England in the late nineteenth and early twentieth centuries, there was a wave of reports from the United States in the early 1960s especially from Pennsylvania and Kansas. One incident hit the news from Alamosa, Colorado, in 1967. A horse named Lady was found skinned. Investigations revealed that mutilations had occurred in about fifteen U.S. States and had caused substantial financial loss of livestock. There was a report from the Panggang District of Gunung Kidul Regency, Yogyakarta, Indonesia in 2001, suggesting that 200 goats had been mutilated.

Some very disturbing cases have arisen of human mutilation. One case dating from 1988 had frightening and graphic photographic records. It occurred in Brazil in the area of Guarapiranga located in the southern area of the city of São Paulo. An autopsy report concluded the procedure occurred while the victim was still alive and he must have died in great pain. The mutilation procedure ultimately may have resulted in cardiac arrest. The left eye, left ear, lips, tongue, parts of the groin and jaw were removed. The torso had two holes in it and no blood was detected. The rectum was 'cored out' leaving a hole. It has been suggested that precision instruments must have been used to carry out the observed mutilation effects.

Alien Autopsy

Ray Santilli based in London, released a low quality seventeen minute black and white film in the 1990s. This film purported to show an authentic alien autopsy. The body was supposedly a being recovered from a crashed disc at Roswell, New Mexico, in 1947. Santilli claimed the film footage was supplied to him by an anonymous retired military cameraman. In 2006, Santilli admitted the film was not authentic. It was actually a staged reconstruction of footage he claimed to have viewed. The footage was aired on television. There was a lot of disagreement despite Santilli's admission as to whether the film was authentic or not. Noted forensic pathologist Cyril Wecht considered the autopsy procedures in the film to be authentic. Alien artefacts supposedly from the crash site were depicted in the footage including alien symbols and six finger control panels.

Alien Species

According to varied sources such as whistleblowers and speakers at disclosure projects (including ex-political, NASA and military staff), the number of alien beings or extraterrestrials that have visited planet Earth is between sixty to over 150 species. It is open to debate as to whether such entities exist at all. If they do, their origins are still unproven at the present time. They might be resident on the Earth itself or be intergalactic, interstellar or interdimensional visitors. They might be temporal in nature, travelling through time. There are other possibilities too including divine or religion related apparitions and paranormal manifestations. Some species may have been on Earth since the distant past and may have influenced mankind's development. There is a belief by some people that aliens have blended into human society and may wield political and financial power.

It is claimed that certain species have a benevolent agenda towards humans. This is commonly ascribed to Nordic aliens who try to guide human spiritual development and lead mankind away from negative actions such as environmental pollution, climate warming and nuclear war. On the other hand, other aliens such as the greys may be malevolent. They may wish to invade the Earth or enslave mankind. Commonly, they are said to be involved in abductions, medical examinations and genetic experiments to produce human-alien hybrids. They may use human extracts as a nutrient food source.

There are claims that the Earth is hollow and this is where certain alien species are based. There have been postulated suggestions that there is a cavernous entry and exit point for alien craft to an underground base in the Antarctic. Alien craft may also utilise portals which are aerial or located in remote mountain sides. Aliens may have underwater bases in deep trenches below the sea or in remote deep freshwater lakes. Many claim that lunar and Martian alien bases exist. It is too vast an area to do a comprehensive review of speculated alien species here so a brief review has been undertaken and a few selected examples mentioned.

Nordics are 'good looking' and healthy human appearing men and women around six feet to seven feet tall. Some

Nordics have long blonde hair and blue eyes. Nordic aliens are purported to have longer lifespans than humans. Their skin is said to range from pale to tanned white. They sometimes wear skin tight clothing or garments like coveralls. Communication with humans is by telepathy. Nordics were commonly reported in the 1950s by contactees such as George Adamski. Nordics have been reported less often after that time but have occasionally been reported observing or assisting some human abductions. However, some abductees claim the Nordics warned them of the bad intentions of the grey species. The Nordics are often called Pleiadians, referring to the Pleiades star cluster from which they supposedly come from. They were once called 'space brothers' by various contactees due to their positive concerns for the future of mankind. Some contactees referred to the Nordics as Venusians because they were under the impression that Venus was their home world.

The greys are supposedly about three feet to four feet tall. The skin colour has been described as grey-white, grey-brown, grey-green and grey-blue. They have been described as robotic and insensitive to human feelings during episodes of abduction. They can communicate telepathically and impose screen memories to mask events from the human memory. They have often been described as deceitful and untrustworthy. Greys have a reptilian nature and may exchange nutrients and excretions through the skin. They sometimes appear to be drone like and act as if they are under external control. They have narrow dark eyes (without eyelids) which are sensitive to light. The eyes are slanted and found on a bulbous and hairless head. The ears are reduced to tiny orifices as are the nostrils while the mouth is a small slit like opening. They may come from zeta reticuli, Orion or Syrius. A taller version or different sub-species of greys have been recorded about five feet to six feet or more tall which 'work' alongside the shorter ones. These tall greys may have a command role.

Every now and again another type of being has independently been reported seen during abductions by grey aliens. These beings come into a category called 'Insectoids'. They appear to be at a high level of extraterrestrial hierarchy since they are usually described as having an overseeing or supervisory role. Most frequently, Insectoids are said to have the appearance of a large Mantis and occur in both male and female genders. Researcher John Carpenter published a description of their appearance which likens them to a preying mantis insect. These beings purportedly have long, narrow faces and large eyes sharply slanted upward and outward. They have a long thin torso with very long thin arms attached to it, sharply bent at the mid-joint. The hand and fingers are positioned almost vertically downward from the wrist. The legs are bent at a right angle to the mid-joint. The overall stance is crouched and very reminiscent of insect life.

The Tall Whites have been reported to interact with humans. These are chalk white humanlike aliens. They have large blue wraparound eyes. Their hair has often been described as blonde and translucent. Height can range up to up to eight feet tall. Charles Hall described these beings and some of their activities (see the section on Whistleblowers and Hackers).

Another group of humanoid entities are known as the Reptilians. Variations of these have been called Reptoids, Reptiloids, Saurians and Draconians. In 1967, a police officer named Herbert Schirmer from Ashland, Nebraska, claimed to have been abducted onto an alien craft by such reptilian beings. They purportedly wore a 'winged serpent' emblem on the left side of their chests. David Icke has suggested that some of the entities in this group drink blood and are shape-shifters. They may relate to or include well known public figures including Presidents and Monarchs. Supposedly, these beings come from the Alpha Draconis star system.

Some entities supposedly viewed on Earth may not have intelligent intellect such as the chupacabra or else may be truly exotic in nature, such as the mothman. These are discussed in the Unworldy Species section. Other named alien species, sub-species, races or hybrids include the following, in no particular order: Agharians or Aghartians, Altarians, Annunaki or Giants, Nephilim, Elohim, Alpha-Draconians, Amphibians, Bernarians, Cetians or Tau Cetians, Burrowers, Booteans, Chameleons, Draco-Borgs, Eva-Borgs, Grails, Greens and Gizan or Gizahn.

J-Rod

Bill Uhouse was a retired mechanical engineer from Las Vegas who passed away in 2009. He claimed there was a crash of an alien aerial craft near Kingman, Arizona, in 1953. Four entities purportedly were recovered. Government agents retrieved these entities but two were injured, one seriously. The four beings that accompanied the craft were taken to Los Alamos and the two that were injured were taken to a medical facility where at least one of them survived. The humans that entered the craft later became sick. The craft itself was loaded on a trailer and taken to a Nevada Test Site north of Las Vegas.

Uhouse claimed to have been involved in reverse-engineering alien technology antigravity systems at various government facilities. He said he worked both at Los Alamos and at Area 51. An effort was made to construct a flight-simulator for human pilots. Due to a communication problem with a surviving being in 1953, a series of symbols were used for this purpose initially. These resembled letters and geometric shapes. Uhouse testified that the first disc tested was a re-engineered craft and the work was overseen by the surviving extraterrestrial biological entity (EBE) who became known as

J-Rod. Extraterrestrials later presented a craft to the U.S. government which was taken to Area 51. J-Rod may have had a role as an exchange ambassador.

A purported document reported on tissue samples taken from J-Rod as part of 'Project Aquarius' under the Majestic 12 group created by U.S. President Harry S. Truman in 1947. (This group was supposedly tasked to research the crashed disc and non-human bodies from the Roswell incident). J-Rod suffered from cell deterioration. He was kept at a facility five floors under the Papoose Mountain (in a region called S4 near Area 51 in Nevada) within a 'clean sphere' containing hydrogen gas. It was necessary for human visitors going down to that level to wear special suits in the underground laboratory which had breathing and urination hoses.

J-Rod was a typical grey alien as described elsewhere in this book and reported to be 200 years old. However, Dan Burisch (who claimed to have been one of the scientists that interacted with J-Rod) suggested that J-Rod was actually a visitor from the future intent upon correcting some mistakes that ultimately might have a negative impact on future history.

Unworldly Species

On November 12th, 1966, five men digging a grave at a cemetery near Clendenin, West Virginia in the USA, said they saw a humanlike figure fly overhead. This creature became known as the Mothman. In 1966, two young couples from Point Pleasant told police they saw a large flying man with ten feet wings and glowing red eyes following their car. Other sightings were also reported. Some press reports claimed the sightings were connected with UFOs and alien beings. Point Pleasant unveiled a metallic statue of the Mothman in 2003.

The chupacabra ('goat-sucker') was originally reported in Puerto Rico as early as 1995. The creature was also later reported in Mexico and several countries in South America. It was said to attack and drink the blood of livestock including goats and sheep leaving puncture marks on the bodies. Pets were also recorded as being killed. The creature was said to be about four feet high with spines along its back. The suggested identity of the creature includes the possibilities of it being a hairless dog or dog with mange and a coyote. Many people believe it is a 'pet' left behind or released onto the Earth by extraterrestrials.

Some Miscelleneous People of Note

Many individuals have already been mentioned in this book who have made significant contributions in the study area or the history related to UFO sightings and crashes, visions of entities and alien abductions. Of course, there are numerous other people worthy of note but it is impossible to include them all in this publication. The list of names is virtually endless. Rather than omit some of these people completely, several further names have been selected for discussion along with more information on a few individuals only mentioned briefly. This does not indicate that individuals not included in this book or mentioned briefly are of any less importance than those selected below.

Nikola Tesla (10th July 1856–7th January 1943) was a Serbian-American inventor, electrical and mechanical engineer. He became well known for his contributions to the design of the alternating current (AC) electricity supply system. His work led to later developments of items like radio, television, fluorescent lighting, radar and microwaves. During his time in his laboratory at Colorado Springs, Tesla observed unusual signals from his receiver which he concluded may have been communications from another planet. Tesla claimed to have worked on plans for a directed energy weapon from the early 1900s until his death. His claims concerned a 'teleforce' weapon which the press called a 'death ray'. According to Tesla "the nozzle would send concentrated beams of particles through the free air of such tremendous energy that they will bring down a fleet of 10,000 enemy airplanes at a distance of 200 miles from a defending nation's border and will cause armies to drop dead in their tracks." Tesla produced a last patent in 1928 for a flying machine that resembled both a helicopter and an airplane. Before he died, Tesla purportedly had plans to make an engine for a spaceship. He called it the anti-electromagnetic field drive or 'Space Drive'. This may have utilised an antigravity effect. Nikola Tesla had plans for a kind of 'flying stove'. One of his quotes to a company read as follows. "You should not be at all surprised if some day you see me fly from New York to Colorado Springs in a contrivance which will resemble a gas stove and weigh as much and could, if necessary, enter and depart through a window."

Robert 'Bob' Lazar claimed to have worked as a scientist and engineer on a U.S. government above top secret programme during 1988 and 1989. This was in an area close to the infamous Area 51 test facility near Groom Dry Lake, Nevada, at a site known as S4, sited at Papoose Lake. He said that he agreed to a warning that if he revealed information about the programme he, or his family, would be executed. He was allowed access to one area of a crashed extraterrestrial craft in an attempt to reverse engineer the technology. He claimed that the craft created a gravitational pull and the fabric of space and time was pulled toward it. He investigated the means of propulsion which utilised fuel in the form of an element with the atomic number 115, called Ununpentium. This element was said to release antimatter particles and generate large amounts of energy. Lazar claimed to have seen nine different extraterrestrial vehicles at the site. A further claim was that he had been briefed about grey aliens from the star system zeta reticuli who have been interacting with the Earth for 100,000 years. There are doubts over Lazar's claims as the universities he says awarded him degrees apparently have no record of him (the California Institute of Technology and Massachusetts Institute of Technology).

Dr Steven Greer hails from Charlotte, North Carolina. As a retired medical doctor and a keen Ufologist, Greer founded the Centre for the Study of Extraterrestrial Intelligence (CSETI). He also instigated the Disclosure Project. This has the aim of disclosing suppressed UFO information to the public. The project also attempts to obtain amnesty for government whistleblowers. Such individuals would have to break security oaths if they shared their knowledge with others. Greer, Apollo astronaut Edgar Mitchell and others gave a briefing to members of Congress in 1997. He organised a press conference at the National Press Club in Washington DC in May 2001. Twenty retired Air Force, Federal Aviation Administration and intelligence officers gave accounts of their UFO knowledge or experiences. Testimony was also obtained from astronaut Gordon Cooper. Greer himself claims to have seen an unidentified flying object at close range when he was a small child.

Benjamin Robert Rich (June 18th 1925–January 5th 1995) was the second director of Lockheed's Skunk Works from 1975 to 1991. He was regarded as the 'father of stealth' and worked on the development of various secret stealth aircraft projects. Just before his death in January 1995, he purportedly revealed that extraterrestrial UFO visitors are real and U.S. military have the capability of travelling to the stars using vehicles that mimic alien craft. The information was hidden away in 'black project' files.

A brief reference is made regarding Stanton Friedman (born July 29th, 1934) from Fredericton, New Brunswick, Canada. Friedman worked as a nuclear physicist on research and development programmes for various large commercial organisations and companies. He was awarded BSc and MSc degrees in physics from the University of Chicago in 1955 and 1956. He has been noted as the original civilian investigator of the famous Roswell alien craft crash incident of 1947. Since around 1970, Friedman has worked steadfastly studying UFO reports such as purported Majestic 12 papers and has given numerous lectures and appeared on many television documentary and radio broadcasts. He has also provided written testimony to Congressional hearings and given testimony at the United Nations on two occasions. Friedman supports the hypothesis that the Earth is, and has been, visited by extraterrestrials in intelligently controlled craft. However, he has strong views against SETI (Search for Extraterrestrial Intelligence) research. He purportedly claimed that SETI only seeks signals rather than extraterrestrial intelligence or beings and this had a negative effect by work undertaken on UFO research by journalists.

Professor Stephen Hawking (born 8th January, 1942) is a well known English theoretical physicist and cosmologist. He has directed research at the Centre for Theoretical Cosmology at the University of Cambridge. He has done work related to the Theory of General Relativity on gravitational singularities and possible radiation emanating from black holes in space (Hawking radiation). Hawking has received various accolades. He authored a book called *A Brief History of Time* which was a best seller. Hawkins has been wheelchair bound during his adult life due to a form of motorneurone disease called Lou Gehrig's disease. He supports the many worlds/dimensions view of quantum mechanics. On a Discovery Channel programme called *Alien Planet* on May 14th 2005, he purportedly stated the following. "The life we have on Earth must have spontaneously generated itself. It must therefore be possible for life to generate spontaneously elsewhere in the Universe." On the National Geographic Channel programme called *Naked Science: Alien Contact* broadcast on the 24th November 2004, he has been quoted as saying "I think contacting an alien civilization would be a disaster. The extraterrestrials would probably be far in advance of us. The history of advanced races meeting more primitive people on this planet is not very happy and they were the same species. I think we should keep our heads low."

Chinese Professor Wang Sichao is an expert astronomer and has worked at Nanjing's Zijinshan Astronomical Observatory. On August 23rd 2010, Professor Sichao stated that he believed extraterrestrial aliens exist. He believed that UFOs have visited planet Earth. He did not agree with the view of British astronomer Stephen Hawking that an encounter between humanity and aliens would be disastrous. He has been quoted as saying "If they (extraterrestrials) are friendly to us, we can promote the human beings' civilization through exchange and cooperation with them. If they are not, as long as we prepared for their invasion, we can beat them back based on their weaknesses." Sichao also concluded that UFOs had antigravity propulsion and he has also presented data related to altitude and UFO speeds.

Dr Michio Kaku (born January 24th, 1947) has been a Professor of Theoretical Physics at the City College of New York. He has written numerous books and appeared on many television documentaries relating to UFOs, extraterrestrial life and so on. Dr Kaku is said to have referred to the 5% of 'spooky' and inexplicable UFO sightings and chronicled the large number of reliable and credible witnesses worldwide. "What if 'they' aren't all from another planet? Even today, we have people living at fairly advanced levels, technology wise, while others remain in the Brazilian rainforest in the Stone Age, seemingly oblivious to our existence. Perhaps they've been here for a very long time and we ourselves are almost oblivious to their existence."

Worthy of note in this section is Nick Pope (born 19th September, 1965). Pope has appeared on numerous television documentaries concerned with UFO sightings and has authored several books related to the subject. From 1985 to 2006, he worked for the British Government's Ministry of Defence (MoD). His brief with the Air Staff during 1991 to 1994 involved investigating reports of UFO sightings in order to determine their defence significance. The MoD's position maintained that it was open minded about the existence of extraterrestrial life forms but there was no evidence that UFO sightings were extraterrestrial in nature or posed any defence threat. It became apparent that in Pope's view, conventional explanations could not account for all UFO sightings. Pope's final posting in the MoD was at the Directorate of Defence Security until his resignation in 2006. In 2009, the MoD claimed that UFO sightings would no longer be investigated.

The Illuminati, Freemasons and the Bilderberg Group

A very brief mention is made of the Illuminati and one or two other groups. The Illuminati ('enlightened') is a suspected secret society founded in Bavaria on May 1st, 1776. The members are often alleged to conspire to control world affairs. Typically, members are claimed to be various world leaders, monarchy, high ranked military staff, prominent business people, lawyers and financiers. Various world events are allegedly masterminded by the group and some individuals wield political power and influence. One aim of the group is to establish a 'New World Order'. A group of about a hundred people in high finance, politics, the judiciary and big business allegedly formed a group called the 'Club of Rome' whose aim is to control all international finance. Certain conspiracy theorists like David Icke also claim that Illuminati members observe Satanic rituals.

Freemasons are also accused of similar intentions to the Illuminati. The Eye of Providence (or the 'All-Seeing Eye') is often associated with this group. It is a symbol showing an eye surrounded by rays of light enclosed by a triangle. Some have interpreted the symbol as representing the eye of God watching over mankind. The image is located on the reverse of the Great Seal of the United States, which appears on the United States one dollar bill. Some people believe that the Eye of Providence indicates evidence for the influence of Freemasonry in the founding of the United States.

Another secretive elite group is the Bilderberg Club. There is an annual private conference of approximately 120–150 members including famous movie stars and musicians. The original conference was held at the Hotel de Bilderberg in Oosterbeek, Netherlands, from 29th to 31st May, 1954. A 2008 press release claimed that Bilderberg's only activity is its annual Conference. No agenda is publicly claimed by the group but many believe that world government is an issue.

Some believe that the organisations mentioned have been infiltrated by alien beings who cannot be distinguished from 'normal' people and who have their own agenda regarding world affairs. They may ultimately have plans to 'depopulate' large areas of the world to make control of society easier. Some claim space arks are being produced to evacuate Illuminati members and individuals from other exclusive groups from Earth to Mars so they can survive any terrestrial catastrophes or invasions.

HAARP

The High Frequency Active Auroral Research Programme (HAARP) is an ionospheric research project. Funding sources include branches of the American military. The mission of the project is said to involve improving radio communications and surveillance. One research facility is located at a base owned by the American air force at Gakona, Alaska, though HAARP stations may be located elsewhere in the USA and possibly some other countries. The full operating system was active in 2007 though work on it began back in 1993. A variety of instrumentation is used to study atmospheric effects following the excitation of areas of the ionosphere. The excitation is caused by a high power frequency transmitter. Reportedly HAARP has now been shut down but there is some controversy regarding this.

A variety of accusations have been made against the HAARP system, principally that it might be used to modify weather and used as a military weapon against enemy countries. It has been blamed for various atmospheric anomalies, floods, droughts, storms and earthquakes. Some claim it can control the mind or disrupt satellites in orbit. This has implications as an anti-UFO device. Conversely, extraterrestrial control of such a system could have significant military consequences on the Earth's population.

Eugenics

Eugenics is a practice which aims at improving the genetic quality of the human population. Francis Galton coined the term itself. Positive eugenics encourages the reproduction of people with desired traits while negative eugenics is the opposite philosophy. The latter might include people deemed unfit to reproduce. Such people might have mental and physical disabilities or a low IQ. They also might be criminals, deviants and members of unpopular minority groups. In Nazi Germany, state policy of racial purity led to the Holocaust and the murder of at least ten million people. In a publication in 2003, claims were made that advances in pre-implantation genetic diagnosis may take society into a 'new era of eugenics'. Modern eugenics is consumer driven and market based. It ultimately might result in 'designer children' and/or an imbalance of the sexes. Eugenics has a strong link with alleged alien activity. Many people believe that celestial visitors altered the evolution of humankind in antiquity which enabled civilization to advance beyond cave dwelling and on to the building of sophisticated cities. Alleged abduction experiences often involve the withdrawal of ova and sperms from the victims, removal of foetuses from the womb and the presentation of hybrid children. It may be that exotic genetic manipulation and engineering is still occurring for purposes unknown.

Religious Worship

In modern times new religions have sprung up based on the worship of extraterrestrials. Such religions take into account possible ancient contacts and also modern day experiences and revelations. The details of these are beyond the present scope so some examples are mentioned in outline only.

Helena Petrovna Blavatsky (12th August 1831–8th May 1891) was an occultist spirit medium and author who co-founded the Theosophical Society in 1875. She gained an international following. Her doctrines influenced the spread of Hindu and Buddhist ideas in the West and helped generate the 'New Age' Movement. Theosophy promoted the concept that intelligent life exists on seven worlds which exist in parallel universes called 'etheric planes'. Venusians came to

Earth some sixteen million years ago to spread their population and inspired the production of ancient Pacific stone monuments.

The founder of the Church of Scientology was L. Ron Hubbard (March 13th 1911–January 24th 1986). He was born in Tilden, Nebraska and was known for his science fiction works. He developed a self-help system called Dianetics proposed in a book in May 1950 discussing "the modern science of mental health." This led to a new religious movement that he called Scientology in 1952. In Scientology, the Universe is controlled by a Galactic Confederation of seventy six linked worlds who came to Earth seventy five million years ago in an armada of space vehicles to reduce their overpopulation. They made buildings in many places and the souls or 'thetans' of the aliens attached themselves to modern human souls. Their physical bodies are destroyed at such times as their leader Xenu detonates hydrogen bombs in volcanoes where they are imprisoned.

Raëlism was founded in 1974 by Claude Vorilhon, now known as Raël. Life on Earth was created by extraterrestrials called the Elohim. In ancient times they informed people they were angels or gods and they brought with them prophets including Buddha and Jesus. The Church espouses world peace, democracy, non-violent behaviour and liberal views of sexuality. The Swastika has been used as a symbol of peace.

Heaven's Gate was a 'New Age' religion founded in the early 1970s. The group was based in San Diego, California and led by Marshall Applewhite (1931–1997) and Bonnie Nettles (1927–1985). Heaven's Gate members believed the planet Earth was about to be 'recycled' and the only chance of survival was to leave the Earth and reach an alien spacecraft following comet Hale-Bopp. They believed their human bodies were only 'vessels' meant to help them on their journey.

A mass suicide occurred. On March 26th 1997, police discovered the bodies of thirty nine members of the group.

Another 'New Age' religion was the Aetherius Society founded by George King in the mid-1950s. The religion expounds an extraterrestrial hierarchy of spiritual 'cosmic masters' and the religion's goal is to prevent worldly destruction by improving cooperation between humanity and these 'masters'. Aetherius was a being King claimed to have telepathically channelled. Aetherius is a cosmic master from Venus, as were Buddha and Jesus. Various disasters may be prevented by prayer aided by 'Spiritual Energy Batteries' which store healing psychic energy. In due course the messianic 'Next Master' will descend upon the Earth in a flying saucer with 'magic' more powerful than the world's military power.

ACKNOWLEDGEMENTS

Many thanks for opinions on the script offered by B Rabeya (formerly Rahman). I would also like to thank sources of information ranging through books, newspaper reports, magazine articles, government publications, television documentaries, numerous online websites and Wikipedia.